John Meade Falkner was born in 1858, the son of a Wiltshire curate, and was brought up in the West Country. His childhood was marked by poverty and tragedy, but he went to Marlborough College and then Hertford College, Oxford. After graduating, he became tutor to the children of Sir Andrew Noble, a partner in a Tyneside arms firm. In time Falkner joined the firm, Armstrong Whitworth, and eventually became a director of the company. On behalf of the firm he travelled widely in Europe and South America.

As well as books on Oxfordshire and Berkshire, Falkner found time to write three classic tales: *The Lost Stradivarius*, *Moonfleet* and *The Nebuly Coat*. The manuscript of a half-written fourth novel was apparently lost on a train.

In 1915, during the First World War, he became chairman of Armstrongs, which was by then one of the largest armaments producers in the world. After the war, in 1921, Falkner stepped down as chairman. In 1925 he became Honorary Reader in Palæography at the University of Durham and Honorary Librarian at Durham Cathedral, and in 1926 he retired from the board of Armstrongs.

John Meade Falkner died in Durham in 1932 and was buried in Burford.

By the same author

The Lost Stradivarius
Moonfleet
Handbook for Travellers in Oxfordshire
Handbook for Berkshire
A History of Oxfordshire
Collected Poems

John Meade Falkner

The Nebuly Coat

Steve Savage
LONDON AND EDINBURGH

Steve Savage Publishers Ltd
The Old Truman Brewery
91 Brick Lane
LONDON
E1 6QL

www.savagepublishers.com

Published in Great Britain by Steve Savage Publishers Ltd 2006
First published by Edward Arnold 1903

ISBN-13: 978-1-904246-22-0
ISBN-10: 1-904246-22-2

Typeset by Steve Savage Publishers
Printed and bound by The Cromwell Press Ltd

The Nebuly Coat

Sir George Farquhar, Baronet, builder of railway-stations, and institutes, and churches, author, antiquarian, and senior partner of Farquhar and Farquhar, leant back in his office chair and turned it sideways to give more point to his remarks. Before him stood an understudy, whom he was sending to superintend the restoration work at Cullerne Minster.

'Well, good-bye, Westray; keep your eyes open, and don't forget that you have an important job before you. The church is too big to hide its light under a bushel, and this Society-for-the-Conservation-of-National-Inheritances has made up its mind to advertise itself at our expense. Ignoramuses who don't know an aumbry from an abacus, charlatans, amateur faddists, they *will* abuse our work. Good, bad, or indifferent, it's all one to them; they are pledged to abuse it.'

His voice rang with a fine professional contempt, but he sobered himself and came back to business.

'The south transept roof and the choir vaulting will want careful watching. There is some old trouble, too, in the central tower; and I should like later on to underpin the main crossing piers, but there is no money. For the moment I have said nothing about the tower; it is no use raising doubts that one can't set at rest; and I don't know how we are going to make ends meet, even with the little that it is proposed to do now. If funds come in, we must tackle the tower; but transept- and choir-vaults are more pressing, and there is no risk from the bells, because the cage is so rotten that they haven't been rung for years.

'You must do your best. It isn't a very profitable stewardship, so try to give as good an account of it as you can. We shan't make a penny out of it, but the church is too well known to play fast-and-loose with. I have written to the parson—a foolish old fellow, who is no more fit than a lady's maid to be trusted with such a church as Cullerne—to say you are coming to-morrow, and will put in an appearance at the church in the afternoon, in case he wishes to see you. The man is an ass, but he is legal guardian of the place, and has not done badly in collecting money for the restoration; so we must bear with him.'

Chapter 1

Cullerne Wharf of the Ordnance maps, or plain Cullerne as known to the country-side, lies two miles from the coast to-day; but it was once much nearer, and figures in history as a seaport of repute, having sent six ships to fight the Armada, and four to withstand the Dutch a century later. But in fulness of time the estuary of the Cull silted up, and a bar formed at the harbour mouth; so that sea-borne commerce was driven to seek other havens. Then the Cull narrowed its channel, and instead of spreading itself out prodigally as heretofore on this side or on that, shrunk to the limits of a well-ordered stream, and this none of the greatest. The burghers, seeing that their livelihood in the port was gone, reflected that they might yet save something by reclaiming the salt-marshes, and built a stone dyke to keep the sea from getting in, with a sluice in the midst of it to let the Cull out. Thus were formed the low-lying meadows called Cullerne Flat, where the Freemen have a right to pasture sheep, and where as good-tasting mutton is bred as on any *pré-salé* on the other side of the Channel. But the sea has not given up its rights without a struggle, for with a south-east wind and spring-tide the waves beat sometimes over the top of the dyke; and sometimes the Cull forgets its good behaviour, and after heavy rainfalls inland breaks all bonds, as in the days of yore. Then anyone looking out from upper windows in Cullerne town would think the little place had moved back once more to the seaboard; for the meadows are under water, and the line of the dyke is scarcely broad enough to make a division in the view, between the inland lake and the open sea beyond.

The main line of the Great Southern Railway passes seven miles to the north of this derelict port, and converse with the outer world was kept up for many years by carriers' carts, which journeyed to and fro between the town and the wayside station of Cullerne Road. But by-and-by deputations of the Corporation of Cullerne, properly introduced by Sir Joseph Carew, the talented and widely-respected member for that ancient borough, persuaded the railway company that better communication was needed, and a branch line was made on which the service was scarcely less primitive than that of the carriers in the past.

The novelty of the railway had not altogether worn off at the time when the restorations of the church were entrusted to Messrs Farquhar and Farquhar; and the arrival of the trains was still attended by Cullerne loungers as a daily ceremonial. But the afternoon on which Westray came was so very wet that there were no spectators. He had taken a third-class ticket from London to Cullerne Road to spare his pocket, and a first-class ticket from the junction to Cullerne to support the dignity of his firm. But this forethought was wasted, for, except certain broken-down railway officials, who were drafted to Cullerne as to an asylum, there were no witnesses of his advent.

He was glad to learn that the enterprise of the Blandamer Arms led that family and commercial hotel to send an omnibus to meet all trains, and he availed himself the more willingly of this conveyance because he found that it would set him down at the very door of the church itself. So he put himself and his modest luggage inside—and there was ample room to do this, for he was the only passenger—plunged his feet into the straw which covered the floor, and endured for ten minutes such a shaking and rattling as only an omnibus moving over cobble-stones can produce.

With the plans of Cullerne Minster Mr Westray was thoroughly familiar, but the reality was as yet unknown to him; and when the omnibus lumbered into the market-place, he could not suppress an exclamation as he first caught sight of the great church of St Sepulchre shutting in the whole south side of the square. The drenching rain had cleared the streets of passengers, and save for some peeping-Toms who looked over the low green blinds as the omnibus passed, the place might indeed have been waiting for Lady Godiva's progress, all was so deserted.

The heavy sheets of rain in the air, the misty water-dust raised by the drops as they struck the roofs, and the vapour steaming from the earth, drew over everything a veil invisible yet visible, which softened outlines like the gauze curtain in a theatre. Through it loomed the Minster, larger and far more mysteriously impressive than Westray had in any moods imagined. A moment later the omnibus drew up before an iron gate, from which a flagged pathway led through the churchyard to the north porch.

The conductor opened the carriage door.

'This is the church, sir,' he said, somewhat superfluously. 'If you get out here, I will drive your bag to the hotel.'

Westray fixed his hat firmly on his head, turned up the collar of his coat, and made a dash through the rain for the door. Deep puddles had formed in the worn places of the gravestones that paved the alley, and he splashed himself in his hurry before he reached the shelter of the porch. He pulled aside the hanging leather mattress that covered a wicket in the great door, and found himself inside the church.

It was not yet four o'clock, but the day was so overcast that dusk was already falling in the building. A little group of men who had been talking in the choir turned round at the sound of the opening door, and made towards the architect. The protagonist was a clergyman past middle age, who wore a stock, and stepped forward to greet the young architect.

'Sir George Farquhar's assistant, I presume. One of Sir George Farquhar's assistants I should perhaps say, for no doubt Sir George has more than one assistant in carrying out his many and varied professional duties.'

Westray made a motion of assent, and the clergyman went on: 'Let me introduce myself as Canon Parkyn. You will no doubt have heard of me from Sir George, with whom I, as rector of this church, have had exceptional opportunities of associating. On one occasion, indeed, Sir George spent the night under my own roof, and I must say that I think any young man should be proud of studying under an architect of such distinguished ability. I shall be able to explain to you very briefly the main views which Sir George has conceived with regard to the restoration; but in the meantime let me make you known to my worthy parishioners—and friends,' he added in a tone which implied some doubt as to whether condescension was not being stretched too far, in qualifying as friends persons so manifestly inferior.

'This is Mr Sharnall, the organist, who under my direction presides over the musical portion of our services; and this is Dr Ennefer, our excellent local practitioner; and this is Mr Joliffe, who, though engaged in trade, finds time as churchwarden to assist me in the supervision of the sacred edifice.'

The doctor and the organist gave effect to the presentation by a nod, and something like a shrug of the shoulders, which deprecated the Rector's conceited pomposity, and implied that if such an exceedingly unlikely contingency as their making friends with Mr Westray should ever happen it would certainly not be due to any introduction of Canon Parkyn. Mr Joliffe, on the other hand, seemed fully to recognize the dignity to which he was called by being numbered among the Rector's friends, and with a gracious bow, and a polite 'Your servant, sir,' made it plain that he understood how to condescend in his turn, and was prepared to extend his full protection to a young and struggling architect.

Beside these leading actors, there were present the clerk, and a handful of walking-gentlemen in the shape of idlers who had strolled in from the street, and who were glad enough to find shelter from the rain, and an afternoon's entertainment gratuitously provided.

'I thought you would like to meet me here,' said the Rector, 'so that I might point out to you at once the more salient features of the building. Sir George Farquhar, on the occasion of his last visit, was pleased to compliment me on the lucidity of the explanations which I ventured to offer.'

There seemed to be no immediate way of escape, so Westray resigned himself to the inevitable, and the little group moved up the nave, enveloped in an atmosphere of its own of which wet overcoats and umbrellas were resolvable constituents. The air in the church was raw and cold, and a smell of sodden matting drew Westray's attention to the fact that the roofs were not water-tight, and that there were pools of rain-water on the floor in many places.

'The nave is the oldest part,' said the cicerone, 'built about 1135 by Walter Le Bec.'

'I am very much afraid our friend is too young and inexperienced for the work here. What do *you* think?' he put in as a rapid aside to the doctor.

'Oh, I dare say if you take him in hand and coach him a little he will do all right,' replied the doctor, raising his eyebrows for the organist's delectation.

'Yes, this is all Le Bec's work,' the Rector went on, turning back to Westray. 'So sublime the simplicity of the Norman style, is it not? The nave arcades will repay your close attention; and look at these wonderful arches in the crossing. Norman, of course, but how light; and yet strong as a rock to bear the enormous weight of the tower which later builders reared on them. Wonderful, wonderful!'

Westray recalled his Chief's doubts about the tower, and looking up into the lantern saw on the north side a seam of old brick filling; and on the south a thin jagged fissure, that ran down from the sill of the lantern-window like the impress of a lightning-flash. There came into his head an old architectural saw, 'The arch never sleeps'; and as he looked up at the four wide and finely drawn semicircles they seemed to say:

'The arch never sleeps, never sleeps. They have bound on us a burden too heavy to be borne. We are shifting it. The arch never sleeps.'

'Wonderful, wonderful!' the Rector still murmured. 'Daring fellows, these Norman builders.'

'Yes, yes,' Westray was constrained to say; 'but they never reckoned that the present tower would be piled upon their arches.'

'What, you think them a little shaky?' put in the organist. 'Well, I have fancied so, many a time, myself.'

'Oh, I don't know. I dare say they will last our time,' Westray answered in a nonchalant and reassuring tone; for he remembered that, as regards the tower, he had been specially cautioned to let sleeping dogs lie, but he thought of the Ossa heaped on Pelion above their heads, and conceived a mistrust of the wide crossing-arches which he never was able entirely to shake off.

'No, no, my young friend,' said the Rector with a smile of forbearance for so mistaken an idea, 'do not alarm yourself about these arches. "Mr Rector," said Sir George to me the very first time we were here together, "you have been at Cullerne forty years; have you ever observed any signs of movement in the tower?" "Sir George," I said, "will you wait for your fees until my tower tumbles down?" Ha, ha, ha! He saw the joke, and we never heard anything more about the tower. Sir George has, no doubt, given you all proper instructions; but as I had the privilege of personally showing him the church, you must forgive me if I ask you to step into the south transept for a moment, while I point out to you what Sir George considered the most pressing matter.'

They moved into the transept, but the doctor managed to buttonhole Westray for a moment *en route*.

'You will be bored to death,' he said, 'with this man's ignorance and conceit. Don't pay the least attention to him, but there is one thing I want to take the first opportunity of pressing on you. Whatever is done or not done, however limited the funds may be, let us at least have a sanitary floor. You must have all these stones up and put a foot or two of concrete under them. Can anything be more monstrous than that the dead should be allowed to poison the living? There must be hundreds of burials close under the floor, and look at the pools of water standing about. Can anything, I say, be more insanitary?'

They were in the south transept, and the Rector had duly pointed out the dilapidations of the roof, which, in truth, wanted but little showing.

'Some call this the Blandamer aisle,' he said, 'from a noble family of that name who have for many years been buried here.'

'*Their* vaults are, no doubt, in a most insanitary condition,' interpolated the doctor.

'These Blandamers ought to restore the whole place,' the organist said bitterly. 'They would, if they had any sense of decency. They are as rich as Croesus, and would miss pounds less than most people would miss pennies. Not that I believe in any of this sanitary talk—things have gone on well enough as they are; and if you go digging up the floors you will only dig up pestilences. Keep the fabric together, make the roofs water-tight, and spend a hundred or two on the organ. That is all we want, and these Blandamers would do it, if they weren't curmudgeons and skinflints.'

'You will forgive me, Mr Sharnall,' said the Rector, 'if I remark that an hereditary peerage is so important an institution, that we should be very careful how we criticize any members of it. At the same time,' he went on, turning apologetically to Westray, 'there is perhaps a modicum of reason in our friend's remarks. I had hoped that Lord Blandamer would have contributed handsomely to the restoration fund, but he has not hitherto done so, though I dare say that his continued absence abroad accounts for some delay. He only succeeded his grandfather last year, and the late lord never showed much interest in this place, and was indeed in many ways a very strange character. But it's no use raking up these stories; the old man is gone, and we must hope for better things from the young one.'

'I don't know why you call him young,' said the doctor. 'He's young, maybe, compared to his grandfather, who died at eighty-five; but he must be forty, if he's a day.'

'Oh, impossible; and yet I don't know. It was in my first year at Cullerne that his father and mother were drowned. You remember that, Mr Sharnall—when the *Corisande* upset in Pallion Bay?'

'Ay, I mind that well enough,' struck in the clerk; 'and I mind their being married, becos' we wor ringing of the bells, when old Mason Parmiter run into the church, and says: "Do'ant-ee, boys—do'ant-ee ring 'em any more. These yere old tower'll never stand it. I see him rock," he says, "and the dust a-running out of the cracks like rain." So out we come, and glad enough to stop it, too, because there was a feast down in the meadows by the London Road, and drinks and dancing, and we wanted to be there. That were two-and-forty years ago come Lady Day, and there was some shook their heads, and said we never ought to have stopped the ring, for a broken peal broke life or happiness. But what was we to do?'

'Did they strengthen the tower afterwards?' Westray asked. 'Do you find any excessive motion when the peal is rung now?'

'Lor' bless you, sir; them bells was never rung for thirty years afore that, and wouldn't a been rung then, only Tom Leech, he says: "The ropes is there, boys; let's have a ring out of these yere tower. He ain't been rung for thirty year. None on us don't recollect the last time he *was* rung, and if 'er were weak then, 'er's had plenty of time to get strong again, and there'll be half a crown a man for ringing of a peal."

So up we got to it, till old Parmiter come in to stop us. And you take my word for it, they never have been rung since. There's only that rope there'—and he pointed to a bell-rope that came down from the lantern far above, and was fastened back against the wall—'wot we tolls the bell with for service, and that ain't the big bell neither.'

'Did Sir George Farquhar know all this?' Westray asked the Rector.

'No, sir; Sir George did not know it,' said the Rector, with some tartness in his voice, 'because it was not material that he should know it; and Sir George's time, when he was here, was taken up with more pressing matters. I never heard this old wife's tale myself till the present moment, and although it is true that we do not ring the bells, this is on account of the supposed weakness of the cage in which they swing, and has nothing whatever to do with the tower itself. You may take *my* word for that. "Sir George," I said, when Sir George asked me—"Sir George, I have been here forty years, and if you will agree not to ask for your fees till my tower tumbles down, why, I shall be very glad." Ha, ha, ha! how Sir George enjoyed that joke! Ha, ha, ha!'

Westray turned away with a firm resolve to report to headquarters the story of the interrupted peal, and to make an early examination of the tower on his own behalf.

The clerk was nettled that the Rector should treat his story with such scant respect, but he saw that the others were listening with interest, and he went on:

'Well, 'tain't for I to say the old tower's a-going to fall, and I hope Sir Jarge won't ever live to larf the wrong side o' his mouth; but stopping of a ring never brought luck with it yet, and it brought no luck to my lord. First he lost his dear son and his son's wife in Cullerne Bay, and I remember as if 'twas yesterday how we grappled for 'em all night, and found their bodies lying close together on the sand in three fathoms, when the tide set inshore in the morning. And then he fell out wi' my lady, and she never spoke to him again—no, not to the day of her death. They lived at Fording—that's the great hall over there,' he said to Westray, jerking his thumb towards the east—'for twenty years in separate wings, like you mid say each in a house to themselves. And then he fell out wi' Mr Fynes, his grandson, and turned him out of house and lands, though he couldn't leave them nowhere else when he died. 'Tis Mr Fynes as is the young lord now, and half his life he's bin a wand'rer in foreign parts, and isn't come home yet. Maybe he never will come back. It's like enough he's got killed out there, or he'd be tied to answer parson's letters. Wouldn't he, Mr Sharnall?' he said, turning abruptly to the organist with a wink, which was meant to retaliate for the slight that the Rector had put on his stories.

'Come, come; we've had enough of these tales,' said the Rector. 'Your listeners are getting tired.'

'The man's in love with his own voice,' he added in a lower tone, as he took Westray by the arm; 'when he's once set off there's no stopping him. There are still a good many points which Sir George and I discussed, and on which I shall hope to give you our conclusions; but we shall have to finish our inspection to-morrow, for this talkative fellow has sadly interrupted us. It is a great pity the light is failing so fast just now; there is some good painted glass in this end window of the transept.'

Westray looked up and saw the great window at the end of the transept shimmering with a dull lustre; light only in comparison with the shadows that were falling inside the church. It was an insertion of Perpendicular date, reaching from wall to wall, and almost from floor to roof. Its vast breadth, parcelled out into eleven lights, and the infinite division of the stonework in the head, impressed the imagination; while mullions and tracery stood out in such inky contrast against the daylight yet lingering outside, that the architect read the scheme of subarcuation and the tracery as easily as if he had been studying a plan. Sundown had brought no gleam to lift the pall of the dying day, but the monotonous grey of the sky was still sufficiently light to enable a practised eye to make out that the head of the window was filled with a broken medley of ancient glass, where translucent blue and amber, pink and green mingled like the harmony of an old patchwork quilt. Of the lower divisions of the window, those at the sides had no colour to clothe their nakedness, and remained in ghostly whiteness; but the three middle lights were filled with strong browns and purples of the seventeenth century. Here and there in the rich colour were introduced medallions, representing apparently scriptural scenes, and at the top of each light, under the cusping, was a coat of arms. The head of the middle division formed the centre of the whole scheme, and seemed to represent a shield of silver-white crossed by waving sea-green bars. Westray's attention was attracted by the unusual colouring, and by the transparency of the glass, which shone as with some innate radiance where all was dim. He turned almost unconsciously to ask whose arms were thus represented, but the Rector had left him for a minute, and he heard an irritating 'Ha, ha, ha!' at some distance down the nave, that convinced him that the story of Sir George Farquhar and the postponed fees was being retold in the dusk to a new victim.

Someone, however, had evidently read the architect's thoughts, for a sharp voice said:

'That is the coat of the Blandamers—barry nebuly of six, argent and vert.' It was the organist who stood near him in the deepening shadows. 'I forgot that such jargon probably conveys no meaning to you, and, indeed, I know no heraldry myself excepting only this one coat of arms, and sometimes wish,' he said with a sigh, 'that I knew nothing of that either. There have been queer tales told of that shield, and maybe there are queerer yet to be told. It has been stamped for good or evil on this church, and on this town, for centuries, and every tavern loafer will talk to you about the "nebuly coat" as if it was a thing he wore. You will be familiar enough with it before you have been a week at Cullerne.'

There was in the voice something of melancholy, and an earnestness that the occasion scarcely warranted. It produced a curious effect on Westray, and led him to look closely at the organist; but it was too dark to read any emotion in his companion's face, and at this moment the Rector rejoined them.

'Eh, what? Ah, yes; the nebuly coat. Nebuly, you know, from the Latin *nebulum, nebulus* I should say, a cloud, referring to the wavy outline of the bars, which are supposed to represent cumulus clouds. Well, well, it is too dark to pursue our studies further this evening, but to-morrow I can accompany you the whole day, and shall be able to tell you much that will interest you.'

Westray was not sorry that the darkness had put a stop to further investigations. The air in the church grew every moment more clammy and chill, and he was tired, hungry, and very cold. He was anxious, if possible, to find lodgings at once, and so avoid the expense of an hotel, for his salary was modest, and Farquhar and Farquhar were not more liberal than other firms in the travelling allowances which they granted their subordinates.

He asked if anyone could tell him of suitable rooms.

'I am sorry,' the Rector said, 'not to be able to offer you the hospitality of my own house, but the indisposition of my wife unfortunately makes that impossible. I have naturally but a very slight acquaintance with lodging-houses or lodging-house keepers; but Mr Sharnall, I dare say, may be able to give you some advice. Perhaps there may be a spare room in the house where Mr Sharnall lodges. I think your landlady is a relation of our worthy friend Joliffe is she not, Mr Sharnall? And no doubt herself a most worthy woman.'

'Pardon, Mr Rector,' said the churchwarden, in as offended a tone as he dared to employ in addressing so superior a dignitary— 'pardon, no relation at all, I assure you. A namesake, or, at the nearest, a very distant connection of whom—I speak with all Christian forbearance—my branch of the family have no cause to be proud.'

The organist had scowled when the Rector was proposing Westray as a fellow-lodger, but Joliffe's disclaimer of the landlady seemed to pique him.

'If no branch of your family brings you more discredit than my landlady, you may hold your head high enough. And if all the pork you sell is as good as her lodgings, your business will thrive. Come along,' he said, taking Westray by the arm; 'I have no wife to be indisposed, so I can offer you the hospitality of *my* house; and we will stop at Mr Joliffe's shop on our way, and buy a pound of sausages for tea.'

Chapter 2

There was a rush of outer air into the building as they opened the door. The rain still fell heavily, but the wind was rising, and had in it a clean salt smell, that contrasted with the close and mouldering atmosphere of the church.

The organist drew a deep breath.

'Ah,' he said, 'what a blessed thing to be in the open air again—to be quit of all their niggling and naggling, to be quit of that pompous old fool the Rector, and of that hypocrite Joliffe, and of that pedant of a doctor! Why does he want to waste money on cementing the vaults? It's only digging up pestilences; and they won't spend a farthing on the organ. Not a penny on the *Father Smith*, clear and sweet-voiced as a mountain brook. Oh,' he cried, 'it's too bad! The naturals are worn down to the quick, you can see the wood in the gutters of the keys, and the pedal-board's too short and all to pieces. Ah well! the organ's like me—old, neglected, worn out. I wish I was dead.' He had been talking half to himself, but he turned to Westray and said: 'Forgive me for being peevish; you'll be peevish too, when you come to my age—at least, if you're as poor then as I am, and as lonely, and have nothing to look forward to. Come along.'

They stepped out into the dark—for night had fallen—and plashed along the flagged path which glimmered like a white streamlet between the dark turves.

'I will take you a short-cut, if you don't mind some badly-lighted lanes,' said the organist, as they left the churchyard; 'it's quicker, and we shall get more shelter.' He turned sharply to the left, and plunged into an alley so narrow and dark that Westray could not keep up with him, and fumbled anxiously in the obscurity. The little man reached up and took him by the arm. 'Let me pilot you,' he said; 'I know the way. You can walk straight on; there are no steps.'

There was no sign of life, nor any light in the houses, but it was not till they reached a corner where an isolated lamp cast a wan and uncertain light that Westray saw that there was no glass in the windows, and that the houses were deserted.

'It's the old part of the town,' said the organist; 'there isn't one house in ten with anyone in it now. All we fashionables have moved farther up. Airs from the river are damp, you know, and wharves so very vulgar.'

They left the narrow street, and came on to what Westray made out to be a long wharf skirting the river. On the right stood abandoned warehouses, square-fronted, and huddled together like a row of gigantic packing-cases; on the left they could hear the gurgle of the current among the mooring-posts, and the flapping of the water against the quay wall, where the east wind drove the wavelets up the river. The lines of what had once been a horse tramway still ran along the quay, and the pair had some ado to thread their way without tripping, till a low building on the right broke the line of lofty warehouses. It seemed to be a church or chapel, having mullioned windows with stone tracery, and a bell-turret at the west end; but its most marked feature was a row of heavy buttresses which shored up the side facing the road. They were built of brick, and formed triangles with the ground and the wall which they supported. The shadows hung heavy under the building, but where all else was black the recesses between the buttresses were blackest. Westray felt his companion's hand tighten on his arm.

'You will think me as great a coward as I am,' said the organist, 'if I tell you that I never come this way after dark, and should not have come here tonight if I had not had you with me. I was always frightened as a boy at the very darkness in the spaces between the buttresses, and I have never got over it. I used to think that devils and hobgoblins lurked in those cavernous depths, and now I fancy evil men may be hiding in the blackness, all ready to spring out and strangle one. It is a lonely place, this old wharf, and after nightfall—' He broke off, and clutched Westray's arm. 'Look,' he said; 'do you see nothing in the last recess?'

His abruptness made Westray shiver involuntarily, and for a moment the architect fancied that he discerned the figure of a man standing in the shadow of the end buttress. But, as he took a few steps nearer, he saw that he had been deceived by a shadow, and that the space was empty.

'Your nerves are sadly overstrung,' he said to the organist. 'There is no one there; it is only some trick of light and shade. What is the building?'

'It was once a chantry of the Grey Friars,' Mr Sharnall answered, 'and afterwards was used for excise purposes when Cullerne was a real port. It is still called the Bonding House, but it has been shut up as long as I remember it. Do you believe in certain things or places being bound up with certain men's destinies? because I have a presentiment that this broken-down old chapel will be connected somehow or other with a crisis of my life.'

Westray remembered the organist's manner in the church and began to suspect that his mind was turned. The other read his thoughts, and said rather reproachfully:

'Oh no, I am not mad—only weak and foolish and very cowardly.'

They had reached the end of the wharf, and were evidently returning to civilization, for a sound of music reached them. It came from a little beer-house, and as they passed they heard a woman singing inside. It was a rich contralto, and the organist stopped for a moment to listen.

'She has a fine voice,' he said, 'and would sing well if she had been taught. I wonder how she comes here.'

The blind was pulled down, but did not quite reach the bottom of the window, and they looked in. The rain blurred the panes on the outside, and the moisture had condensed within, so that it was not easy to see clearly; but they made out that a Creole woman was singing to a group of topers who sat by the fire in a corner of the room. She was middle-aged, but sang sweetly, and was accompanied on the harp by an old man:

> *Oh, take me back to those I love!*
> *Or bring them here to me!*
> *I have no heart to rove, to rove*
> *Across the rolling sea.*

'Poor thing!' said the organist; 'she has fallen on bad days to have so scurvy a company to sing to. Let us move on.'

They turned to the right, and came in a few minutes to the highroad. Facing them stood a house which had once been of some pretensions, for it had a porch carried on pillars, under which a semi-circular flight of steps led up to the double door. A street-lamp, which stood before it had been washed so clean in the rain that the light was shed with unusual brilliance, and showed even at night that the house was fallen from its high estate. It was not ruinous, but *Ichabod** was written on the paintless window-frames and on the rough-cast front, from which the plaster had fallen away in more than one place. The pillars of the porch had been painted to imitate marble, but they were marked with scabrous patches, where the brick core showed through the broken stucco.

The organist opened the door, and they found themselves in a stone-floored hall, out of which dingy doors opened on both sides. A broad stone staircase, with shallow steps and iron balustrades, led from the hall to the next storey, and there was a little pathway of worn matting that threaded its way across the flags, and finally ascended the stairs.

'Here is my town house,' said Mr Sharnall. 'It used to be a coaching inn called The Hand of God, but you must never breathe a word of that, because it is now a private mansion, and Miss Joliffe has christened it Bellevue Lodge.'

A door opened while he was speaking, and a girl stepped into the hall. She was about nineteen, and had a tall and graceful figure. Her warm brown hair was parted in the middle, and its profusion was gathered loosely up behind in the half-formal, half-natural style of a preceding generation. Her face had lost neither the rounded outline nor the delicate bloom of girlhood, but there was something in it that negatived any impression of inexperience, and suggested that her life had not been free from trouble. She wore a close-fitting dress of black, and had a string of pale corals round her neck.

'Good-evening, Mr Sharnall,' she said. 'I hope you are not very wet'—and gave a quick glance of inquiry at Westray.

The organist did not appear pleased at seeing her. He grunted testily, and, saying, 'Where is your aunt? Tell her I want to speak to her,' led Westray into one of the rooms opening out of the hall.

It was a large room, with an upright piano in one corner, and a great litter of books and manuscript music. A table in the middle was set for tea; a bright fire was burning in the grate, and on either side of it stood a rush-bottomed armchair.

'Sit down,' he said to Westray; 'this is my reception-room, and we will see in a minute what Miss Joliffe can do for *you*.' He glanced at his companion and added, 'That was her niece we met in the passage,' in so unconcerned a tone as to produce an effect opposite to that intended, and to lead Westray to wonder whether there was any reason for his wishing to keep the girl in the background.

In a few moments the landlady appeared. She was a woman of sixty, tall and spare, with a sweet and even distinguished face. She, too, was dressed in black, well worn and shabby, but her appearance

* I Samuel 4, 21 'The glory is departed'

suggested that her thinness might be attributed to privation or self-denial, rather than to natural habit.

Preliminaries were easily arranged; indeed, the only point of discussion was raised by Westray, who was disturbed by scruples lest the terms which Miss Joliffe offered were too low to be fair to herself. He said so openly and suggested a slight increase, which, after some demur, was gratefully accepted.

'You are too poor to have so fine a conscience,' said the organist snappishly. 'If you are so scrupulous now, you will be quite unbearable when you get rich with battening and fattening on this restoration.' But he was evidently pleased with Westray's consideration for Miss Joliffe, and added with more cordiality: 'You had better come down and share my meal; your rooms will be like an ice-house such a night as this. Don't be long, or the turtle will be cold, and the ortolans baked to a cinder. I will excuse evening dress, unless you happen to have your court suit with you.'

Westray accepted the invitation with some willingness, and an hour later he and the organist were sitting in the rush-bottomed armchairs at either side of the fireplace. Miss Joliffe had herself cleared the table, and brought two tumblers, wine-glasses, sugar, and a jug of water, as if they were natural properties of the organist's sitting-room.

'I did Churchwarden Joliffe an injustice,' said Mr Sharnall, with the reflective mood that succeeds a hearty meal; 'his sausages are good. Put on some more coal, Mr Westray; it is a sinful luxury, a fire in September, and coal at twenty-five shillings a ton; but we must have *some* festivity to inaugurate the restoration and your advent. Fill a pipe yourself, and then pass me the tobacco.'

'Thank you, I do not smoke,' Westray said; and, indeed, he did not look like a smoker. He had something of the thin, unsympathetic traits of the professional water-drinker in his face, and spoke as if he regarded smoking as a crime for himself, and an offence for those of less lofty principles than his own.

The organist lighted his pipe, and went on:

'This is an airy house—sanitary enough to suit our friend the doctor; every window carefully ventilated on the crack-and-crevice principle. It was an old inn once, when there were more people hereabouts; and if the rain beats on the front, you can still read the name through the colouring—the Hand of God. There used to be a market held outside, and a century or more ago an apple-woman sold some pippins to a customer just before this very door. He said he had paid for them, and she said he had not; they came to wrangling, and she called Heaven to justify her. "God strike me dead if I have ever touched your money!" She was taken at her word, and fell dead on the cobbles. They found clenched in her hand the two coppers for which she had lost her soul, and it was recognized at once that nothing less than an inn could properly commemorate such an exhibition of Divine justice. So the Hand of God was built, and flourished while Cullerne flourished, and fell when Cullerne fell. It stood empty ever since I can remember it, till Miss Joliffe took it fifteen years ago. She elevated it into Bellevue Lodge, a select boarding-house, and spent what little money that niggardly landlord old Blandamer would give for repairs, in painting out the Hand of God on the front. It was to be a house of resort for Americans who came to Cullerne. They say in our guide-book that Americans come to see Cullerne Church because some of the Pilgrim Fathers' fathers are buried in it; but I've never seen any Americans about. They never come to me; I have been here boy and man for sixty years, and never knew an American do a pennyworth of good to Cullerne Church; and they never did a pennyworth of good for Miss Joliffe, for none of them ever came to Bellevue Lodge, and the select boarding-house is so select that you and I are the only boarders.' He paused for a minute and went on: 'Americans—no, I don't think much of Americans; they're too hard for me—spend a lot of money on their own pleasure, and sometimes cut a dash with a big donation, where they think it will be properly trumpeted. But they haven't got warm hearts. I don't care for Americans. Still, if you know any about, you can say I am quite venal; and if any one of them restores my organ, I am prepared to admire the whole lot. Only they must have a little water-engine for blowing it into the bargain. Shutter, the organist of Carisbury Cathedral, has just had a water-engine put in, and, now we've got our own new waterworks at Cullerne, we could manage it very well here too.'

The subject did not interest Westray, and he flung back:

'Is Miss Joliffe very badly off?' he asked, 'she looks like one of those people who have seen better days.'

'She is worse than badly off—I believe she is half starved. I don't know how she lives at all. I wish I could help her, but I haven't a copper myself to jingle on a tombstone, and she is too proud to take it it if I had.'

He went to a cupboard in a recess at the back of the room, and took out a squat black bottle.

'Poverty's a chilly theme,' he said; 'let's take something to warm us before we go on with the variations.'

He pushed the bottle towards his friend, but, though Westray felt inclined to give way, the principles of severe moderation which he had recently adopted restrained him, and he courteously waived the temptation.

'You're hopeless,' said the organist. 'What are we to do for you, who neither smoke nor drink, and yet want to talk about poverty? This is some *eau-de-vie* old Martelet the solicitor gave me for playing the Wedding March at his daughter's marriage. "The Wedding March was magnificently rendered by the organist, Mr Sharnall," you know, as if it was the Fourth Organ-Sonata. I misdoubt this ever having paid duty; he's not the man to give away six bottles of anything he'd paid the excise upon.'

He poured out a portion of spirit far larger than Westray had expected, and then, becoming intuitively aware of his companion's surprise, said rather sharply: 'If you despise good stuff, I must do duty for us both. Up to the top of the church windows is a good maxim.' And he poured in yet more, till the spirit rose to the top of the cuts, which ran higher than half-way up the sides of the tumbler. There was silence for a few minutes, while the organist puffed testily at his pipe; but a copious draught from the tumbler melted his chagrin, and he spoke again:

'I've had a precious hard life, but Miss Joliffe's had a harder; and I've got myself to thank for my bad luck, while hers is due to other people. First, her father died. He had a farm at Wydcombe, and people thought he was well off; but when they came to reckon up, he only left just enough to go round among his creditors; so Miss Euphemia gave up the house, and came into Cullerne. She took this rambling great place because it was cheap at twenty pounds a year, and lived, or half lived, from hand to mouth, giving her niece (the girl you saw) all the grains, and keeping the husks for herself. Then a year ago turned up her brother Martin, penniless and broken, with paralysis upon him. He was a harum-scarum ne'er-do-well. Don't stare at me with that Saul-among-the-prophets look; *he* never drank; he would have been a better man if he had.' And the organist made a further call on the squat bottle. 'He would have given her less bother if he had drunk, but he was always getting into debt and trouble, and then used to come back to his sister, as to a refuge, because he knew she loved him. He was clever enough—brilliant they call it now—but unstable as water, with no lasting power. I don't believe he meant to sponge on his sister; I don't think he knew he did sponge, only he sponged. He would go off on his travels, no one knew where, though they knew well what he was seeking. Sometimes he was away two months, and sometimes he was away two years; and then when Miss Joliffe had kept Anastasia—I mean her niece—all the time, and perhaps got a summer lodger, and seemed to be turning the corner, back would come Martin again to beg money for debts, and eat them out of house and home. I've seen that many a time, and many a time my heart has ached for them; but what could I do to help? I haven't a farthing. Last he came back a year ago, with death written on his face. I was glad enough to read it there, and think he was come for the last time to worry them; but it was paralysis, and he a strong man, so that it took that fool Ennefer a long time to kill him. He only died two months ago; here's better luck to him where he's gone.'

The organist drank as deeply as the occasion warranted.

'Don't look so glum, man,' he said; 'I'm not always as bad as this, because I haven't always the means. Old Martelet doesn't give me brandy every day.'

Westray smoothed away the deprecating expression with which he had felt constrained to discountenance such excesses, and set Mr Sharnall's tongue going again with a question:

'What did you say Joliffe used to go away for?'

'Oh, it's a long story; it's the nebuly coat again. I spoke of it in the church—the silver and sea-green that turned his head. He would have it he wasn't a Joliffe at all, but a Blandamer, and rightful heir to Fording. As a boy, he went to Cullerne Grammar School, and did well, and got a scholarship at Oxford. He did still better there, and just when he seemed starting strong in the race of life, this nebuly-coat craze seized him and crept over his mind, like the paralysis that crept over his body later on.'

'I don't quite follow you,' Westray said. 'Why did he think he was a Blandamer? Did he not know who his father was?'

'He was brought up as a son of old Michael Joliffe, a yeoman who died fifteen years ago. But Michael married a woman who called herself a widow, and brought a three-year-old son ready-made to his wedding; and that son was Martin. Old Michael made the boy his own, was proud of his cleverness, would have him go to college, and left him all he had. There was no talk of Martin being anything but a Joliffe till Oxford puffed him up, and then he got this crank, and spent the rest of his life trying to find out who his father was. It was a forty-years' wandering in the wilderness; he found this clue and that, and thought at last he had climbed Pisgah and could see the promised land. But he had to be content with the sight, or mirage I suppose it was, and died before he tasted the milk and honey.'

'What was his connection with the nebuly coat? What made him think he was a Blandamer?'

'Oh, I can't go into that now,' the organist said; 'I have told you too much, perhaps, already. You won't let Miss Joliffe guess I have said anything, will you? She is Michael Joliffe's own child—his only child—but she loved her half-brother dearly, and doesn't like his cranks being talked about. Of course, the Cullerne wags had many a tale to tell of him, and when he came back, greyer each time and wilder-looking, from his wanderings, they called him "Old Nebuly", and the boys would make their bow in the streets, and say "Good-morning, Lord Blandamer." You'll hear stories enough about him, and it was a bitter thing for his poor sister to bear, to see her brother a butt and laughing-stock, all the time that he was frittering away her savings. But it's all over now, and Martin's gone where they don't wear nebuly coats.'

'There was nothing in his fancies, I suppose?' Westray asked.

'You must put that to wiser folk than me,' said the organist lightly; 'ask the Rector, or the doctor, or some really clever man.'

He had fallen back into his sneering tone, but there was something in his words that recalled a previous doubt, and led Westray to wonder whether Mr Sharnall had not lived so long with the Joliffes as to have become himself infected with Martin's delusions.

His companion was pouring out more brandy, and the architect wished him good-night.

Mr Westray's apartment was on the floor above, and he went at once to his bedroom; for he was very tired with his journey, and with standing so long in the church during the afternoon. He was pleased to find that his portmanteau had been unpacked, and that his clothes were carefully arranged in the drawers. This was a luxury to which he was little accustomed; there was, moreover, a fire to fling cheerful flickerings on spotlessly white curtains and bed-linen.

Miss Joliffe and Anastasia had between them carried the portmanteau up the great well-staircase of stone, which ran from top to bottom of the house. It was a task of some difficulty, and there were frequent pauses to take breath, and settings-down of the portmanteau to rest aching arms. But they got it up at last, and when the straps were undone Miss Euphemia dismissed her niece.

'No, my dear,' she said; 'let *me* set the things in order. It is not seemly that a young girl should arrange men's clothes. There was a time when I should not have liked to do so myself, but now I am so old it does not very much matter.'

She gave a glance at the mirror as she spoke, adjusted a little bit of grizzled hair which had strayed from under her cap, and tried to arrange the bow of ribbon round her neck so that the frayed part should be as far as possible concealed. Anastasia Joliffe thought, as she left the room, that there were fewer wrinkles and a sweeter look than usual in the old face, and wondered that her aunt had never married. Youth looking at an old maid traces spinsterhood to man's neglect. It is so hard to read in sixty's plainness the beauty of sixteen—to think that underneath the placidity of advancing years may lie buried, yet unforgotten, the memory of suits urged ardently, and quenched so long ago in tears.

Miss Euphemia put everything carefully away. The architect's wardrobe was of the most modest proportions, but to her it seemed well furnished, and even costly. She noted, however, with the eye of a sportsman marking down a covey, sundry holes, rents, and missing buttons, and resolved to devote her first leisure to their rectification. Such mending, in anticipation and accomplishment, forms, indeed, a well-defined and important pleasure of all properly constituted women above a certain age.

'Poor young man!' she said to herself. 'I am afraid he has had no one to look after his clothes for a long time.' And in her pity she rushed into the extravagance of lighting the bedroom fire.

After things were arranged upstairs, she went down to see that all was in order in Mr Westray's sitting-room, and, as she moved about there, she heard the organist talking to the architect in the room below. His voice was so deep and raucous that it seemed to jar the soles of her feet. She dusted lightly a certain structure which, resting in tiers above the chimney-piece, served to surround a looking-glass with meaningless little shelves and niches. Miss Joliffe had purchased this piece-of-resistance when Mrs Cazel, the widow of the ironmonger, had sold her household effects preparatory to leaving Cullerne.

'It is an overmantel, my dear,' she had said to dubious Anastasia, when it was brought home. 'I did not really mean to buy it, but I had not bought anything the whole morning, and the auctioneer looked so fiercely at me that I felt I must make a bid. Then no one else said anything, so here it is; but I dare say it will serve to smarten the room a little, and perhaps attract lodgers.'

Since then it had been brightened with a coat of blue enamel paint, and a strip of Brusa silk which Martin had brought back from one of his wanderings was festooned at the side, so as to hide a patch where the quicksilver showed signs of peeling off. Miss Joliffe pulled the festoon a little forward, and adjusted in one of the side niches a present-for-a-good-girl cup and saucer which had been bought for herself at Beacon Hill Fair half a century ago. She wiped the glass dome that covered the basket of artificial fruit, she screwed up the 'banner-screen' that projected from the mantelpiece, she straightened out the bead mat on which the stereoscope stood, and at last surveyed the room with an expression of complete satisfaction on her kindly face.

An hour later Westray was asleep, and Miss Joliffe was saying her prayers. She added a special thanksgiving for the providential direction to her house of so suitable and gentlemanly a lodger, and a special request that he might be happy whilst he should be under her roof. But her devotions were disturbed by the sound of Mr Sharnall's piano.

'He plays most beautifully,' she said to her niece, as she put out the candle; 'but I wish he would not play so late. I am afraid I have not thought so earnestly as I should at my prayers.'

Anastasia Joliffe said nothing. She was grieved because the organist was thumping out old waltzes, and she knew by his playing that he had been drinking.

Chapter 3

The Hand of God stood on the highest point in all the borough, and Mr Westray's apartments were in the third storey. From the window of his sitting-room he could look out over the houses on to Cullerne Flat, the great tract of salt-meadows that separated the town from the sea. In the foreground was a broad expanse of red-tiled roofs; in the middle distance St Sepulchre's Church, with its tower and soaring ridges, stood out so enormous that it seemed as if every house in the place could have been packed within its walls; in the background was the blue sea.

In summer the purple haze hangs over the mouth of the estuary, and through the shimmer of the heat off the marsh, can be seen the silver windings of the Cull as it makes its way out to sea, and snow-white flocks of geese, and here and there the gleaming sail of a pleasure-boat. But in autumn, as Westray saw it for the first time, the rank grass is of a deeper green, and the face of the salt-meadows is seamed with irregular clay-brown channels, which at high-tide show out like crows'-feet on an ancient countenance, but at the ebb dwindle to little gullies with greasy-looking banks and a dribble of iridescent water in the bottom. It is in the autumn that the moles heap up meanders of miniature barrows, built of the softest brown loam; and in the turbaries the turf-cutters pile larger and darker stacks of peat.

Once upon a time there was another feature in the view, for there could have been seen the masts and yards of many stately ships, of timber vessels in the Baltic trade, of tea-clippers, and Indiamen, and emigrant ships, and now and then the raking spars of a privateer owned by Cullerne adventurers. All these had long since sailed for their last port, and of ships nothing more imposing met the eye than the mast of Dr Ennefer's centre-board laid up for the winter in a backwater. Yet the scene was striking enough, and those who knew best said that nowhere in the town was there so fine an outlook as from the upper windows of the Hand of God.

Many had looked out from those windows upon that scene: the skipper's wife as her eyes followed her husband's barque warping down the river for the voyage from which he never came back; honeymoon couples who broke the posting journey from the West at Cullerne, and sat hand in hand in summer twilight, gazing seaward till the white mists rose over the meadows and Venus hung brightening in the violet sky; old Captain Frobisher, who raised the Cullerne Yeomanry, and watched with his spy-glass for the French vanguard to appear; and, lastly, Martin Joliffe, as he sat dying day by day in his easy-chair, and scheming how he would spend the money when he should come into the inheritance of all the Blandamers.

Westray had finished breakfast, and stood for a time at the open window. The morning was soft and fine, and there was that brilliant clearness in the air that so often follows heavy autumn rain. His full enjoyment of the scene was, however, marred by an obstruction which impeded free access to the window. It was a case of ferns, which seemed to be formed of an aquarium turned upside down, and supported by a plain wooden table. Westray took a dislike to the dank-looking plants, and to the moisture beaded on the glass inside, and made up his mind that the ferns must be banished. He would ask Miss Joliffe if she could take them away, and this determination prompted him to consider whether there were any other articles of furniture with which it would be advisable to dispense.

He made a mental inventory of his surroundings. There were several pieces of good mahogany furniture, including some open-backed chairs, and a glass-fronted bookcase, which were survivals from the yeoman's equipment at Wydcombe Farm. They had been put up for auction with the rest of Michael Joliffe's effects, but Cullerne taste considered them old-fashioned, and no bidders were found for them. Many things, on the other hand, such as bead mats, and wool-work mats, and fluff mats, a case of wax fruit, a basket of shell flowers, chairs with worsted-work backs, sofa-cushions with worsted-work fronts, two cheap vases full of pampas-grass, and two candlesticks with dangling prisms, grated sadly on Westray's taste, which he had long since been convinced was of all tastes the most impeccable. There were a few pictures on the walls—a coloured representation of young Martin Joliffe in Black Forest costume, a faded photograph of a boating crew, and another of a group in front of some ruins, which was taken when the Carisbury Field Club made an expedition to Wydcombe Abbey. Besides these, there were conventional copies in oils of a shipwreck, and an avalanche, and a painting of still-life representing a bowl full of flowers.

This last picture weighed on Westray's mind by reason of its size, its faulty drawing, and vulgar, flashy colours. It hung full in front of him while he sat at breakfast, and though its details amused him for the time, he felt it would become an eyesore if he should continue to occupy the room. In it was represented the polished top of a mahogany table on which stood a blue and white china bowl filled with impossible flowers. The bowl occupied one side of the picture, and the other side was given up to a meaningless expanse of table-top. The artist had perceived, but apparently too late, the bad balance of the composition, and had endeavoured to redress this by a few more flowers thrown loose upon the table. Towards these flowers a bulbous green caterpillar was wriggling, at the very edge of the table, and of the picture.

The result of Westray's meditations was that the fern-case and the flower picture stood entirely condemned. He would approach Miss Joliffe at the earliest opportunity about their removal. He anticipated little trouble in modifying by degrees many other smaller details, but previous experience in lodgings had taught him that the removal of pictures is sometimes a difficult and delicate problem.

He opened his rolls of plans, and selecting those which he required, prepared to start for the church, where he had to arrange with the builder for the erection of scaffolding. He wished to order dinner before he left, and pulled a broad worsted-work bell-pull to summon his landlady. For some little time he had been aware of the sound of a fiddle, and as he listened, waiting for the bell to be answered, the intermittence and reiteration of the music convinced him that the organist was giving a violin lesson. His first summons remained unanswered, and when a second attempt met with no better success, he gave several testy pulls in quick succession. This time he heard the music cease, and made no doubt that his indignant ringing had attracted the notice of the musicians, and that the organist had gone to tell Miss Joliffe that she was wanted.

He was ruffled by such want of attention, and when there came at last a knock at his door, was quite prepared to expostulate with his landlady on her remissness. As she entered the room, he began, without turning from his drawings:

'Never knock, please, when you answer the bell; but I do wish you—'

Here he broke off, for on looking up he found he was speaking not to the elder Miss Joliffe, but to her niece Anastasia. The girl was graceful, as he had seen the evening before, and again he noticed the peculiar fineness of her waving brown hair. His annoyance had instantaneously vanished, and he experienced to the full the embarrassment natural to a sensitive mind on finding a servant's role played by a lady, for that Anastasia Joliffe was a lady he had no doubt at all. Instead of blaming her, he seemed to be himself in fault for having somehow brought about an anomalous position.

She stood with downcast eyes, but his chiding tone had brought a slight flush to her cheeks, and this flush began a discomfiture for Westray, that was turned into a rout when she spoke.

'I am very sorry, I am afraid I have kept you waiting. I did not hear your bell at first, because I was busy in another part of the house, and then I thought my aunt had answered it. I did not know she was out.'

It was a low, sweet voice, with more of weariness in it than of humility. If he chose to blame her, she was ready to take the blame; but it was Westray who now stammered some incoherent apologies. Would she kindly tell Miss Joliffe that he would be in for dinner at one o'clock, and that he was quite indifferent as to what was provided for him. The girl showed some relief at his blundering courtesy, and it was not till she had left the room that Westray recollected that he had heard that Cullerne was celebrated for its red mullet; he had meant to order red mullet for dinner. Now that he was mortifying the flesh by drinking only water, he was proportionately particular to please his appetite in eating. Yet he was not sorry that he had forgotten the fish; it would surely have been a bathos to discuss the properties and application of red mullet with a young lady who found herself in so tragically lowly a position.

After Westray had set out for the church, Anastasia Joliffe went back to Mr Sharnall's room, for it was she who had been playing the violin. The organist sat at the piano, drumming chords in an impatient and irritated way.

'Well,' he said, without looking at her as she came in—'well, what does my lord want with my lady? What has he made you run up to the top of the house for now? I wish I could wring his neck for him. Here we are out of breath, as usual, and our hands shaking; we shan't be able to play even as well as we did before, and that isn't saying much. Why,' he cried, as he looked at her, 'you're as red as a turkey-cock. I believe he's been making love to you.'

'Mr Sharnall,' she retorted quickly, 'if you say those things I will never come to your room again. I hate you when you speak like that and fancy you are not yourself.'

She took her violin, and putting it under her arm, plucked arpeggi sharply.

'There,' he said, 'don't take all I say so seriously; it is only because I am out of health and out of temper. Forgive me, child; I know well enough that there'll be no love-making with you till the right man comes, and I hope he never will come, Anastasia—I hope he never will.'

She did not accept or refuse his excuses, but turned a string that had gone down.

'Good heavens!' he said, as she walked to the music-stand to play; 'can't you hear the A's as flat as a pancake?'

She tightened the string again without speaking, and began the movement in which they had been interrupted. But her thoughts were not with the music and mistake followed mistake.

'What *are* you doing?' said the organist. 'You're worse than you were when we began five years ago. It's mere waste of time for you to go on, and for me, too.'

Then he saw that she was crying in the bitterness of vexation, and swung round on his music-stool without getting up.

'Anstice, I didn't mean it, dear. I didn't mean to be such a brute. You are getting on well—well; and as for wasting my time, why, I haven't got anything to do, nor anyone to teach except you, and you know I would slave all day and all night, too, if I could give you any pleasure by it. Don't cry. Why are you crying?'

She laid the violin on the table, and sitting down in that rush-bottomed chair in which Westray had sat the night before, put her head between her hands and burst into tears.

'Oh,' she said between her sobs in a strange and uncontrolled voice—'oh, I am so miserable—*everything* is so miserable. There are father's debts not paid, not even the undertaker's bill paid for his funeral, and no money for anything, and poor Aunt Euphemia working herself to death. And now she says she will have to sell the little things we have in the house, and then when there is a chance of a decent lodger, a quiet, gentlemanly man, you go and abuse him, and say these rude things to me, because he rings the bell. How does he know aunt is out? How does he know she won't let me answer the bell when she's in? Of course, he thinks we have a servant, and then *you* make me so sad. I couldn't sleep last night, because I knew you were drinking. I heard you when we went to bed playing trashy things that you hate except when you are not yourself. It makes me ill to think that you have been with us all these years, and been so kind to me, and now are come to this. Oh, do not do it! Surely we all are wretched enough, without your adding this to our wretchedness.'

He got up from the stool and took her hand.

'Don't, Anstice—don't! I broke myself of it before, and I will break myself again. It was a woman drove me to it then, and sent me down the hill, and now I didn't know there was a living soul would care whether old Sharnall drank himself to death or not. If I could only think there was someone who cared; if I could only think you cared.'

'Of course I care'—and as she felt his hand tighten she drew her own lightly away—'of course we care—poor aunt and I—or she would care, if she knew, only she is so good she doesn't guess. I hate to see those horrid glasses taken in after your supper. It used to be so different, and I loved to hear the "Pastoral" and "Les Adieux" going when the house was still.'

It is sad when man's unhappiness veils from him the smiling face of nature. The promise of the early morning was maintained. The sky was of a translucent blue, broken with islands and continents of clouds, dazzling white like cotton-wool. A soft, warm breeze blew from the west, a bird forgot that autumn had come and sang merrily in a garden bush, and Cullerne was a town of gardens, where men could sit each under his own vine and fig-tree. The bees issued forth from their hives, and hummed with cheery droning chorus in the ivy-berries that covered the wall-tops with deep purple. The old vanes on the corner pinnacles of St Sepulchre's tower shone as if they had been regilt. Great flocks of plovers flew wheeling over Cullerne marsh, and flashed with a blinking silver gleam as they changed their course suddenly. Even through the open window of the organist's room fell a shaft of golden sunlight that lit up the peonies of the faded, threadbare carpet.

But inside beat two poor human hearts, one unhappy and one hopeless, and saw nothing of the gold vanes, or the purple ivy-berries, or the plovers, or the sunlight, and heard nothing of the birds or the bees.

'Yes, I will give it up,' said the organist, though not quite so enthusiastically as before; and as he moved closer to Anastasia Joliffe, she got up and left the room, laughing as she went out.

'I must get the potatoes peeled, or you will have none for dinner.'

Mr Westray, being afflicted neither with poverty nor age, but having a good digestion and entire confidence both in himself and in his prospects, could fully enjoy the beauty of the day. He walked this morning as a child of the light forsaking the devious back-ways through which the organist had let him on the previous night, and choosing the main streets on his road to the church. He received this time a different impression of the town. The heavy rain had washed the pavements and roadway, and as he entered the Market Square he was struck with the cheerfulness of the prospect, and with the air of quiet prosperity which pervaded the place.

On two sides of the square the houses overhung the pavement, and formed an arcade supported on squat pillars of wood. Here were situated some of the best 'establishments', as their owners delighted to call them. Custance, the grocer; Rose and Storey, the drapers, who occupied the fronts of no less than three houses, and had besides a 'department' round the corner 'exclusively devoted to tailoring'; Lucy, the bookseller, who printed the *Cullerne Examiner*, and had published several of Canon Parkyn's sermons, as well as a tractate by Dr Ennefer on the means adopted in Cullerne for the suppression of cholera during the recent outbreak; Calvin, the saddler; Miss Adcutt, of the toy-shop; and Prior, the chemist, who was also postmaster. In the middle of the third side stood the Blandamer Arms, with a long front of buff, low green blinds, and window-sashes grained to imitate oak. At the edge of the pavement before the inn were some stone mounting-steps, and by them stood a tall white pole, on which swung the green and silver of the nebuly coat itself. On either side of the Blandamer Arms clustered a few more modern shops, which, possessing no arcade, had to be content with awnings of brown stuff with red stripes. One of these places of business was occupied by Mr Joliffe, the pork-butcher. He greeted Westray through the open window.

'Good morning. About your work betimes, I see,' pointing to the roll of drawings which the architect carried under his arm. 'It is a great privilege, this restoration to which you are called,' and here he shifted a chop into a more attractive position on the show-board—'and I trust blessing will attend your efforts. I often manage to snatch a few minutes from the whirl of business about mid-day myself, and seek a little quiet meditation in the church. If you are there then, I shall be glad to give you any help in my power. Meanwhile, we must both be busy with our own duties.'

He began to turn the handle of a sausage-machine, and Westray was glad to be quit of his pious words, and still more of his insufferable patronage.

Chapter 4

The north side of Cullerne Church, which faced the square, was still in shadow, but, as Westray stepped inside, he found the sunshine pouring through the south windows, and the whole building bathed in a flood of most mellow light. There are in England churches larger than that of St Sepulchre, and fault has been found with its proportions, because the roof is lower than in some other conventual buildings of its size. Yet, for all this, it is doubtful whether architecture has ever produced a composition more truly dignified and imposing.

The nave was begun by Walter Le Bec in 1135, and has on either side an arcade of low, round-headed arches. These arches are divided from one another by cylindrical pillars, which have no incised ornamentation, as at Durham or Waltham or Lindisfarne, nor are masked with Perpendicular work, as in the nave of Winchester or in the choir of Gloucester, but rely for effect on severe plainness and great diameter. Above them is seen the dark and cavernous depth of the triforium, and higher yet the clerestory with minute and infrequent openings. Over all broods a stone vault, divided across and diagonally by the chevron-mouldings of heavy vaulting-ribs.

Westray sat down near the door, and was so engrossed in the study of the building and in the strange play of the shafts of sunlight across the massive stonework, that half an hour passed before he rose to walk up the church.

A solid stone screen separates the choir from the nave, making, as it were, two churches out of one; but as Westray opened the doors between them, he heard four voices calling to him, and looking up, saw above his head the four tower arches. 'The arch never sleeps,' cried one. 'They have bound on us a burden too heavy to be borne,' answered another. 'We are shifting it,' said the third; and the fourth returned to the old refrain. 'The arch never sleeps, never sleeps.'

As he considered them in the daylight he wondered still more at their breadth and slenderness, and was still more surprised that his Chief had made so light of the settlement and of the ominous crack in the south wall.

The choir is a hundred and forty years later than the nave, ornate Early English, with a multiplication of lancet windows, which rich hood-mouldings group into twos and threes, and at the east end into seven. Here are innumerable shafts of dark-grey Purbeck marble, elaborate capitals, deeply under-cut foliage, and broad-winged angels bearing up the vaulting shafts on which rests the sharply-pointed roof.

The spiritual needs of Cullerne were amply served by this portion of the church alone, and, except at confirmations or on Militia Sunday, the congregation never overflowed into the nave. All who came to the minster found there full accommodation, and could indeed worship in much comfort; for in front of the canopied stalls erected by Abbot Vinnicomb in 1530 were ranged long rows of pews, in which green baize and brass nails, cushions and hassocks, and Prayer-Book boxes ministered to the devotion of the occupants. Anybody who aspired to social status in Cullerne rented one of these pews, but for as many as could not afford such luxury in their religion there were provided other seats of deal, which had, indeed, no baize or hassocks, nor any numbers on the doors, but were, for all that, exceedingly appropriate and commodious.

The clerk was dusting the stalls as the architect entered the choir, and made for him at once as the hawk swoops on its quarry. Westray did not attempt to escape his fate, and hoped, indeed, that from the old man's garrulity he might glean some facts of interest about the building, which was to be the scene of his work for many months to come. But the clerk preferred to talk of people rather than of things, and the conversation drifted by easy stages to the family with whom Westray had taken up his abode.

The doubt as to the Joliffe ancestry, in the discussion of which Mr Sharnall had shown such commendable reticence, was not so sacred to the clerk. He rushed in where the organist had feared to tread, nor did Westray feel constrained to check him, but rather led the talk to Martin Joliffe and his imaginary claims.

'Lor' bless you!' said the clerk, 'I was a little boy myself when Martin's mother runned away with the soldier, yet mind well how it was in everybody's mouth. But folks in Cullerne like novelties; it's all old-world talk now, and there ain't one perhaps, beside me and Rector, could tell you *that* tale. Sophia Flannery her name was when Farmer Joliffe married her, and where he found her no one knew. He lived up at Wydcombe Farm, did Michael Joliffe, where his father lived afore him, and a gay one he was, and dressed in yellow breeches and a blue waistcoat all his time. Well, one day he gave out he was to be married, and came into Cullerne, and there was Sophia waiting for him at the

Blandamer Arms, and they were married in this very church. She had a three-year-old boy with her then, and put about she was a widow, though there were many who thought she couldn't show her marriage lines if she'd been asked for them. But p'raps Farmer Joliffe never asked to see 'em, or p'raps he knew all about it. A fine upstanding woman she was, with a word and a laugh for everyone, as my father told me many a time; and she had a bit of money beside. Every quarter, up she'd go to London town to collect her rents, so she said, and every time she'd come back with terrible grand new clothes. She dressed that fine, and had such a way with her, the people called her Queen of Wydcombe. Wherever she come from, she had a boarding-school education, and could play and sing beautiful. Many a time of a summer evening we lads would walk up to Wydcombe, and sit on the fence near the farm, to hear Sophy a-singing through the open window. She'd a pianoforty, too, and would sing powerful long songs about captains and moustachers and broken hearts, till people was nearly fit to cry over it. And when she wasn't singing she was painting. My old missis had a picture of flowers what she painted, and there was a lot more sold when they had to give up the farm. But Miss Joliffe wouldn't part with the biggest of 'em, though there was many would ha' liked to buy it. No, she kep' that one, and has it by her to this day—a picture so big as a signboard, all covered with flowers most beautiful.'

'Yes, I've seen that,' Westray put in; 'it's in my room at Miss Joliffe's.'

He said nothing about its ugliness, or that he meant to banish it, not wishing to wound the narrator's artistic susceptibilities, or to interrupt a story which began to interest him in spite of himself.

'Well, to be sure!' said the clerk, 'it used to hang in the best parlour at Wydcombe over the sideboard; I seed'n there when I was a boy, and my mother was helping spring-clean up at the farm. "Look, Tom," my mother said to me, "did 'ee ever see such flowers? And such a pritty caterpillar a-going to eat them!" You mind, a green caterpillar down in the corner.'

Westray nodded, and the clerk went on:

'"Well, Mrs Joliffe," says my mother to Sophia, "I never want for to see a more beautiful picture than that." And Sophia laughed, and said my mother know'd a good picture when she saw one. Some folks 'ud stand her out, she said, that 'tweren't worth much, but she knew she could get fifty or a hundred pound or more for't any day she liked to sell, if she took it to the right people. *Then* she'd soon have the laugh of those that said it were only a daub; and with that she laughed herself, for she were always laughing and always jolly.

'Michael were well pleased with his strapping wife, and used to like to see the people stare when he drove her into Cullerne Market in the high cart, and hear her crack jokes with the farmers what they passed on the way. Very proud he was of her, and prouder still when one Saturday he stood all comers glasses round at the Blandamer, and bid 'em drink to a pritty little lass what his wife had given him. Now he'd got a brace of 'em, he said; for he'd kep' that other little boy what Sophia brought when she married him, and treated the child for all the world as if he was his very son.

'So 'twas for a year or two, till the practice-camp was put up on Wydcombe Down. I mind that summer well, for 'twere a fearful hot one, and Joey Garland and me taught ourselves to swim in the sheepwash down in Mayo's Meads. And there was the white tents all up the hillside, and the brass band a-playing in the evenings before the officers' dinner-tent. And sometimes they would play Sunday afternoons too; and Parson were terrible put about, and wrote to the Colonel to say as how the music took the folk away from church, and likened it to the worship of the golden calf, when "the people sat down to eat and drink, and rose up again to play." But Colonel never took no notice of it, and when 'twas a fine evening there was a mort of people trapesing over the Downs, and some poor lasses wished afterwards they'd never heard no music sweeter than the clar'net and bassoon up in the gallery of Wydcombe Church.

'Sophia was there, too, a good few times, walking round first on her husband's arm, and afterwards on other people's; and some of the boys said they had seen her sitting with a redcoat up among the juniper-bushes. 'Twas Michaelmas Eve before they moved the camp, and 'twas a sorry goose was eat that Michaelmas Day at Wydcombe Farm; for when the soldiers went, Sophia went too, and left Michael and the farm and the children, and never said goodbye to anyone, not even to the baby in the cot. 'Twas said she ran off with a sargeant, but no one rightly knew; and if Farmer Joliffe made any search and found out, he never told a soul; and she never come back to Wydcombe.

'She never come back to Wydcombe,' he said under his breath, with something that sounded like a sigh. Perhaps the long-forgotten break-up of Farmer Joliffe's home had touched him, but perhaps he was only thinking of his own loss, for he went on: 'Ay, many's the time she would give a poor fellow an ounce of baccy, and many's the pound of tea she sent to a labourer's cottage. If she bought herself fine clothes, she'd give away the old ones; my missis has a fur tippet yet that her mother got from Sophy Joliffe. She was free with her money, whatever else she mid have been. There wasn't a labourer on the farm but what had a good word for her; there wasn't one was glad to see her back turned.

'Poor Michael took on dreadful at the first, though he wasn't the man to say much. He wore his yellow breeches and blue waistcoat just the same, but lost heart for business, and didn't go to market so reg'lar as he should. Only he seemed to stick closer by the children by Martin that never know'd his father, and little Phemie that never know'd her mother. Sophy never come back to visit 'em by what I could learn; but once I seed her myself twenty years later, when I took the hosses over to sell at Beacon Hill Fair.

'That was a black day, too, for 'twas the first time Michael had to raise the wind by selling aught of his'n. He'd got powerful thin then, had poor master, and couldn't fill the blue waistcoat and yellow breeches like he used to, and *they* weren't nothing so gay by then themselves neither.

'"Tom," he said—that's me, you know—"take these here hosses over to Beacon Hill, and sell 'em for as much as 'ee can get, for I want the money."

'"What, sell the best team, dad!" says Miss Phemie—for she was standing by—"you'll never sell the best team with White-face and old Strike-a-light!" And the hosses looked up, for they know'd their names very well when she said 'em.

'"Don't 'ee take on, lass," he said; "we'll buy 'em back again come Lady Day."

'And so I took 'em over, and knew very well why he wanted the money; for Mr Martin had come back from Oxford, wi' a nice bit of debt about his neck, and couldn't turn his hand to the farm, but went about saying he was a Blandamer, and Fording and all the lands belonged to he by right. 'Quiries he was making, he said, and gadded about here and there, spending a mort of time and money in making 'quiries that never came to nothing. 'Twas a black day, that day, and a thick rain falling at Beacon Hill, and all the turf cut up terrible. The poor beasts was wet through, too, and couldn't look their best, because they knowed they was going to be sold; and so the afternoon came, and never a bid for one of 'em. "Poor old master," says I to the horses, 'what'll 'e say when we get back again?" And yet I was gladlike to think me and they weren't going to part.

'Well, there we was a-standing in the rain, and the farmers and the dealers just give us a glimpse, and passed by without a word, till I see someone come along, and that was Sophia Joliffe. She didn't look a year older nor when I met her last, and her face was the only cheerful thing we saw that afternoon, as fresh and jolly as ever. She wore a yellow mackintosh with big buttons, and everybody turned to measure her up as she passed. There was a horse-dealer walking with her, and when the people stared, he looked at her just so proud as Michael used to look when he drove her in to Cullerne Market. She didn't take any heed of the hosses, but she looked hard at me, and when she was passed turned her head to have another look, and then she come back.

"'Bain't you Tom Janaway," says she, "what used to work up to Wydcombe Farm?"

"'Ay, that I be," says I, but stiff-like, for it galled me to think what she'd a-done for master, and yet could look so jolly with it all.

'She took no note that I were glum, but "Whose hosses is these?" she asked.

"'Your husband's, mum," I made bold to say, thinking to take her down a peg. But lor'! she didn't care a rush for that, but "Which o' my husbands?" says she, and laughed fit to bust, and poked the horse-dealer in the side. He looked as if he'd like to throttle her, but she didn't mind that neither. "What for does Michael want to sell his hosses?"

'And then I lost my pluck, and didn't think to humble her any more, but just told her how things was, and how I'd stood the blessed day, and never got a bid. She never asked no questions, but I see her eyes twinkle when I spoke of Master Martin and Miss Phemie; and then she turned sharp to the horse-dealer and said:

"'John, these is fine hosses; you buy these cheap-like, and we can sell 'em again tomorrow."

'Then he cursed and swore, and said the hosses was old scraws, and he'd be damned afore he'd buy such hounds'-meat.

"'John," says she, quite quiet, "'tain't polite to swear afore ladies. These here is good hosses, and I want you to buy 'em."

'Then he swore again, but she'd got his measure, and there was a mighty firm look in her face, for all she laughed so; and by degrees he quieted down and let her talk.

"'How much do you want for the four of 'em, young man?" she says; and I had a mind to say eighty pounds, thinking maybe she'd rise to that for old times' sake, but didn't like to say so much for fear of spoiling the bargain. "Come," she says, "how much? Art thou dumb? Well, if thou won't fix the price, I'll do it for 'ee. Here, John, you bid a hundred for this lot."

'He stared stupid-like but didn't speak.

'Then she looked at him hard.

"'You've got to do it," she says speaking low, but very firm; and out he comes with, "Here, I'll give 'ee a hundred." But before I had time to say "Done," she went on: "No—this young man says no; I can see it in his face; he don't think 'tis enough; you try him with a hundred and twenty."

"Twas as if he were overlooked, for he says quite mild, "Well, I'll give 'ee a hundred and twenty."

"'Ay, that's better," says she; "he says that's better." And she takes out a little leather wallet from her bosom, holding it under the flap of her waterproof so that the rain shouldn't get in, and counts out two dozen clean banknotes, and puts 'em into my hand. There was many more where they come from, for I could see the book was full of 'em; and when she saw my eyes on them, she takes out another, and gives it me, with, "There's one for thee, and good luck to 'ee; take that, and buy a fairing for thy sweetheart, Tom Janaway, and never say Sophy Flannery forgot an old friend."

"'Thank 'ee kindly, mum," says I; "thank 'ee kindly, and may you never miss it! I hope your rents do still come in reg'lar, mum."

'She laughed out loud, and said there was no fear of that; and then she called a lad, and he led off White-face and Strike-a-light and Jenny and the Cutler, and they was all gone, and the horse-dealer and Sophia, afore I had time to say good-night. She never come into these parts again—at least, I never seed her; but I heard tell she lived a score of years more after that, and died of a broken blood-vessel at Beriton Races.'

He moved a little further down the choir, and went on with his dusting, but Westray followed, and started him again.

'What happened when you got back? You haven't told me what Farmer Joliffe said, nor how you came to leave farming and turn clerk.'

The old man wiped his forehead.

'I wasn't going to tell 'ee that,' he said, 'for it do fair make I sweat still to think o' it; but you can have it if you like. Well, when they was gone, I was nigh dazed with such a stroke of luck, and said the Lord's Prayer to see I wasn't dreaming. But 'twas no such thing, and so I cut a slit in the lining of my waistcoat and dropped the notes in, all except the one she give me for myself, and that I put in my fob pocket. 'Twas getting dark, and I felt numb with cold and wet, what with standing so long in the rain and not having bite nor sup all day.

"'Tis a bleak place, Beacon Hill, and 'twas so soft underfoot that day the water'd got inside my boots, till they fair bubbled if I took a step. The rain was falling steady, and sputtered in the naphtha-lamps that they was beginning to light up outside the booths. There was one powerful flare outside a long tent, and from inside there come a smell of fried onions that made my belly cry "Please, master, please!"

"'Yes, my lad," I said to un, "I'm darned if I don't humour 'ee; thou shan't go back to Wydcombe empty." So in I step, and found the tent mighty warm and well lit, with men smoking and women laughing, and a great smell of cooking. There were long tables set on trestles down the tent, and long benches beside 'em, and folks eating and drinking, and a counter across the head of the room, and great tin dishes simmering a-top of it—trotters and sausages and tripe, bacon and beef and colliflowers, cabbage and onions, blood-puddings and plum-duff. It seemed like a chance to change my banknote, and see whether 'twere good and not elf-money that folks have found turn to leaves in their pocket. So up I walks, and bids 'em gi'e me a plate of beef and jack-pudding, and holds out my note for't. The maid—for 'twas a maid behind the counter—took it, and then she looks at it and then at me, for I were very wet and muddy; and then she carries it to the gaffer, and he shows it to his wife, who holds it up to the light, and they they all fall to talking, and showed it to a 'cise-man what was there marking down the casks.

The people sitting nigh saw what was up, and fell to staring at me till I felt hot enough, and lief to leave my note where 'twas, and get out and back to Wydcombe. But the 'cise-man must have said 'twere all right, for the gaffer comes back with four gold sovereigns and nineteen shillings, and makes a bow and says:

"'Your servant, sir; can I give you summat to drink?"

'I looked round to see what liquor there was, being main glad all the while to find the note were good; and he says:

"'Rum and milk is very helping, sir; try the rum and milk hot."

'So I took a pint of rum and milk, and sat down at the nighest table, and the people as were waiting to see me took up, made room now, and stared as if I'd been a lord. I had another plate o' beef and another rum-and-milk, and then smoked a pipe, knowing they wouldn't make no bother of my being late that night at Wydcombe when I brought back two dozen banknotes.

'The meat and drink heartened me, and the pipe and the warmth of the tent seemed to dry my clothes and take away the damp, and I didn't feel the water any longer in my boots. The company was pleasant, too, and some very genteel dealers sitting near.

"'My respec's to you, sir," says one, holding up his glass to me— "best respec's. These pore folk isn't used to the flimsies, and was a bit surprised at your paper-money; but directly I see you, I says to my friends, 'Mates, that gentleman's one of us; that's a monied man, if ever I see one.' I knew you for a gentleman the minute you come in."

'So I was flattered like, and thought if they made so much o' one banknote, what'd they say to know I'd got a pocket full of them. But didn't speak nothing, only chuckled a bit to think I could buy up half the tent if I had a mind to. After that I stood 'em drinks, and they stood me, and we passed a very pleasant evening—the more so because when we got confidential, and I knew they were men of honour, I proved that I was worthy to mix with such by showing 'em I had a packet of banknotes handy. They drank more respec's, and one of them said as how the liquor we were swallowing weren't fit for such a gentleman as me; so he took a flask out o' his pocket, and filled me a glass of his own tap, what his father 'ud bought in the same year as Waterloo. 'Twas powerful strong stuff that, and made me blink to get it down; but I took it with a good face, not liking to show I didn't know old liquor when it come my way.

'So we sat till the tent was very close, and them hissing naphtha-lamps burnt dim with tobacco-smoke. 'Twas still raining outside, for you could hear the patter heavy on the roof; and where there was a belly in the canvas, the water began to come through and drip inside. There was some rough talking and wrangling among folk who had been drinking; and I knew I'd had as much as I could carry myself, 'cause my voice sounded like someone's else, and I had to think a good bit before I could get out the words. 'Twas then a bell rang, and the 'cise-man called out, "Closing time," and the gaffer behind the counter said, "Now, my lads, good-night to 'ee; hope the fleas won't bite 'ee. God save the Queen and give us a merry meeting tomorrow." So all got up, and pulled their coats over their ears to go out, except half a dozen what was too heavy, and was let lie for the night on the grass under the trestles.

I couldn't walk very firm myself, but my friends took me one under each arm; and very kind of them it was, for when we got into the open air, I turned sleepy and giddy-like. I told 'em where I lived to, and they said never fear, they'd see me home, and knew a cut through the fields what'd take us to Wydcombe much shorter. We started off, and went a bit into the dark; and then the very next thing I know'd was something blowing in my face, and woke up and found a white heifer snuffing at me. 'Twas broad daylight, and me lying under a hedge in among the cuckoo-pints. I was wet through and muddy (for 'twas a loamy ditch), and a bit dazed still, and sore ashamed; but when I thought of the bargain I'd made for master, and of the money I'd got in my waistcoat, I took heart, and reached in my hand to take out the notes, and see they weren't wasted with the wet.

'But there was no notes there—no, not a bit of paper, for all I turned my waistcoat inside out, and ripped up the lining. 'Twas only half a mile from Beacon Hill that I was lying, and I soon made my way back to the fair-ground, but couldn't find my friends of the evening before, and the gaffer in the drinking-tent said he couldn't remember as he'd ever seen any such. I spent the livelong day searching here and there, till the folks laughed at me, because I looked so wild with drinking the night before, and with sleeping out, and with having nothing to eat; for every penny was took from me. I told the constable, and he took it all down, but I see him looking at me the while, and at the torn lining hanging out under my waistcoat, and knew he thought 'twas only a light tale, and that I had the drink still in me. 'Twas dark afore I give it up, and turned to go back.

"Tis seven mile good by the nigh way from Beacon Hill to Wydcombe; and I was dog-tired, and hungry, and that shamed I stopped a half-hour on the bridge over Proud's mill-head, wishing to throw myself in and ha' done with it, but couldn't bring my mind to that, and so went on, and got to Wydcombe just as they was going to bed. They stared at me, Farmer Michael, and Master Martin, and Miss Phemie, as if I was a spirit, while I told my tale; but I never said as how 'twas Sophia Joliffe as had bought the horses. Old Michael, he said nothing, but had a very blank look on his face, and Miss Phemie was crying; but Master Martin broke out saying 'twas all make-up, and I'd stole the money, and they must send for a constable.

'"'Tis lies," he said. "This fellow's a rogue, and too great a fool even to make up a tale that'll hang together. Who's going to believe a woman 'ud buy the team, and give a hundred and twenty pounds in note for hosses that 'ud be dear at seventy pounds? Who was the woman? Did 'ee know her? There must be many in the fair 'ud know such a woman. They ain't so common as go about with their pockets full of banknotes, and pay double price for hosses what they buy."

'I knew well enough who'd bought 'em, but didn't want to give her name for fear of grieving Farmer Joliffe more nor he was grieved already, so said nothing, but held my peace.

'Then the farmer says: "Tom, I believe 'ee; I've know'd 'ee thirty year, and never know'd 'ee tell a lie, and I believe 'ee now. But if thou knows her name, tell it us, and if thou doesn't know, tell us what she looked like, and maybe some of us 'll guess her."

'But still I didn't say aught till Master Martin goes on:

'"Out with her name. He must know her name right enough, if there ever was a woman as did buy the hosses; and don't you be so soft, father, as to trust such fool's tales. We'll get a constable for 'ee. Out with her name, I say."

'Then I was nettled like, at his speaking so rough, when the man that suffered had forgiven me, and said:

'"Yes, I know her name right enough, if 'ee will have it. 'Twas the missis."

'"Missis?" he says, "what missis?"

'"Your mother," says I. "She was with a man, but he weren't the man she runned away from here with, and she made he buy the team."

'Master Martin didn't say any more, and Miss Phemie went on crying; but there was a blanker look come on old master's face, and he said very quiet:

'"There, that'll do, lad. I believe 'ee, and forgive thee. Don't matter much to I now if I have lost a hundred pound. 'Tis only my luck, and if 'tweren't lost there, 'twould just as like be lost somewhere else. Go in and wash thyself, and get summat to eat; and if I forgive 'ee this time, don't 'ee ever touch the drink again."

'"Master," I says, "I thank 'ee, and if I ever get a bit o' money I'll pay thee back what I can; and there's my sacred word I'll never touch the drink again."

'I held him out my hand, and he took it, for all 'twas so dirty.

'"That's right, lad; and to-morrow we'll put the p'leece on to trace them fellows down."

'I kep' my promise, Mr— Mr— Mr—.'

'Westray,' the architect suggested.

'I didn't know your name, you see, because Rector never introduced *me* yesterday. I kep' my promise, Mr Westray, and bin teetotal ever since; but he never put the p'leece on the track, for he was took with a stroke next morning early, and died a fortnight later. They laid him up to Wydcombe nigh his father and grandfather, what have green rails round their graves; and give his yellow breeches and blue waistcoat to Timothy Foord the shepherd, and he wore them o' Sundays for many a year after that. I left farming the same day as old master was put underground, and come into Cullerne, and took odd jobs till the sexton fell sick, and then I helped dig graves; and when he died they made I sexton, and that were forty years ago come Whitsun.'

'Did Martin Joliffe keep on the farm after his father's death?' Westray asked, after an interval of silence.

They had wandered along the length of the stalls as they talked, and were passing through the stone screen which divides the minster into two parts. The floor of the choir at Cullerne is higher by some feet than that of the rest of the church, and when they stood on the steps which led down into the nave, the great length of the transepts opened before them on either side. The end of the north transept, on the outside of which once stood the chapter-house and dormitories of the monastery, has only three small lancet-windows high up in the wall, but at the south end of the cross-piece there is no wall at all, for the whole space is occupied by Abbot Vinnicomb's window, with its double transoms and infinite subdivisions of tracery. Thus is produced a curious contrast, for, while the light in the rest of the church is subdued to sadness by the smallness of the windows, and while the north transept is the most sombre part of all the building, the south transept, or Blandamer aisle, is constantly in clear daylight. Moreover, while the nave is of the Norman style, and the transepts and choir of the Early English, this window is of the latest Perpendicular, complicated in its scheme, and in the elaboration of its detail. The difference is so great as to force itself upon the attention even of those entirely unacquainted with architecture, and it has naturally more significance for the professional eye. Westray stood a moment on the steps as he repeated his question:

'Did Martin keep on the farm?'

'Ay, he kep' it on, but he never had his heart in it. Miss Phemie did the work, and would have been a better farmer than her father, if Martin had let her be; but he spent a penny for every ha'penny she made, till all came to the hammer. Oxford puffed him up, and there was no one to check him; so he must needs be a gentleman, and give himself all kinds of airs, till people called him "Gentleman Joliffe", and later on "Old Neb'ly" when his mind was weaker. 'Twas that turned his brain,' said the sexton, pointing to the great window; ''twas the silver and green what done it.'

Westray looked up, and in the head of the centre light saw the nebuly coat shining among the darker painted glass with a luminosity which was even more striking in daylight than in the dusk of the previous evening.

Chapter 5

After a week's trial, Westray made up his mind that Miss Joliffe's lodgings would suit him. It was true that the Hand of God was somewhat distant from the church, but, then, it stood higher than the rest of the town, and the architect's fads were not confined to matters of eating and drinking, but attached exaggerated importance to bracing air and the avoidance of low-lying situations. He was pleased also by the scrupulous cleanliness pervading the place, and by

Miss Joliffe's cooking, which a long experience had brought to some perfection, so far as plain dishes were concerned.

He found that no servant was kept, and that Miss Joliffe never allowed her niece to wait at table, so long as she herself was in the house. This occasioned him some little inconvenience, for his naturally considerate disposition made him careful of overtaxing a landlady no longer young. He rang his bell with reluctance, and when he did so, often went out on to the landing and shouted directions down the well staircase, in the hopes of sparing any unnecessary climbing of the great flights of stone steps. This consideration was not lost upon Miss Joliffe, and Westray was flattered by an evident anxiety which she displayed to retain him as a lodger.

It was, then, with a proper appreciation of the favour which he was conferring, that he summoned her one evening near teatime, to communicate to her his intention of remaining at Bellevue Lodge. As an outward and visible sign of more permanent tenure, he decided to ask for the removal of some of those articles which did not meet his taste, and especially of the great flower-picture that hung over the sideboard.

Miss Joliffe was sitting in what she called her study. It was a little apartment at the back of the house (once the still-room of the old inn), to which she retreated when any financial problem had to be grappled. Such problems had presented themselves with unpleasant frequency for many years past, and now her brother's long illness and death brought about something like a crisis in the weary struggle to make two and two into five. She had spared him no luxury that illness is supposed to justify, nor was Martin himself a man to be overscrupulous in such matters. Bedroom fires, beef-tea, champagne, the thousand and one little matters which scarcely come within the cognizance of the rich, but tax so heavily the devotion of the poor, had all left their mark on the score. That such items should figure in her domestic accounts, seemed to Miss Joliffe so great a violation of the rules which govern prudent housekeeping that all the urgency of the situation was needed to free her conscience from the guilt of extravagance—from that *luxuria* or wantonness, which leads the van among the seven deadly sins.

Philpotts the butcher had half smiled, half sighed to see sweetbreads entered in Miss Joliffe's book, and had, indeed, forgotten to keep record of many a similar purchase; using that kindly, quiet charity which the recipient is none the less aware of, and values the more from its very unostentation. So, too, did Custance the grocer tremble in executing champagne orders for the thin and wayworn old lady, and gave her full measure pressed down and running over in teas and sugars, to make up for the price which he was compelled to charge for such refinements in the way of wine. Yet the total had mounted up in spite of all forbearance, and Miss Joliffe was at this moment reminded of its gravity by the gold-foil necks of three bottles of the universally-appreciated Duc de Bentivoglio brand, which still projected from a shelf above her head. Of Dr Ennefer's account she scarcely dared even to think; and there was perhaps less need of her doing so, for he never sent it in, knowing very well that she would pay it as she could, and being quite prepared to remit it entirely if she could never pay it at all.

She appreciated his consideration, and overlooked with rare tolerance a peculiarly irritating breach of propriety of which he was constantly guilty. This was nothing less than addressing medicines to her house as if it were still an inn. Before Miss Joliffe moved into the Hand of God, she had spent much of the little allowed her for repairs, in covering up the name of the inn painted on the front. But after heavy rains the great black letters stared perversely through their veil, and the organist made small jokes about it being a difficult thing to thwart the Hand of God. Silly and indecorous, Miss Joliffe termed such witticisms, and had Bellevue House painted in gold upon the fanlight over the door. But the Cullerne painter wrote Bellevue too small, and had to fill up the space by writing House too large; and the organist sneered again at the disproportion, saying it should have been the other way, for everyone knew it was a house, but none knew it was Bellevue.

And then Dr Ennefer addressed his medicine to 'Mr Joliffe, The Hand'—not even to The Hand of God, but simply The Hand; and Miss Joliffe eyed the bottles askance as they lay on the table in the dreary hall, and tore the wrappers off them quickly, holding her breath the while that no exclamation of impatience might escape her. Thus, the kindly doctor, in the hurry of his workaday life, vexed, without knowing it, the heart of the kindly lady, till she was constrained to retire to her study, and read the precepts about turning the other cheek to the smiters, before she could quite recover her serenity.

Miss Joliffe sat in her study considering how Martin's accounts were to be met. Her brother, throughout his disorderly and unbusinesslike life, had prided himself on orderly and business habits. It was true that these were only manifested in the neat and methodical arrangement of his bills, but there he certainly excelled. He never paid a bill; it was believed it never occurred to him to pay one; but he folded each account to exactly the same breadth, using the cover of an old pencil-box as a gauge, wrote very neatly on the outside the date, the name of the creditor, and the amount of the debt, and with an indiarubber band enrolled it in a company of its fellows. Miss Joliffe found drawers full of such disheartening packets after his death, for Martin had a talent for distributing his favours, and of planting small debts far and wide, which by-and-by grew up into a very upas forest.

Miss Joliffe's difficulties were increased a thousand-fold by a letter which had reached her some days before, and which raised a case of conscience. It lay open on the little table before her:

139, New Bond Street

Madam

We are entrusted with a commission to purchase several pictures of still-life, and believe that you have a large painting of flowers for the acquiring of which we should be glad to treat. The picture to which we refer was formerly in the possession of the late Michael Joliffe, Esq., and consists of a basket of flowers on a mahogany table, with a caterpillar in the left-hand corner. We are so sure of our client's taste and of the excellence of the painting that we are prepared to offer for it a sum of fifty pounds, and to dispense with any previous inspection.

We shall be glad to receive a reply at your early convenience, and in the meantime

We remain, madam

Your most obedient servants,
BAUNTON & LUTTERWORTH.

Miss Joliffe read this letter for the hundredth time, and dwelt with unabated complacency on the 'formerly in the possession of the late Michael Joliffe, Esq.' There was about the phrase something of ancestral dignity and importance that gratified her, and dulled the sordid bitterness of her surroundings. 'The late Michael Joliffe, Esq.'—it read like a banker's will; and she was once more Euphemia Joliffe, a romantic girl sitting in Wydcombe Church of a summer Sunday morning, proud of a new sprigged muslin, and proud of many tablets to older Joliffes on the walls about her; for yeomen in Southavonshire have pedigrees as well as Dukes.

At first sight it seemed as if Providence had offered her in this letter a special solution of her difficulties, but afterwards scruples had arisen that barred the way of escape. 'A large painting of flowers'—her father had been proud of it—proud of his worthless wife's work; and when she herself was a little child, had often held her up in his arms to see the shining table-top and touch the caterpillar. The wound his wife had given him must still have been raw, for that was only a year after Sophia had left him and the children, yet he was proud of her cleverness, and perhaps not without hope of her coming back. And when he died he left to poor Euphemia, then half-way through the dark gorge of middle age, an old writing-desk full of little tokens of her mother—the pair of gloves she wore at her wedding, a flashy brooch, a pair of flashy ear-rings, and many other unconsidered trifles that he had cherished. He left her, too, Sophia's long wood paint-box, with its little bottles of coloured powders for mixing oil-paints, and this same 'basket of flowers on a mahogany table, with a caterpillar in the left-hand corner'.

There had always been a tradition as to the value of this picture. Her father had spoken little of his wife to the children, and it was only piecemeal, as she grew into womanhood, that Miss Euphemia learnt from hints and half-told truths the story of her mother's shame. But Michael Joliffe was known to have considered this painting his wife's masterpiece, and old Mrs Janaway reported that Sophia had told her many a time it would fetch a hundred pounds. Miss Euphemia herself never had any doubts as to its worth, and so the offer in this letter occasioned her no surprise. She thought, in fact, that the sum named was considerably less than its market value, but sell it she could not. It was a sacred trust, and the last link (except the silver spoons marked 'J') that bound the squalid present to the comfortable past. It was an heirloom, and she could never bring herself to part with it.

Then the bell rang, and she slipped the letter into her pocket, smoothed the front of her dress, and climbed the stone stairs to see what Mr Westray wanted. The architect told her that he hoped to remain as her lodger during his stay in Cullerne, and he was pleased at his own magnanimity when he saw what pleasure the announcement gave Miss Joliffe. She felt it as a great relief, and consented readily enough to take away the ferns, and the mats, and the shell flowers, and the wax fruit, and to make sundry small alterations of the furniture which he desired. It seemed to her, indeed, that considering he was an architect, Mr Westray's taste was strangely at fault; but she extended to him all possible forbearance, in view of his kindly manner and of his intention to remain with her. Then the architect approached the removal of the flower-painting. He hinted delicately that it was perhaps rather too large for the room, and that he should be glad of the space to hang a plan of Cullerne Church, to which he would have constantly to refer. The rays of the setting sun fell full on the picture at the time, and, lighting up its vulgar showiness, strengthened him in his resolution to be free of it at any cost. But the courage of his attack flagged a little, as he saw the look of dismay which overspread Miss Joliffe's face.

'I think, you know, it is a little too bright and distracting for this room, which will really be my workshop.'

Miss Joliffe was now convinced that her lodger was devoid of all appreciation, and she could not altogether conceal her surprise and sadness in replying:

'I am sure I want to oblige you in every way, sir, and to make you comfortable, for I always hope to have gentlefolk for my lodgers, and could never bring myself to letting the rooms down by taking anyone who was not a gentleman; but I hope you will not ask me to move the picture. It has hung here ever since I took the house, and my brother, "the late Martin Joliffe"'—she was unconsciously influenced by the letter which she had in her pocket, and almost said 'the late Martin Joliffe, Esq.'—'thought very highly of it, and used to sit here for hours in his last illness studying it. I hope you will not ask me to move the picture. You may not be aware, perhaps, that, besides being painted by my mother, it is in itself a very valuable work of art.'

There was a suggestion, however faint, in her words, of condescension for her lodger's bad taste, and a desire to enlighten his ignorance which nettled Westray; and he contrived in his turn to throw a tone of superciliousness into his reply.

'Oh, of course, if you wish it to remain from sentimental reasons, I have nothing more to say, and I must not criticize your mother's work; but—' And he broke off, seeing that the old lady took the matter so much to heart, and being sorry that he had been ruffled at a trifle.

Miss Joliffe gulped down her chagrin. It was the first time she had heard the picture openly disparaged, though she had thought that on more than one occasion it had not been appreciated so much as it deserved. But she carried a guarantee of its value in her pocket, and could afford to be magnanimous.

'It has always been considered very valuable,' she went on, 'though I dare say I do not myself understand all its beauties, because I have not been sufficiently trained in art. But I am quite sure that it could be sold for a great deal of money, if I could only bring myself to part with it.'

Westray was irritated by the hint that he knew little of art, and his sympathy for his landlady in her family attachment to the picture was much discounted by what he knew must be wilful exaggeration as to its selling value.

Miss Joliffe read his thoughts, and took a piece of paper from her pocket.

'I have here,' she said, 'an offer of fifty pounds for the picture from some gentlemen in London. Please read it, that you may see it is not I who am mistaken.'

She held him out the dealers' letter, and Westray took it to humour her. He read it carefully, and wondered more and more as he went on. What could be the explanation? Could the offer refer to some other picture? for he knew Baunton and Lutterworth as being most reputable among London picture-dealers; and the idea of the letter being a hoax was precluded by the headed paper and general style of the communication. He glanced at the picture. The sunlight was still on it, and it stood out more hideous than ever; but his tone was altered as he spoke again to Miss Joliffe.

'Do you think,' he said, 'that this is the picture mentioned? Have you no other pictures?'

'No, nothing of this sort. It is certainly this one; you see, they speak of the caterpillar in the corner.' And she pointed to the bulbous green animal that wriggled on the table-top.

'So they do,' he said; 'but how did they know anything about it?'—quite forgetting the question of its removal in the new problem that was presented.

'Oh, I fancy that most really good paintings are well known to dealers. This is not the first inquiry we have had, for the very day of my dear brother's death a gentleman called here about it. None of us were at home except my brother, so I did not see him; but I believe he wanted to buy it, only my dear brother would never have consented to its being sold.'

'It seems to me a handsome offer,' Westray said; 'I should think very seriously before I refused it.'

'Yes, it is very serious to me in my position,' answered Miss Joliffe; 'for I am not rich; but I *could* not sell this picture. You see, I have known it ever since I was a little girl, and my father set such store by it. I hope, Mr Westray, you will not want it moved. I think, if you let it stop a little, you will get to like it very much yourself.'

Westray did not press the matter further; he saw it was a sore point with his landlady, and reflected that he might hang a plan in front of the painting, if need be, as a temporary measure. So a concordat was established, and Miss Joliffe put Baunton and Lutterworth's letter back into her pocket, and returned to her accounts with equanimity at least partially restored.

After she had left the room, Westray examined the picture once more, and more than ever was he convinced of its worthlessness. It had all the crude colouring and hard outlines of the worst amateur work, and gave the impression of being painted with no other object than to cover a given space. This view was, moreover, supported by the fact that the gilt frame was exceptionally elaborate and well made, and he came to the conclusion that Sophia must somehow have come into possession of the frame, and had painted the flower-piece to fill it.

The sun was a red ball on the horizon as he flung up the window and looked out over the roofs towards the sea. The evening was very still, and the town lay steeped in deep repose. The smoke hung blue above it in long, level strata, and there was perceptible in the air a faint smell of burning weeds. The belfry storey of the centre tower glowed with a pink flush in the sunset, and a cloud of jackdaws wheeled round the golden vanes, chattering and fluttering before they went to bed.

'It is a striking scene, is it not?' said a voice at his elbow; 'there is a curious aromatic scent in this autumn air that makes one catch one's breath.' It was the organist who had slipped in unawares. 'I feel down on my luck,' he said. 'Take your supper in my room tonight, and let us have a talk.'

Westray had not seen much of him for the last few days and agreed gladly enough that they should spend the evening together; only the venue was changed, and supper taken in the architect's room. They talked over many things that night, and Westray let his companion ramble on to his heart's content about Cullerne men and manners; for he was of a receptive mind, and anxious to learn what he could about those among whom he had taken up his abode.

He told Mr Sharnall of his conversation with Miss Joliffe, and of the unsuccessful attempt to get the picture removed. The organist knew all about Baunton and Lutterworth's letter.

'The poor thing has made the question a matter of conscience for the last fortnight,' he said, 'and worried herself into many a sleepless night over that picture. "Shall I sell it, or shall I not?" "Yes," says poverty—"sell it, and show a brave front to your creditors." "Yes," say Martin's debts, clamouring about her with open mouths, like a nest of young starlings, "sell it, and satisfy us." "No," says pride, "don't sell it; it is a patent of respectability to have an oil-painting in the house." "No," says family affection, and the queer little piping voice of her own childhood—"don't sell it. Don't you remember how fond poor daddy was of it, and how dear Martin treasured it?" "Dear Martin,"— psh! Martin never did her anything but evil turns all his threescore years, but women canonize their own folk when they die. Haven't you seen what they call a religious woman damn the whole world for evil-doers? and then her husband or her brother dies, and may have lived as ill a life as any other upon earth, but she don't damn him. Love bids her penal code halt; she makes a way of escape for her own, and speaks of dear Dick and dear Tom for all the world as if they had been double Baxter-saints. No, blood is thicker than water; damnation doesn't hold good for her own. Love is stronger than hell-fire, and works a miracle for Dick and Tom; only *she* has to make up the balance by giving other folks an extra dose of brimstone.

'Lastly, worldly wisdom, or what Miss Joliffe thinks wisdom says, "No, don't sell it; you should get more than fifty pounds for such a gem." So she is tossed about, and if she'd lived when there were monks in Cullerne Church, she would have asked her father confessor, and he would have taken down his "Summa Angelica", and looked it out under V—"*Vendetur? utrum vendetur an non?*"—and set her mind at rest. You didn't know I could chaffer Latin with the best of them, did you? Ah, but I can, even with the Rector, for all his *nebulus* and *nebulum*; only I don't trot it out too often. I'll show you a copy of the "Summa" when you come down to my room; but there aren't any confessors now, and dear Protestant Parkyn couldn't read the "Summa" if he had it, so there is no one to settle the case for her.'

The little man had worked himself into a state of exaltation, and his eyes twinkled as he spoke of his scholastic attainments. 'Latin,' he said—'damn it! I can talk Latin against anyone—yes, with Beza himself—and could tell you tales in it which would make you stop your ears. Ah, well, more fool I—more fool I. "*Contentus esto, Paule mi, lasciva, Paule, pagina*",' he muttered to himself, and drummed nervously with his fingers on the table.

Westray was apprehensive of these fits of excitement, and led the conversation back to the old theme.

'It baffles me to understand how *anyone* with eyes at all could think a daub like this was valuable—that is strange enough; but how come these London people to have made an offer for it? I know the firm quite well; they are first-rate dealers.'

'There are some people,' said the organist, 'who can't tell "Pop goes the weasel" from the "Hallelujah Chorus", and others are as bad with pictures. I'm very much that way myself. No doubt all you say is right, and this picture an eyesore to any respectable person, but I've been used to it so long I've got to like it, and should be sorry to see her sell it. And as for these London buyers, I suppose some other ignoramus has taken a fancy to it, and wants to buy. You see, there *have* been chance visitors staying in this room a night or two between whiles—perhaps even Americans, for all I said about them—and you can never reckon what *they'll* do. The very day Martin Joliffe died there was a story of someone coming to buy the picture of him. I was at church in the afternoon, and Miss Joliffe at the Dorcas meeting, and Anastasia gone out to the chemist. When I got back, I came up to see Martin in this same room, and found him full of a tale that he had heard the bell ring, and after that someone walking in the house, and last his door opened, and in walked a stranger. Martin was sitting in the chair I'm using now, and was too weak then to move out of it; so he was forced to sit until this man came in. The stranger talked kindly to him, so he said, and wanted to buy the picture of the flowers, bidding as high as twenty pounds for it; but Martin wouldn't hear him, and said he wouldn't let him have it for ten times that, and then the man went away. That was the story, and I thought at the time 'twas all a cock-and-bull tale, and that Martin's mind was wandering; for he was very weak, and seemed flushed too, like one just woken from a dream. But he had a cunning look in his eye when he told me, and said if he lived another week he would be Lord Blandamer himself, and wouldn't want then to sell any pictures. He spoke of it again when his sister came back, but couldn't say what the man was like, except that his hair reminded him of Anastasia's.

'But Martin's time was come, he died that very night, and Miss Joliffe was terribly cast down, because she feared she had given him an overdose of sleeping-draught; for Ennefer told her he had taken too much, and she didn't see where he had got it from unless she gave it him by mistake. Ennefer wrote the death certificate, and so there was no inquest; but that put the stranger out of our thoughts until it was too late to find him, if, indeed, he ever was anything more than the phantom of a sick man's brain. No one beside had seen him, and all we had to ask for was a man with wavy hair, because he reminded Martin of Anastasia. But if 'twas true, then there was someone else who had a fancy for the painting, and poor old Michael must have thought a lot of it to frame it in such handsome style.'

'I don't know,' Westray said; 'it looks to me as if the picture was painted to fill the frame.'

'Perhaps so, perhaps so,' answered the organist dryly.

'What made Martin Joliffe think he was so near success?'

'Ah, that I can't tell you. He was always thinking he had squared the circle, or found the missing bit to fit into the puzzle; but he kept his schemes very dark. He left boxes full of papers behind him when he died, and Miss Joliffe handed me them to look over, instead of burning them. I shall go through them some day; but no doubt the whole thing is moonshine, and if he ever had a clue it died with him.'

There was a little pause; the chimes of St Sepulchre's played 'Mount Ephraim', and the great bell tolled out midnight over Cullerne Flat.

'It's time to be turning in. You haven't a drop of whisky, I suppose?' he said, with a glance at the kettle which stood on a trivet in front of the fire; 'I have talked myself thirsty.'

There was a pathos in his appeal that would have melted many a stony heart, but Westray's principles were unassailable, and he remained obdurate.

'No, I am afraid I have not,' he said; 'you see, I never take spirits myself. Will you not join me in a cup of cocoa? The kettle boils.'

Mr Sharnall's face fell.

'You ought to have been an old woman,' he said; 'only old women drink cocoa. Well, I don't mind if I do; any port in a storm.'

The organist went to bed that night in a state of exemplary sobriety, for when he got down to his own room he could find no spirit in the cupboard, and remembered that he had finished the last bottle of old Martelet's *eau-de-vie* at his tea, and that he had no money to buy another.

Chapter 6

A month later the restoration work at St Sepulchre's was fairly begun, and in the south transept a wooden platform had been raised on scaffold-poles to such a height as allowed the masons to work at the vault from the inside. This roof was no doubt the portion of the fabric that called most urgently for repair, but Westray could not disguise from himself that delay might prove dangerous in other directions, and he drew Sir George Farquhar's attention to more than one weak spot which had escaped the great architect's cursory inspection.

But behind all Westray's anxieties lurked that dark misgiving as to the tower arches, and in his fancy the enormous weight of the central tower brooded like the incubus over the whole building. Sir George Farquhar paid sufficient attention to his deputy's representations to visit Cullerne with a special view to examining the tower. He spent an autumn day in making measurements and calculations, he listed to the story of the interrupted peal, and probed the cracks in the walls, but saw no reason to reconsider his former verdict or to impugn the stability of the tower. He gently rallied Westray on his nervousness, and, whilst he agreed that in other places repair was certainly needed, he pointed out that lack of funds must unfortunately limit for the present both the scope of operations and the rate of progress.

Cullerne Abbey was dissolved with the larger religious houses in 1539, when Nicholas Vinnicomb, the last abbot, being recalcitrant, and refusing to surrender his house, was hanged as a traitor in front of the great West Gate-house. The general revenues were impropriated by the King's Court of Augmentations, and the abbey lands in the immediate vicinity were given to Shearman, the King's Physician. Spellman, in his book on sacrilege, cites Cullerne as an instance where church lands brought ruin to their new owner's family; for Shearman had a spendthrift son who squandered his patrimony, and then, caballing with Spanish intriguants, came to the block in Queen Elizabeth's days.

> *For evil hands have abbey lands,*
> *Such evil fate in store;*
> *Such is the heritage that waits*
> *Church-robbers evermore.*

Thus in the next generation the name of Shearman was clean put away; but Sir John Fynes, purchasing the property, founded the Grammar School and almshouses as a sin-offering for the misdoings of his predecessors. This measure of atonement succeeded admirably, for Horatio Fynes was ennobled by James I, and his family, with the title of Blandamer, endures to this present.

On the day before the formal dissolution of their house the monks sang the last service in the abbey church. It was held late in the evening, partly because this time seemed to befit such a farewell, and partly that less public attention might be attracted; for there was a doubt whether the King's servants would permit any further ceremonies. Six tall candles burnt upon the altar, and the usual sconces lit the service-books that lay before the brothers in the choir-stalls. It was a sad service, as every good and amiable thing is sad when done for the last time. There were agonizing hearts among the brothers, especially among the older monks, who knew not whither to go on the morrow, and the voice of the sub-prior was broken with grief, and failed him as he read the lesson.

The nave was in darkness except for the warming-braziers, which here and there cast a ruddy glow on the vast Norman pillars. In the obscurity were gathered little groups of townsmen. The nave had always been open for their devotions in happier days, and at the altars of its various chapels they were accustomed to seek the means of grace. That night they met for the last time—some few as curious spectators, but most in bitterness of heart and profound sorrow, that the great church with its splendid services was lost to them for ever. They clustered between the pillars of the arcades; and, the doors that separated the nave from the choir being open, they could look through the stone screen, and see the serges twinkling far away on the high altar.

Among all the sad hearts in the abbey church, there was none sadder than that of Richard Vinnicomb, merchant and woolstapler. He was the abbot's elder brother, and to all the bitterness naturally incident to the occasion was added in his case the grief that his brother was a prisoner in London, and would certainly be tried for his life.

He stood in the deep shadow of the pier that supported the north-west corner of the tower, weighed down with sorrow for the abbot and for the fall of the abbey, and uncertain whether his brother's condemnation would not involve his own ruin. It was December 6, St Nicholas' Day, the day of the abbot's patron saint. He was near enough to the choir to hear the collect being read on the other side of the screen:

'*Deus qui beatum Nicolaum pontificem innumeris decorasti miraculis: tribue quæsumus ut ejus meritis, et precibus, a gehennæ incendiis liberemur, per Dominum nostrum Jesum Christum. Amen.*'

'Amen,' he said in the shadow of his pillar. 'Blessed Nicholas, save me; blessed Nicholas, save us all; blessed Nicholas, save my brother, and, if he must lose this temporal life, pray to our Lord Christ that He will shortly accomplish the number of His elect, and reunite us in His eternal Paradise.'

He clenched his hands in his distress, and, as a flicker from the brazier fell upon him, those standing near saw the tears run down his cheeks.

'*Nicholas qui omnem terram doctrina replevisti, intercede pro peccatis nostris,*' said the officiant; and the monks gave the antiphon:

'*Iste est qui contempsit vitam mundi et pervenit ad cœlestia regna.*'

One by one a server put out the altar-lights, and as the last was extinguished the monks rose in their places, and walked out in procession, while the organ played a dirge as sad as the wind in a ruined window.

The abbot was hanged before his abbey gate, but Richard Vinnicomb's goods escaped confiscation; and when the great church was sold, as it stood, for building material, he bought it for three hundred pounds, and gave it to the parish. One part of his prayer was granted, for within a year death reunited him to his brother; and in his pious will he bequeathed his 'sowle to Allmyhtie God his Maker and Redemer, to have the fruition of the Deitie with Our Blessed Ladie and all Saints and the Abbey Churche of St Sepulchre with the implements thereof, to the Paryshe of Cullerne, so that the said Parishioners shall not sell, alter, or alienate the said Churche, or Implements or anye part or parcell thereof for ever.' Thus it was that the church which Westray had to restore was preserved at a critical period of its history.

Richard Vinnicomb's generosity extended beyond the mere purchase of the building, for he left in addition a great sum to support the dignity of a daily service, with a complement of three chaplains, an organist, ten singing-men, and sixteen choristers. But the negligence of trustees and the zeal of much more religious minded men than poor old superstitious Richard had sadly diminished these funds. Successive rectors of Cullerne became convinced that the spiritual interests of the town would be better served by placing a larger income at their own disposal for good works, and by devoting less to the mere lip-service of much daily singing. Thus, the stipend of the Rector was gradually augmented, and Canon Parkyn found an opportunity soon after his installation to increase the income of the living to a round two thousand by curtailing extravagance in the payment of an organist, and by reducing the emoluments of that office from two hundred to eighty pounds a year.

It was true that this scheme of economy included the abolition of the week-day morning service, but at three o'clock in the afternoon evensong was still rehearsed in Cullerne Church. It was the thin and vanishing shadow of a cathedral service, and Canon Parkyn hoped that it might gradually dwindle away until it was dispersed to nought. Such formalism must certainly throttle any real devotion, and it was regrettable that many of the prayers in which his own fine voice and personal magnetism must have had a moving effect upon his hearers should be constantly obscured by vain intonations. It was only by doing violence to his own high principles that he constrained himself to accept the emoluments which poor Richard Vinnicomb had provided for a singing foundation, and he was scrupulous in showing his disapproval of such vanities by punctilious absence from the week-day service. This ceremony was therefore entrusted to white-haired Mr Noot, whose zeal in his Master's cause had left him so little opportunity for pushing his own interests that at sixty-five he was stranded as an underpaid curate in the backwater of Cullerne.

At four o'clock, therefore, on a week-day afternoon, anyone who happened to be in St Sepulchre's Church might see a little surpliced procession issue from the vestries in the south transept, and wind its way towards the choir. It was headed by Clerk Janaway, who carried a silver-headed mace; then followed eight choristers (for the number fixed by Richard Vinnicomb had been diminished by half); then five singing-men, of whom the youngest was fifty, and the rear was brought up by Mr Noot. The procession having once entered the choir, the clerk shut the doors of the screen behind it, that the minds of the officiants might be properly removed from contemplation of the outer world, and that devotion might not be interrupted by any intrusion of profane persons from the nave. These outside Profane existed rather in theory than fact, for, except in the height of summer, visitors were rarely seen in the nave or any other part of the building. Cullerne lay remote from large centres, and archæologic interest was at this time in so languishing a condition that few, except professed antiquaries, were aware of the grandeur of the abbey church. If strangers troubled little about Cullerne, the interest of the inhabitants in the week-day service was still more lukewarm, and the pews in front of the canopied stalls remained consistently empty.

Thus, Mr Noot read, and Mr Sharnall the organist played, and the choirmen and choristers sang, day by day, entirely for Clerk Janaway's benefit, because there was no one else to listen to them. Yet, if a stranger given to music ever entered the church at such times, he was struck with the service; for, like the Homeric housewife who did the best with what she had by her, Mr Sharnall made the most of his defective organ and inadequate choir. He was a man of much taste and resource, and, as the echoes of the singing rolled round the vaulted roofs, a generous critic thought little of cracked voices and leaky bellows and rattling trackers, but took away with him an harmonious memory of sunlight and coloured glass and eighteenth-century music; and perhaps of some clear treble, for Mr Sharnall was famed for training boys and discovering the gift of song.

St Luke's little summer, in the October that followed the commencement of the restoration, amply justified its name. In the middle of the month there were several days of such unusual beauty as to recall the real summer, and the air was so still and the sunshine so warm that anyone looking at the soft haze on Cullerne Flat might well have thought that August had returned.

Cullerne Minster was, as a rule, refreshingly cool in the warmth of summer, but something of the heat and oppressiveness of the outside air seemed to have filtered into the church on these unseasonably warm autumn days. On a certain Saturday a more than usual drowsiness marked the afternoon service. The choir plumped down into their places when the Psalms were finished, and abandoned themselves to slumber with little attempt at concealment, as Mr Noot began the first lesson. There were, indeed, honourable exceptions to the general somnolence. On the cantoris side the worn-out alto held an animated conversation with the cracked tenor. They were comparing some specially fine onions under the desk, for both were gardeners, and the autumn leek-show was near at hand. On the decani side Patrick Ovens, a red-haired little treble, was kept awake by the necessity for altering *Magnificat* into *Magnified Cat* in his copy of Aldrich in G.

The lesson was a long one. Mr Noot, mildest and most beneficent of men, believed that he was at his best in denunciatory passages of Scripture. The Prayer Book, it was true, had appointed a portion of the Book of Wisdom for the afternoon lesson, but Mr Noot made light of authorities, and read instead a chapter from Isaiah. If he had been questioned as to this proceeding, he would have excused himself by saying that he disapproved of the Apocrypha, even for instruction of manners (and there was no one at Cullerne at all likely to question this right of private judgment), but his real, though perhaps unconscious, motive was to find a suitable passage for declamation. He thundered forth judgments in a manner which combined, he believed, the terrors of supreme justice with an infinite commiseration for the blindness of errant, but long-forgotten peoples. He had, in fact, that 'Bible voice' which seeks to communicate additional solemnity to the Scriptures by reciting them in a tone never employed in ordinary life, as the fledgling curate adds gravity to the Litany by whispering 'the hour of death and Day of Judgment.'

Mr Noot, being short-sighted, did not see how lightly the punishments of these ancient races passed over the heads of his dozing audience, and was bringing the long lesson to a properly dramatic close when the unexpected happened: the screen-door opened and a stranger entered. As the blowing of a horn by the paladin broke the repose of a century, and called back to life the spell-bound princess and her court, so these slumbering churchmen were startled from their dreams by the intruder. The choir-boys fell to giggling, the choir-men stared, Clerk Janaway grasped his mace as if he would brain so rash an adventurer, and the general movement made Mr Sharnall glance nervously at his stops; for he thought that he had overslept himself, and that the choir had stood up for the *Magnificat*.

The stranger seemed unconscious of the attention which his appearance provoked. He was no doubt some casual sightseer, and had possibly been unaware that any service was in progress until he opened the screen-door. But once there, he made up his mind to join in the devotions, and was walking to the steps which led up to the stalls when Clerk Janaway popped out of his place and accosted him, quoting the official regulations in something louder than a stage whisper:

'Ye cannot enter the choir during the hours of Divine service. Ye cannot come in.'

The stranger was amused at the old man's officiousness.

'I am in,' he whispered back, 'and, being in, will take a seat, if you please, until the service is over.'

The clerk looked at him doubtfully for a moment, but if there was amusement to be read in the other's countenance, there was also a decision that did not encourage opposition. So he thought better of the matter and opened the door of one of the pews that run below the stalls in Cullerne Church.

But the stranger did not appear to notice that a place was being shown him, and walked past the pew and up the little steps that lead to the stalls on the cantoris side. Directly behind the singing-men were five stalls, which had canopies richer and more elaborate than those of the others, with heraldic escutcheons painted on the backs. From these seats the vulgar herd was excluded by a faded crimson cord, but the stranger lifted the cord from its hook, and sat down in the first reserved seat, as if the place belonged to him.

Clerk Janaway was outraged, and bustled up the steps after him like an angry turkey-cock.

'Come, come!' he said, touching the intruder on the shoulder; 'you cannot sit here; these are the Fording seats, and kep' for Lord Blandamer's family.'

'I will make room if Lord Blandamer brings his family,' the stranger said; and, seeing that the old man was returning to the attack, added, 'Hush! that is enough.'

The clerk looked at him again, and then turned back to his own place, routed.

'*And in that day they shall roar against thee like the roaring of the sea, and if one look unto the land behold darkness and sorrow, and the light is darkened in the heavens thereof,*' said Mr Noot, and shut the book, with a glance of general fulmination through his great round spectacles

The choir, who had been interested spectators of this conflict of lawlessness as personified in the intruder, and authority as in the clerk, rose to their feet as the organ began the *Magnificat*.

The singing-men exchanged glances of amusement, for they were not altogether averse to seeing the clerk worsted. He was an autocrat in his own church, and ruffled them now and again with what they called his bumptiousness. Perhaps he did assume a little as he led the procession, for he forgot at times that he was a peaceable servant of the sanctuary, and fancied, as he marched mace in hand to the music of the organ, that he was a daring officer leading a forlorn hope. That very afternoon he had had a heated discussion in the vestry with Mr Milligan, the bass, on a question of gardening, and the singer, who still smarted under the clerk's overbearing tongue, was glad to emphasise his adversary's defeat by paying attention to the intruder.

The tenor on the cantoris side was taking holiday that day, and Mr Milligan availed himself of the opportunity to offer the absentee's copy of the service to the intruder, who was sitting immediately behind him. He turned round, and placed the book, open at the *Magnificat*, before the stranger with much deference, casting as he faced round again a look of misprision at Janaway, of which the latter was quick to appreciate the meaning.

This by-play was lost upon the stranger, who nodded his acknowledgment of the civility, and turned to the study of the score which had been offered him.

Mr Sharnall's resources in the way of men's voices were so limited that he was by no means unused to finding himself short of a voice-part on the one side or the other. He had done his best to remedy the deficiency in the Psalms by supplying the missing part with his left hand, but as he began the *Magnificat* he was amazed to hear a mellow and fairly strong tenor taking part in the service with feeling and precision. It was the stranger who stood in the gap, and when the first surprise was past, the choir welcomed him as being versed in their own arts, and Clerk Janaway forgot the presumption of his entrance and even the rebellious conduct of Mr Milligan. The men and boys sang with new life; they wished, in fact, that so knowledgeable a person should be favourably impressed, and the service was rendered in a more creditable way than Cullerne Church had known for many a long day. Only the stranger was perfectly unmoved. He sang as if he had been a lay-vicar all his life, and when the *Magnificat* was ended, and Mr Sharnall could look through the curtains of the organ-loft, the organist saw him with a Bible devoutly following Mr Noot in the second lesson.

He was a man of forty, rather above the middle height, with dark eyebrows and dark hair, that was beginning to turn grey. His hair, indeed, at once attracted the observer's attention by its thick profusion and natural wavy curl. He was clean-shaven, his features were sharply cut without being thin, and there was something contemptuous about the firm mouth. His nose was straight, and a powerful face gave the impression of a man who was accustomed to be obeyed. To anyone looking at him from the other side of the choir, he presented a remarkable picture, for which the black oak of Abbot Vinnicomb's stalls supplied a frame. Above his head the canopy went soaring up into crockets and finials, and on the woodwork at the back was painted a shield which nearer inspection would have shown to be the Blandamer cognizance, with its nebuly bars of green and silver. It was, perhaps, so commanding an appearance that made red-haired Patrick Ovens take out an Australian postage-stamp which he had acquired that very day, and point out to the boy next to him the effigy of Queen Victoria sitting crowned in a gothic chair.

The stranger seemed to enter thoroughly into the spirit of the performance; he bore his part in the service bravely, and, being furnished with another book, lent effective aid with the anthem. He stood up decorously as the choir filed out after the Grace, and then sat down again in his seat to listen to the voluntary. Mr Sharnall determined to play something of quality as a tribute to the unknown tenor, and gave as good a rendering of the St Anne's fugue as the state of the organ would permit. It was true that the trackers rattled terribly, and that a cipher marred the effect of the second subject; but when he got to the bottom of the little winding stairs that led down from the loft, he found the stranger waiting with a compliment.

'Thank you very much,' he said; 'it is very kind of you to give us so fine a fugue. It is many years since I was last in this church, and I am fortunate to have chosen so sunny an afternoon, and to have been in time for your service.'

'Not at all, not at all,' said the organist; 'it is we who are fortunate in having you to help us. You read well, and have a useful voice, though I caught you tripping a little in the lead of the *Nunc Dimittis* Gloria.' And he sung it over by way of reminder. 'You understand church music, and have sung many a service before I am sure, though you don't look much given that way,' he added, scanning him up and down.

The stranger was amused rather than offended at these blunt criticisms, and the catechizing went on.

'Are you stopping in Cullerne?'

'No,' the other replied courteously; 'I am only here for the day, but I hope I may find other occasions to visit the place and to hear your service. You will have your full complement of voices next time I come, no doubt, and I shall be able to listen more at my ease than to-day?'

'Oh no, you won't. It's ten to one you will find us still worse off. We are a poverty-stricken lot, and no one to come over into Macedonia to help us. These cursed priests eat up our substance like canker-worms, and grow sleek on the money that was left to keep the music going. I don't mean the old woman that read this afternoon; he's got *his* nose on the grindstone like the rest of us—poor Noot! He has to put brown paper in his boots because he can't afford to have them resoled. No, it's the Barabbas in the rectory-house, that buys his stocks and shares, and starves the service.'

This tirade fell lightly on the stranger's ears. He looked as if his thoughts were a thousand miles away, and the organist broke off:

'Do you play the organ? Do you understand an organ?' he asked quickly.

'Alas! I do not play,' the stranger said, bringing his mind back with a jerk for the answer, 'and understand little about the instrument.'

'Well, next time you are here come up into the loft, and I will show you what a chest of rattletraps I have to work with. We are lucky to get through a service without a breakdown; the pedal-board is too short and past its work, and now the bellows are worn out.'

'Surely you can get that altered,' the stranger said; 'the bellows shouldn't cost so much to mend.'

'They are patched already past mending. Those who would like to pay for new ones haven't got the money, and those who have the money won't pay. Why, that very stall you sat in belongs to a man who could give us a new church, if we wanted it. Blandamer, that's his name—Lord Blandamer. If you had looked you could have seen his great coat of arms on the back of the seat; and he won't spend a halfpenny to keep the roofs from falling on our heads.'

'Ah,' said the stranger, 'it seems a very sad case.' They had reached the north door, and, as they stepped out, he repeated meditatively: 'It seems a very sad case; you must tell me more about it next time we meet.'

The organist took the hint, and wished his companion good afternoon, turning down towards the wharves for a constitutional on the riverside. The stranger raised his hat with something of foreign courtesy, and walked back into the town.

Chapter 7

Miss Euphemia Joliffe devoted Saturday afternoon to St Sepulchre's Dorcas Society. The meetings were held in a class-room of the Girls' National School, and there a band of devoted females gathered week by week to make garments for the poor. If there was in Cullerne some thread-bare gentility, and a great deal of middle-class struggling, there was happily little actual poverty, as it is understood in great towns. Thus the poor, to whom the clothes made by the Dorcas Society were ultimately distributed, could sometimes afford to look the gift-horse in the mouth, and to lament that good material had been marred in the making. 'They wept,' the organist said, 'when they showed the coats and garments that Dorcas made, because they were so badly cut'; but this was a libel, for there were many excellent needlewomen in the society, and among the very best was Miss Euphemia Joliffe.

She was a staunch supporter of the church, and, had her circumstances permitted, would have been a Scripture-reader or at least a district visitor. But the world was so much with her, in the shape of domestic necessities at Bellevue Lodge, as to render parish work impossible, and so the Dorcas meeting was the only systematic philanthropy in which she could venture to indulge. But in the discharge of this duty she was regularity personified; neither wind nor rain, snow nor heat, sickness nor amusement, stopped her, and she was to be found each and every Saturday afternoon, from three to five, in the National School.

If the Dorcas Society was a duty for the little old lady, it was also a pleasure—one of her few pleasures, and perhaps the greatest. She liked the meeting, because on such occasions she felt herself to be the equal of her more prosperous neighbours. It is the same feeling that makes the half-witted attend funerals and church services. At such times they feel themselves to be for once on an equal footing with their fellow-men; all are reduced to the same level; there are no speeches to be made, no accounts to be added up, no counsels to be given, no decisions to be taken; all are as fools in the sight of God.

At the Dorcas meeting Miss Joliffe wore her 'best things' with the exception only of head-gear, for the wearing of her best bonnet was a crowning grace reserved exclusively for the Sabbath. Her wardrobe was too straitened to allow her 'best' to follow the shifting seasons closely. If it was bought as best for winter, it might have to play the same role also in summer, and thus it fell sometimes to her lot to wear alpaca in December, or, as on this day, to be adorned with a fur necklet when the weather asked for muslin. Yet 'in her best' she always felt 'fit to be seen'; and when it came to cutting out, or sewing, there were none that excelled her.

Most of the members greeted her with a kind word, for even in a place where envy, hatred, and malice walked the streets arm in arm from sunrise to sunset, Miss Euphemia had few enemies. Lying and slandering, and speaking evil of their fellows, formed a staple occupation of the ladies of Cullerne, as of many another small town; and to Miss Joliffe, who was foolish and old-fashioned enough to think evil of no one, it had seemed at first the only drawback of these delightful meetings that a great deal of such highly-spiced talk was to be heard at them. But even this fly was afterwards removed from the amber; for Mrs Bulteel—the brewer's lady—who wore London dresses, and was much the most fashionable person in Cullerne, proposed that some edifying book should be read aloud on Dorcas afternoons to the assembled workers. It was true that Mrs Flint said she only did so because she thought she had a fine voice; but however that might be, she proposed it, and no one cared to run counter to her. So Mrs Bulteel read properly religious stories, of so touching a nature that an afternoon seldom passed without her being herself dissolved in tears, and evoking sympathetic sniffs and sobs from such as wished to stand in her good books. If Miss Joliffe was not herself so easily moved by imaginary sorrow, she set it down to some lack of loving-kindness in her own disposition, and mentally congratulated the others on their superior sensitiveness.

Miss Joliffe was at the Dorcas meeting, Mr Sharnall was walking by the river-side, Mr Westray was with the masons on the roof of the transept; only Anastasia Joliffe was at Bellevue Lodge when the front-door bell rang. When her aunt was at home, Anastasia was not allowed to 'wait on the gentlemen', nor to answer the bell; but her aunt being absent, and there being no one else in the house, she duly opened one leaf of the great front-door, and found a gentleman standing on the semi-circular flight of steps outside. That he was a gentleman she knew at a glance, for she had a *flair* for such useless distinctions, though the genus was not sufficiently common at Cullerne to allow her much practice in its identification near home. It was, in fact, the stranger of the tenor voice, and such is the quickness of woman's wit, that she learnt in a moment as much concerning his outward appearance as the organist and the choir-men and the clerk had learnt in an hour; and more besides, for she saw that he was well dressed. There was about him a complete absence of personal adornment. He wore no rings and no scarf-pin, even his watch-chain was only of leather. His clothes were of so dark a grey as to be almost black, but Miss Anastasia Joliffe knew that the cloth was good, and the cut of the best. She had thrust a pencil into the pages of *Northanger Abbey* to keep the place while she answered the bell, and as the stranger stood before her, it seemed to her he might be a Henry Tilney, and she was prepared, like a Catherine Morland, for some momentous announcement when he opened his lips. Yet there came nothing very weighty from them; he did not even inquire for lodgings, as she half hoped that he would.

'Does the architect in charge of the works at the church lodge here? Is Mr Westray at home?' was all he said.

'He does live here,' she answered, 'but is out just now, and we do not expect him back till six. I think you will probably find him at the church if you desire to see him.'

'I have just come from the minster, but could see nothing of him there.'

It served the stranger right that he should have missed the architect, and been put to the trouble of walking as far as Bellevue Lodge, for his inquiries must have been very perfunctory. If he had taken the trouble to ask either organist or clerk, he would have learnt at once where Mr Westray was.

'I wonder if you would allow me to write a note. If you could give me a sheet of paper I should be glad to leave a message for him.'

Anastasia gave him a glance from head to foot, rapid as an instantaneous exposure. 'Tramps' were a permanent bugbear to the ladies of Cullerne, and a proper dread of such miscreants had been instilled into Anastasia Joliffe by her aunt. It was, moreover, a standing rule of the house that no strange men were to be admitted on any pretence, unless there was some man-lodger at home, to grapple with them if occasion arose. But the glance was sufficient to confirm her first verdict—he was a gentleman; there surely could not be such things as gentlemen-tramps. So she answered 'Oh, certainly,' and showed him into Mr Sharnall's room, because that was on the ground floor.

The visitor gave a quick look round the room. If he had ever been in the house before, Anastasia would have thought he was trying to identify something that he remembered; but there was little to be seen except an open piano, and the usual litter of music-books and manuscript paper.

'Thank you,' he said; 'can I write here? Is this Mr Westray's room?'

'No, another gentleman lodges here, but you can use this room to write in. He is out, and would not mind in any case; he is a friend of Mr Westray.'

'I had rather write in Mr Westray's room if I may. You see I have nothing to do with this other gentleman, and it might be awkward if he came in and found me in his apartment.'

It seemed to Anastasia that the information that the room in which they stood was not Mr Westray's had in some way or other removed an anxiety from the stranger's mind. There was a faint and indefinable indication of relief in his manner, however much he professed to be embarrassed at the discovery. It might have been, she thought, that he was a great friend of Mr Westray, and had been sorry to think that his room should be littered and untidy as Mr Sharnall's certainly was, and so was glad when he found out his mistake.

'Mr Westray's room is at the top of the house,' she said deprecatingly.

'It is no trouble to me, I assure you, to go up,' he answered.

Anastasia hesitated again for an instant. If there were no gentlemen-tramps perhaps there were gentlemen-burglars, and she hastily made a mental inventory of Mr Westray's belongings, but could think of nothing among them likely to act as an incentive to crime. Still she would not venture to show a strange man to the top of the house, when there was no one at home but herself.

The stranger ought not to have asked her. He could not be a gentleman after all, or he would have seen how irregular was such a request, unless he had indeed some particular motive for wishing to see Mr Westray's room.

The stranger perceived her hesitation, and read her thoughts easily enough.

'I beg your pardon,' he said. 'I ought, of course, to have explained who it is who has the honour of speaking to you. I am Lord Blandamer, and wish to write a few words to Mr Westray on questions connected with the restoration of the church. Here is my card.'

There was probably no lady in the town that would have received this information with as great composure as did Anastasia Joliffe. Since the death of his grandfather, the new Lord Blandamer had been a constant theme of local gossip and surmise. He was a territorial magnate, he owned the whole of the town, and the whole of the surrounding country. His stately house of Fording could be seen on a clear day from the minster tower. He was reputed to be a man of great talents and distinguished appearance; he was not more than forty, and he was unmarried. Yet no one had seen him since he came to man's estate; it was said he had not been in Cullerne for twenty years.

There was a tale of some mysterious quarrel with his grandfather, which had banished the young man from his home, and there had been no one to take his part, for both his father and mother were drowned when he was a baby. For a quarter of a century he had been a wanderer abroad: in France and Germany, in Russia and Greece, in Italy and Spain. He was believed to have visited the East, to have fought in Egypt, to have run blockades in South America, to have found priceless diamonds in South Africa. He had suffered the awful penances of the Fakirs, he had fasted with the monks of Mount Athos;

he had endured the silence of La Trappe; men said that the Sheik-ul-Islam had himself bound the green turban round Lord Blandamer's head. He could shoot, he could hunt, he could fish, he could fight, he could sing, he could play all instruments; he could speak all languages as fluently as his own; he was the very wisest and the very handsomest, and—some hinted—the very wickedest man that ever lived, yet no one had ever seen him. Here was indeed a conjunction of romance for Anastasia, to find so mysterious and distinguished a stranger face to face with her alone under the same roof; yet she showed none of those hesitations, tremblings, or faintings that the situation certainly demanded.

Martin Joliffe, her father, had been a handsome man all his life, and had known it. In youth he prided himself on his good looks, and in old age he was careful of his personal appearance. Even when his circumstances were at their worst he had managed to obtain well-cut clothes. They were not always of the newest, but they sat well on his tall and upright figure; 'Gentleman Joliffe' people called him, and laughed, though perhaps something less ill-naturedly than was often the case in Cullerne, and wondered whence a farmer's son had gotten such manners. To Martin himself an aristocratic bearing was less an affectation than a duty; his position demanded it, for he was in his own eyes a Blandamer kept out of his rights.

It was his good appearance, even at five-and-forty, which induced Miss Hunter of the Grove to run away with him, though Colonel Hunter had promised to disown her if she ever married so far beneath her. She did not, it is true, live long to endure her father's displeasure, but died in giving birth to her first child. Even this sad result had failed to melt the Colonel's heart. Contrary to all precedents of fiction, he would have nothing to do with his little granddaughter, and sought refuge from so untenable a position in removing from Cullerne. Nor was Martin himself a man to feel a parent's obligations too acutely; so the child was left to be brought up by Miss Joliffe, and to become an addition to her cares, but much more to her joys. Martin Joliffe considered that he had amply fulfilled his responsibilities in christening his daughter Anastasia, a name which Debrett shows to have been borne for generations by ladies of the Blandamer family; and, having given so striking a proof of affection, he started off on one of those periodic wanderings which were connected with his genealogical researches, and was not seen again in Cullerne for a lustre.

For many years afterwards Martin showed but little interest in the child. He came back to Cullerne at intervals; but was always absorbed in his efforts to establish a right to the nebuly coat, and content to leave the education and support of Anastasia entirely to his sister. It was not till his daughter was fifteen that he exercised any paternal authority; but, on his return from a long absence about that period, he pointed out to Miss Joliffe, senior, that she had shamefully neglected her niece's education, and that so lamentable a state of affairs must be remedied at once. Miss Joliffe most sorrowfully admitted her shortcomings, and asked Martin's forgiveness for her remissness. Nor did it ever occur to her to plead, in excuse, that the duties of a lodging-house, and the necessity of providing sustenance for herself and Anastasia, made serious inroads on the time that ought, no doubt, to have been devoted to education; or that the lack of means prevented her from engaging teachers to supplement her own too limited instructions. She had, in fact, been able to impart to Anastasia little except reading, writing and arithmetic, some geography, a slight knowledge of Miss Magnall's questions, a wonderful proficiency with the needle, an unquenchable love of poetry and fiction, a charity for her neighbours which was rare enough in Cullerne, and a fear of God which was sadly inconsistent with the best Blandamer traditions.

The girl was not being brought up as became a Blandamer, Martin had said; how was she to fill her position when she became the Honourable Anastasia? She must learn French, not such rudiments as Miss Joliffe had taught her, and he travestied his sister's 'Doo, dellah, derlapostrof, day' with a laugh that flushed her withered cheeks with crimson, and made Anastasia cry as she held her aunt's hand under the table; not *that* kind of French, but something that would really pass muster in society. And music, she *must* study that; and Miss Joliffe blushed again as she thought very humbly of some elementary duets in which she had played a bass for Anastasia till household work and gout conspired to rob her knotty fingers of all pliancy. It had been a great pleasure to her, the playing of these duets with her niece; but they must, of course, be very poor things, and quite out of date now, for she had played them when she was a child herself, and on the very same piano in the parlour at Wydcombe.

So she listened with attention while Martin revealed his scheme of reform, and this was nothing less than the sending of Anastasia to Mrs Howard's boarding-school at the county town of Carisbury. The project took away his sister's breath, for Mrs Howard's was a finishing school of repute, to which only Mrs Bulteel among Cullerne ladies could afford to send her daughters. But Martin's high-minded generosity knew no limits. 'It was no use making two bites at a cherry; what had to be done had better be done quickly.' And he clinched the argument by taking a canvas bag from his pocket, and pouring out a little heap of sovereigns on to the table. Miss Joliffe's wonder as to how her brother had become possessed of such wealth was lost in admiration of his magnanimity, and if for an instant she thought wistfully of the relief that a small portion of these riches would bring to the poverty-stricken menage at Bellevue Lodge, she silenced such murmurings in a burst of gratitude for the means of improvement that Providence had vouchsafed to Anastasia. Martin counted out the sovereigns on the table; it was better to pay in advance and so make an impression in Anastasia's favour, and to this Miss Joliffe agreed with much relief, for she had feared that before the end of the term Martin would be off on his travels again, and that she herself would be left to pay.

So Anastasia went to Carisbury, and Miss Joliffe broke her own rules, and herself incurred a number of small debts because she could not bear to think of her niece going to school with so meagre an equipment as she then possessed, and yet had no ready money to buy better. Anastasia remained for two half-years at Carisbury. She made such progress with her music that after much wearisome and lifeless practising she could stumble through Thalberg's variations on the air of 'Home, Sweet Home'; but in French she never acquired the true Parisian accent, and would revert at times to the 'Doo, dellah, derlapostrof, day,' of her earlier teaching, though there is no record that these shortcomings were ever a serious drawback to her in after-life. Besides such opportunities of improvement, she enjoyed the privilege of association with thirty girls of the upper middle-classes, and ate of the tree of knowledge of good and evil, the fruits of which had hitherto escaped her notice. At the end of her second term, however, she was forced to forgo these advantages, for Martin had left Cullerne without making any permanent provision for his daughter's schooling, and there was in Mrs Howard's propectus a law, inexorable as that of gravity, that no pupil shall be permitted to return to the academy whose account for the previous term remains unsettled.

Thus Anastasia's schooling came to an end. There was some excuse put forward that the air of Carisbury did not agree with her; and she never knew the real reason till nearly two years later, by which time Miss Joliffe's industry and self-denial had discharged the greater part of Martin's obligation to Mrs Howard. The girl was glad to remain at Cullerne, for she was deeply attached to Miss Joliffe; but she came back much older in experience; her horizon had widened, and she was beginning to take a more prospective view of life. These enlarged ideas bore fruit both pleasant and unpleasant, for she was led to form a juster estimate of her father's character, and when he next returned she found it difficult to tolerate his selfishness and his abuse of his sister's devotion.

That this should be so was a cause of great grief to Miss Joliffe. Though she herself felt for her niece a love which had in it something of adoration, she was at the same time conscientious enough to remember that a child's first duty should be towards its parents. Thus she forced herself to lament that Anastasia should be more closely attached to her than to Martin, and if there were times when she could not feel properly dissatisfied that she possessed the first place in her niece's affections, she tried to atone for this frailty by sacrificing opportunities of being with the girl herself, and using every opportunity of bringing her into her father's company. It was a fruitless endeavour, as every endeavour to cultivate affection, where no real basis for it exists, must eternally remain fruitless. Martin was wearied by his daughter's society, for he preferred to be alone, and set no store by her except as a cooking, house-cleaning, and clothes-mending machine; and Anastasia resented this attitude, and could find, moreover, no interest in the torn peerage which was her father's Bible, or in the genealogical research and jargon about the nebuly coat which formed the staple of his conversation. Later on, when he came back for the last time, her sense of duty enabled her to tend and nurse him with exemplary patience, and to fulfil all those offices of affection which even the most tender filial devotion could have suggested. She tried to believe that his death brought her sorrow and not relief, and succeeded so well that her aunt had no doubts at all upon the subject.

Martin Joliffe's illness and death had added to Anastasia's experience of life by bringing her into contact with doctors and clergymen; and it was no doubt this training, and the association with the superior classes afforded by Mrs Howard's academy, that enabled her to stand the shock of Lord Blandamer's announcement without giving any more perceptible token of embarrassment than a very slight blush.

'Oh, of course there is no objection,' she said, 'to your writing in Mr Westray's room. I will show you the way to it.'

She accompanied him to the room, and having provided writing materials, left him comfortably ensconced in Mr Westray's chair. As she pulled the door to behind her in going out, something prompted her to look round—perhaps it was merely a girl's light fancy, perhaps it was that indefinite fascination which the consciousness that we are being looked at sometimes exercises over us; but as she looked back her eyes met those of Lord Blandamer and she shut the door sharply, being annoyed at her own foolishness.

She went back to the kitchen, for the kitchen of the Hand of God was so large that Miss Joliffe and Anastasia used part of it for their sitting-room, took the pencil out of *Northanger Abbey*, and tried to transport herself to Bath. Five minutes ago she had been in the Grand Pump Room herself, and knew exactly where Mrs Allen and Isabella Thorpe and Edward Morland were sitting; where Catherine was standing, and what John Thorpe was saying to her when Tilney walked up. But alas! Anastasia found no re-admission; the lights were put out, the Pump Room was in darkness. A sad change to have happened in five minutes; but no doubt the charmed circle had dispersed in a huff on finding that they no longer occupied the first place in Miss Anastasia Joliffe's interest. And, indeed, she missed them the less because she had discovered that she herself possessed a wonderful talent for romance, and had already begun the first chapter of a thrilling story.

Nearly half an hour passed before her aunt returned, and in the interval Miss Austen's knights and dames had retired still farther into the background, and Miss Anastasia's hero had entirely monopolized the stage. It was twenty minutes past five when Miss Joliffe, senior, returned from the Dorcas meeting; 'precisely twenty minutes past five,' as she remarked many times subsequently, with that factitious importance which the ordinary mind attaches to the exact moment of any epoch-making event.

'Is the water boiling, my dear?' she asked, sitting down at the kitchen table. 'I should like to have tea to-day before the gentlemen come in, if you do not mind. The weather is quite oppressive, and the schoolroom was very close because we only had one window open. Poor Mrs Bulteel is so subject to take cold from draughts, and I very nearly fell asleep while she was reading.'

'I will get tea at once,' Anastasia said; and then added, in a tone of fine unconcern: 'There is a gentleman waiting upstairs to see Mr Westray.'

'My dear,' Miss Joliffe exclaimed deprecatingly, 'how could you let anyone in when I was not at home? It is exceedingly dangerous with so many doubtful characters about. There is Mr Westray's presentation inkstand, and the flower-picture for which I have been offered so much money. Valuable paintings are often cut out of their frames; one never has an idea what thieves may do.'

There was the faintest trace of a smile about Anastasia's lips.

'I do not think we need trouble about that, dear Aunt Phemie, because I am sure he is a gentleman. Here is his card. Look!' She handed Miss Joliffe the insignificant little piece of white cardboard that held so momentous a secret, and watched her aunt put on her spectacles to read it.

Miss Joliffe focussed the card. There were only two words printed on it, only 'Lord Blandamer' in the most unpretending and simple characters, but their effect was magical. Doubt and suspicion melted suddenly away, and a look of radiant surprise overspread her countenance, such as would have become a Constantine at the vision of the Labarum. She was a thoroughly unworldly woman, thinking little of the things of this life in general, and keeping her affections on that which is to come, with the constancy and realization that is so often denied to those possessed of larger temporal means. Her views as to right and wrong were defined and inflexible; she would have gone to the stake most cheerfully rather than violate them, and unconsciously lamented perhaps that civilization has robbed the faithful of the luxury of burning. Yet with all this were inextricably bound up certain little weaknesses among which figured a fondness for great names, and a somewhat exaggerated consideration for the lofty ones of this earth. Had she been privileged to be within the same four walls as a peer at a bazaar or missionary meeting, she would have revelled in a great opportunity; but to find Lord Blandamer under her own roof was a grace so wondrous and surprising as almost to overwhelm her.

'Lord Blandamer!' she faltered as soon as she had collected herself a little. 'I hope Mr Westray's room was tidy. I dusted it thoroughly this morning, but I wish he had given some notice of his intention to call. I should be so vexed if he found anything dusty. What is he doing, Anastasia? Did he say he would wait till Mr Westray came back?'

'He said he would write a note for Mr Westray. I found him writing things.'

'I hope you gave his lordship Mr Westray's presentation inkstand.'

'No, I did not think of that; but there was the little black inkstand, and plenty of ink in it.'

'Dear me, dear me!' Miss Joliffe said, ruminating on so extraordinary a position, 'to think that Lord Blandamer, whom no one has ever seen, should have come to Cullerne at last, and is now in this very house. I will just change this bonnet for my Sunday one,' she added, looking at herself in the glass, 'and then tell his lordship how very welcome he is, and ask him if I can get anything for him. He will see at once, from my bonnet, that I have only just returned, otherwise it would appear to him very remiss of me not to have paid him my respects before. Yes, I think it is undoubtedly more fitting to appear in a bonnet.'

Anastasia was a little perturbed at the idea of her aunt's interview with Lord Blandamer. She pictured to herself Miss Joliffe's excess of zeal, the compliments, which she would think it necessary to shower upon him, the marked attention and homage which he might interpret as servility, though it was only intended as proper deference to exalted rank. Anastasia was quite unaccountably anxious that the family should appear to the distinguished visitor in as favourable a light as possible, and thought for a moment of trying to persuade Miss Joliffe that there was no need for her to see Lord Blandamer at all, unless he summoned her. But she was of a philosophic temperament, and in a moment had rebuked her own folly. What could any impression of Lord Blandamer's matter to her? She would probably never see him again unless she opened the door when he went out. Why should he think anything at all about a commonplace lodging-house, and its inmates? And if such trivial matters did ever enter his thoughts, a man so clever as he would make allowance for those of a different station to himself, and would see what a good woman her aunt was in spite of any little mannerisms.

So she made no remonstrance, but sat heroically quiet in her chair, and re-opened *Northanger Abbey* with a determination to entirely forget Lord Blandamer, and the foolish excitement which his visit had created.

Chapter 8

Miss Joliffe must have had a protracted conversation with Lord Blandamer. To Anastasia, waiting in the kitchen, it seemed as if her aunt would never come down. She devoted herself to *Northanger Abbey* with fierce resolution, but though her eyes followed the lines of type, she had no idea what she was reading, and found herself at last turning the pages so frequently and with so much rustling as to disturb her own reverie. Then she shut the book with a bang, got up from her chair, and paced the kitchen till her aunt came back.

Miss Joliffe was full of the visitor's affability.

'It is *always* the way with these really great people, my dear,' she said with effusion. 'I have *always* noticed that the nobility are condescending; they adapt themselves so entirely to their surroundings.' Miss Joliffe fell into a common hyperbole in qualifying an isolated action as a habit. She had never before been brought face to face with a peer, yet she represented her first impression of Lord Blandamer's manner as if it were a mature judgment based upon long experience of those of his rank and position.

'I insisted on his using the presentation inkstand, and took away that shabby little black thing; and I could see at once that the silver one was far more like what he had been accustomed to use. He seemed to know something about us, and even asked if the young lady who had shown him in was my niece. That was you; he meant you, Anastasia; he asked it if was *you*. I think he must have met dear Martin somewhere, but I really was so agitated by such a very unexpected visit that I scarcely took in all he said. Yet he was so careful all the time to put me at my ease that at last I ventured to ask him if he would take some light refreshment. "My lord," I said, "may I be so bold as to offer your lordship a cup of tea? It would be a great honour if you would partake of our humble hospitality." And what do you think he answered, my dear? "Miss Joliffe"—and he had such a winning look—"there is nothing I should like better. I am very tired with walking about in the church, and have still some little time to wait, for I am going to London by the evening train." Poor young man! (for Lord Blandamer was still young in Cullerne, which had only known his octogenarian predecessor) he is no doubt called to London on some public business— the House of Lords, or the Court, or something like that. I wish he would take as much care of himself as he seems to take for others. He looked so very tired, and a sad face too, Anastasia, and yet is most considerate. "I should like a cup of tea very much"—those were his exact words—"but you must not trouble to come all the way upstairs again to bring it to me. Let me come down and take it with you."

'"Forgive me, my lord," was my answer, "but I could not permit that. Our establishment is much too homely, and I shall feel it a privilege to wait on you, if you will kindly excuse my walking clothes, as I have just come back from an afternoon meeting. My niece often wishes to relieve me, but I tell her my old legs are more active than her young ones even still."'

Anastasia's cheeks were red, but she said nothing, and her aunt went on: 'So I will take him some tea at once. You can make it, my dear, if you like, but put a great deal more in than what we use ourselves. The upper classes have no call to practise economy in such matters, and he is no doubt used to take his tea very strong. I think Mr Sharnall's teapot is the best, and I will get out the silver sugar-tongs and one of the spoons with the "J" on them.'

As Miss Joliffe was taking up the tea, she met Westray in the hall. He had just come back from the church, and was not a little concerned at his landlady's greeting. She put down her tray, and, with a fateful gesture and an 'Oh, Mr Westray, what do you think?' beckoned him aside into Mr Sharnall's room. His first impression was that some grave accident had happened, that the organist was dead, or that Anastasia Joliffe had sprained an ankle; and he was relieved to hear the true state of affairs. He waited a few minutes while Miss Joliffe took the visitor his tea, and then went upstairs himself.

Lord Blandamer rose.

'I must apologize,' he said, 'for making myself at home in your room; but I hope your landlady may have explained who I am, and how I come to take so great a liberty. I am naturally interested in Cullerne and all that concerns it, and hope ere long to get better acquainted with the place—and the people,' he added as an afterthought. 'At present I know disgracefully little about it, but that is due to my having been abroad for many years; I only came back a few months ago. But I need not bother you with all this; what I really wanted was to ask you if you would give me some idea of the scheme of restoration which it is proposed to undertake at the minster. Until last week I had not heard that anything of the kind was in contemplation.'

His tone was measured, and a clear, deep voice gave weight and sincerity to his words. His clean-shaven face and olive complexion, his regular features and dark eyebrows, suggested a Spaniard to Westray as he spoke, and the impression was strengthened by the decorous and grave courtesy of his manner.

'I shall be delighted to explain anything I can,' said the architect, and took down a bundle of plans and papers from a shelf.

'I fear I shall not be able to do much this evening,' Lord Blandamer said; 'for I have to catch the train to London in a short time; but, if you will allow me, I will take an early opportunity of coming over again. We might then, perhaps, go to the church together. The building has a great fascination for me, not only on account of its own magnificence, but also from old associations. When I was a boy, and sometimes a very unhappy boy, I used often to come over from Fording and spend hours rambling about the minster. Its winding staircases, its dark wall-passages, its mysterious screens and stalls, brought me romantic dreams, from which I think I have never entirely wakened. I am told the building stands in need of extensive restoration, though to the outsider it looks much the same as ever. It always had a dilapidated air.'

Westray gave a short outline of what it was considered should ultimately be done, and of what it was proposed to attack for the present.

'You see, we have our work cut out for us,' he said. 'The transept roof is undoubtedly the most urgent matter, but there are lots of other things that cannot be left to themselves for long. I have grave doubts about the stability of the tower, though my Chief doesn't share them to anything like the same extent: and perhaps that is just as well, for we are hampered on every side by lack of funds. They are going to have a bazaar next week to try to give the thing a lift, but a hundred bazaars would not produce half that is wanted.'

'I gathered that there were difficulties of this kind,' the visitor said reflectively. 'As I came out of the church after service to-day I met the organist. He had no idea who I was, but gave his views very strongly as to Lord Blandamer's responsibilities for things in general, and for the organ in particular. We are, I suppose, under some sort of moral obligation for the north transept, from having annexed it as a burying place. It used to be called, I fancy, the Blandamer Aisle.'

'Yes, it is called so still,' Westray answered. He was glad to see the turn the conversation had taken, and hoped that a *deus ex machina* had appeared. Lord Blandamer's next question was still more encouraging.

'At what do you estimate the cost of the transept repairs?'

Westray ran through his papers till he found a printed leaflet with a view of Cullerne Minster on the outside.

'Here are Sir George Farquhar's figures,' he said. 'This was a circular that was sent everywhere to invite subscriptions, but it scarcely paid the cost of printing. No one will give a penny to these things nowadays. Here it is, you see—seven thousand eight hundred pounds for the north transept.'

There was a little pause. Westray did not look up, being awkwardly conscious that the sum was larger than Lord Blandamer had anticipated, and fearing that such an abrupt disclosure might have damped the generosity of an intended contributor.

Lord Blandamer changed the subject.

'Who is the organist? I rather liked his manner, for all he took me so sharply, if impersonally, to task. He seems a clever musician, but his instrument is in a shocking state.'

'He *is* a very clever organist,' Westray answered. It was evident that Lord Blandamer was in a subscribing frame of mind, and if his generosity did not extend to undertaking the cost of the transept, he might at least give something towards the organ. The architect tried to do his friend Mr Sharnall a service. 'He is a very clever organist,' he repeated; 'his name is Sharnall, and he lodges in this house. Shall I call him? Would you like to ask him about the organ?'

'Oh, no, not now; I have so little time; another day we can have a chat. Surely a very little money—comparatively little money, I mean—would put the organ in proper repair. Did they never approach my grandfather, the late Lord Blandamer, on the question of funds for these restorations?'

Westray's hopes of a contribution were again dashed, and he felt a little contemptuous at such evasions. They came with an ill grace after Lord Blandamer's needlessly affectionate panegyric of the church.

'Yes,' he said; 'Canon Parkyn, the Rector here, wrote to the late Lord Blandamer begging for a subscription to the restoration fund for the church, but never got any answer.'

Westray flung something like a sneer into his tone, and was already sorry for his ungracious words before he had finished speaking. But the other seemed to take no offence, where some would have been offended.

'Ah,' he said, 'my grandfather was no doubt a very sad old man indeed. I must go now, or I shall miss my train. You shall introduce me to Mr Sharnall the next time I come to Cullerne; I have your promise, remember, to take me over the church. Is it not so?'

'Yes—oh yes, certainly,' Westray said, though with less cordiality perhaps than he had used on the previous occasion. He was disappointed that Lord Blandamer had promised no subscription, and accompanied him to the foot of the stairs with much the same feelings as a shop-assistant entertains for the lady who, having turned over goods for half an hour, retreats with the promise that she will consider the matter and call again.

Miss Joliffe had been waiting on the kitchen stairs, and so was able to meet Lord Blandamer in the hall quite accidentally. She showed him out of the front door with renewed professions of respect, for she knew nothing of his niggardly evasions of a subscription, and in her eyes a lord was still a lord. He added the comble* to all his graces and courtesies by shaking her hand as he left the house, and expressing a hope that she would be so kind as to give him another cup of tea, the very next time he was in Cullerne.

The light was falling as Lord Blandamer descended the flight of steps outside the door of Bellevue Lodge. The evening must have closed in earlier than usual, for very soon after the visitor had gone upstairs Anastasia found it too dark to read in the kitchen; so she took her book, and sat in the window-seat of Mr Sharnall's room.

It was a favourite resort of hers, both when Mr Sharnall was out, and also when he was at home; for he had known her from childhood, and liked to watch the graceful girlish form as she read quietly while

* apex

he worked at his music. The deep window-seat was panelled in painted deal, and along the side of it hung a faded cushion, which could be turned over on to the sill when the sash was thrown up, so as to form a rest for the arms of anyone who desired to look out on a summer evening.

The window was still open, though it was dusk; but Anastasia's head, which just appeared above the sill, was screened from observation by a low blind. This blind was formed of a number of little green wooden slats, faded and blistered by the suns of many summers, and so arranged that, by the turning of a brass, urn-shaped knob, they could be made to open and afford a prospect of the outer world to anyone sitting inside.

It had been for some time too dark for Anastasia to read, but she still sat in the window-seat; and as she heard Lord Blandamer come down the stairs, she turned the brass urn so as to command a view of the street. She felt herself blushing in the dark, at the reiterated and voluminous compliments which her aunt was paying in the hall. She blushed because Westray's tone was too off-handed and easy towards so important a personage to please her critical mood; and then she blushed again at her own folly in blushing. The front door shut at last, and the gaslight fell on Lord Blandamer's active figure and straight, square shoulders as he went down the steps. Three thousand years before, another maiden had looked between the doorpost and the door, at the straight broad back of another great stranger as he left her father's palace; but Anastasia was more fortunate than Nausicaa, for there is no record that Ulysses cast any backward glance as he walked down to the Phæacian ship, and Lord Blandamer did turn and look back.

He turned and looked back; he seemed to Anastasia to look between the little blistered slats into her very eyes. Of course, he could not have guessed that a very foolish girl, the niece of a very foolish landlady in a very commonplace lodging-house, in a very commonplace town, was watching him behind a shutter; but he turned and looked, and Anastasia stayed for half an hour after he had gone, thinking of the hard and clean-cut face that she had seen for an instant in the flickering gaslight.

It was a hard face, and as she sat in the dark with closed eyes, and saw that face again and again in her mind, she knew that it was hard. It was hard—it was almost cruel. No, it was not cruel, but only recklessly resolved, with a resolution that would not swerve from cruelty, if cruelty were needed to accomplish its purpose. Thus she reasoned in the approved manner of fiction. She knew that such reasonings were demanded of heroines. A heroine must be sadly unworthy of her lofty rôle if she could not with a glance unmask even the most enigmatic countenance, and trace the passions writ on it, clearly as a page of *Reading without Tears*. And was she, Anastasia, to fall short in such a simple craft? No, she had measured the man's face in a moment; it was resolved, even to cruelty. It was hard, but ah! how handsome! and she remembered how the grey eyes had met hers and blinded them with power, when she first saw him on the doorstep. Wondrous musings, wondrous thought-reading, by a countrified young lady in her teens; but is it not out of the mouths of babes and sucklings that strength has been eternally ordained?

She was awakened from her reverie by the door being flung open, and she leapt from her perch as Mr Sharnall entered the room.

'Heyday! heyday!' he said. 'What have we here? Fire out, and window open; missy dreaming of Sir Arthur Bedevere, and catching a cold—a very poetic cold in the head.'

His words jarred on her mood like the sharpening of a slate pencil. She said nothing, but brushed by him, shut the door behind her, and left him muttering in the dark.

The excitement of Lord Blandamer's visit had overtaxed Miss Joliffe. She took the gentlemen their supper—and Mr Westray was supping in Mr Sharnall's room that evening—and assured Anastasia that she was not in the least tired. But ere long she was forced to give up this pretence, and to take refuge in a certain high-backed chair with ears, which stood in a corner of the kitchen, and was only brought into use in illness or other emergency. The bell rang for supper to be taken away, but Miss Joliffe was fast asleep, and did not hear it. Anastasia was not allowed to 'wait' under ordinary circumstances, but her aunt must not be disturbed when she was so tired, and she took the tray herself and went upstairs.

'He is a striking-looking man enough,' Westray was saying as she entered the room; 'but I must say he did not impress me favourably in other respects. He spoke too enthusiastically about the church. It would have sat on him with a very good grace if he had afterwards come down with five hundred pounds, but ecstasies are out of place when a man won't give a halfpenny to turn them into reality.'

'He is a chip of the old block,' said the organist.

> *"Leap year's February twenty-nine days,*
> *And on the thirtieth Blandamer pays."*

'That's a saw about here. Well, I rubbed it into him this afternoon, and all the harder because I hadn't the least idea who he was.'

There was a fierce colour in Anastasia's cheeks as she packed the dirty plates and supper débris into the tray, and a fiercer feeling in her heart. She tried hard to conceal her confusion, and grew more confused in the effort. The organist watched her closely, without ever turning his eyes in her direction. He was a cunning little man, and before the table was cleared had guessed who was the hero of those dreams, from which he had roused her an hour earlier.

Westray waved away with his hand a puff of smoke which drifted into his face from Mr Sharnall's pipe.

'He asked me whether anyone had ever approached the old lord about the restoration, and I said the Rector had written, and never got an answer.'

'It wasn't to the *old* lord he wrote,' Mr Sharnall cut in; 'it was to this very man. Didn't you know it was to this very man? No one ever thought it worth ink and paper to write to *old* Blandamer. I was the only one fool enough to do that. I had an appeal for the organ printed once upon a time, and sent him a copy, and asked him to head the list. After a bit he sent me a cheque for ten shillings and sixpence; and then I wrote and thanked him, and said it would do very nicely to mend a leg of the organ-stool which had broken. But he had the last word, for when I went to the bank to cash the cheque, I found it stopped.'

Westray laughed with a thin and tinkling merriment that irritated Anastasia more than an honest guffaw.

'When he stuck at seven thousand eight hundred pounds for the church, I tried to give *you* a helping hand with the organ. I told him you lived in the house; would he not like to see you? "Oh no, not *now*," he said; "some other day."'

'He is a chip of the old block,' the organist said again bitterly. 'Gather figs of thistles, if you will, but don't expect money from Blandamers.'

Anastasia's thumb went into the curry as she lifted a plate but she did not notice it. She was only eager to get away, to place herself outside the reach of these slanderous tongues, to hide herself where she could unburden her heart of its bitterness. Mr Sharnall fired one more shaft at her as she left the room.

'He takes after his grandfather in other ways besides closefistedness. The old man had a bad enough name with women, and this man has a worse. They are a poor lot—lock, stock, and barrel.'

Lord Blandamer had certainly been unhappy in the impression which he created at Bellevue Lodge; a young lady had diagnosed his countenance as hard and cruel, an architect had detected niggardliness in his disposition, and an organist was resolved to regard him at all hazards as a personal foe. It was fortunate indeed for his peace of mind that he was completely unaware of this, but, then, he might not perhaps have troubled much even if he had known all about it. The only person who had a good word for him was Miss Euphemia Joliffe. She woke up flushed, but refreshed, after her nap, and found the supper-things washed and put away in their places.

'My dear, my dear,' she said deprecatingly, 'I am afraid I have been asleep and left all the work to you. You should not have done this, Anastasia. You ought to have awakened me.' The flesh was weak, and she was forced to hold her hand before her mouth for a moment to conceal a yawn; but her mind reverted instinctively to the great doings of the day, and she said with serene reflection: 'A very remarkable man, so dignified and yet so affable, and *very* handsome too, my dear.'

Chapter 9

Among the letters which the postman brought to Bellevue Lodge on the morning following these remarkable events was an envelope which possessed a dreadful fascination. It bore a little coronet stamped in black upon the flap, and 'Edward Westray, Esq., Bellevue Lodge, Cullerne,' written on the front in a bold and clear hand. But this was not all, for low in the left corner was the inscription 'Blandamer'. A single word, yet fraught with so mystical an import that it set Anastasia's heart beating fast as she gave it to her aunt, to be taken upstairs with the architect's breakfast.

'There is a letter for you, sir, from Lord Blandamer,' Miss Joliffe said, as she put down the tray on the table.

But the architect only grunted, and went on with ruler and compass at the plan with which he was busy. Miss Joliffe would have been more than woman had she not felt a burning curiosity to know the contents of so important a missive; and to leave a nobleman's letter neglected on the table seemed to her little short of sacrilege.

Never had breakfast taken longer to lay, and still there was the letter lying by the tin cover, which (so near is grandeur to our dust) concealed a simple bloater. Poor Miss Joliffe made a last effort ere she left the room to bring Westray to a proper appreciation of the situation.

'There is a letter for you, sir; I think it is from Lord Blandamer.'

'Yes, yes,' the architect said sharply; 'I will attend to it presently.'

And so she retired, routed.

Westray's nonchalance had been in part assumed. He was anxious to show that he, at any rate, could rise superior to artificial distinctions of rank, and was no more to be impressed by peers than peasants. He kept up this philosophic indifference even after Miss Joliffe left the room; for he took life very seriously, and felt his duty towards himself to be at least as important as that towards his neighbours. Resolution lasted till the second cup of tea, and then he opened the letter.

Dear Sir [it began],

I understood from you yesterday that the repairs to the north transept of Cullerne Minster are estimated to cost £7,800. This charge I should like to bear myself, and thus release for other purposes of restoration the sum already collected. I am also prepared to undertake whatever additional outlay is required to put the whole building in a state of substantial repair. Will you kindly inform Sir George Farquhar of this, and ask him to review the scheme of restoration as modified by these considerations? I shall be in Cullerne on Saturday next, and hope I may find you at home if I call about five in the afternoon, and that you may then have time to show me the church.

I am, dear sir,

Very truly yours,

BLANDAMER.

Westray had scanned the letter so rapidly that he knew its contents by intuition rather than by the more prosaic method of reading. Nor did he re-read it several times, as is generally postulated by important communications in fiction; he simply held it in his hand, and crumpled it unconsciously while he thought. He was surprised, and he was pleased—pleased at the wider vista of activity that Lord Blandamer's offer opened, and pleased that he should be chosen as the channel through which an announcement of such gravity was to be made. He felt, in short, that pleasurable and confused excitement, that mental inebriation which unexpected good fortune is apt to produce in any except the strongest minds, and went down to Mr Sharnall's room still crumpling the letter in his hand. The bloater was left to waste its sweetness on the morning air.

'I have just received some extraordinary news,' he said, as he opened the door.

Mr Sharnall was not altogether unprepared, for Miss Joliffe had already informed him that a letter from Lord Blandamer had arrived for Mr Westray; so he only said 'Ah!' in a tone that implied compassion for the lack of mental balance which allowed Westray to be so easily astonished, and added 'Ah, yes?' as a manifesto that no sublunary catastrophe could possibly astonish him, Mr Sharnall. But Westray's excitement was cold-waterproof, and he read the letter aloud with much jubilation.

'Well,' said the organist, 'I don't see much in it; seven thousand pounds is nothing to him. When we have done all that we ought to do, we are unprofitable servants.'

'It isn't only seven thousand pounds; don't you see he gives carte-blanche for repairs in general? Why, it may be thirty or forty thousand, or even more.'

'Don't you wish you may get it?' the organist said, raising his eyebrows and shutting his eyelids.

Westray was nettled.

'Oh, I think it's mean to sneer at everything the man does. We abused him yesterday as a niggard; let us have the grace to-day to say we were mistaken.' He was afflicted with the over-scrupulosity of a refined, but strictly limited mind, and his conscience smote him. 'I, at any rate, was quite mistaken,' he went on; 'I quite misinterpreted his hesitation when I mentioned the cost of the transept repairs.'

'Your chivalrous sentiments do you the greatest credit,' the organist said, 'and I congratulate you on being able to change your ideas so quickly. As for me, I prefer to stick to my first opinion. It is all humbug; either he doesn't mean to pay, or else he has some plan of his own to push. I wouldn't touch his money with a barge-pole.'

'Oh no, of course not,' Westray said, with the exaggerated sarcasm of a schoolboy in his tone. 'If he was to offer a thousand pounds to restore the organ, you wouldn't take a penny of it.'

'He hasn't offered a thousand yet,' rejoined the organist; 'and when he does, I'll send him away with a flea in his ear.'

'That's a very encouraging announcement for would-be contributors,' Westray sneered; 'they ought to come forward very strongly after that.'

'Well, I must get on with some copying,' the organist said dryly; and Westray went back to the bloater.

If Mr Sharnall was thus pitiably wanting in appreciation of a munificent offer, the rest of Culerne made no pretence of imitating his example. Westray was too elated to keep the good news to himself, nor did there appear, indeed, to be any reason for making a secret of it. So he told the foreman-mason, and Mr Janaway the clerk, and Mr Noot the curate, and lastly Canon Parkyn the rector, whom he certainly ought to have told the first of all. Thus, before the carillon of

St Sepulchre's played 'New Sabbath'* at three o'clock that afternoon, the whole town was aware that the new Lord Blandamer had been among them, and had promised to bear the cost of restoring the great minster of which they were all so proud—so very much more proud when their pride entailed no sordid considerations of personal subscription.

Canon Parkyn was ruffled. Mrs Parkyn perceived it when he came in to dinner at one o'clock, but, being a prudent woman she did not allude directly to his ill-humour, though she tried to dispel it by leading the conversation to topics which experience had shown her were soothing to him. Among such the historic visit of Sir George Farquhar, and the deference which he had paid to the Rector's suggestions, occupied a leading position; but the mention of the great architect's name was a signal for a fresh exhibition of vexation on her husband's part.

'I wish,' he said, 'that Sir George would pay a little more personal attention to the work at the minster. His representative, this Mr— er—er—this Mr Westray, besides being, I fear, very inexperienced and deficient in architectural knowledge, is a most conceited young man, and constantly putting himself forward in an unbecoming way. He came to me this morning with an exceedingly strange communication—a letter from Lord Blandamer.'

Mrs Parkyn laid down her knife and fork.

'A letter from Lord Blandamer?' she said in unconcealed amazement —'a letter from Lord Blandamer to Mr Westray!'

'Yes,' the Rector went on, losing some of his annoyance in the pleasurable consciousness that his words created a profound sensation—'a letter in which his lordship offers to bear in the first place the cost of the repairs of the north transept, and afterwards to make good any deficiency in the funds required for the restoration of the rest of the fabric. Of course, I am very loth to question any action taken by a member of the Upper House, but at the same time I am compelled to characterize the proceeding as most irregular. That such a communication should be made to a mere clerk of the works instead of to the Rector and duly appointed guardian of the sacred edifice, is so grave a breach of propriety that I am tempted to veto the matter entirely, and to refuse to accept this offer.'

His face wore a look of sublime dignity, and he addressed his wife as if she were a public meeting. *Ruat cœlum*, Canon Parkyn was not to be moved a hair's breadth from the line traced by propriety and rectitude. He knew in his inmost heart that under no possible circumstances would he have refused any gift that was offered him, yet his own words had about them so heroic a ring that for a moment he was himself dashing Lord Blandamer's money on the floor, as early

84

* See Appendix at the end of the story.

Christians had flung to the wind that pinch of incense that would have saved them from the lions.

'I think I *must* refuse this offer,' he repeated.

Mrs Parkyn knew her husband intimately—more intimately, perhaps, than he knew himself—and had an additional guarantee that the discussion was merely academic in the certainty that, even were he really purposed to refuse the offer, she would not *allow* him to do so. Yet she played the game, and feigned to take him seriously.

'I quite appreciate your scruples, my dear; they are just what anyone who knew you would expect. It is a positive affront that you should be told of such a proposal by this impertinent young man; and Lord Blandamer has so strange a reputation himself that one scarcely knows how far it is right to accept anything from him for sacred purposes. I honour your reluctance. Perhaps it *would* be right for you to decline this proposal, or, at any rate to take time for consideration.'

The Rector looked furtively at his wife. He was a little alarmed at her taking him so readily at his word. He had hoped that she would be dismayed—that she could have brought proper arguments to bear to shake his high resolve.

'Ah, your words have unwittingly reminded me of my chief difficulty in refusing. It is the sacred purpose which makes me doubt my own judgment. It would be a painful reflection to think that the temple should suffer by my refusing this gift. Maybe I should be yielding to my own petulance or personal motives if I were to decline. I must not let my pride stand in the way of higher obligations.'

He concluded in his best pulpit manner, and the farce was soon at an end. It was agreed that the gift must be accepted, that proper measures should be taken to rebuke Mr Westray's presumption as *he* had no doubt induced Lord Blandamer to select so improper a channel of communication, and that the Rector should himself write direct to thank the noble donor. So after dinner, Canon Parkyn retired to his 'study', and composed a properly fulsome letter, in which he attributed all the noblest possible motives and qualities to Lord Blandamer, and invoked all the most unctuously conceived blessings upon his head. And at tea-time the letter was perused and revised by Mrs Parkyn, who added some finishing touches of her own, especially a preamble which stated that Canon Parkyn had been informed by the clerk of the works that Lord Blandamer had expressed a desire to write to Canon Parkyn to make a certain offer but had asked the clerk of the works to find out first whether such an offer would be acceptable to Canon Parkyn, and a peroration which hoped that Lord Blandamer would accept the hospitality of the Rectory on the occasion of his next visit to Cullerne.

The letter reached Lord Blandamer at Fording the next morning as he sat over a late breakfast, with a Virgil open on the table by his coffee-cup. He read the Rector's stilted periods without a smile, and made a mental note that he would at once send a specially civil acknowledgment. Then he put it carefully into his pocket, and turned back to the *Di patrii indigetes et Romule Vestaque Mater* of the First Georgic, which he was committing to memory, and banished the invitation so completely from his mind that he never thought of it again till he was in Cullerne a week later.

Lord Blandamer's visit, and the offer which he had made for the restoration of the church, formed the staple of Cullerne conversation for a week. All those who had been fortunate enough to see or to speak to him discussed him with one another, and compared notes. Scarcely a detail of his personal appearance, of his voice or manner escaped them; and so infectious was this interest that some who had never seen him at all were misled by their excitement into narrating how he had stopped them in the street to ask the way to the architect's lodgings, and how he had made so many striking and authentic remarks that it was wonderful that he had ever reached Bellevue Lodge at all that night. Clerk Janaway, who was sorely chagrined to think that he should have missed an opportunity of distinguished converse, declared that he had felt the stranger's grey eyes go through and through him like a knife, and had only made believe to stop him entering the choir, in order to convince himself by the other's masterful insistence that his own intuition was correct. He had known all the time, he said, that he was speaking to none other than Lord Blandamer.

Westray thought the matter important enough to justify him in going to London to consult Sir George Farquhar, as to the changes in the scheme of restoration which Lord Blandamer's munificence made possible; but Mr Sharnall, at any rate, was left to listen to Miss Joliffe's recollections, surmises, and panegyrics.

In spite of all the indifference which the organist had affected when he first heard the news, he showed a surprising readiness to discuss the affair with all comers, and exhibited no trace of his usual impatience with Miss Joliffe, so long as she was talking of Lord Blandamer. To Anastasia it seemed as if he could talk of nothing else, and the more she tried to check him by her silence or by change of subject, the more bitterly did he return to the attack.

The only person to exhibit no interest in this unhappy nobleman, who had outraged propriety by offering to contribute to the restoration of the minster, was Anastasia herself; and even tolerant Miss Joliffe was moved to chide her niece's apathy in this particular.

'I do not think it becomes us, love, young or old, to take so little notice of great and good deeds. Mr Sharnall is, I fear, discontented with the station of life to which it has pleased Providence to call him, and I am less surprised at *his* not always giving praise where praise should be given; but with the young it is different. I am sure if anyone had offered to restore Wydcombe Church when I was a girl—and specially a nobleman—I should have been as delighted, or nearly as delighted, as if he—as if I had been given a new frock.' She altered the 'as if he had given me' which was upon her tongue because the proposition, even for purposes of illustration, that a nobleman could ever have offered her a new frock seemed to have in itself something of the scandalous and unfitting.

'I should have been delighted, but, dear me! in those days people were so blind as never to think of restorations. We used to sit in quite *comfortable* seats every Sunday, with cushions and hassocks, and the aisles were paved with flagstones—simple worn flagstones, and none of the caustic tiles which look so much more handsome; though I am always afraid I am going to slip, and glad to be off them, they are so hard and shiny. Church matters were very behindhand then. All round the walls were tablets that people had put up to their relations, white caskets on black marble slates, and urns and cherubs' heads, and just opposite where I used to sit a poor lady, whose name I have forgotten, weeping under a willow-tree. No doubt they were very much out of place in the sanctuary, as the young gentleman said in his lecture on "How to make our Churches Beautiful" in the Town Hall last winter. He called them "mural blisters", my dear, but there was no talk of removing them in my young days, and that was, I dare say, because there was no one to give the money for it. But now, here is this good young nobleman, Lord Blandamer, come forward so handsomely, and I have no doubt at all Cullerne will be much improved ere long. We are not meant to *loll* at our devotions, as the lecturer told us. That was his word, to "*loll*"; and they will be sure to take away the baize and hassocks, though I do hope there will be a little strip of *something* on the seats; the bare wood is apt to make one ache sometimes. I should not say it to anyone else in the world but you, but it *does* make me ache a little sometimes; and when the caustic is put down in the aisle, I shall take your arm, my dear, to save me from slipping. Here is Lord Blandamer going to do all this for us, and you do not show yourself in the least grateful. It is not becoming in a young girl.'

'Dear aunt, what would you have me do? I cannot go and thank him publicly in the name of the town. That would be still more unbecoming; and I am sure I hope they will not do all the dreadful things in the church that you speak of. I love the old monuments, and like *lolling* much better than bare forms.'

So she would laugh the matter off; but if she could not be induced to talk of Lord Blandamer, she thought of him the more, and rehearsed again and again in day-dreams and in night-dreams every incident of that momentous Saturday afternoon, from the first bars of the overture, when he had revealed in so easy and simple a way that he was none other than Lord Blandamer, to the ringing down of the curtain, when he turned to look back—to that glance when his eyes had seemed to meet hers, although she was hidden behind a blind, and he could not have guessed that she was there.

Westray came back from London with the scheme of restoration reconsidered and amplified in the light of altered circumstances, and with a letter for Lord Blandamer in which Sir George Farquhar hoped that the munificent donor would fix a day on which Sir George might come down to Cullerne to offer his respects, and to discuss the matter in person. Westray had looked forward all the week to the appointment which he had with Lord Blandamer for five o'clock on the Saturday afternoon, and had carefully thought out the route which he would pursue in taking him round the church. He returned to Bellevue Lodge at a quarter to five, and found his visitor already awaiting him. Miss Joliffe was, as usual, at her Saturday meeting, but Anastasia told Westray that Lord Blandamer had been waiting more than half an hour.

'I must apologize, my lord, for keeping you waiting,' Westray said, as he went in. 'I feared I had made some mistake in the time of our meeting, but I see it *was* five that your note named.' And he held out the open letter which he had taken from his pocket.

'The mistake is entirely mine,' Lord Blandamer admitted with a smile, as he glanced at his own instructions; 'I fancied I had said four o'clock; but I have been very glad of a few minutes to write one or two letters.'

'We can post them on our way to the church; they will just catch the mail.'

'Ah, then I must wait till to-morrow; there are some enclosures which I have not ready at this moment.'

They set out together for the minster, and Lord Blandamer looked back as they crossed the street.

'The house has a good deal of character,' he said, 'and might be made comfortable enough with a little repair. I must ask my agent to see what can be arranged; it does not do me much credit as landlord in its present state.'

'Yes, it has a good many interesting features,' Westray answered; 'you know its history, of course—I mean that it was an old inn.'

He had turned round as his companion turned, and for an instant thought he saw something moving behind the blind in Mr Sharnall's room. But he must have been mistaken; only Anastasia was in the house, and she was in the kitchen, for he had called to her as they went out to say that he might be late for tea.

Westray thoroughly enjoyed the hour and a half which the light allowed him for showing and explaining the church. Lord Blandamer exhibited what is called, so often by euphemism, an intelligent interest in all that he saw, and was at no pains either to conceal or display a very adequate architectural knowledge. Westray wondered where he had acquired it, though he asked no questions; but before the inspection was ended he found himself unconsciously talking to his companion of technical points, as to a professional equal and not to an amateur. They stopped for a moment under the central tower.

'I feel especially grateful,' Westray said, 'for your generosity in giving us a free hand for all fabric work. because we shall now be able to tackle the tower. Nothing will ever induce me to believe that all is right up there. The arches are extraordinarily wide and thin for their date. You will laugh when I tell you that I sometimes think I hear them crying for repair, and expecially that one on the south with the jagged crack in the wall above it. Now and then, when I am alone in the church or the tower, I seem to catch their very words. "The arch never sleeps," they say; "we never sleep."'

'It is a romantic idea,' Lord Blandamer said. 'Architecture is poetry turned into stone, according to the old aphorism, and you, no doubt, have much of the poet in you.'

He glanced at the thin and rather bloodless face, and at the high cheekbones of the water-drinker as he spoke. Lord Blandamer never made jokes, and very seldom was known to smile, yet if anyone but Westray had been with him, they might have fancied that there was a whimsical tone in his words, and a trace of amusement in the corners of his eyes. But the architect did not see it, and coloured slightly as he went on:

'Well, perhaps you are right; I suppose architecture does inspire one. The first verses I ever wrote, or the first, at least, that I ever printed, were on the Apse of Tewkesbury Abbey. They came out in the *Gloucester Herald*, and I dare say I shall scribble something about these arches some day.'

'Do,' said Lord Blandamer, 'and send me a copy. This place ought to have its poet, and it is much safer to write verses to arches than to arched eyebrows.'

Westray coloured again, and put his hand in his breast-pocket. Could he have been so foolish as to leave those half-finished lines on his desk for Lord Blandamer or anyone else to see? No, they were quite safe; he could feel the sharp edge of the paper folded lengthways, which differentiated them from ordinary letters.

'We shall just have time to go up to the roof-space, if you care to do so,' he suggested, changing the subject. 'I should like to show you the top of the transept groining, and explain what we are busy with at present. It is always more or less dark up there, but we shall find lanterns.'

'Certainly, with much pleasure.' And they climbed the newel staircase that was carried in the north-east pier.

Clerk Janaway had been hovering within a safe distance of them as they went their round. He was nominally busy in 'putting things straight' for the Sunday, before the church was shut up; and had kept as much out of sight as was possible, remembering how he had withstood Lord Blandamer to the face a week before. Yet he was anxious to meet him, as it were, by accident, and explain that he had acted in ignorance of the real state of affairs; but no favourable opportunity for such an explanation presented itself. The pair had gone up to the roof, and the clerk was preparing to lock up—for Westray had a key of his own—when he heard someone coming up the nave.

It was Mr Sharnall, who carried a pile of music-books under his arm.

'Hallo!' he said to the clerk, 'what makes *you* so late? I expected to have to let myself in. I thought you would have been off an hour ago.'

'Well, things took a bit longer to-night than usual to put away.' He broke off, for there was a little noise somewhere above them in the scaffolding, and went on in what was meant for a whisper: 'Mr Westray's taking his lordship round; they're up in the roof now. D'ye hear 'em?'

'Lordship! What lordship? D'you mean that fellow Blandamer?'

'Yes, that's just who I do mean. But I don't know as how he's a fellow, and he *is* a lordship; so that's why I call him a lordship and not a fellow. And mid I ask what he's been doing to set *your* back up? Why don't you wait here for him, and talk to him about the organ? Maybe, now he's in the giving mood, he'd set it right for 'ee, or anyways give 'ee that little blowin'-engine you talk so much about. Why do 'ee always go about showin' your teeth?—metaforally, I mean, for you haven't that many real ones left to make much show—why ain't you like other folk sometimes? Shall I tell 'ee? 'Cause you wants to be young when you be old, and rich when you be poor. That's why. That makes 'ee miserable, and then you drinks to drown it. Take my advice, and act like other folk. I'm nigh a score of years older than you, and take a vast more pleasure in my life than when I was twenty. The neighbours and their ways tickle me now, and my pipe's sweeter; and there's many a foolish thing a young man does that age don't give an old one the chanst to. You've spoke straight to me, and now I've spoke straight to you, 'cause I'm a straight-speaking man, and have no call to be afraid of anyone—lord or fellow or organist. So take an old man's word: cheer up, and wait on my lord, and get him to give 'ee a new organ.'

'Bah!' said Mr Sharnall, who was far too used to Janaway's manner to take umbrage or pay attention to it. 'Bah! I hate all Blandamers. I wish they were as dead and buried as dodos; and I'm not at all sure they aren't. I'm not at all sure, mind you, that this strutting peacock has any more right to the name of Blandamer than you or I have. I'm sick of all this wealth. No one's thought anything of today, who can't build a church or a museum or a hospital. "So long as thou doest well unto *thyself*, men will speak good of thee." If you've got the money, you're everything that's wonderful, and if you haven't you may go rot. I wish all Blandamers were in their graves,' he said, raising his thin and strident voice till it rang again in the vault above, 'and wrapped up in their nebuly coat for a shroud. I should like to fling a stone through their damned badge.' And he pointed to the sea-green and silver shield high up in the transept window. 'Sunlight and moonlight, it is always there. I used to like to come down and play here to the bats of a full moon, till I saw *that* would always look into the loft and haunt me.'

He thumped his pile of books down on the seat, and flung out of the church. He had evidently been drinking, and the clerk made his escape at the same time, being anxious not to be identified with sentiments which had been so loudly enunciated that he feared those in the roof might have overheard them.

Lord Blandamer wished Westray good-night at the church-door, excusing himself from an invitation to tea on the ground of business which necessitated his return to Fording.

'We must spend another afternoon in the minster,' he said. 'I hope you will allow me to write and make an appointment. I am afraid that it may possibly be for a Saturday again, for I am much occupied at present during the week.'

Clerk Janaway lived not far from the church, in Governour's Lane. No one knew whence its name was derived, though Dr Ennefer thought that the Military Governour might have had his quarters thereabouts when Cullerne was held for the Parliament. Serving as a means of communication between two quiet back-streets, it was itself more quiet than either, and yet, for all this, had about it a certain air of comfort and well-being. The passage of vehicles was barred at either end by old cannon. Their breeches were buried in the ground, and their muzzles stood up as sturdy iron posts, while the brown cobbles of the roadway sloped to a shallow stone gutter which ran down the middle of the lane. Custom ordained that the houses should be coloured with a pink wash; and the shutters, which were a feature of the place, shone in such bright colours as to recall a Dutch town.

Shutter-painting was indeed an event of some importance in Governour's Lane. Not a few of its inhabitants had followed the sea as fishermen or smack-owners, and when fortune so smiled on them that they could retire, and there were no more boats to be painted, shutters and doors and window frames came in to fill the gap. So, on a fine morning, when the turpentine oozing from cracks and the warm smell of blistering varnish brought to Governour's Lane the first tokens of returning summer, might have been seen sexagenarians and septuagenarians, and some so strong that they had come to fourscore years, standing paint-pot and paint-brush in hand, while they gave a new coat to the woodwork of their homes.

They were a kindly folk, open of face, and fresh-complexioned, broad in the beam, and vested as to their bodies in dark blue, brass-buttoned pilot coats. Insuperable smokers, inexhaustible yarn-spinners, they had long welcomed Janaway as a kindred spirit—the more so that in their view a clerk and grave-digger was in some measure an expert in things unseen, who might anon assist in piloting them on the last cruise for which some had already the Blue Peter at the fore.

A myrtle-bush which grew out of a hole in the cobbles was carefully trained against the front of a cottage in the middle of the row, and a brass plate on the door informed the wayfarer and ignorant man that 'T. Janaway, Sexton' dwelt within. About eight o'clock on the Saturday evening some two hours after Lord Blandamer and Westray had parted, the door of the myrtle-fronted cottage was open, and the clerk stood on the threshold smoking his pipe, while from within came a cheerful, ruddy light and a well-defined smell of cooking; for Mrs Janaway was preparing supper.

'Tom,' she called, 'shut the door, and come to thy victuals.'

'Ay,' he answered, 'I'll be with 'ee directly; but gi'e me a minute. I want to see who this is coming up the lane.'

Someone that the clerk knew at once for a stranger had entered the little street at the bottom. There was half a moon, and light enough to see that he was in search of some particular house; for he crossed from one side of the lane to the other, and peered at the numbers on the doors. As he came nearer, the clerk saw that he was of spare build, and wore a loose overcoat or cape, which fluttered in the breeze that blew at evening from the sea. A moment later Janaway knew that the stranger was Lord Blandamer, and stepped back instinctively to let him pass. But the open door had caught the attention of the passer-by; he stopped, and greeted the householder cheerily.

'A beautiful night, but with a cold touch in the air that makes your warm room look very cheerful.' He recognized the clerk's face as he spoke, and went on: 'Ah, ha! we are old friends already; we met in the minster a week ago, did we not?'

Mr Janaway was a little disconcerted at the unexpectedness of the meeting, and returned the salutation in a confused way. The attempt which he had made to prevent Lord Blandamer from entering the choir was fresh in his memory, and he stammered some unready excuses.

Lord Blandamer smiled with much courtesy.

'You were quite right to stop me; you would have been neglecting your duty if you had not done so. I had no idea that service was going on, or I should not have come in; you may make your mind quite easy on that score. I hope you will have many more opportunities of finding a place for me in Cullerne Church.'

'No need to find any place for *you*, my Lord. You have your own seat appointed and fixed, as sure as Canon Parkyn, and your own arms painted up clear on the back of it. Don't you trouble for that. It is all laid down in the statutes, and I shall make the very same obeisance for your lordship when you take your seat as for my Lord Bishop. "Two inclinations of the body, the mace being held in the right hand, and supported on the left arm." I cannot say more fair than that, for only royalties have three inclinations, and none of them has ever been to church in my time—no, nor yet a Lord Blandamer neither, since the day that your dear father and mother, what you never knew, was buried.'

Mrs Janaway drummed with her knuckles on the supper-table, in amazement that her husband should dare to stand chattering at the door when she had told him that the meal was ready. But, as the conversation revealed by degrees the stranger's identity, curiosity to see the man whose name was in all Cullerne mouths got the better of her, and she came curtseying to the door.

Lord Blandamer flung the flapping cape of his overcoat over the left shoulder in a way that made the clerk think of foreigners, and of woodcuts of Italian opera in a bound volume of the *Illustrated London News* which he studied on Sunday evenings.

'I must be moving on,' said the visitor, with a shiver. 'I must not keep you standing here; there is a very chill air this evening.'

Then Mrs Janaway was seized with a sudden temerity.

'Will your lordship not step in and warm yourself for a moment?' she interposed. 'We have a clear fire burning if you will overlook the smell of cooking.'

The clerk trembled for a moment at his wife's boldness, but Lord Blandamer accepted the invitation with alacrity.

'Thank you very much,' said he; 'I should be very glad to rest a few minutes before my train leaves. Pray make no apology for the smell of cookery; it is very appetizing, especially at supper time.'

He spoke as if he took supper every evening, and had never heard of a late dinner in his life; and five minutes later he sat at table with Mr and Mrs Janaway. The cloth was of roughest homespun, but clean; the knives and forks handled in old green horn, and the piece-of-resistance tripe; but the guest made an excellent meal.

'Some folk think highly of squash tripe or ribband tripe,' the clerk said meditatively, looking at the empty dish; 'but they don't compare, according to my taste, with cushion tripe.' He was emboldened to make these culinary remarks by that moral elevation which comes to every properly constituted host, when a guest has eaten heartily of the viands set before him.

'No,' Lord Blandamer said, 'there can be no doubt that cushion tripe is the best.'

'Quite as much depends upon the cooking as upon the tripe itself,' remarked Mrs Janaway, bridling at the thought that her art had been left out of the reckoning; 'a bad cook will spoil the best tripe. There are many ways of doing it, but a little milk and a leek is the best for me.'

'You cannot beat it,' Lord Blandamer assented—'you cannot beat it'—and then went on suggestively: 'Have you ever tried a sprig of mace with it?'

No, Mrs Janaway had never heard of that; nor, indeed, had Lord Blandamer either, if the point had been pushed; but she promised to use it the very next time, and hoped that the august visitor would honour them again when it was to be tasted.

''Tis only Saturday nights that we can get the cushion,' she went on; 'and it's well it don't come oftener, for we couldn't afford it. No woman ever had a call to have a better husband nor Thomas, who spends little enough on hisself. He don't touch nothing but tea, sir, but Saturday nights we treat ourselves to a little tripe, which is all the more convenient in that it is very strengthening, and my husband's duties on Sunday being that urgent-like. So, if your lordship is fond of tripe, and passing another Saturday night, and will do us the honour, you will always find something ready.'

'Thank you very much for your kind invitation,' Lord Blandamer said; 'I shall certainly take you at your word, the more so that Saturday is the day on which I am oftenest in Cullerne, or, I should say, have happened to be lately.'

'There's poor and poor,' said the clerk reflectively; 'and *we're* poor, but we're happy; but there's Mr Sharnall poor and unhappy. "Mr Sharnall," says I to him, "many a time have I heard my father say over a pot of tenpenny, 'Here's to poverty in a plug-hole, and a man with a wooden leg to trample it down;' but you never puts your poverty in a plug-hole, much less tramples it down. You always has it out and airs it, and makes yourself sad with thinking of it. 'Tisn't because you're poor that you're sad; 'tis because you *think* you're poor, and talk so much about it. You're not so poor as we, only you have so many grievances."'

'Ah, you are speaking of the organist?' Lord Blandamer asked. 'I fancy it was he who was talking with you in the minster this afternoon, was it not?'

The clerk felt embarrassed once more, for he remembered Mr Sharnall's violent talk, and how his anathema of all Blandamers had rung out in the church.

'Yes,' he said; 'poor organist was talking a little wild; he gets took that way sometimes, what with his grievances, and a little drop of the swanky* what he takes to drown them. Then he talks loud; but I hope your lordship didn't hear all his foolishness.'

'Oh dear no; I was engaged at the time with the architect,' Lord Blandamer said; but his tone made Janaway think that Mr Sharnall's voice had carried farther than was convenient. 'I did not hear what he said, but he seemed to be much put out. I chatted with him in the church some days ago; he did not know who I was, but I gathered that he bore no very good will to my family.'

Mrs Janaway saw it was a moment for prudent words.

'Don't pay no manner of attention to him, if I may make so bold as to advise your lordship,' she said, 'he talks against my husband just as well. He is crazy about his organ, and thinks he ought to have

* small beer

a new one, or, at least, a waterworks to blow it, like what they have at Carisbury. Don't pay no attention to him; no one minds what Sharnall says in Cullerne.'

The clerk was astonished at his wife's wisdom, yet apprehensive as to how it might be taken. But Lord Blandamer bowed his head graciously by way of thanks for sage counsel, and went on:

'Was there not some queer man at Cullerne who thought he was kept out of his rights, and should be in my place—who thought, I mean, he ought to be Lord Blandamer?'

The question was full of indifference, and there was a little smile of pity on his face; but the clerk remembered how Mr Sharnall had said something about a strutting peacock, and that there were no real Blandamers left, and was particularly ill at ease.

'Oh, yes,' he answered after a moment's pause, 'there was a poor doited body who, saving your presence, had some cranks of that kind; and, more by token, Mr Sharnall lived in the same house with him, and so I dare say he has got touched with the same craze.'

Lord Blandamer took out a cigar instinctively, and then, remembering that there was a lady present, put it back into his case and went on:

'Oh, he lived in the same house with Mr Sharnall, did he? I should like to hear more of this story; it naturally interests me. What was his name?'

'His name was Martin Joliffe,' said the clerk quickly, being surprised into eagerness by the chance of telling a story; and then the whole tale of Martin, and Martin's father and mother and daughter, as he had told it to Westray, was repeated for Lord Blandamer.

The night was far advanced before the history came to an end, and the local policeman walked several times up and down Governour's Lane, and made pauses before Mr Janaway's house, being surprised to see a window lighted so late. Lord Blandamer must have changed his intention of going by train, for the gates of Cullerne station had been locked for hours, and the boiler of the decrepit branch-line engine was cooling in its shed.

'It is an interesting tale, and you tell tales well,' he said, as he got up and put on his coat. 'All good things must have an end, but I hope to see you again ere long.' He shook hands with hostess and host, drained the pot of beer that had been fetched from a public-house, with a 'Here's to poverty in a plug-hole, and a man with a wooden leg to trample it down,' and was gone.

A minute later the policeman, coming back for yet another inspection of the lighted window, passed a man of middle height, who wore a loose overcoat, with the cape tossed lightly over the left shoulder. The stranger walked briskly, and hummed an air as he went, turning his face up to the stars and the wind-swept sky, as if entirely oblivious of all sublunary things. A midnight stranger in Governour's Lane was even more surprising than a lighted window, and the policeman had it in his mind to stop him and ask his business. But before he could decide on so vigorous a course of action, the moment was past, and the footsteps were dying away in the distance.

The clerk was pleased with himself, and proud of his success as a story-teller.

'That's a clever, understanding sort of chap,' he said to his wife, as they went to bed; 'he knows a good tale when he hears one.'

'Don't you be too proud of yourself, my man,' answered she; 'there's more in that tale than your telling, I warrant you, for my lord to think about.'

Chapter 10

The extension of the scheme of restoration which Lord Blandamer's liberality involved, made it necessary that Westray should more than once consult Sir George Farquhar in London. On coming back to Cullerne from one of these visits on a Saturday night, he found his meal laid in Mr Shamall's room.

'I thought you would not mind our having supper together,' Mr Sharnall said. 'I don't know how it is, I always feel gloomy just when the winter begins, and the dark sets in so soon. It is all right later on; I rather enjoy the long evenings and a good fire, when I can afford a good one, but at first it is a little gloomy. So come and have supper with me. There *is* a good fire to-night, and a bit of driftwood that I got specially for your benefit.'

They talked of indifferent subjects during the meal, though once or twice it seemed to Westray that the organist gave inconsequential replies, as though he were thinking of something else. This was no doubt the case, for, after they had settled before the fire, and the lambent blue flames of the driftwood had been properly admired, Mr Sharnall began with a hesitating cough:

'A rather curious thing happened this afternoon. When I got back here after evening service, who should I find waiting in my room but that Blandamer fellow. There was no light and no fire, for I had thought if we lit the fire late we could afford a better one. He was sitting at one end of the window-seat, damn him!'—(the expletive was caused by Mr Sharnall remembering that this was Anastasia's favourite seat, and his desire to reprobate the use of it by anyone else)—'but got up, of course, as I came in, and made a vast lot of soft speeches. He must really apologize for such an intrusion. He had come to see Mr Westray, but found that Mr Westray had unfortunately been called away. He had taken the liberty of waiting a few minutes in Mr Sharnall's room. He was anxious to have a few moments' conversation with Mr Sharnall, and so on, and so on. You know how I hate palaver, and how I disliked—how I dislike' (he corrected himself)—'the man; but he took me at a disadvantage, you see, for here he was actually in my room, and one cannot be so rude in one's own room as one can in other people's. I felt responsible, too, to some extent for his having had to wait without fire or light, though why he shouldn't have lit the gas himself I'm sure I don't know. So I talked more civilly than I meant to, and then, just at the moment when I was hoping to get rid of him, Anastasia, who it seems was the only person at home, must needs come in and ask if I was ready for my tea. You may imagine my disgust, but there was nothing for it but to ask him if he would like a cup of tea. I never dreamt of his taking it, but he did; and so, behold! there we were hobnobbing over the tea-table as if we were cronies.'

Westray was astonished. Mr Sharnall had rebuked him so short a time before for not having repulsed Lord Blandamer's advances that he could scarcely understand such a serious falling away from all the higher principles of hatred and malice as were implied in this tea-drinking. His experience of life had been as yet too limited to convince him that most enmities and antipathies, being theoretical rather than actual, are apt to become mitigated, or to disappear altogether on personal contact—that it is, in fact, exceedingly hard to keep hatred at concert-pitch, or to be consistently rude to a person face to face who has a pleasant manner and a desire to conciliate.

Perhaps Mr Sharnall read Westray's surprise in his face, for he went on with a still more apologetic manner:

'That is not the worst of it; he has put me in a most awkward position. I must admit that I found his conversation amusing enough. We spoke a good deal of music, and he showed a surprising knowledge of the subject, and a correct taste; I do not know where he has got it from.'

'I found exactly the same thing with his architecture,' Westray said. 'We started to go round the minster as master and pupil, but before we finished I had an uncomfortable impression that he knew more about it than I did—at least, from the archaeologic point of view.'

'Ah!' said the organist, with the indifference with which a person who wishes to recount his own experiences listens to those of someone else, however thrilling they may be. 'Well, his taste was singularly refined. He showed a good acquaintance with the contrapuntists of the last century, and knew several of my own works. A very curious thing this. He said he had been in some cathedral—I forget which—heard the service, and been so struck with it that he went afterwards to look it up on the bill, and found it was Sharnall in D flat. He hadn't the least idea that it was mine till we began to talk. I haven't had that service by me for years. I wrote it at Oxford for the Gibbons' prize; it has a fugal movement in the *Gloria* ending with a tonic pedal-point that you would like. I must look it up.'

'Yes, I should like to hear it,' Westray said, more to fill the interval while the speaker took breath than from any great interest in the matter.

'So you shall—so you shall,' went on the organist; 'you will find the pedal-point adds immensely to the effect. Well, by degrees we came to talking of the organ. It so happens that we had spoken of it the very first day I met him in the church, though you know I *never* talk about my instrument, do I? At that time it didn't strike me that he was so well up in the matter, but now he seemed to know all about it, and so I gave him my ideas as to what ought to be done. Then, before I knew where I was, he cut in with, "Mr Sharnall, what you say interests me immensely; you put things in such a lucid way that even an outsider like myself can understand them. It would be a thousand pities if neglect were permanently to injure this sweet-toned instrument that Father Smith made so long ago. It is no use restoring the church without the organ, so you must draw up a specification of the repairs and additions required, and understand that anything you suggest shall be done. In the meantime pray order at once the water-engine and new pedal-board of which you speak, and inform me as to the cost." He took me quite aback, and was gone before I had time to say anything. It puts me in a very equivocal position; I have such an antipathy to the man. I shall refuse his offer point-blank. I will not put myself under any obligation to such a man. You would refuse in my position? You would write a strong letter of refusal at once, would you not?'

Westray was of a guileless disposition, and apt to assume that people meant what they said. It seemed to him a matter for much regret that Mr Sharnall's independence, however lofty, should stand in the way of so handsome a benefaction, and he was at pains to elaborate and press home all the arguments that he could muster to shake the organist's resolve. The offer was kindly meant; he was sure that Mr Sharnall took a wrong view of Lord Blandamer's character —that Mr Sharnall was wrong in imputing motives to Lord Blandamer. What motives could he have except the best? and however much Mr Sharnall might personally refuse, how was a man to be stopped eventually from repairing an organ which stood so manifestly in need of repair?

Westray spoke earnestly, and was gratified to see the effect which his eloquence produced on Mr Sharnall. It is so rarely that argument prevails to change opinion that the young man was flattered to see that the considerations which he was able to marshal were strong enough, at any rate, to influence Mr Sharnall's determination.

Well, perhaps there was something in what Mr Westray said. Mr Sharnall would think it over. He would not write the letter of refusal that night; he could write to refuse the next day quite as well. In the meantime he *would* see to the new pedal-board, and order the water-engine. Ever since he had seen the water-engine at Carisbury, he had been convinced that sooner or later they must have one at Cullerne. It *must* be ordered; they could decide later on whether it should be paid for by Lord Blandamer, or should be charged to the general restoration fund.

This conclusion, however inconclusive, was certainly a triumph for Westray's persuasive oratory, but his satisfaction was chastened by some doubts as to how far he was justified in assailing the scrupulous independence which had originally prompted Mr Sharnall to refuse to have anything to do with Lord Blandamer's offer. If Mr Sharnall had scruples in the matter, ought not he, Westray, to have respected those scruples? Was it not tampering with rectitude to have overcome them by a too persuasive rhetoric?

His doubts were not allayed by the observation that Mr Sharnall himself had severely felt the strain of this mental quandary, for the organist said that he was upset by so difficult a question, and filled himself a bumper of whisky to steady his nerves. At the same time he took down from a shelf two or three note-books and a mass of loose papers, which he spread open upon the table before him. Westray looked at them with a glance of unconscious inquiry.

'I must really get to work at these things again,' said the organist; 'I have been dreadfully negligent of late. They are a lot of papers and notes that Martin Joliffe left behind him. Poor Miss Euphemia never had the heart to go through them. She was going to burn them just as they were, but I said, "Oh, you mustn't do that; turn them over to me. I will look into them, and see whether there is anything worth keeping." So I took them, but haven't done nearly as much as I ought, what with one interruption and another. It's always sad going through a dead man's papers, but sadder when they're all that's left of a life's labour—lost labour, so far as Martin was concerned, for he was taken away just when he began to see daylight. "We brought nothing into this world, and it is certain that we shall carry nothing out." When that comes into my mind, I think rather of the *little* things than of gold or lands. Intimate letters that a man treasured more than money; little tokens of which the clue had died with him; the unfinished work to which he was coming back, and never came; even the unpaid bills that worried him; for death transfigures all, and makes the commonplace pathetic.'

He stopped for a moment. Westray said nothing, being surprised at this momentary softening of the other's mood.

'Yes, it's sad enough,' the organist resumed; 'all these papers are nebuly coat—the sea-green and silver.'

'He was quite mad, I suppose?' Westray said.

'Everyone except me will tell you so,' replied the organist; 'but I'm not so very sure after all that there wasn't a good deal more in it than madness. That's all that I can say just now, but those of us who live will see. There is a queer tradition hereabout. I don't know how long ago it started, but people say that there *is* some mystery about the Blandamer descent, and that those in possession have no right to what they hold. But there is something else. Many have tried to solve the riddle, and some, you may depend, have been very hot on the track. But just as they come to the touch, something takes them off; that's what happened to Martin. I saw him the very day he died. "Sharnall," he said to me, "if I can last out forty-eight hours more, you may take off you hat to me, and say 'my lord.'"

'But the nebuly coat was too much for him; he had to die. So don't you be surprised if I drop off the hooks some of these fine days; if I don't I'm going to get to the bottom, and you will see some changes here before so very long.'

He sat down at the table, and made a show for a minute of looking at the papers.

'Poor Martin!' he said, and got up again, opened the cupboard, and took out the bottle. 'You'll have a drop,' he asked Westray, 'won't you?'

'No, thanks, not I,' Westray said, with something as near contempt as his thin voice was capable of expressing.

'Just a drop—do! I must have just a drop myself; I find it a great strain working at these papers; there may be more at stake in the reading than I care to think of.'

He poured out half a tumbler of spirit. Westray hesitated for a moment, and then his conscience and an early puritan training forced him to speak.

'Sharnall,' he said, 'put it away. That bottle is your evil angel. Play the man, and put it away. You force me to speak. I cannot sit by with hands folded and see you going down the hill.'

The organist gave him a quick glance; then he filled up the tumbler to the brim with neat spirit.

'Look you,' he said: 'I was going to drink half a glass; now I'm going to drink a whole one. That much for your advice! Going down the hill indeed! Go to the devil with your impertinence! If you can't keep a civil tongue in your head, you had better get your supper in someone else's room.'

A momentary irritation dragged Westray down from the high podium of judicial reproof into the arena of retort.

'Don't worry yourself,' he said sharply; 'you may rely on my not troubling you with my company again.' And he got up and opened the door. As he turned to go out, Anastasia Joliffe passed through the passage on her way to bed.

The glimpse of her as she went by seemed still further to aggravate Mr Sharnall. He signed to Westray to stay where he was, and to shut the door again.

'Damn you!' he said; 'that's what I called you back to say. Damn you! Damn Blandamer! Damn everybody! Damn poverty! Damn wealth! I will not touch a farthing of his money for the organ. Now you can go.'

Westray had been cleanly bred. He had been used neither to the vulgarity of ill-temper nor to the coarser insolence of personal abuse. He shrank by natural habit even from gross adjectives, from the 'beastly' and 'filthy' which modern manners too often condone, and still more from the abomination of swearing. So Mr Sharnall's obloquy wounded him to the quick. He went to bed in a flutter of agitation, and lay awake half the night mourning over a friendship so irreparably broken, bitter with the resentment of an unjustified attack, yet reproaching himself lest through his unwittingness he might have brought it all upon himself.

The morning found him unrefreshed and dejected but, whilst he sat at breakfast, the sun came out brightly, and he began to take a less despondent view of the situation. It was possible that Mr Sharnall's friendship might not after all be lost beyond repair; he would be sorry if it were, for he had grown fond of the old man, in spite of all his faults of life and manner. It was he, Westray, who had been entirely to blame. In another man's room he had lectured the other man. He, a young man, had lectured the other, who was an old man. It was true that he had done so with the best motives; he had only spoken from a painful sense of duty. But he had shown no tact, he had spoken too strongly; he had imperilled his own good cause by the injudicious manner in which he had put it forward. At the risk of all rebuffs, he would express his regret; he would go down and apologise to Mr Sharnall, and offer, if need be, the other cheek to the smiter.

Good resolves, if formed with the earnest intention of carrying them into effect, seldom fail to restore a measure of peace to the troubled mind. It is only when a regular and ghastly see-saw of wrongdoing and repentance has been established, and when the mind can no longer deceive even itself as to the possibility of permanent uprightness of life, that good resolves cease to tranquillize. Such a see-saw must gradually lose its regularity; the set towards evil grows more and more preponderant; the return to virtue rarer and more brief. Despair of any continuity of godliness follows, and then it is that good resolves, becoming a mere reflex action of the mind, fail in their gracious influence, and cease to bring quiet. These conditions can scarcely occur before middle age, and Westray, being young and eminently conscientious, was feeling the full peacefulness of his high-minded intention steal over him, when the door opened, and the organist entered.

An outbreak of temper and a night of hard drinking had left their tokens on Mr Sharnall's face. He looked haggard, and the rings that a weak heart had drawn under his eyes were darker and more puffed. He came in awkwardly, and walked quickly to the architect, holding out his hand.

'Forgive me, Westray,' he said; 'I behaved last night like a fool and a cad. You were quite right to speak to me as you did; I honour you for it. I wish to God there had been someone to speak to me like that years ago.'

His outstretched hand was not so white as it should have been, the nails were not so well trimmed as a more fastidious mood might have demanded; but Westray did not notice these things. He took the shaky old hand, and gripped it warmly, not saying anything, because he could not speak.

'We *must* be friends,' the organist went on, after a moment's pause; 'we must be friends, because I can't afford to lose you. I haven't known you long, but you are the only friend I have in the world. Is it not an awful thing to confess?' he said, with a tremulous little laugh. 'I have no other friend in the world. Say those things you said last night whenever you like; the oftener you say them the better.'

He sat down, and, the situation being too strained to remain longer at so high a pitch, the conversation drifted, however awkwardly, to less personal topics.

'There is a thing I wanted to speak about last night,' the organist said. 'Poor old Miss Joliffe is very hard up. She hasn't said a word to me about it—she never would to anyone—but I happen to know it for a fact: she *is* hard up. She is in a chronic state of hard-upishness always, and that we all are; but this is an acute attack—she has her back against the wall. It is the fag-end of Martin's debts that bother her; these blood-sucking tradesmen are dunning her, and she hasn't the pluck to tell them go hang, though they know well enough she isn't responsible for a farthing. She has got it into her head that she hasn't a right to keep that flower-and-caterpillar picture so long as Martin's debts are unpaid, because she could raise money on it. You remember those people, Baunton and Lutterworth, offered her fifty pounds for it.'

'Yes, I remember,' Westray said; 'more fools they.'

'More fools, by all means,' rejoined the organist; 'but still they offer it, and I believe our poor old landlady will come to selling it. "All the better for her," you will say, and anyone with an ounce of common sense would have sold it long ago for fifty pounds or fifty pence. But, then, she has no common sense, and I do believe it would break her pride and worry her into a fever to part with it. Well, I have been at the pains to find out what sum of money would pull her through, and I fancy something like twenty pounds would tide over the crisis.'

He paused a moment, as if he half expected Westray to speak; but the architect making no suggestion, he went on.

'I didn't know,' he said timidly; 'I wasn't quite sure whether you had been here long enough to take much interest in the matter. I had an idea of buying the picture myself, so that we could still keep it here. I would be no good offering Miss Euphemia money as a *gift*; she wouldn't accept it on any condition. I know her quite well enough to be sure of that. But if I was to offer her twenty pounds for it, and tell her it must always stop here, and that she could buy it back from me when she was able, I think she would feel such an offer to be a godsend, and accept it readily.'

'Yes,' Westray said dubitatively; 'I suppose it couldn't be construed into attempting to outwit her, could it? It seems rather funny at first sight to get her to sell a picture for twenty pounds for which others have offered fifty pounds.'

'No, I don't think so,' replied the organist. 'It wouldn't be a real sale at all, you know, but only just a colour for helping her.'

'Well, as you have been kind enough to ask my advice, I see no further objection, and think it very good of you to show such thoughtfulness for poor Miss Joliffe.'

'Thank you,' said the organist hesitatingly—'thank you; I had hoped you would take that view of the matter. There is a further little difficulty: I am as poor as a church mouse. I live like an old screw, and never spend a penny, but, then, I haven't got a penny to spend, and so can't save.'

Westray had already wondered how Mr Sharnall could command so large a sum as twenty pounds, but thought it more prudent to make no comments.

Then the organist took the bull by the horns.

'I didn't know,' he said, 'whether you would feel inclined to join me in the purchase. I have got ten pounds in the savings-bank; if you could find the other ten pounds, we could go shares in the picture: and, after all, that wouldn't much matter, for Miss Euphemia is quite sure to buy it back from us before very long.'

He stopped and looked at Westray. The architect was taken aback. He was of a cautious and calculating disposition, and a natural inclination to save had been reinforced by the conviction that any unnecessary expenditure was in itself to be severely reprobated. As the Bible was to him the foundation of the world to come, so the keeping of meticulous accounts and the putting by of however trifling sums, were the foundation of the world that is. He had so carefully governed his life as to have been already able, out of a scanty salary, to invest more than a hundred pounds in Railway Debentures. He set much store by the half-yearly receipt of an exiguous interest cheque, and derived a certain dignity and feeling of commercial stability from envelopes headed the 'Great Southern

Railway,' which brought him from time to time a proxy form or a notice of shareholders' meetings. A recent examination of his bank-book had filled him with the hope of being able ere long to invest a second hundred pounds, and he had been turning over in his mind for some days the question of the stocks to be selected; it seemed financially unsound to put so large a sum in any single security.

This suddenly presented proposal that he should make a serious inroad on his capital filled him with dismay; it was equivalent to granting a loan of ten pounds without any tangible security. No one in their senses could regard this miserable picture as a security; and the bulbous green caterpillar seemed to give a wriggle of derision as he looked at it across the breakfast-table. He had it on his tongue to refuse Mr Sharnall's request, with the sympathetic but judicial firmness with which all high-minded persons refuse to lend. There is a tone of sad resolution particularly applicable to such occasions, which should convey to the borrower that only motives of great moral altitude constrain us for the moment to override an earnest desire to part with our money. If it had not been for considerations of the public good, we would most readily have given him ten times as much as was asked.

Westray was about to express sentiments of this nature when he glanced at the organist's face, and saw written in its folds and wrinkles so paramount and pathetic an anxiety that his resolution was shaken. He remembered the quarrel of the night before, and how Mr Sharnall, in coming to beg his pardon that morning, had humbled himself before a younger man. He remembered how they had made up their differences; surely an hour ago he would willingly have paid ten pounds to know that their differences could be made up. Perhaps, after all, he might agree to make this loan as a thank-offering for friendship restored. Perhaps, after all, the picture *was* a security: someone *had* offered fifty pounds for it.

The organist had not followed the change of Westray's mind; he retained only the first impression of reluctance, and was very anxious—curiously anxious, it might have seemed, if his only motive in the acquiring of the picture was to do a kindness to Miss Euphemia.

'It *is* a large sum, I know,' he said in a low voice. 'I am very sorry to ask you to do this. It is not for myself; I never asked a penny for myself in my life, and never will, till I go to the workhouse. Don't answer at once, if you don't see your way. Think it over. Take time to think it over; but do try, Westray, to help in the matter, if you can. It would be a sad pity to let the picture go out of the house just now.'

The eagerness with which he spoke surprised Westray. Could it be that Mr Sharnall had motives other than mere kindness? Could it be that the picture *was* valuable after all? He walked across the room to look closer at the tawdry flowers and the caterpillar. No, it could not be that; the painting was absolutely worthless. Mr Sharnall had followed him, and they stood side by side looking out of the window. Westray was passing through a very brief interval of indecision. His emotional and perhaps better feelings told him that he ought to accede to Mr Sharnall's request; caution and the hoarding instinct reminded him that ten pounds was a large proportion of his whole available capital.

Bright sunshine had succeeded the rain. The puddles flashed on the pavements; the long rows of raindrops glistened on the ledges which overhung the shop-windows, and a warm steam rose from the sandy roadway as it dried in the sun. The front door of Bellevue Lodge closed below them, and Anastasia, in a broad straw hat and a pink print dress, went lightly down the steps. On that bright morning she looked the brightest thing of all, as she walked briskly to the market with a basket on her arm, unconscious that two men were watching her from an upper window.

It was at that minute that thrift was finally elbowed by sentiment out of Westray's mind.

'Yes,' he said, 'by all means let us buy the picture. You negotiate the matter with Miss Joliffe, and I will give you two five-pound notes this evening.'

'Thank you—thank you,' said the organist, with much relief. 'I will tell Miss Euphemia that she can buy it back from us whenever it suits her to do so; and if she should not buy it back before one of us dies, then it shall remain the sole property of the survivor.'

So that very day the purchase of a rare work of art was concluded by a private treaty between Miss Euphemia Joliffe of the one part, and Messrs Nicholas Sharnall and Edward Westray of the other. The hammer never fell upon the showy flowers with the green caterpillar wriggling in the corner; and Messrs Baunton and Lutterworth received a polite note from Miss Joliffe to say that the painting late in the possession of Martin Joliffe, Esq, deceased, was not for sale.

Chapter 11

The old Bishop of Carisbury was dead, and a new Bishop of Carisbury reigned in his stead. The appointment had caused some chagrin in Low-Church circles, for Dr Willis, the new Bishop, was a High Churchman of pronounced views. But he had a reputation for deep personal piety, and a very short experience sufficed to show that he was full of Christian tolerance and tactful loving-kindness.

One day, as Mr Sharnall was playing a voluntary after the Sunday morning service, a chorister stole up the little winding steps, and appeared in the organ-loft just as his master had pulled out a handful of stops and dashed into the *stretto*. The organist had not heard the boy on the stairs, and gave a violent start as he suddenly caught sight of the white surplice. Hands and feet for an instant lost their place, and the music came perilously near breaking down. It was only for an instant; he pulled himself together, and played the fugue to its logical conclusion.

Then the boy began, 'Canon Parkyn's compliments,' but broke off; for the organist greeted him with a sound cuff and a 'How many times have I told you, sir, not to come creeping up those stairs when I am in the middle of a voluntary? You startle me out of my senses, coming round the corner like a ghost.'

'I'm very sorry sir,' the boy said, whimpering. 'I'm sure I never meant—I never thought—'

'You never *do* think,' Mr Sharnall said. 'Well, well, don't go on whining. Old heads don't grow on young shoulders; don't do it again, and there's a sixpence for you. And now let's hear what you have to say.'

Sixpences were rare things among Cullerne boys, and the gift consoled more speedily than any balm in Gilead.

'Canon Parkyn's compliments to you, sir, and he would be glad to have a word with you in the clergy-vestry.'

'All in good time. Tell him I'll be down as soon as I've put my books away.'

Mr Sharnall did not hurry. There were the Psalter and the chant-book to be put open on the desk for the afternoon; there were the morning-service and anthem-book to be put away, and the evening-service and anthem-book to be got out.

The establishment had once been able to afford good music books, and in the list of subscribers to the first edition Boyce—the list which so mortified poor Dr Boyce by its smallness—you may see to this day, 'The Rector and Foundation of Cullerne Minster (6 copies).' Mr Sharnall loved the great Boyce, with its parchment paper and largest of large margins. He loved the crisp sound of the leaves as he turned them, and he loved the old-world clefs that he could read nine staves at a time as easily as a short score. He looked at the weekly list to check his memory—'Awake up my Glory' (*Wise*). No, it was in Volume III instead of II; he had taken down the wrong volume—a stupid mistake for one who knew the copy so well. How the rough calf backs were crumbling away! The rusty red-leather dust had come off on his coat-sleeves; he really was not fit to be seen, and he took some minutes more to brush it all off. So it was that Canon Parkyn chafed at being kept waiting in the clergy-vestry, and greeted Mr Sharnall on his appearance with a certain tartness:

'I wish you could be a little quicker when you are sent for. I am particularly busy just now, and you have kept me waiting a quarter of an hour at least.'

As this was precisely what Mr Sharnall had intended to do, he took no umbrage at the Rector's remarks, but merely said:

'Pardon me; scarcely so long as a quarter of an hour, I think.'

'Well, do not let us waste words. What I wanted to tell you was that it has been arranged for the Lord Bishop of Carisbury to hold a confirmation in the minster on the eighteenth of next month, at three o'clock in the afternoon. We must have a full musical service, and I shall be glad if you will submit a sketch of what you propose for my approval. There is one point to which I must call your attention particularly. As his lordship walks up the nave, we must have a becoming march on the organ—not any of this old-fashioned stuff of which I have had so often to complain, but something really dignified and with a tune in it.'

'Oh yes, we can easily arrange that,' Mr Sharnall said obsequiously. '"See the Conquering Hero comes," by Handel, would be very appropriate; or there is an air out of one of Offenbach's Operas that I think I could adapt to the purpose. It is a very sweet thing if rendered with proper feeling; or I could play a "Danse Macabre" slowly on the full organ.'

'Ah, that is from the "Judas Maccabæus", I conclude,' said the Rector, a little mollified at this unexpected acquiescence in his views. 'Well, I see that you understand my wishes, so I hope I may leave that matter in your hands. By the way,' he said, turning back as he left the vestry, 'what *was* the piece which you played after the service just now?'

'Oh, only a fugal movement—just a fugue of Kirnberger's.'

'I *wish* you would not give us so much of this fugal style. No doubt it is all very fine from a scholastic point of view, but to most it seems merely confused. So far from assisting me and the choir to go out with dignity, it really fetters our movements. We want something with pathos and dignity, such as befits the end of a solemn service, yet with a marked rhythm, so that it may time our footsteps as we leave the choir. Forgive these suggestions; the *practical* utility of the organ is so much overlooked in these days. When Mr Noot is taking the service it does not so much matter, but when I am here myself I beg that there may be no more fugue.'

The visit of the Bishop of Carisbury to Cullerne was an important matter, and necessitated some forethought and arrangement.

'The Bishop must, of course, lunch with us,' Mrs Parkyn said to her husband; 'you will ask him, of course, to lunch, my dear.'

'Oh yes, certainly,' replied the canon; 'I wrote yesterday to ask him to lunch.'

He assumed an unconcerned air, but with only indifferent success, for his heart misgave him that he had been guilty of an unpardonable breach of etiquette in writing on so important a subject without reference to his wife.

'Really, my dear!' she rejoined—'really! I hope at least that your note was couched in proper terms.'

'Psha!' he said, a little nettled in his turn, 'do you suppose I have never written to a Bishop before?'

'That is not the point; *any* invitation of this kind should always be given by me. The Bishop, if he has any *breeding*, will be very much astonished to receive an invitation to lunch that is not given by the lady of the house. This, at least, is the usage that prevails among persons of *breeding*.'

There was just enough emphasis in the repetition of the last formidable word to have afforded a *casus belli*, if the Rector had been minded for the fray; but he was a man of peace.

'You are quite right, my dear,' was the soft answer; 'it was a slip of mine, which we must hope the Bishop will overlook. I wrote in a hurry yesterday afternoon, as soon as I received the official information of his coming. You were out calling, if you recollect, and I had to catch the post. One never knows what tuft-hunting may not lead people to do; and if I had not caught the post, some pushing person or other might quite possibly have asked him sooner. I meant, of course, to have reported the matter to you, but it slipped my memory.'

'Really,' she said, with fine deprecation, being only half pacified, 'I do not see who there *could* be to ask the Bishop except ourselves. Where should the Bishop of Carisbury lunch in Cullerne except at the Rectory?' In this unanswerable conundrum she quenched the smouldering embers of her wrath. 'I have no doubt, dear, that you did it all for the best, and I hate these vulgar pushing nobodies, who try to get hold of everyone of the least position, quite as much as you can hate them. So let us consider whom we *ought* to ask to meet him. A small party, I think it should be; he would take it as a greater compliment if the party were small.'

She had that shallow and ungenerous mind which shrinks instinctively from admitting any beauty or intellect in others, and which grudges any participation in benefits, however amply sufficient they may be for all. Thus, few must be asked to meet the Bishop, that it might the better appear that few indeed, beside the Rector and Mrs Parkyn, were fit to associate with so distinguished a man.

'I quite agree with you,' said the Rector, considerably relieved to find that his own temerity in asking the Bishop might now be considered as condoned. 'Our party must above all things be select; indeed, I do not know how we could make it anything but very small; there are so few people whom we *could* ask to meet the Bishop.'

'Let me see,' his wife said, making a show of reckoning Cullerne respectability with the fingers of one hand on the fingers of the other. There is—' She broke off as a sudden idea seized her. 'Why, of course, we must ask Lord Blandamer. He has shown such marked interest in ecclesiastical matters that he is sure to wish to meet the Bishop.'

'A most fortunate suggestion—admirable in every way. It may strengthen his interest in the church; and it must certainly be beneficial to him to associate with correct society after his wandering and Bohemian life. I hear all kinds of strange tales of his hobnobbing with this Mr Westray, the clerk of the works, and with other persons entirely out of his own rank. Mrs Flint, who happened to be visiting a poor woman in a back lane, assures me that she has every reason to believe that he spent an hour or more in the clerk's house, and even ate there. They say he positively ate tripe.'

'Well, it will certainly do him good to meet the Bishop,' the lady said. 'That would make four with ourselves; and we can ask Mrs Bulteel. We need not ask her husband; he is painfully rough, and the Bishop might not like to meet a brewer. It will not be at all strange to ask her alone; there is always the excuse of not liking to take a business-man away from his work in the middle of the day.'

'That would be five; we ought to make it up to six. I suppose it would not do to ask this architect fellow or Mr Sharnall.'

'My dear! what can you be thinking of? On no account whatever. Such guests would be *most* inappropriate.'

The rector looked so properly humble and cast down at this reproof that his wife relented a little.

'Not that there is any *harm* in asking them, but they would be so very ill at ease themselves, I fear, in such surroundings. If you think the number should be even, we might perhaps ask old Noot. He *is* a gentleman, and would pass as your chaplain, and say grace.'

Thus the party was made up, and Lord Blandamer accepted, and Mrs Bulteel accepted; and there was no need to trouble about the curate's acceptance—he was merely ordered to come to lunch. But, after all had gone so well up to this point, the unexpected happened—the Bishop could not come. He regretted that he could not accept the hospitality so kindly offered him by Canon Parkyn; he had an engagement which would occupy him for any spare time that he would have in Cullerne; he had made other arrangements for lunch; he would call at the Rectory half an hour before the service.

The Rector and his wife sat in the 'study', a dark room on the north side of the rectory house, made sinister from without by dank laurestinus, and from within by glass cases of badly stuffed birds. A Bradshaw lay on the table before them.

'He cannot be *driving* from Carisbury,' Mrs Parkyn said. 'Dr Willis does not keep at all the same sort of stables that his predecessor kept. Mrs Flint, when she was attending the annual Christian Endeavour meeting at Carisbury, was told that Dr Willis thinks it wrong that a Bishop should do more in the way of keeping carriage than is absolutely necessary for church purposes. She said she had passed the Bishop's carriage herself, and that the coachman was a most unkempt creature, and the horses two wretched screws.'

'I heard much the same thing,' assented the Rector. 'They say he would not have his own coat of arms painted on the carriage, for what was there already was quite good enough for him. He cannot possibly be driving here from Carisbury; it is a good twenty miles.'

'Well, if he does not drive, he must come by the 12.15 train; that would give him two hours and a quarter before the service. What business can he have in Cullerne? Where can he be lunching? What can he be doing with himself for two mortal hours and a quarter?'

Here was another conundrum to which probably only one person in Cullerne town could have supplied an answer, and that was Mr Sharnall. A letter had come for the organist that very day:

My dear Sharnall,

(I had almost written, 'My dear Nick'; forty years have made my pen a little stiff, but you must give me your official permission to write 'My dear Nick' the very next time.) You may have forgotten my hand, but you will not have forgotten me. Do you know, it is I, Willis, who am your new Bishop? It is only a fortnight since I learnt that you were so near me

> *'Quam dulce amicitias,*
> *Redintegrare nitidas'* —

and the very first point of it is that I am going to sponge on you, and ask myself to lunch. I am coming to Cullerne at 12.45 to-day fortnight for the Confirmation, and have to be at the Rectory at 2.30, but till then an old friend, Nicholas Sharnall, will give me food and shelter, will he not? Make no excuses, for I shall not accept them; but send me word to say that in this you will not fail of your duty, and believe me always to be

Yours,

JOHN CARUM.

There was something that moved strangely inside Mr Sharnall's battered body as he read the letter—an upheaval of emotion; the child's heart within the man's; his young hopeful self calling to his old hopeless self. He sat back in his arm-chair, and shut his eyes, and the organ-loft in a little college chapel came back to him, and long, long practisings, and Willis content to stand by and listen as long as he should play. How it pleased Willis to stand by, and pull the stops, and fancy he knew something of music! No, Willis never knew any music, and yet he had a good taste, and loved a fugue.

There came to him country rambles and country churches and Willis with an *A.B.C. of Gothic Architecture*, trying to tell an Early English from a Decorated moulding. There came to him illimitably long summer evenings, with the sky clearest yellow in the north, hours after sunset; dusty white roads, with broad galloping-paths at the side, drenched with heavy dew; the dark, mysterious boskage of Stow Wood; the scent of the syringa in the lane at Beckley; the white mist sheeting the Cherwell vale. And supper when they got home— for memory is so powerful an alchemist as to transmute suppers as well as sunsets. What suppers! Cider-cup with borage floating in it, cold lamb and mint sauce, watercress, and a triangular commons of Stilton. Why, he had not tasted Stilton for forty years!

No, Willis never knew any music, but he loved a fugue. Ah, the fugues Willis had listened to! And then a voice crossed Mr Sharnall's memory, saying, 'When I am here myself, I beg that there may be no more fugue.' 'No more fugue'—there was a finality in the phrase uncompromising as the 'no more sea' of the Apocalyptic vision. It made Mr Sharnall smile bitterly; he woke from his day-dream, and was back in the present.

Oh yes, he knew very well that it was his old friend when he first saw on whom the choice had fallen for the Bishopric. He was glad Willis was coming to see him. Willis knew all about the row, and how it was that Sharnall had to leave Oxford. Ay, but the Bishop was too generous and broadminded to remember that now. Willis must know very well that he was only a poor, out-at-elbows old fellow, and yet he was coming to lunch with him; but did Willis know that he still— He did not follow the thought farther, but glanced in a mirror, adjusted his tie, fastened the top button of his coat, and with his uncertain hands brushed the hair back on either side of his head. No, Willis did not know that; he never should know; it was *never* too late to mend.

He went to the cupboard, and took out a bottle and a tumbler. Only very little spirit was left, and he poured it all into the glass. There was a moment's hesitation, a moment while enfeebled will-power was nerving itself for the effort. He was apparently engaged in making sure that not one minim of this most costly liquor was wasted. He held the bottle carefully inverted, and watched the very last and smallest drop detach itself and fall into the glass. No, his will-power was not yet altogether paralysed—not yet; and he dashed the contents of the glass into the fire. There was a great blaze of light-blue flame, and a puff in the air that made the window-panes rattle; but the heroic deed was done, and he heard a mental blast of trumpets, and the acclaiming voice of the *Victor Sui*. Willis should never know that he still—because he *never* would again.

He rang the bell, and when Miss Euphemia answered it she found him walking briskly, almost tripping, to and fro in the room. He stopped as she entered, drew his heels together, and made her a profound bow.

'Hail, most fair chastelaine! Bid the varlets lower the draw-bridge and raise the portcullis. Order pasties and souse-fish and a butt of malmsey; see the great hall is properly decored for my Lord Bishop of Carisbury, who will take his *ambigue* and bait his steeds at this castle.'

Miss Joliffe stared; she saw a bottle and an empty tumbler on the table, and smelt a strong smell of whisky; and the mirth faded from Mr Sharnall's face as he read her thoughts.

'No, wrong,' he said—'wrong this once; I am sober as a judge, but excited. A Bishop is coming to lunch with me. *You* are excited when Lord Blandamer takes tea with you—a mere trashy temporal peer; am I not to be excited when a real spiritual lord pays me a visit? Hear, O woman! The Bishop of Carisbury has written to ask, not me to lunch with him, but him to lunch with me. You will have a Bishop lunching at Bellevue Lodge.'

'Oh, Mr Sharnall! pray, sir, speak plainly. I am so old and stupid, I can never tell whether you are joking or in earnest.'

So he put off his exaltation, and told her the actual facts.

'I am sure I don't know, sir, what you will give him for lunch,' Miss Joliffe said. She was always careful to put in a proper number of 'sirs', for, though she was proud of her descent, and considered that so far as birth went she need not fear comparison with other Cullerne dames, she thought it a Christian duty to accept fully the position of landlady to which circumstances had led her. 'I am sure I don't know what you will give him for lunch; it is always so difficult to arrange meals for the clergy. If one provides *too* much of the good things of this world, it seems as if one was not considering sufficiently their sacred calling; it seems like Martha, too cumbered with much serving, too careful and troubled, to gain all the spiritual advantage that must come from clergymen's society. But, of course, even the most spiritually minded must nourish their *bodies*, or they would not be able to do so much good. But when less provision has been made, I have sometimes seen clergymen eat it all up, and become quite wearied, poor things! for want of food. It was so, I remember, when Mrs Sharp invited the parishioners to meet the "deputation" after the Church Missionary Meeting. All the patties were eaten before the "deputation" came, and he was so tired, poor man! with his long speech that when he found there was nothing to eat he got quite annoyed. It was only for a moment, of course, but I heard him say to someone, whose name I forget, that he had much better have trusted to a ham-sandwich in the station refreshment-room.

'And if it is difficult with the food, it is worse still with what they are to drink. Some clergymen do so dislike wine, and others feel they need it before the exertion of speaking. Only last year, when Mrs Bulteel gave a drawing-room meeting, and champagne with biscuits was served before it, Dr Stimey said quite openly that though he did not consider all who drank to be *reprobate*, yet he must regard alcohol as the Mark of the Beast, and that people did not come to drawing-room meetings to drink themselves sleepy before the speaking. With Bishops it must be much worse; so I don't know what we shall give him.'

'Don't distress yourself too much,' the organist said, having at last spied a gap in the serried ranks of words; 'I have found out what Bishops eat; it is all in a little book. We must give him cold lamb—cold ribs of lamb—and mint sauce, boiled potatoes, and after that Stilton cheese.'

'Stilton?' Miss Joliffe asked with some trepidation. 'I am afraid it will be very expensive.'

As a drowning man in one moment passes in review the events of a lifetime, so her mind took an instantaneous conspectus of all cheeses that had ever stood in the cheese-cradle in the palmy days of Wydcombe, when hams and plum-puddings hung in bags from the rafters, when there was cream in the dairy and beer in the cellar. Blue Vinny, little Gloucesters, double Besants, even sometimes a cream-cheese with rushes on the bottom, but Stilton never!

'I am afraid it is a very expensive cheese; I do not think anyone in Cullerne keeps it.'

'It is a pity,' Mr Sharnall said; 'but we cannot help ourselves, for Bishops *must* have Stilton for lunch; the book says so. You must ask Mr Custance to get you a piece, and I will tell you later how it is to be cut, for there are rules about that too.'

He laughed to himself with a queer little chuckle. Cold lamb and mint sauce, with a piece of Stilton afterwards—they would have an Oxford lunch; they would be young again, and undefiled.

The stimulus that the Bishop's letter had brought Mr Sharnall soon wore off. He was a man of moods, and in his nervous temperament depression walked close at the heels of exaltation. Westray felt sure in those days that followed that his friend was drinking to excess, and feared something more serious than a mere nervous break-down, from the agitation and strangeness that he could not fail to observe in the organist's manner.

The door of the architect's room opened one night, as he sat late over his work, and Mr Sharnall entered. His face was pale, and there was a startled wide-open look in his eyes that Westray did not like.

'I wish you would come down to my room for a minute,' the organist said; 'I want to change the place of my piano, and can't move it by myself.'

'Isn't it rather late to-night?' Westray said, pulling at his watch, while the deep and slow melodious chimes of St Sepulchre told the dreaming town and the silent sea-marshes that it lacked but a quarter of an hour to midnight. 'Wouldn't it be better to do it to-morrow morning?'

'Couldn't you come down to-night?' the organist asked; 'it wouldn't take you a minute.'

Westray caught the disappointment in the tone.

'Very well,' he said, putting his drawing-board aside. 'I've worked at this quite long enough; let us shift your piano.'

They went down to the ground floor.

'I want to turn the piano right-about-face,' the organist said, 'with its back to the room and the keyboard to the wall—the keyboard quite close to the wall, with just room for me to sit.'

'It seems a curious arrangement,' Westray criticized; 'is it better acoustically?'

'Oh, I don't know; but, if I want to rest a bit, I can put my back against the wall, you see.'

The change was soon accomplished, and they sat down for a moment before the fire.

'You keep a good fire,' Westray said, 'considering it is bed-time.' And, indeed, the coals were piled high, and burning fiercely.

The organist gave them a poke, and looked round as if to make sure that they were alone.

'You'll think me a fool,' he said; 'and I am. You'll think I've been drinking, and I have. You'll think I'm drunk, but I'm not. Listen to me: I'm not drunk; I'm only a coward. Do you remember the very first night you and I walked home to this house together? Do you remember the darkness and the driving rain, and how scared I was when we passed the Old Bonding-house? Well, it was beginning then, but it's much worse now. I had a horrible idea even then that there was something always following me—following me close. I didn't know what it was—I only knew there was *something* close behind me.'

His manner and appearance alarmed Westray. The organist's face was very pale, and a curious raising of the eyelids, which showed the whites of the eyes above the pupils, gave him the staring appearance of one confronted suddenly with some ghastly spectacle. Westray remembered that the hallucination of pursuant enemies is one of the most common symptoms of incipient madness, and put his hand gently on the organist's arm.

'Don't excite yourself,' he said; 'this is all nonsense. Don't get excited so late at night.'

Mr Sharnall brushed the hand aside.

'I only used to have that feeling when I was out of doors, but now I have it often indoors—even in this very room. Before, I never knew what it was following me—I only knew it was *something*. But now I know what it is: it is a man—a man with a hammer. Don't laugh. You don't *want* to laugh; you only laugh because you think it will quiet me, but it won't. I think it is a man with a hammer. I have never seen his face yet, but I shall some day. Only I know it is an evil face—not hideous, like pictures of devils or anything of that kind, but worse—a dreadful, disguised face, looking all right, but wearing a mask. He walks constantly behind me, and I feel every moment that the hammer may brain me.'

'Come, come!' Westray said in what is commonly supposed to be a soothing tone, 'let us change this subject, or go to bed. I wonder how you will find the new position of your piano answer.'

The organist smiled.

'Do you know why I really put it like that?' he said. 'It is because I am such a coward. I like to have my back against the wall, and then I know there can be no one behind me. There are many nights, when it gets late, that it is only with a great effort I can sit here. I grow so nervous that I should go to bed at once, only I say to myself, "Nick"—that's what they used to call me at home, you know, when I was a, boy—"Nick, you're not going to be beat; you're not going to be scared out of your own room by ghosts surely." And then I sit tight, and play on, but very often don't think much of what I'm playing. It is a sad state for a man to get into, is it not?' And Westray could not traverse the statement.

'Even in the church,' Mr Sharnall went on, 'I don't care to practise much in the evening by myself. It used to be all right when Cutlow was there to blow for me. He is a daft fellow, but still was some sort of company; but now the water-engine is put in, I feel lonely there, and don't care to go as often as I used. Something made me tell Lord Blandamer how his water-engine contrived to make me frightened, and he said he should have to come up to the loft himself sometimes to keep me company.'

'Well, let me know the first evening you want to practise,' Westray said, 'and I will come, too, and sit in the loft. Take care of yourself, and you will soon grow out of all these fancies, and laugh at them as much as I do.' And he feigned a smile. But it was late at night; he was high-strung and nervous himself, and the fact that Mr Sharnall should have been brought to such a pitiable state of mental instability depressed him.

The report that the Bishop was going to lunch with Mr Sharnall on the day of the Confirmation soon spread in Cullerne. Miss Joliffe had told Mr Joliffe the pork-butcher, as her cousin, and Mr Joliffe, as churchwarden, had told Canon Parkyn. It was the second time within a few weeks that a piece of important news had reached the Rector at second-hand. But on this occasion he experienced little of the chagrin that had possessed him when Lord Blandamer made the great offer to the restoration fund through Westray. He did not feel resentment against Mr Sharnall; the affair was of too solemn an importance for any such personal and petty sentiments to find a place. Any act of any Bishop was vicariously an act of God, and to chafe at this dispensation would have been as out of place as to be incensed at a shipwreck or an earthquake. The fact of being selected as the entertainer of the Bishop of Carisbury invested Mr Sharnall in the Rector's eyes with a distinction which could not have been possibly attained by mere intellect or technical skill or devoted drudgery. The organist became *ipso facto* a person to be taken into account.

The Rectory had divined and discussed, and discussed and divined, how it was, could, would, should, have been that the Bishop could be lunching with Mr Sharnall. Could it be that the Bishop had thought that Mr Sharnall kept an eating-house, or that the Bishop took some special diet which only Mr Sharnall knew how to prepare? Could it be that the Bishop had some idea of making Mr Sharnall organist in his private chapel, for there was no vacancy in the Cathedral? Conjecture charged the blank wall of mystery full tilt, and retired broken from the assault. After talking of nothing else for many hours, Mrs Parkyn declared that the matter had no interest at all for her.

'For my part, I cannot profess to understand such goings on,' she said in that convincing and convicting tone which implies that the speaker knows far more than he cares to state, and that the solution of the mystery must in any case be discreditable to all concerned.

'I wonder, my dear,' the Rector said to his wife, 'whether Mr Sharnall has the means to entertain the Bishop properly.'

'Properly!' said Mrs Parkyn—'properly! I think the whole proceeding entirely improper. Do you mean has Mr Sharnall money enough to purchase a proper repast? I should say certainly not. Or has he proper plates or forks or spoons, or a proper room in which to eat? Of course he has not. Or do you mean can he get things properly cooked? Who is to do it? There is only feckless old Miss Joliffe and her stuck-up niece.'

The Canon was much perturbed by the vision of discomfort which his wife had called up.

'The Bishop ought to be spared as much as *possible*,' he said; 'we ought to do all we *can* to save him annoyance. What do you think? Should we not put up with a little inconvenience, and ask Sharnall to bring the Bishop here, and lunch himself? He must know perfectly well that entertaining a Bishop in a lodging-house is an unheard-of thing, and he would do to make up the sixth instead of old Noot. We could easily tell Noot he was not wanted.'

'Sharnall is such a disreputable creature,' Mrs Parkyn answered; 'he is quite as likely as not to come tipsy; and, if he does not, he has no *breeding* or education, and would scarcely understand polite conversation.'

'You forget, my dear, that the Bishop is already pledged to lunch with Mr Sharnall, so that we should not be held responsible for introducing him. And Sharnall has managed to pick up some sort of an education—I can't imagine where; but I found on one occasion that he could understand a little Latin. It was the Blandamer motto, "*Aut Fynes, aut finis.*" He may have been told what it meant, but certainly seemed to know. Of course, no real knowledge of Latin can be obtained without a *University* education'— and the Rector pulled up his tie and collar—'but still chemists and persons of that sort do manage to get a smattering of it.'

'Well, well, I don't suppose we are going to talk Latin all through lunch,' interrupted his wife. 'You can do precisely as you please about asking him.'

The Rector contented himself with the permission, however, ungraciously accorded, and found himself a little later in Mr Sharnall's room.

'Mrs Parkyn was hoping that she might have prevailed on you to lunch with us on the day of the Confirmation. She was only waiting for the Bishop's acceptance to send you an invitation; but we hear now,' he said in a dubitative and tentative way—'we hear now that it is possible that the Bishop may be lunching with you.'

There was a twitch about the corners of Canon Parkyn's mouth. The position that a Bishop should be lunching with Mr Sharnall in a common lodging-house was so exquisitely funny that he could only restrain his laughter with difficulty.

Mr Sharnall gave an assenting nod.

'Mrs Parkyn was not quite sure whether you might have in your lodgings exactly everything that might be necessary for entertaining his lordship.'

'Oh dear, yes,' Mr Sharnall said. 'It looks a little dowdy just this minute, because the chairs are at the upholsterers to have the gilt touched up; we are putting up new curtains, of *course*, and the housekeeper has already begun to polish the best silver.'

'It occurred to Mrs Parkyn,' the Rector continued, being too bent on saying what he had to say to pay much attention to the organist's remarks—'it occurred to Mrs Parkyn that it might perhaps be more convenient to you to bring the Bishop to lunch at the Rectory. It would spare you all trouble in preparation, and you would of course lunch with us yourself. It would be putting us to no inconvenience; Mrs Parkyn would be glad that you should lunch with us yourself.'

Mr Sharnall nodded, this time deprecatingly.

'You are very kind. Mrs Parkyn is very considerate, but the Bishop has signified his intention of lunching in *this* house; I could scarcely venture to contravene his lordship's wishes.'

'The Bishop is a friend of yours?' the Rector asked.

'You can scarcely say that; I do not think I have set eyes on the man for forty years.'

The Rector was puzzled.

'Perhaps the Bishop is under some misconception; perhaps he thinks that this house is still an inn—the Hand of God, you know.'

'Perhaps,' said the organist; and there was a little pause.

'I hope you will consider the matter. May I not tell Mrs Parkyn that you will urge the Bishop to lunch at the Rectory—that you both'—and he brought out the word bravely, though it cost him a pang to yoke the Bishop with so unworthy a mate, and to fling the door of select hospitality open to Mr Sharnall—'that you both will lunch with us?'

'I fear not,' the organist said; 'I fear I must say no. I shall be very busy preparing for the extra service, and if I am to play "See the Conquering Hero" as the Bishop enters the church, I shall need time for practice. A piece like that takes some playing, you know.'

'I hope you will endeavour to render it in the very best manner,' the Rector said, and withdrew his forces *re infecta*.

The story of Mr Sharnall's mental illusions, and particularly of the hallucination as to someone following him, had left an unpleasant impression on Westray's mind. He was anxious about his fellow lodger, and endeavoured to keep a kindly supervision over him, as he felt it to be possible that a person in such a state might do himself a mischief. On most evenings he either went down to Mr Sharnall's room, or asked the organist to come upstairs to his, considering that the solitude incident to bachelor life in advancing years was doubtless to blame to a large extent for these wandering fancies. Mr Sharnall occupied himself at night in sorting and reading the documents which had once belonged to Martin Joliffe. There was a vast number of them, representing the accumulation of a lifetime, and consisting of loose memoranda, of extracts from registers, of manuscript-books full of pedigrees and similar material. When he had first begun to examine them with a view to their classification or destruction, he showed that the task was distinctly uncongenial to him; he was glad enough to make any excuse for interruption or for invoking Westray's aid. The architect, on the other hand, was by nature inclined to archæologic and genealogic studies, and would not have been displeased if Mr Sharnall had handed over to him the perusal of these papers entirely. He was curious to trace the origin of that chimera which had wasted a whole life—to discover what had led

Martin originally to believe that he had a claim to the Blandamer peerage. He found, perhaps, an additional incentive in an interest which he was beginning unconsciously to take in Anastasia Joliffe, whose fortunes might be supposed to be affected by these investigations.

But in a little while Westray noticed a change in the organist's attitude as touching the papers. Mr Sharnall evinced a dislike to the architect examining them further; he began himself to devote a good deal more time and attention to their study, and he kept them jealously under lock and key. Westray's nature led him to resent anything that suggested suspicion; he at once ceased to concern himself with the matter, and took care to show Mr Sharnall that he had no wish whatever to see more of the documents.

As for Anastasia, she laughed at the idea of there being any foundation underlying these fancies; she laughed at Mr Sharnall, and rallied Westray, saying she believed that they both were going to embark on the quest of the nebuly coat. To Miss Euphemia it was no laughing matter.

'I think, my dear,' she said to her niece, 'that all these searchings after wealth and fortune are not of God. I believe that trying to discover things'—and she used 'things' with the majestic comprehensiveness of the female mind—'is generally bad for man. If it is good for us to be noblemen and rich, then Providence will bring us to that station; but to try to prove one's self a nobleman is like star-gazing and fortune-telling. Idolatry is as the sin of witchcraft. There can be no *blessing* on it, and I reproach myself for ever having given dear Martin's papers to Mr Sharnall at all. I only did so because I could not bear to go through them myself, and thought perhaps that there might be cheques or something valuable among them. I wish I had burnt everything at first, and now Mr Sharnall says he will not have the papers destroyed till he has been through them. I am sure they were no *blessing* at all to dear Martin. I hope they may not bewitch these two gentlemen as well.'

Chapter 12

The scheme of restoration had been duly revised in the light of Lord Blandamer's generosity, and the work had now entered on such a methodical progress that Westray was able on occasion to relax something of that close personal supervision which had been at first so exacting. Mr Sharnall often played for half an hour or more after the evening service, and on such occasions Westray found time, now and then, to make his way to the organ-loft. The organist liked to have him there; he was grateful for the token of interest, however slight, that was implied in such visits; and Westray, though without technical knowledge, found much to interest him in the unfamiliar surroundings of the loft. It was a curious little kingdom of itself, situate over the great stone screen, which at Cullerne divides the choir from the nave, but as remote and cut off from the outside world as a desert island. Access was gained to it by a narrow, round, stone staircase, which led up from the nave at the south end of the screen. After the bottom door of this windowless staircase was opened and shut, anyone ascending was left for a moment in bewildering darkness. He had to grope the way by his feet feeling the stairs, and by his hand laid on the central stone shaft which had been polished to the smoothness of marble by countless other hands of past times.

But, after half a dozen steps, the darkness resolved; there was first the dusk of dawn, and soon a burst of mellow light, when he reached the stairhead and stepped out into the loft. Then there were two things which he noticed before any other—the bow of that vast Norman arch which spanned the opening into the south transept, with its lofty and over-delicate mouldings; and behind it the head of the Blandamer window, where in the centre of the infinite multiplication of the tracery shone the sea-green and silver of the nebuly coat. Afterwards he might remark the long-drawn roof of the nave, and the chevroned ribs of the Norman vault, delimiting bay and bay with a saltire as they crossed, or his eyes might be led up to the lantern of the central tower, and follow the lighter ascending lines of Abbot Vinnicomb's Perpendicular panelling, till they vanished in the windows far above.

Inside the loft there was room and to spare. It was formed on ample lines, and had space for a stool or two beside the performer's seat, while at the sides ran low bookcases which held the music library. In these shelves rested the great folios of Boyce, and Croft, and Arnold, Page and Greene, Battishill and Crotch—all those splendid and ungrudging tomes for which the 'Rectors and Foundation of Cullerne' had subscribed in older and richer days. Yet these were but the children of a later birth. Round about them stood elder brethren, for Cullerne Minster was still left in possession of its seventeenth-century music-books. A famous set they were, a hundred or more bound in their old black polished calf, with a great gold medallion, and 'Tenor: Dec.', or 'Contra-tenor: Can.', 'Basso', or 'Sopra', stamped in the middle of every cover. And inside was parchment with red-ruled margins, and on the parchment were inscribed services and 'verse-anthems' and 'ffull-anthems', all in engrossing hand and the most uncompromising of black ink. Therein was a generous table of contents—Mr Batten and Mr Gibbons, Mr Munday and Mr Tomkins, Doctor Bull and Doctor Giles, all neatly filed and paged; and Mr Byrd would incite singers long since turned to churchyard mould to 'bring forthe ye timbrell, ye pleasant harp and ye violl,' and reinsist with six parts, and a red capital letter, 'ye pleasant harp and ye violl.'

It was a great place for dust, the organ-loft—dust that fell, and dust that rose; dust of wormy wood, dust of crumbling leather, dust of tattered mothy curtains that were dropping to pieces, dust of primeval green baize; but Mr Sharnall had breathed the dust for forty years, and felt more at home in that place than anywhere else. If it was Crusoe's island, he was Crusoe, monarch of all he surveyed.

'Here, you can take this key,' he said one day to Westray; 'it unlocks the staircase-door; but either tell me when to expect you, or make a noise as you come up the steps. I don't like being startled. Be sure you push the door to after you; it fastens itself. I am always particular about keeping the door locked, otherwise one doesn't know what stranger may take it into his head to walk up. I can't bear being startled.' And he glanced behind him with a strange look in his eyes.

A few days before the Bishop's visit Westray was with Mr Sharnall in the organ-loft. He had been there through most of the service, and, as he sat on his stool in the corner, had watched the curious diamond pattern of light and dark that the clerestory windows made with the vaulting ribs. Anyone outside would have seen islands of white cloud drifting across the blue sky, and each cloud as it passed threw the heavy chevroned diagonals inside into bold relief, and picked out that rebus of a carding-comb encircled by wreath of vine-leaves which Nicholas Vinnicomb had inserted for a vaulting-boss.

The architect had learned to regard the beetling roof with an almost superstitious awe, and was this day so fascinated with the strange effect as to be scarcely aware that the service was over till Mr Sharnall spoke.

'You said you would like to hear my service in D flat—"Sharnall in D flat", did you not? I will play it through to you now, if you care to listen. Of course, I can only give you the general effect, without voices, though, after all, I don't know that you won't get quite as good an idea of it as you could with any voices that we have here.'

Westray woke up from his dreams and put himself into an attitude of proper attention, while Mr Sharnall played the service from a faded manuscript.

'Now,' he said, as he came towards the end—'now listen. This is the best part of it—a fugal *Gloria*, ending with a pedal-point. Here you are, you see—a tonic pedal-point, this D flat, the very last raised note in my new pedal-board, held down right through.' And he set his left foot on the pedal. 'What do you think of *that* for a *Magnificat?*' he said, when it was finished; and Westray was ready with all the conventional expressions of admiration. 'It is not bad, is it?' Mr Sharnall asked; 'but the gem of it is the *Gloria*—not real fugue, but fugal, with a pedal-point. Did you catch the effect of that point? I will keep the note down by itself for a second, so that you may get thoroughly hold of it, and then play the *Gloria* again.'

He held down the D flat, and the open pipe went booming and throbbing through the long nave arcades, and in the dark recesses of the triforium, and under the beetling vaulting, and quavered away high up in the lantern, till it seemed like the death-groan of a giant.

'Take it up,' Westray said; 'I can't bear the throbbing.'

'Very well; now listen while I give you the *Gloria*. No, I really think I had better go through the whole service again; you see, it leads up more naturally to the finale.'

He began the service again, and played it with all the conscientious attention and sympathy that the creative artist must necessarily give to his own work. He enjoyed, too, that pleasurable surprise which awaits the discovery that a composition laid aside for many years and half forgotten is better and stronger than had been imagined, even as a disused dress brought out of the wardrobe sometimes astonishes us with its freshness and value.

Westray stood on a foot-pace at the end of the loft which allowed him to look over the curtain into the church. His eyes roamed through the building as he listened, but he did not appreciate the music the less. Nay, rather, he appreciated it the more, as some writers find literary perception and power of expression quickened at the influence of music itself. The great church was empty. Janaway had left for his tea; the doors were locked, no strangers could intrude; there was no sound, no murmur, no voice, save only the voices of the organ-pipes. So Westray listened. Stay, were there no other voices? was there nothing he heard—nothing that spoke within him? At first he was only conscious of *something*—something that drew his attention away from the music, and then the disturbing influence was resolved into another voice, small but rising very clear even above 'Sharnall in D flat'. 'The arch never sleeps,' said that still and ominous voice. 'The arch never sleeps; they have bound on us a burden too heavy to be borne. We are shifting it; we never sleep.' And his eyes turned to the cross arches under the tower. There, above the bow of the south transept, showed the great crack, black and writhen to a lightning-flash, just as it had showed any time for a century—just the same to the ordinary observer, but not to the architect. He looked at it fixedly for a moment, and then, forgetting Mr Sharnall and the music, left the loft, and made his way to the wooden platform that the masons had built up under the roof.

Mr Sharnall did not even perceive that he had gone down, and dashed *con furore* into the *Gloria*. 'Give me the full great,' he called to the architect, who he thought was behind him; 'give me the full great, all but the reed,' and snatched the stops out himself when there was no response. 'It went better that time—distinctly better,' he said, as the last note ceased to sound, and then turned round for Westray's comment; but the loft was empty—he was alone.

'Curse the fellow!' he said; 'he might at least have let me know that he was going away. Ah, well, it's all poor stuff, no doubt.' And he shut up the manuscript with a lingering and affectionate touch, that contrasted with so severe a criticism: 'It's poor stuff; why should I expect anyone to listen to it?'

It was full two hours later that Westray came quickly into the organist's room at Bellevue Lodge.

'I beg your pardon, Sharnall,' he said, 'for leaving you so cavalierly. You must have thought me rude and inappreciative; but the fact is I was so startled that I forgot to tell you why I went. While you were playing I happened to look up at that great crack over the south transept arch, and saw something very like recent movement. I went up at once to the scaffolding, and have been there ever since. I don't like it at all; it seems to me that the crack is opening, and extending. It may mean very serious mischief, and I have made up my mind to go up to London by the last train tonight. I must get Sir George Farquhar's opinion at once.'

The organist grunted. The wound inflicted on his susceptibility had rankled deeply, and indignation had been tenderly nursed. A piece of his mind was to have been given to Westray, and he regretted the very reasonableness of the explanation that robbed him of his opportunity.

'Pray don't apologize,' he said; 'I never noticed that you had gone. I really quite forgot that you had been there.'

Westray was too full of his discovery to take note of the other's annoyance. He was one of those excitable persons who mistake hurry for decision of action.

'Yes,' he said, 'I must be off to London in half an hour. The matter is far too serious to play fast-and-loose with. It is quite possible that we shall have to stop the organ, or even to forbid the use of the church altogether, till we can shore and strut the arch. I must go and put my things together.'

So, with heroic promptness and determination, he flung himself into the last train, and spent the greater part of the night in stopping at every wayside station, when his purpose would have been equally served by a letter or by taking the express at Cullerne Road the next morning.

Chapter 13

The organ was not silenced, nor was the service suspended. Sir George came down to Cullerne, inspected the arch, and rallied his subordinate for an anxiety which was considered to be unjustifiable. Yes, the wall above the arch *had* moved a little, but not more than was to be expected from the repairs which were being undertaken with the vaulting. It was only the old wall coming to its proper bearings—he would have been surprised, in fact, if no movement had taken place; it was much safer as it was.

Canon Parkyn was in high good-humour. He rejoiced in seeing the pert and officious young clerk of the works put in his proper place; and Sir George had lunched at the Rectory. There was a repetition of the facetious proposal that Sir George should wait for payment of his fees until the tower should fall, which acquired fresh point from the circumstance that all payments were now provided for by Lord Blandamer. The ha-ha-ing which accompanied this witticism palled at length even upon the robust Sir George, and he winced under a dig in the ribs, which an extra glass of port had emboldened the Canon to administer.

'Well, well, Mr Rector,' he said, 'we cannot put old heads on young shoulders. Mr Westray was quite justified in referring the matter to me. It *has* an ugly look; one needs *experience* to be able to see through things like this.' And he pulled up his collar, and adjusted his tie.

Westray was content to accept his Chief's decision as a matter of faith, though not of conviction. The black lightning-flash was impressed on his mental retina, the restless cry of the arches was continually in his ear; he seldom passed the transept-crossing without hearing it. But he bore his rebuke with exemplary resignation—the more so that he was much interested in some visits which Lord

Blandamer paid him at this period. Lord Blandamer called more than once at Bellevue Lodge in the evenings, even as late as nine o'clock, and would sit with Westray for two hours together, turning over plans and discussing the restoration. The architect learnt to appreciate the charm of his manner, and was continually astonished at the architectural knowledge and critical power which he displayed. Mr Sharnall would sometimes join them for a few minutes, but Lord Blandamer never appeared quite at his ease when the organist was present; and Westray could not help thinking that Mr Sharnall was sometimes tactless, and even rude, considering that he was beholden to Lord Blandamer for new pedals and new bellows and a water-engine *in esse*, and for the entire repair of the organ *in posse*.

'I can't help being "beholden to him", as you genteelly put it,' Mr Sharnall said one evening when Lord Blandamer had gone. 'I can't stop his giving new bellows or a new pedal-board. And we do want the new board and the additional pipes. As it is, I can't play German music, can't touch a good deal of Bach's organ work. Who is to say this man "nay", if he chooses to alter the organ? But I'm not going to truckle to anyone, and least of all to him. Do you want me to fall flat on my face because he is a lord? Pooh! we would all be lords like him. Give me another week with Martin's papers, and I'll open your eyes. Ay, you may stare and sniff if you please, but you'll open your eyes then. *Ex oriente lux*—that's where the light's coming from, out of Martin's papers. Once get this Confirmation over, and you'll see. I can't settle to the papers till that's done with. What do people want to confirm these boys and girls for? It only makes hypocrites of wholesome children. I hate the whole business. If people want to make their views public, let them do it at five-and-twenty; then we should believe that they knew something of what they were about.'

The day of the Bishop's visit had arrived; the Bishop had arrived himself; he had entered the door of Bellevue Lodge; he had been received by Miss Euphemia Joliffe as one who receives an angel awares; he had lunched in Mr Sharnall's room, and had partaken of the cold lamb, and the Stilton, and even of the cider-cup, to just such extent as became a healthy and good-hearted and host-considering bishop.

'You have given me a regular Oxford lunch,' he said. 'Your landlady has been brought up in the good tradition.' And he smiled, never doubting that he was partaking of the ordinary provision of the house, and that Mr Sharnall fared thus sumptuously every day. He knew not that the meal was as much a set piece as a dinner on the stage, and that cold lamb and Stilton and cider-cup were more often represented by the bottom of a tin of potted meat and—a gill of cheap whisky.

'A regular Oxford lunch.' And then they fell to talking of old and the Bishop called Mr Sharnall 'Nick,' and Mr Sharnall called the Bishop of Carisbury 'John'; and they walked round the room looking at pictures of college groups and college eights, and the Bishop examined very tenderly the little water-colour sketch that Mr Sharnall had once made of the inner quad; and they identified in it their own old rooms, and the rooms of several other men of their acquaintance.

The talk did Mr Sharnall good; he felt the better for it every moment. He had meant to be very proud and reserved with the Bishop—to be most dignified and coldly courteous. He had meant to show that, though John Willis might wear the gaiters, Nicholas Sharnall could retain his sturdy independence, and was not going to fawn or to admit himself to be the mental inferior of any man. He had meant to give a tirade against Confirmation, against the neglect of music, against rectors, with perhaps a back-thrust at the Bench of Bishops itself. But he had done none of these things, because neither pride nor reserve nor assertiveness were possible in John Willis's company. He had merely eaten a good lunch, and talked with a kindly, broad-minded gentleman, long enough to warm his withered heart, and make him feel that there were still possibilities in life.

There is a bell that rings for a few strokes three-quarters of an hour before every service at Cullerne. It is called the Burgess Bell—some say because it was meant to warn such burgesses as dwelt at a distance that it was time to start for church; whilst others will have that Burgess is but a broken-down form of *expergiscere*—'Awake, awake!'—that those who dozed might rise for prayer. The still air of the afternoon was yet vibrating with the Burgess bell, and the Bishop rose to take his leave.

If it was the organist of Cullerne who had been ill at ease when their interview began, it was the Bishop of Carisbury who was embarrassed at the end of it. He had asked himself to lunch with Mr Sharnall with a definite object, and towards the attainment of that object nothing had been done. He had learnt that his old friend had fallen upon evil times, and, worse, had fallen into evil courses—that the failing which had ruined his Oxford career had broken out again with a fresh fire in advancing age, that Nicholas Sharnall was in danger of a drunkard's judgment.

There had been lucid intervals in the organist's life; the plague would lie dormant for months and then break out, to cancel all the progress that had been made. It was like a 'race-game' where the little leaden horse is moved steadily forward, till at last the die falls on the fatal number, and the racer must lose a turn, or go back six or, even in the worst issue, begin his whole course again. It was in the forlorn hope of doing something, however little, to arrest a man on the downward slope that the Bishop had come to Bellevue Lodge; he hoped to speak the word in season that should avail. Yet nothing had been said. He felt like a clerk who had sought an interview with his principal to ask for an increase of salary, and then, fearing to broach the subject, pretends to have come on other business. He felt like a son longing to ask his father's counsel in some grievous scrape, or like an extravagant wife waiting her opportunity to confess some heavy debt.

'A quarter past two,' the Bishop said; 'I must be going. It has been a great pleasure to recall the old times. I hope we shall meet again soon; but remember it is your turn now to come and see me. Carisbury is not so very far off, so do come. There is always a bed ready for you. Will you walk up the street with me now? I have to go to the Rectory, and I suppose you will be going to the church, will you not?'

'Yes,' said Mr Sharnall; 'I'll come with you if you wait one minute. I think I'll take just a drop of something before I go, if you'll excuse me. I feel rather run down, and the service is a long one. You won't join me, of course?' And he went to the cupboard.

The Bishop's opportunity was come.

'Don't, Sharnall. Don't, Nick,' he said; 'don't take that stuff. Forgive me for speaking openly, the time is so short. I am not speaking professionally or from the religious standpoint, but only just as one man of the world to another, just as one friend to another, because I cannot bear to see you going on like this without trying to stop you. Don't take offence, Nick,' he added, as he saw the change of the other's countenance; 'our old friendship gives me a right to speak; the story you are writing on your own face gives me a right to speak. Give it up. There is time yet to turn; give it up. Let me help you; is there nothing I can do to help?'

The angry look that crossed Mr Sharnall's face had given way to sadness.

'It is all very easy for you,' he said; 'you've done everything in life and have a long row of mile-stones behind you to show how you've moved on. I have done nothing, only gone back, and have all the milestones in front to show how I've failed. It's easy to twit me when you've got everything you want—position, reputation, fortune, a living faith to keep you up to it. I am nobody, miserably poor, have no friends, and don't believe half we say in church. What am I to do? No one cares a fig about me; what have I got to live for? To drink is the only chance I have of feeling a little pleasure in life; of losing for a few moments the dreadful consciousness of being an outcast; of losing for a moment the remembrance of happy days long ago; that's the greatest torment of all, Willis. Don't blame me if I drink; it's the *elixir vitæ* for me just as much as for Paracelsus.' And he turned the handle of the cupboard.

'Don't,' the Bishop said again, putting his hand on the organist's arm; 'don't do it; don't touch it. Don't make success any criterion of life; don't talk about "getting on". We shan't be judged by how we have got on. Come along with me; show you've got your old resolution, your old will-power.'

'I *haven't* got the power,' Mr Sharnall said; 'I can't help it.' But he took his hand from the cupboard-door.

'Then let me help it for you,' said the Bishop; and he opened the cupboard, found a half-used bottle of whisky, drove the cork firmly into it, and put it under his arm inside the lappet of his coat. 'Come along.'

So the Bishop of Carisbury walked up the High Street of Cullerne with a bottle of whisky under his left arm. But no one could see that because it was hid under his coat; they only saw that he had his arm inside Mr Sharnall's. Some thought this an act of Christian condescension, but others praised the times that were past; bishops were losing caste, they said, and it was a sad day for the Church when they were found associating openly with persons so manifestly their inferiors.

'We must see more of each other,' the Bishop said, as they walked under the arcade in front of the shops. 'You must get out of this quag somehow. You can't expect to do it all at once, but we must make a beginning. I have taken away your temptation under my coat, and you must make a start from this minute; you must make me a promise *now*. I have to be in Cullerne again in six days' time, and will come and see you. You must promise me not to touch anything for these six days, and you must drive back with me to Carisbury when I go back then, and spend a few days with me. Promise me this, Nick; the time is pressing, and I must leave you, but you must promise me this first.'

The organist hesitated for a moment, but the Bishop gripped his arm.

'Promise me this; I will not go till you promise.'

'Yes, I promise.'

And lying-and-mischief-making Mrs Flint, who was passing, told afterwards how she had overheard the Bishop discussing with Mr Sharnall the best means for introducing ritualism into the minster, and how the organist had promised to do his very best to help him so far as the musical part of the service was concerned.

The Confirmation was concluded without any contretemps, save that two of the grammar-school boys incurred an open and well-merited rebuke from the master for appearing in gloves of a much lighter slate colour than was in any way decorous, and that this circumstance reduced the youngest Miss Bulteel to such a state of hysteric giggling that her mother was forced to remove her from the church, and thus deprive her of spiritual privileges for another year.

Mr Sharnall bore his probation bravely. Three days passed, and he had not broken his vow—no, not in one jot or tittle. They had been days of fine weather, brilliantly clear autumn days of blue sky and exhilarating air. They had been bright days for Mr Sharnall; he was himself exhilarated; he felt a new life coursing in his veins. The Bishop's talk had done him good; from his heart he thanked the Bishop for it. Giving up drinking had done him no harm; he felt all the better for his abstinence. It had not depressed him at all; on the contrary, he was more cheerful than he had been for years. Scales had fallen from his eyes since that talk; he had regained his true bearings; he began to see the verities of life. How he had wasted his time! Why *had* he been so sour? Why *had* he indulged his spleen? Why *had* he taken such a jaundiced view of life? He would put aside all jealousies; he would have no enmities; he would be broader-minded—oh, so much broader-minded; he would embrace all mankind—yes, even Canon Parkyn. Above all, he would recognize that he was well advanced in life; he would be more sober-thinking, would leave childish things, would resolutely renounce his absurd infatuation for Anastasia. What a ridiculous idea—a crabbed old sexagenarian harbouring affection for a young girl! Henceforth she should be nothing to him—absolutely nothing. No, that would be foolish; it would not be fair to her to cut her off from all friendship; he could feel for her a fatherly affection—it should be paternal and nothing more. He would bid adieu to all that folly, and his life should not be a whit the emptier for the loss. He would fill it with interests—all kinds of interests, and his music should be the first. He would take up again, and carry out to the end, that oratorio which he had turned over in his mind for years—the 'Absalom'. He had several numbers at his fingers' ends; he would work out the bass solo, 'Oh, Absalom, my son, my son!' and the double chorus that followed it, 'Make ready, ye mighty; up and bare your swords!'

So he discoursed joyfully with his own heart, and felt above measure elated at the great and sudden change that was wrought in him, not recognizing that the clouds return after the rain, and that the leopard may change his spots as easily as man may change his habits.

To change a habit at fifty-five or forty-five or thirty-five; to ordain that rivers shall flow uphill; to divert the relentless sequence of cause and effect—how often dare we say this happens? *Nemo repente*—no man ever suddenly became good. A moment's spiritual agony may blunt our instincts and paralyse the evil in us—for a while, even as chloroform may dull our bodily sense; but for permanence there is no sudden turning of the mind; sudden repentances in life or death are equally impossible.

Three halcyon days were followed by one of those dark and lowering mornings when the blank life seems blanker, and when the gloom of nature is too accurately reflected in the nervous temperament of man. On healthy youth climatic influences have no effect, and robust middle age, if it perceive them, goes on its way steadfast or stolid, with a *cela passera, tout passera*. But on the feeble and the failing such times fall with a weight of fretful despondency; and so they fell on Mr Sharnall.

He was very restless about the time of the mid-day meal. There came up a thick, dark fog from the sea, which went rolling in great masses over Cullerne Flat, till its fringe caught the outskirts of the town. After that, it settled in the streets, and took up its special abode in Bellevue Lodge; till Miss Euphemia coughed so that she had to take two ipecacuanha lozenges, and Mr Sharnall was forced to ring for a lamp to see his victuals. He went up to Westray's room to ask if he might eat his dinner upstairs, but he found that the architect had gone to London, and would not be back till the evening train; so he was thrown upon his own resources.

He ate little, and by the end of the meal depression had so far got the better of him, that he found himself standing before a well-known cupboard. Perhaps the abstemiousness of the last three days had told upon him, and drove him for refuge to his usual comforter. It was by instinct that he went to the cupboard; he was not even conscious of doing so till he had the open door in his hand. Then resolution returned to him, aided, it may be, by the reflection that the cupboard was bare (for the Bishop had taken away the whisky), and he shut the door sharply. Was it possible that he had so soon forgotten his promise—had come so perilously near falling back into the mire, after the bright prospects of the last days, after so lucid an interval? He went to his bureau and buried himself in Martin Joliffe's papers, till the Burgess Bell gave warning of the afternoon service.

The gloom and fog made way by degrees for a drizzling rain, which resolved itself into a steady downpour as the afternoon wore on. It was so heavy that Mr Sharnall could hear the indistinct murmur of millions of raindrops on the long lead roofs, and their noisy splash and spatter as they struck the windows in the lantern and north transept. He was in a bad humour as he came down from the loft. The boys had sung sleepily and flat; Jaques had murdered the tenor solo with his strained and raucous voice; and old Janaway remembered afterwards that Mr Sharnall had never vouchsafed a good afternoon as he strode angrily down the aisle.

Things were no better when he reached Bellevue Lodge. He was wet and chilled, and there was no fire in the grate, because it was too early in the year for such luxuries to be afforded. He would go to the kitchen, and take his tea there. It was Saturday afternoon. Miss Joliffe would be at the Dorcas meeting, but Anastasia would be in; and this reflection came to him as a ray of sunlight in a dark and lowering time. Anastasia would be in, and alone; he would sit by the fire and drink a cup of hot tea, while Anastasia should talk to him and gladden his heart. He tapped lightly at the kitchen door, and as he opened it a gusty buffet of damp air smote him on the face; the room was empty. Through a half-open sash the wet had driven in, and darkened the top of the deal table which stood against the window; the fire was but a smouldering ash. He shut the window instinctively while he reflected. Where could Anastasia be? She must have left the kitchen some time, otherwise the fire would not be so low, and she would have seen that the rain was beating in. She must be upstairs; she had no doubt taken advantage of Westray's absence to set his room in order. He would go up to her; perhaps there was a fire in Westray's room.

He went up the circular stone staircase, that ran like a wide well from top to bottom of the old Hand of God. The stone steps and the stone floor of the hall, the stuccoed walls, and the coved stucco roof which held the skylight at the top, made a whispering-gallery of that gaunt staircase; and before Mr Sharnall had climbed half-way up he heard voices.

They were voices in conversation; Anastasia had company. And then he heard that one was a man's voice. What right had any man to be in Westray's room? What man had any right to be talking to Anastasia? A wild suspicion passed through his mind—no, that was quite impossible. He would not play the eavesdropper or creep near them to listen; but, as he reflected, he had mounted a step or two higher, and the voices were now more distinct. Anastasia had finished speaking, and the man began again. There was one second of uncertainty in Mr Sharnall's mind, while the hope that it was not, balanced the fear that it was; and then doubt vanished, and he knew the voice to be Lord Blandamer's.

The organist sprang up two or three steps very quickly. He would go straight to them—straight into Westray's room; he would— And then he paused; he would do, what? What right had he to go there at all? What had he to do with them? What was there for anyone to do? He paused, then turned and went downstairs again, telling himself that he was a fool—that he was making mountains of molehills, that there did not exist, in fact, even a molehill; yet having all the while a sickening feeling within him, as if some gripping hand had got hold of his poor physical and material heart, and was squeezing it. His room looked more gloomy than ever when he got back to it, but it did not matter now, because he was not going to remain there. He only stopped for a minute to sweep back into the bureau all those loose papers of Martin Joliffe's that were lying in a tumble on the open desk-flap. He smiled grimly as he put them back and locked them in. *Le jour viendra qui tout paiera.* These papers held a vengeance that would atone for all wrongs.

He took down his heavy and wet-sodden overcoat from the peg in the hall, and reflected with some satisfaction that the bad weather could not seriously damage it, for it had turned green with wear, and *must* be replaced as soon as he got his next quarter's salary. The rain still fell heavily, but he *must* go out. Four walls were too narrow to hold his chafing mood, and the sadness of outward nature accorded well with a gloomy spirit. So he shut the street-door noiselessly, and went down the semicircular flight of stone steps in front of the Hand of God, just as Lord Blandamer had gone down them on that historic evening when Anastasia first saw him. He turned back to look at the house, just as Lord Blandamer had turned back then; but was not so fortunate as his illustrious predecessor, for Westray's window was tight shut, and there was no one to be seen.

'I wish I may never look upon the place again,' he said to himself, half in earnest, and half with that cynicism which men affect because they know Fate seldom takes them at their word.

For an hour or more he wandered aimlessly, and found himself, as night fell, on the western outskirts of the town, where a small tannery carries on the last pretence of commercial activity in Cullerne. It is here that the Cull, which has run for miles under willow and alder, through deep pastures golden with marsh marigolds or scented with meadowsweet, past cuckoo-flower and pitcher-plant and iris and nodding bulrush, forsakes better traditions, and becomes a common town-sluice before it deepens at the wharves, and meets the sandy churn of the tideway. Mr Sharnall had become aware that he was tired, and he stood and leant over the iron paling that divides the roadway from the stream. He did not know how tired he was till he stopped walking, nor how the rain had wetted him till he bent his head a little forward, and a cascade of water fell from the brim of his worn-out hat.

It was a forlorn and dismal stream at which he looked. The low tannery buildings of wood projected in part over the water, and were supported on iron props, to which were attached water-whitened skins and repulsive portions of entrails, that swung slowly from side to side as the river took them. The water here is little more than three feet deep, and beneath its soiled current can be seen a sandy bottom on which grow patches of coarse duckweed. To Mr Sharnall these patches of a green so dark and drain-soiled as to be almost black in the failing light, seemed tresses of drowned hair, and he weaved stories about them for himself as the stream now swayed them to and fro, and now carried them out at length.

He observed things with that vacant observation which the body at times insists on maintaining, when the mind is busy with some overmastering preoccupation. He observed the most trivial details; he made an inventory of the things which he could see lying on the dirty bed of the river underneath the dirty water. There was a tin bucket with a hole in the bottom; there was a brown teapot without a spout; there was an earthenware blacking-bottle too strong to be broken; there were other shattered glass bottles and shards of crockery; there was a rim of a silk hat, and more than one toeless boot. He turned away, and looked down the road towards the town. They were beginning to light the lamps, and the reflections showed a criss-cross of white lines on the muddy road, where the water stood in the wheel-tracks. There was a dark vehicle coming down the road now, making a fresh track in the mud, and leaving two shimmering lines behind it as it went. He gave a little start when it came nearer, and he saw that it was the undertaker's cart carrying out a coffin for some pauper at the Union Workhouse.

He gave a start and a shiver; the wet had come through his overcoat; he could feel it on his arms; he could feel the cold and clinging wet striking at his knees. He was stiff with standing so long, and a rheumatic pain checked him suddenly as he tried to straighten himself. He would walk quickly to warm himself—he would go home at once. Home—what *home* had he? That great, gaunt Hand of God. He detested it and all that were within its walls. That was no home. Yet he was walking briskly towards it, having no other whither to go.

He was in the mean little streets, he was within five minutes of his goal, when he heard singing. He was passing the same little inn which he had passed the first night that Westray came. The same voice was singing inside which had sung the night that Westray came. Westray had brought discomfort; Westray had brought Lord

Blandamer. Things had never been the same since; he wished Westray had never come at all; he wished—oh, how he wished!—that all might be as it was before—that all might jog along quietly as it had for a generation before. She certainly had a fine voice, this woman. It really would be worth while seeing who she was; he wished he could just look inside the door. Stay, he could easily make an excuse for looking in: he would order a little hot whisky-and-water. He was so wet, it was prudent to take something to drink. It might ward off a bad chill. He would only take a very little, and only as a medicine, of course; there could be no harm in *that*—it was mere prudence.

He took off his hat, shook the rain from it, turned the handle of the door very gently, with the consideration of a musician who will do nothing to interrupt another who is making music, and went in.

He found himself in that sanded parlour which he had seen once before through the window. It was a long, low room, with heavy beams crossing the roof, and at the end was an open fireplace where a kettle hung above a smouldering fire. In a corner sat an old man playing on a fiddle, and near him the Creole woman stood singing; there were some tables round the room, and behind them benches on which a dozen men were sitting. There was no young man among them, and most had long passed the meridian of life. Their faces were suntanned and mahogany-coloured; some wore ear-rings in their ears, and strange curls of grey hair at the side of their heads. They looked as if they might have been sitting there for years—as if they might be the crew of some long-foundered vessel to whom had been accorded a Nirvana of endless tavern-fellowship. None of them took any notice of Mr Sharnall, for music was exercising its transporting power, and their thoughts were far away. Some were with old Cullerne whalers, with the harpoon and the ice-floe; some dreamt of square-stemmed timber-brigs, of the Baltic and the white Memel-logs, of wild nights at sea and wilder nights ashore; and some, remembering violet skies and moonlight through the mango-groves, looked on the Creole woman, and tried to recall in her faded features, sweet, swart faces that had kindled youthful fires a generation since.

> *Then the grog, boys — the grog, boys, bring hither,*

sang the Creole.

> *Fill it up true to the brim.*
> *May the mem'ry of Nelson ne'er wither*
> *Nor the star of his glory grow dim.*

There were rummers standing on the tables, and now and then a drinking-brother would break the sugar-knobs in his liquor with a glass stirrer, or take a deep draught of the brown jorum that steamed before him. No one spoke to Mr Sharnall; only the landlord, without asking what he would take, set before him a glass filled with the same hot spirit as the other guests were drinking.

The organist accepted his fate with less reluctance than he ought perhaps to have displayed, and a few minutes later was drinking and smoking with the rest. He found the liquor to his liking, and soon experienced the restoring influences of the warm room and of the spirit. He hung his coat up on a peg, and in its dripping condition, and in the wet which had penetrated to his skin, found ample justification for accepting without demur a second bumper with which the landlord replaced his empty glass. Rummer followed rummer, and still the Creole woman sang at intervals, and still the company smoked and drank.

Mr Sharnall drank too, but by-and-by saw things less clearly, as the room grew hotter and more clouded with tobacco-smoke. Then he found the Creole woman standing before him, and holding out a shell for contributions. He had in his pocket only one single coin—a half-crown that was meant to be a fortnight's pocket-money; but he was excited, and had no hesitation.

'There,' he said, with an air of one who gives a kingdom—'there, take that: you deserve it; but sing me a song that I heard you sing once before, something about the rolling sea.'

She nodded that she understood, and after the collection was finished, gave the money to the blind man, and bade him play for her.

It was a long ballad, with many verses and a refrain of

> *Oh, take me back to those I love,*
> *Or bring them here to me;*
> *I have no heart to rove, to rove*
> *Across the rolling sea.*

At the end she came back, and sat down on the bench by Mr Sharnall.

'Will you not give me something to drink?' she said, speaking in very good English. 'You all drink; why should not I?'

He beckoned to the landlord to bring her a glass, and she drank of it, pledging the organist.

'You sing well,' he said, 'and with a little training should sing very well indeed. How do you come to be here? You ought to do better than this; if I were you, I would not sing in such company.'

She looked at him angrily.

'How do *I* come to be here? How do *you* come to be here? If I had a little training, I should sing better, and if I had your training, Mr Sharnall'—and she brought out his name with a sneering emphasis—'I should not be here at all drinking myself silly in a place like this.'

She got up, and went back to the old fiddler, but her words had a sobering influence on the organist, and cut him to the quick. So all his good resolutions had vanished. His promise to the Bishop was broken; the Bishop would be back again on Monday, and find him as bad as ever—would find him worse; for the devil had returned, and was making riot in the garnished house. He turned to pay his reckoning, but his half-crown had gone to the Creole; he had no money, he was forced to explain to the landlord, to humiliate himself, to tell his name and address. The man grumbled and made demur. Gentlemen who drank in good company, he said, should be prepared to pay their shot like gentlemen. Mr Sharnall had drunk enough to make it a serious thing for a poor man not to get paid. Mr Sharnall's story might be true, but it was a funny thing for an organist to come and drink at the Merrymouth, and have no money in his pocket. It had stopped raining; he could leave his overcoat as a pledge of good faith, and come back and fetch it later. So Mr Sharnall was constrained to leave this part of his equipment, and was severed from a well-worn overcoat, which had been the companion of years. He smiled sadly to himself as he turned at the open door, and saw his coat still hang dripping on the peg. If it were put up to auction, would it ever fetch enough to pay for what he had drunk?

It was true that it had stopped raining, and though the sky was still overcast, there was a lightness diffused behind the clouds that spoke of a rising moon. What should he do? Whither should he turn? He could not go back to the Hand of God; there were some there who did not want him—whom he did not want. Westray would not be home, or, if he were, Westray would know that he had been drinking; he could not bear that they should see that he had been drinking again.

And then there came into his mind another thought; he would go to the church, the water-engine should blow for him, and he would play himself sober. Stay, *should* he go to the church—the great church of St Sepulchre alone? Would he be alone there? If he thought that he would be alone, he would feel more secure; but might there not be someone else there, or something else? He gave a little shiver, but the drink was in his veins; he laughed pot-valiantly, and turned up an alley towards the centre tower, that loomed dark in the wet, misty whiteness of the cloud-screened moon.

Chapter 14

Westray returned to Cullerne by the evening train. It was near ten o'clock, and he was finishing his supper, when someone tapped at the door, and Miss Euphemia Joliffe came in.

'I beg your pardon for interrupting you, sir,' she said; 'I am a little anxious about Mr Sharnall. He was not in at teatime, and has not come back since. I thought you might know perhaps where he was. It is years since he has been out so late in the evening.'

'I haven't the least idea where he is,' Westray said rather testily, for he was tired with a long day's work. 'I suppose he has gone out somewhere to supper.'

'No one ever asks Mr Sharnall out. I do not think he can be gone out to supper.'

'Oh well, I dare say he will turn up in due course; let me hear before you go to bed if he has come back;' and he poured himself out another cup of tea, for he was one of those thin-blooded and old-womanly men who elevate the drinking of tea instead of other liquids into a special merit. He could not understand, he said, why everybody did not drink tea. It was so much more refreshing—one could work so much better after drinking tea.

He turned to some calculations for the section of a tie-rod, with which Sir George Farquhar had at last consented to strengthen the south side of the tower, and did not notice how time passed till there came another irritating tap, and his landlady reappeared.

'It is nearly twelve o'clock,' she said, 'and we have seen nothing of Mr Sharnall. I am so alarmed! I am sure I am very sorry to trouble you, Mr Westray, but my niece and I are so alarmed.'

'I don't quite see what I am to do,' Westray said, looking up. 'Could he have gone out with Lord Blandamer? Do you think Lord Blandamer could have asked him to Fording?'

'Lord Blandamer was here this afternoon,' Miss Joliffe answered, 'but he never saw Mr Sharnall, because Mr Sharnall was not at home.'

'Oh, Lord Blandamer was here, was he?' asked Westray. 'Did he leave no message for me?'

'He asked if you were in, but he left no message for you. He drank a cup of tea with us. I think he came in merely as a friendly visitor,' Miss Joliffe said with some dignity. 'I think he came in to drink a cup of tea with me. I was unfortunately at the Dorcas meeting when he first arrived, but on my return drank tea with me.

'It is curious; he seems generally to come on Saturday afternoons,' said Westray. 'Are you *always* at the Dorcas meeting on Saturday afternoons?'

'Yes,' Miss Joliffe said, 'I am always at the meeting on Saturday afternoons.'

There was a minute's pause—Westray and Miss Joliffe were both thinking.

'Well, well,' Westray said, 'I shall be working for some time yet, and will let Mr Sharnall in if he comes; but I suspect that he has been invited to spend the night at Fording. Anyhow, you can go to bed with a clear conscience, Miss Joliffe; you have waited up far beyond your usual time.'

So Miss Euphemia went to bed, and left Westray alone; and a few minutes later the four quarter-chimes rang, and the tenor struck twelve, and then the bells fell to playing a tune, as they did every three hours day and night. Those who dwell near St Sepulchre's take no note of the bells. The ear grows so accustomed to them, that quarter by quarter and hour by hour strike unperceived. If strangers come to stop under the shadow of the church the clangour disturbs their sleep for the first night, and after that they, too, hear nothing. So Westray would sit working late night by night, and could not say whether the bells had rung or not. It was only when attention was too wide awake that he heard them, but he heard them this night, and listened while they played the sober melody of 'Mount Ephraim'.*

He got up, flung his window open, and looked out. The storm had passed; the moon, which was within a few hours of the full, rode serenely in the blue heaven with a long bank of dappled white cloud below, whose edge shone with an amber iridescence. Westray looked over the clustered roofs and chimneys of the town; the upward glow from the market-place showed that the lamps were still burning, though he could not see them. Then, as the glow lessened gradually and finally became extinct, he knew that the lights were being put out because midnight was past. The moonlight glittered on the roofs, which were still wet, and above all towered in gigantic sable mass the centre tower of St Sepulchre's.

The architect felt a curious physical tension. He was excited, he could not tell why; he knew that sleep would be impossible if he were

* See Appendix at end of story for tune

141

to go to bed. It *was* an odd thing that Sharnall had not come home; Sharnall *must* have gone to Fording. He had spoken vaguely of an invitation to Fording that he had received; but if he had gone there he must have taken some things with him for the night, and he had not taken anything, or Miss Euphemia would have said so. Stay, he would go down to Sharnall's room and see if he could find any trace of his taking luggage; perhaps he had left some message to explain his absence. He lit a candle and went down, down the great well staircase where the stone steps echoed under his feet. A patch of bright moonshine fell on the stairs from the skylight at the top, and a noise of someone moving in the attics told him that Miss Joliffe was not yet asleep. There was nothing in the organist's room to give any explanation of his absence. The light of the candle was reflected on the side of the piano, and Westray shuddered involuntarily as he remembered the conversation which he had a few weeks before with his friend, and Mr Sharnall's strange hallucinations as to the man that walked behind him with a hammer. He looked into the bedroom with a momentary apprehension that his friend might have been seized with illness, and be lying all this time unconscious; but there was no one there—the bed was undisturbed. So he went back to his room upstairs, but the night had turned so chill that he could no longer bear the open window. He stood with his hand upon the sash looking out for a moment before he pulled it down, and noticed how the centre tower dominated and prevailed over all the town. It was impossible, surely, that this rock-like mass could be insecure; how puny and insufficient to uphold such a tottering giant seemed the tie-rods whose section he was working out. And then he thought of the crack above the south transept arch that he had seen from the organ-loft, and remembered how 'Sharnall in D flat' had been interrupted by the discovery. Why, Mr Sharnall might be in the church; perhaps he had gone down to practise and been shut in. Perhaps his key had broken, and he could not get out; he wondered that he had not thought of the church before.

In a minute he had made up his mind to go to the minster. As resident architect he possessed a master key which opened all the doors; he would walk round, and see if he could find anything of the missing organist before going to bed. He strode quickly through the deserted streets. The lamps were all put out, for Cullerne economized gas at times of full-moon. There was nothing moving, his footsteps rang on the pavement, and echoed from wall to wall. He took the short-cut by the wharves, and in a few minutes came to the old Bonding-house.

The shadows hung like black velvet in the spaces between the brick buttresses that shored up the wall towards the quay. He smiled to himself as he thought of the organist's nervousness, of those strange fancies as to someone lurking in the black hiding-holes, and as to buildings being in some way connected with man's fate. Yet he knew that his smile was assumed, for he felt all the while the oppression of the loneliness, of the sadness of a half-ruined building, of the gurgling mutter of the river, and instinctively quickened his pace. He was glad when he had passed the spot, and again that night, as he looked back, he saw the strange effect of light and darkness which produced the impression of someone standing in the shadow of the last buttress space. The illusion was so perfect that he thought he could make out the figure of a man, in a long loose cape that flapped in the wind.

He had passed the wrought-iron gates now—he was in the churchyard, and it was then that he first became aware of a soft, low, droning sound which seemed to fill the air all about him. He stopped for a moment to listen; what was it? Where was the noise? It grew more distinct as he passed along the flagged stone path which led to the north door. Yes, it certainly came from inside the church. What could it be? What could anyone be doing in the church at this hour of night?

He was in the north porch now, and then he knew what it was. It was a low note of the organ—a pedal-note; he was almost sure it was that very pedal-point which the organist had explained to him with such pride. The sound reassured him nothing had happened to Mr Sharnall—he was practising in the church; it was only some mad freak of his to be playing so late; he was practising that service 'Sharnall in D flat'.

He took his key to unlock the wicket, and was surprised to find it already open, because he knew that it was the organist's habit to lock himself in. He passed into the great church. It was strange, there was no sound of music; there was no one playing; there was only the intolerably monotonous booming of a single pedal-note, with an occasional muffled thud when the water-engine turned spasmodically to replenish the emptying bellows.

'Sharnall!' he shouted—'Sharnall, what are you doing? Don't you know how late it is?'

He paused and thought at first that someone was answering him—he thought that he heard people muttering in the choir; but it was only the echo of his own voice, his own voice tossed from pillar to pillar and arch to arch, till it faded into a wail of 'Sharnall, Sharnall!' in the lantern.

It was the first time that he had been in the church at night, and he stood for a moment overcome with the mystery of the place, while he gazed at the columns of the nave standing white in the moonlight like a row of vast shrouded figures. He called again to Mr Sharnall, and again received no answer, and then he made his way up the nave to the little doorway that leads to the organ-loft stairs.

This door also was open, and he felt sure now that Mr Sharnall was not in the organ-loft at all, for had he been he would certainly have locked himself in. The pedal-note must be merely ciphering, or something, perhaps a book, might have fallen upon it, and was holding it down. He need not go up to the loft now; he would not go up. The throbbing of the low note had on him the same unpleasant effect as on a previous occasion. He tried to reassure himself, yet felt all the while a growing premonition that something might be wrong, something might be terribly wrong. The lateness of the hour, the isolation from all things living, the spectral moonlight which made the darkness darker—this combination of utter silence, with the distressing vibration of the pedal-note, filled him with something akin to panic. It seemed to him as if the place was full of phantoms, as if the monks of St Sepulchre's were risen from under their grave-stones, as if there were other dire faces appearing such as wait continually on deeds of evil. He checked his alarm before it mastered him. Come what might, he would go up to the organ-loft, and he plunged into the staircase that leads up out of the nave.

It is a circular stair, twisted round a central pillar, of which mention has already been made, and though short, is very dark even in bright daylight. But at night the blackness is inky and impenetrable, and Westray fumbled for an appreciable time before he had climbed sufficiently far up to perceive the glimmer of moonlight at the top. He stepped out at last into the loft, and saw that the organ seat was empty. The great window at the end of the south transept shone full in front of him; it seemed as if it must be day, and not night—the light from the window was so strong in comparison with the darkness which he had left. There was a subdued shimmer in the tracery where the stained glass gleamed diaphanous—amethyst and topaz, chrysoprase and jasper, a dozen jewels as in the foundations of the city of God. And in the midst, in the head of the centre light, shone out brighter than all, with an inherent radiance of its own, the cognizance of the Blandamers, the sea-green and silver of the nebuly coat.

Westray gave a step forward into the loft, and then his foot struck against something, and he nearly fell. It was something soft and yielding that he had struck, something of which the mere touch filled him with horrible surmise. He bent down to see what it was, and a white object met his eyes. It was the white face of a man turned up towards the vaulting; he had stumbled over the body of Mr Sharnall, who lay on the floor with the back of his head on the pedal-note. Westray had bent low down, and he looked full in the eyes of the organist, but they were fixed and glazing.

The moonlight that shone on the dead face seemed to fall on it through that brighter spot in the head of the middle light; it was as if the nebuly coat had blighted the very life out of the man who lay so still upon the floor.

Chapter 15

No evidence of any importance was given at the inquest except Westray's and the doctor's and no other evidence was, in fact, required. Dr Ennefer had made an autopsy, and found that the immediate cause of death was a blow on the back of the head. But the organs showed traces of alcoholic habit, and the heart was distinctly diseased. It was probable that Mr Sharnall had been seized with a fainting fit as he left the organ stool, and had fallen backwards with his head on the pedal-board. He must have fallen with much violence, and the pedal-note had made a bad wound, such as would be produced by a blunt instrument.

The inquest was nearly finished when, without any warning, Westray found himself, as by intuition, asking:

'The wound was such a one, you mean, as might have been produced by the blow of a hammer?'

The doctor seemed surprised, the jury and the little audience stared, but most surprised of all was Westray at his own question.

'You have no *locus standi*, sir,' the coroner said severely; 'such an interrogation is irregular. You are to esteem it an act of grace if I allow the medical man to reply.'

'Yes,' said Dr Ennefer, with a reserve in his voice that implied that he was not there to answer every irrelevant question that it might please foolish people to put him—'yes, such a wound as might have been caused by a hammer, or by any other blunt instrument used with violence.'

'Even by a heavy stick?' Westray suggested.

'The doctor maintained a dignified silence, and the coroner struck in:

'I must say I think you are wasting our time, Mr Westray. I am the last person to stifle legitimate inquiry, but no inquiry is really needed here; it is quite certain that this poor man came to his end by falling heavily, and dashing his head against this wooden note in the pedals.'

'*Is* it quite certain?' Westray asked. 'Is Dr Ennefer quite sure that the wound *could* have been caused by a mere fall? I only want to know that Dr Ennefer is quite sure.'

The coroner looked at the doctor with a deprecating glance, which implied apologies that so much unnecessary trouble should be given, and a hope that he would be graciously pleased to put an end to it by an authoritative statement.

'Oh, I am quite sure,' the doctor responded. 'Yes'—and he hesitated for the fraction of a second—'oh yes, there is no doubt such a wound could be caused by a fall.'

'I merely wish to point out,' said Westray, 'that the pedal-note on which he fell is to a certain extent a yielding substance; it would yield, you must remember, at the first impact.'

'That is quite true,' the doctor said; 'I had taken that into account, and admit that one would scarcely expect so serious an injury to have been caused. But, of course, it *was* so caused, because there is no other explanation; you don't suggest, I presume, that there was any foul play? It is certainly a case of accident or foul play.'

'Oh, no, I don't suggest anything.'

The coroner raised his eyebrows; he was tired, and could not understand such waste of time. But the doctor, curiously enough, seemed to have grown more tolerant of interruption.

'I have examined the injury very carefully,' he said, 'and have come to the deliberate conclusion that it must have been caused by the wooden key. We must also recollect that the effect of any blow would be intensified by a weak state of health. I don't wish to rake up anything against the poor fellow's memory, or to say any word that may cause you pain, Mr Westray, as his friend; but an examination of the body revealed traces of chronic alcoholism. We must recollect that.'

'The man was, in fact, a confirmed drunkard,' the coroner said. He lived at Carisbury, and, being a stranger both to Cullerne and its inhabitants, had no scruple in speaking plainly; and, besides this, he was nettled at the architect's interference. 'You mean the man was a confirmed drunkard,' he repeated.

'He was nothing of the kind,' Westray said hotly. 'I do not say that he never took more than was good for him, but he was in no sense an habitual drunkard.'

'I did not ask *your* opinion,' retorted the coroner; 'we do not want any lay conjectures. What do you say, Mr Ennefer?'

The surgeon was vexed in his turn at not receiving the conventional title of doctor, the more so because he knew that he had no legal right to it. To be called 'Mr' demeaned him, he considered, in the eyes of present or prospective patients, and he passed at once into an attitude of opposition.

'Oh no, you mistake me, Mr Coroner. I did not mean that our poor friend was an habitual drunkard. I never remember to have actually seen him the worse for liquor.'

'Well, what do you mean? You say the body shows traces of alcoholism, but that he was not a drunkard.'

'Have we any evidence as to Mr Sharnall's state on the evening of his death?' a juror asked, with a pleasant consciousness that he was taking a dispassionate view, and making a point of importance.

'Yes, we have considerable evidence,' said the coroner. 'Call Charles White!'

There stepped forward a little man with a red face and blinking eyes. His name was Charles White; he was landlord of the Merrymouth Inn. The deceased visited his inn on the evening in question. He did not know deceased by sight, but found out afterwards who he was. It was a bad night, deceased was very wet, and took something to drink; he drank a fairish amount, but not *that* much, not more than a gentleman should drink. Deceased was not drunk when he went away.

'He was drunk enough to leave his top-coat behind him, was he not?' the coroner asked. 'Did you not find this coat after he was gone?' and he pointed to a poor masterless garment, that looked greener and more outworn than ever as it hung over the back of a chair.

'Yes, deceased had certainly left his coat behind him, but he was not drunk.'

'There are different standards of drunkenness, gentlemen,' said the coroner, imitating as well as he might the facetious cogency of a real judge, 'and I imagine that the standard of the Merrymouth may be more advanced than in some other places. I don't think'—and he looked sarcastically at Westray—'I do *not* think we need carry this inquiry farther. We have a man who drinks, not an habitual drunkard, Mr Ennefer says, but one who drinks enough to bring himself into a thoroughly diseased state. This man sits fuddling in a low public-house all the evening, and is so far overtaken by liquor when he goes away, that he leaves his overcoat behind him. He actually leaves his coat behind him, though we have it that it was a pouring wet night. He goes to the organ-loft in a tipsy state, slips as he is getting on to his stool, falls heavily with the back of his head on a piece of wood, and is found dead some hours later by an unimpeachable and careful witness'—and he gave a little sniff—'with his head still on this piece of wood. Take note of that—when he was found his head was still on this very pedal which had caused the fatal injury. Gentlemen, I do not think we need any further evidence; I think your course is pretty clear.'

All was, indeed, very clear. The jury with a unanimous verdict of accidental death put the colophon to the sad history of Mr Sharnall, and ruled that the same failing which had blighted his life, had brought him at last to a drunkard's end.

Westray walked back to the Hand of God with the forlorn old top-coat over his arm. The coroner had formally handed it over to him. He was evidently a close friend of the deceased, he would perhaps take charge of his wearing apparel. The architect's thoughts were too preoccupied to allow him to resent the sneer which accompanied these remarks; he went off full of sorrow and gloomy forebodings.

Death in so strange a shape formed a topic of tavern discussion in Cullerne, second only to a murder itself. Not since Mr Leveritt, the timber-merchant, shot a barmaid at the Blandamer Arms, a generation since, had any such dramatic action taken place on Cullerne boards. The loafers swore over it in all its bearings as they spat upon the pavement at the corner of the market square. Mr Smiles, the shopwalker in Rose and Storey's general drapery mart, discussed it genteelly with the ladies who sat before the counter on the high wicker-seated chairs.

Dr Ennefer was betrayed into ill-advised conversation while being shaved, and got his chin cut. Mr Joliffe gave away a packet of moral reflections gratis with every pound of sausage, and turned up the whites of his eyes over the sin of intemperance, which had called away his poor friend in so terrible a state of unpreparedness. Quite a crowd followed the coffin to its last resting-place, and the church was unusually full on the Sunday morning which followed the catastrophe. People expected a 'pulpit reference' from Canon Parkyn, and there were the additional, though subordinate, attractions of the playing of the Dead March, and the possibility of an amateur organist breaking down in the anthem.

Church-going, which sprung from such unworthy motives, was very properly disappointed. Canon Parkyn would not, he said, pander to sensationalism by any allusion in his discourse, nor could the Dead March, he conceived, be played with propriety under such very unpleasant circumstances. The new organist got through the service with provokingly colourless mediocrity, and the congregation came out of St Sepulchre's in a disappointed mood, as people who had been defrauded of their rights.

Then the nine days' wonder ceased, and Mr Sharnall passed into the great oblivion of middle-class dead. His successor was not immediately appointed. Canon Parkyn arranged that the second master at the National School, who had a pretty notion of music, and was a pupil of Mr Sharnall, should be spared to fill the gap. As Queen Elizabeth, of pious memory, recruited the privy purse by keeping in her own hand vacant bishoprics, so the rector farmed the post of organist at Cullerne Minster. He thus managed to effect so important a reduction in the sordid emoluments of that office, that he was five pounds in pocket before a year was ended.

But if the public had forgotten Mr Sharnall, Westray had not. The architect was a man of gregarious instinct. As there is a tradition and bonding of common interest about the Universities, and in a less degree about army, navy, public schools, and professions, which draws together and marks with its impress those who are attached to them, so there is a certain cabala and membership among lodgers which none can understand except those who are free of that guild.

The lodging-house life, call it squalid, mean, dreary if you will, is not without its alleviations and counterpoises. It is a life of youth for the most part, for lodgers of Mr Sharnall's age are comparatively rare; it is a life of simple needs and simple tastes, for lodgings are not artistic, nor favourable to the development of any undue refinement; it is not a rich life, for men as a rule set up their own houses as soon as they are able to do so; it is a life of work and buoyant anticipation, where men are equipping for the struggle, and laying the foundations of fortune, or digging the pit of indigence. Such conditions beget and foster good fellowship, and those who have spent time in lodgings can look back to whole-hearted and disinterested friendships, when all were equal before high heaven, hail-fellows well met, who knew no artificial distinctions of rank when all were travelling the first stage of life's journey in happy chorus together, and had not reached that point where the high road bifurcates, and the diverging branches of success and failure lead old comrades so very far apart. Ah, what a camaraderie and fellowship, knit close by the urgency of making both ends meet, strengthened by the necessity of withstanding rapacious, or negligent, or tyrannous landladies, sweetened by kindnesses and courtesies which cost the giver little, but mean much to the receiver! Did sickness of a transitory sort (for grievous illness is little known in lodgings) fall on the ground-floor tenant, then did not the first-floor come down to comfort him in the evenings? First-floor might be tired after a long day's work, and note when his frugal meal was done that 'twas a fine evening or that a good company was billed for the local theatre; yet he would grudge not his leisure, but go down to sit with ground-floor, and tell him the news of the day, perhaps even would take him a few oranges or a tin of sardines. And ground-floor, who had chafed all the day at being shut in, and had read himself stupid for want of anything else to do, how glad he was to see first-floor, and how the chat did him more good than all the doctor's stuff!

And later on, when some ladies came to lunch with first-floor on the day of the flower-show, did not ground-floor go out and place his sitting-room completely at his fellow-lodger's disposal, so that the company might find greater convenience and change of air after meat? They were fearful joys, these feminine visits, when ladies who were kind enough to ask a young man to spend a Sunday with them, still further added to their kindness, by accepting with all possible effusion the invitation which he one day ventured to give. It was a fearful joy, and cost the host more anxious preparation than a state funerals brings to Earl-Marshal. As brave a face as might be must be put on everything; so many details were to be thought out, so many little insufficiencies were to be masked. But did not the result recompense all? Was not the young man conscious that, though his rooms might be small, there was about them a delicate touch which made up for much, that everything breathed of refinement, from the photographs and silver toddy-spoon upon the mantelpiece to Rossetti's poems and *Marius the Epicurean* which covered negligently a stain on the green tablecloth? And these kindly ladies came in riant mood, well knowing all his little anxieties and preparations, yet showing they knew none of them; resolved to praise his rooms, his puny treasures, even his cookery and perilous wine, and skilful to turn little contretemps into interesting novelties. Householders, yours is a noble lot, ye are the men, and wisdom shall die with you. Yet pity not too profoundly him that inhabiteth lodgings, lest he turn and rend you, pitying you in turn that have bound on your shoulders heavy burdens of which he knows nothing; saying to you that seed time is more profitable than harvest, and the wandering years than the practice of the master. Refrain from too much pity, and believe that loneliness is not always lonely.

Westray was of gregarious temperament, and missed his fellow-lodger. The cranky little man, with all his soured outlook, must still have had some power of evoking sympathy, some attractive element in his composition. He concealed it under sharp words and moody bitterness, but it must still have been there, for Westray felt his loss more than he had thought possible. The organist and he had met twice and thrice a day for a year past. They had discussed the minster that both loved so well, within whose walls both were occupied; they had discussed the nebuly coat, and the Blandamers and Miss Euphemia. There was only one subject which they did not discuss—namely, Miss Anastasia Joliffe, though she was very often in the thoughts of both.

It was all over now, yet every day Westray found himself making a mental note to tell this to Mr Sharnall, to ask Mr Sharnall's advice on that, and then remembering that there is no knowledge in the grave. The gaunt Hand of God was ten times gaunter now that there was no lodger on the ground-floor. Footfalls sounded more hollow at night on the stone steps of the staircase, and Miss Joliffe and Anastasia went early to bed.

'Let us go upstairs, my dear,' Miss Euphemia would say when the chimes sounded a quarter to ten. 'These long evenings are so lonely, are they not? and be sure you see that the windows are properly hasped.' And then they hurried through the hall, and went up the staircase together side by side, as if they were afraid to be separated by a single step. Even Westray knew something of the same feeling when he returned late at night to the cavernous great house. He tried to put his hand as quickly as he might upon the matchbox, which lay ready for him on the marble-topped sideboard in the dark hall; and sometimes when he had lit the candle would instinctively glance at the door of Mr Sharnall's room, half expecting to see it open, and the old face look out that had so often greeted him on such occasions. Miss Joliffe had made no attempt to find a new lodger. No 'Apartments to Let' was put in the window, and such chattels as Mr Sharnall possessed remained exactly as he left them. Only one thing was moved—the collection of Martin Joliffe's papers, and these Westray had taken upstairs to his own room.

When they opened the dead man's bureau with the keys found in his pocket to see whether he had left any will or instructions, there was discovered in one of the drawers a note addressed to Westray. It was dated a fortnight before his death, and was very short:

> *If I go away and am not heard of, or if anything happens to me, get hold of Martin Joliffe's papers at once. Take them up to your own room, lock them up, and don't let them out of your hands. Tell Miss Joliffe it is my wish, and she will hand them over to you. Be very careful there isn't a fire, or lest they should be destroyed in any other way. Read them carefully, and draw your own conclusions; you will find some notes of mine in the little red pocket-book.*

The architect had read these words many times. They were no doubt the outcome of the delusions of which Mr Sharnall had more than once spoken—of that dread of some enemy pursuing him, which had darkened the organist's latter days. Yet to read these things set out in black and white, after what had happened, might well give rise to curious thoughts. The coincidence was so strange, so terribly strange. A man following with a hammer—that had been the organist's hallucination; the vision of an assailant creeping up behind, and doing him to death with an awful, stealthy blow. And the reality—an end sudden and unexpected, a blow on the back of the head, which had been caused by a heavy fall. Was it mere coincidence, was it some inexplicable presentiment, or was it more than either? Had there, in fact, existed a reason why the organist should think that someone had a grudge against him, that he was likely to be attacked? Had some dreadful scene been really enacted in the loneliness of the great church that night? Had the organist been taken unawares, or heard some movement in the silence, and, turning round, found himself alone with his murderer? And if a murderer, whose was the face into which the victim looked? And as Westray thought he shuddered; it seemed it might have been no human face at all, but some fearful presence, some visible presentment of the evil that walketh in darkness.

Then the architect would brush such follies away like cobwebs, and, turning back, consider who could have found his interest in such a deed. Against whom did the dead man urge him to be on guard lest Martin's papers should be spirited away? Was there some other claimant of that ill-omened peerage of whom he knew nothing, or was it— And Westray resolutely quenched the thought that had risen a hundred times before his mind, and cast it aside as a malign and baseless suspicion.

If there was any clue it must lie in those same papers, and he followed the instruction given him, and took them to his own room. He did not show Miss Joliffe the note; to do so could only have shaken her further, and she had felt the shock too severely already. He only told her of Mr Sharnall's wishes for the temporary disposal of her brother's papers. She begged him not to take them.

'Dear Mr Westray,' she said, 'do not touch them, do not let us have anything to do with them. I wanted poor dear Mr Sharnall not to go meddling with them, and now see what has happened. Perhaps it is a judgment'—and she uttered the word under her breath, having a medieval faith in the vengeful irritability of Providence, and seeing manifestations of it in any untoward event, from the overturning of an inkstand to the death of a lodger. 'Perhaps it is a judgment, and he might have been alive now if he had refrained. What good would it do us if all dear Martin hoped should turn out true? He always said, poor fellow, that he would be "my lord" some day; but now he is gone there is no one except Anastasia, and she would never wish to be "my lady", I am sure, poor girl. You would not, darling, wish to be "my lady", even if you could, would you?

Anastasia looked up from her book with a deprecating smile, which lost itself in an air of vexation, when she found that the architect's eyes were fixed steadfastly upon her, and that a responsive smile spread over his face. She flushed very slightly, and turned back abruptly to her book, feeling quite unjustifiably annoyed at the interest in her doings which the young man's gaze was meant to imply. What right had he to express concern, even with a look, in matters which affected *her*? She almost wished she *was* indeed a peeress, and could slay him with her noble birth, as did one Lady Clara of old times. It was only lately that she had become conscious of this interested, would-be interesting, look, which Westray assumed in her presence. Was it possible that *he* was falling in love with her? And at the thought there rose before her fancy the features of someone else, haughty, hard, perhaps malign, but oh, so powerful, and quite eclipsed and blotted out the lifeless amiability of this young man who hung upon her lips.

Could Mr Westray be thinking of falling in love with her? It was impossible, and yet this following her with his eyes, and the mellific manner which he adopted when speaking to her, insisted on its possibility. She ran over hastily in her mind, as she had done several times of late, the course of their relations. Was she to blame? Could anything that she had ever done be wrested into predilection or even into appreciation? Could natural kindness or courtesy have been so utterly misunderstood? She was victoriously acquitted by this commission of mental inquiry, and left the court without a stain upon her character. She certainly had never given him the very least encouragement. At the risk of rudeness she *must* check these attentions in their beginning. Short of actual discourtesy, she must show him that this warm interest in her doings, these sympathetic glances, were exceedingly distasteful. She never would look near him again, she would keep her eyes rigorously cast down whenever he was present, and as she made this prudent resolution she quite unintentionally looked up, and found his patient gaze again fixed upon her.

'Oh, you are too severe, Miss Joliffe,' the architect said; 'we should all be delighted to see a title come to Miss Anastasia, and he added softly, 'I am sure no one would become it better.'

He longed to drop the formal prefix of Miss, and to speak of her simply as Anastasia. A few months before he would have done so naturally and without reflection, but there was something in the girl's manner which led him more recently to forgo this pleasure.

Then the potential peeress got up and left the room.

'I am just going to look after the bread,' she said; 'I think it ought to be baked by this time.'

Miss Joliffe's scruples were at last overborne, and Westray retained the papers, partly because it was represented to her that if he did not examine them it would be a flagrant neglect of the wishes of a dead man—wishes that are held sacred above all others in the circle to which Miss Joliffe belonged—and partly because possession is nine points of the law, and the architect already had them safe under lock and key in his own room. But he was not able to devote any immediate attention to them, for a crisis in his life was approaching, which tended for the present to engross his thoughts.

He had entertained for some time an attachment to Anastasia Joliffe. When he originally became aware of this feeling he battled vigorously against it, and his efforts were at first attended with some success. He was profoundly conscious that any connection with the Joliffes would be derogatory to his dignity; he feared that the discrepancy between their relative positions was sufficiently marked to attract attention, if not to provoke hostile criticism. People would certainly say that an architect was marrying strangely below him, in choosing a landlady's niece. If he were to do such a thing, he would no doubt be throwing himself away socially. His father, who was dead, had been a Wesleyan pastor; and his mother, who survived, entertained so great a respect for the high position of that ministry that she had impressed upon Westray from boyhood the privilege and responsibilities of his birth. But apart from this objection, there was the further drawback that an early marriage might unduly burden him with domestic cares, and so arrest his professional progress. Such considerations had due weight with an equally balanced mind, and Westray was soon able to congratulate himself on having effectually extinguished any dangerous inclinations by sheer strength and reason.

This happy and philosophic state of things was not of long duration. His admiration smouldered only, and was not quenched, but it was a totally extraneous influence, rather than the constant contemplation of Anastasia's beauty and excellences, which fanned the flame into renewed activity. This extraneous factor was the entrance of Lord Blandamer into the little circle of Bellevue Lodge. Westray had lately become doubtful as to the real object of Lord Blandamer's visits, and nursed a latent idea that he was using the church, and the restoration, and Westray himself, to gain a *pied-à-terre* at Bellevue Lodge for a prosecution of other plans. The long conversations in which the architect and the munificent donor still indulged, the examination of plans, the discussion of details, had lost something of their old savour. Westray had done his best to convince himself that his own suspicions were groundless; he had continually pointed out to himself, and insisted to himself, that the mere fact of Lord Blandamer contributing such sums to the restoration as he either had contributed, or had promised to contribute, showed that the church was indeed his primary concern. It was impossible to conceive that any man, however wealthy, should spend many thousand pounds to obtain an entrée to Bellevue Lodge; moreover, it was impossible to conceive that Lord Blandamer should ever marry Anastasia—the disparity in such a match would, Westray admitted, be still greater than in his own. Yet he was convinced that Anastasia was often in Lord Blandamer's thoughts. It was true that the Master of Fording gave no definite outward sign of any predilection when Westray was present. He never singled Anastasia out either for regard or conversation on such occasions as chance brought her into his company. At times he even made a show of turning away from her, of studiously neglecting her presence.

But Westray felt that the fact was there.

There is some subtle effluence of love which hovers about one who entertains a strong affection for another. Looks may be carefully guarded, speech may be framed to mislead, yet that pervading ambient of affection is strong to betray where perception is sharpened by jealousy.

Now and then the architect would persuade himself that he was mistaken; he would reproach himself with his own suspicious disposition, with his own lack of generosity. But then some little episode would occur, some wholly undemonstrable trifle, which swept his cooler judgment to the winds, and gave him a quite incommensurate heartburn. He would recall, for instance, the fact that for their interviews Lord Blandamer had commonly selected a Saturday afternoon. Lord Blandamer had explained this by saying that he was busy through the week; but then a lord was not like a schoolboy with a Saturday half-holiday. What business could he have to occupy him all the week, and leave him free on Saturdays? It was strange enough, and stranger from the fact that Miss Euphemia Joliffe was invariably occupied on that particular afternoon at the Dorcas meeting; stranger from the fact that there had been some unaccountable misunderstandings between Lord Blandamer and Westray as to the exact hour fixed for their interviews, and that more than once when the architect had returned at five, he had found that Lord Blandamer had taken four as the time of their meeting, and had been already waiting an hour at Bellevue Lodge.

Poor Mr Sharnall also must have noticed that something was going on, for he had hinted as much to Westray a fortnight or so before he died. Westray was uncertain as to Lord Blandamer's feelings; he gave the architect the idea of a man who had some definite object to pursue in making himself interesting to Anastasia, while his own affections were not compromised. That object could certainly not be marriage, and if it was not marriage, what was it? In ordinary cases an answer might have been easy, yet Westray hesitated to give it. It was hard to think that this grave man, of great wealth and great position, who had roamed the world, and known men and manners, should stoop to common lures. Yet Westray came to think it, and his own feelings towards Anastasia were elevated by the resolve to be her knightly champion against all base attempts.

Can man's deepest love be deepened? Then it must surely be by the knowledge that he is protector as well as lover, by the knowledge that he is rescuing innocence, and rescuing it for himself. Thoughts such as these bring exaltation to the humblest-minded, and they quickened the slow-flowing and thin fluid that filled the architect's veins.

He came back one evening from the church weary with a long day's work, and was sitting by the fire immersed in a medley of sleepy and half-conscious consideration, now of the crack in the centre tower, now of the tragedy of the organ-loft, now of Anastasia, when the elder Miss Joliffe entered.

'Dear me, sir,' she said, 'I did not know you were in! I only came to see your fire was burning. Are you ready for your tea? Would you like anything special tonight? You do look so very tired. I am sure you are working too hard; all the running about on ladders and scaffolds must be very trying. I think indeed, sir, if I may make so bold, that you should take a holiday; you have not had a holiday since you came to live with us.'

'It is not impossible, Miss Joliffe, that I may take your advice before very long. It is not impossible that I may before long go for a holiday.'

He spoke with that preternatural gravity which people are accustomed to throw into their reply, if asked a trivial question when their own thoughts are secretly occupied with some matter that they consider of deep importance. How could this commonplace woman guess that he was thinking of death and love? He must be gentle with her and forgive her interruption. Yes, fate might, indeed, drive him to take a holiday. He had nearly made up his mind to propose to Anastasia. It was scarcely to be doubted that she would at once accept him, but there must be no half-measures, he would brook no shilly-shallying, he would not be played fast-and-loose with. She must either accept him fully and freely, and at once, or he would withdraw his offer, and in that case, or still more in the entirely improbable case of refusal, he would leave Bellevue Lodge forthwith.

'Yes, indeed, I may ere long have to go away for a holiday.'

The conscious forbearance of replying at all gave a quiet dignity to his tone, and an involuntary sigh that accompanied his words was not lost upon Miss Joliffe. To her this speech seemed oracular and ominous; there was a sepulchral mystery in so vague an expression. He might *have* to take a holiday. What could this mean? Was this poor young man completely broken by the loss of his friend Mr Sharnall, or was he conscious of the seeds of some fell disease that others knew nothing of? He might *have* to take a holiday. Ah, it was not a mere holiday of which he spoke—he meant something more serious than that; his grave, sad manner could only mean some long absence. Perhaps he was going to leave Cullerne.

To lose him would be a very serious matter to Miss Joliffe from the material point of view; he was her sheet-anchor, the last anchor that kept Bellevue Lodge from drifting into bankruptcy. Mr Sharnall was dead, and with him had died the tiny pittance which he contributed to the upkeep of the place, and lodgers were few and far between in Cullerne. Miss Joliffe might well have remembered these things, but she did not. The only thought that crossed her mind was, that if Mr Westray went away she would lose yet another friend. She did not approach the matter from the material point of view, she looked on him only as a friend; she viewed him as no money-making machine, but only as that most precious of all treasures—a last friend.

'I may have to leave you for a while,' he said again, with the same portentous solemnity.

'I hope not, sir,' she interrupted, as though by her very eagerness she might avert threatened evil— 'I hope not; we should miss you terribly, Mr Westray, with dear Mr Sharnall gone too. I do not know what we should do having no man in the house. It is so very lonely if you are away even for a night. I am an old woman now, and it does not matter much for me, but Anastasia is so nervous at night since the dreadful accident.'

Westray's face brightened a little at the mention of Anastasia's name. Yes, his must certainly be a very deep affection, that the naming of her very name should bring him such pleasure. It was on his protection, then, that she leant; she looked on *him* as her defender. The muscles of his not gigantic arms seemed to swell and leap to bursting in his coat-sleeves. Those arms should screen his loved one from all evil. Visions of Perseus, and Sir Galahad, and Cophetua, swept before his eyes; he had almost cried to Miss Euphemia, 'You need have no fear, I love your niece. I shall bow down and raise her to my throne. They that would touch her shall only do so over my dead body,' when hesitating common sense plucked him by the sleeve; he must consult his mother before taking this grave step.

It was well that reason thus restrained him, for such a declaration might have brought Miss Joliffe to a swoon. As it was, she noticed the cloud lifting on his face, and was pleased to think that her conversation cheered him. A little company was no doubt good for him, and she sought in her mind for some further topic of interest. Yes, of course, she had it.

'Lord Blandamer was here this afternoon. He came just like anyone else might have come, in such a very kind and condescending way to ask after me. He feared that dear Mr Sharnall's death might have been too severe a shock for us both, and, indeed, it has been a terrible blow. He was so considerate, and sat for nearly an hour—for forty-seven minutes I should say by the clock, and took tea with us in the kitchen as if he were one of the family. I never could have expected such condescension, and when he went away he left a most polite message for you, sir, to say that he was sorry that you were not in, but he hoped to call again before long.'

The cloud had returned to Westray's face. If he had been the hero of a novel his brow would have been black as night; as it was he only looked rather sulky.

'I shall have to go to London tonight,' he said stiffly, without acknowledging Miss Joliffe's remarks; 'I shall not be back tomorrow, and may be away a few days. I will write to let you know when I shall be back.'

Miss Joliffe started as if she had received an electric shock.

'To London tonight,' she began— 'this very night?'

'Yes,' Westray said, with a dryness that would have suggested of itself that the interview was to be terminated, even if he had not added: 'I shall be glad to be left alone now; I have several letters to write before I can get away.'

So Miss Euphemia went to impart this strange matter to the maiden who was *ex hypothesi* leaning on the architect's strong arm.

'What *do* you think, Anastasia?' she said. 'Mr Westray is going to London tonight, perhaps for some days.'

'Is he?' was all her niece's comment; but there was a languor and indifference in the voice, that might have sent the thermometer of the architect's affection from boiling-point to below blood-heat, if he could have heard her speak.

Westray sat moodily for a few moments after his landlady had gone. For the first time in his life he wished he was a smoker. He wished he had a pipe in his mouth, and could pull in and puff out smoke as he had seen Sharnall do when *he* was moody. He wanted some work for his restless body while his restless mind was turning things over. It was the news of Lord Blandamer's visit, as on this very afternoon, that fanned smouldering thoughts into flame. This was the first time, so far as Westray knew, that Lord Blandamer had come to Bellevue Lodge without at least a formal excuse of business. With that painful effort which we use to convince ourselves of things of which we wish to be convinced in the face of all difficulties; with that blind, stumbling hope against hope with which we try to reconcile things irreconcilable, if only by so doing we can conjure away a haunting spectre, or lull to sleep a bitter suspicion; the architect had hitherto resolved to believe that if Lord Blandamer came with some frequency to Bellevue Lodge, he was only prompted to do so by a desire to keep in touch with the restoration, to follow with intelligence the expenditure of money which he was so lavishly providing. It had been the easier for Westray to persuade himself that Lord Blandamer's motives were legitimate, because he felt that the other must find a natural attraction in the society of a talented young professional man. An occasional conversation with a clever architect on things architectural, or on other affairs of common interest (for Westray was careful to avoid harping unduly on any single topic) must undoubtedly prove a relief to Lord Blandamer from the monotony of bachelor life in the country; and in such considerations Westray found a subsidiary, and sometimes he was inclined to imagine primary, interest for these visits to Bellevue Lodge.

If various circumstances had conspired of late to impugn the sufficiency of these motives, Westray had not admitted as much in his own mind; if he had been disquieted, he had constantly assured himself that disquietude was unreasonable. But now disillusion had befallen him. Lord Blandamer had visited Bellevue Lodge as it were in his own right; he had definitely abandoned the pretence of coming to see Westray; he had been drinking tea with Miss Joliffe; he had spent an hour in the kitchen with Miss Joliffe and—Anastasia. It could only mean one thing, and Westray's resolution was taken.

An object which had seemed at best but mildly desirable, became of singular value when he believed that another was trying to possess himself of it; jealousy had quickened love, duty and conscience insisted that he should save the girl from the snare that was being set for her. The great renunciation must be made; he, Westray, must marry beneath him, but before doing so he would take his mother into his confidence, though there is no record of Perseus doing as much before he cut loose Andromeda.

Meanwhile, no time must be lost; he would start this very night. The last train for London had already left, but he would walk to Cullerne Road Station and catch the night mail from thence. He liked walking, and need take no luggage, for there were things that he could use at his mother's house. It was seven o'clock when he came to this resolve, and an hour later he had left the last house in Cullerne behind him, and entered upon his night excursion.

The line of the Roman way which connected Carauna (Carisbury) with its port Culurnum (Cullerne) is still followed by the modern road, and runs as nearly straight as may be for the sixteen miles which separate those places. About half-way between them the Great Southern main line crosses the highway at right angles, and here is Cullerne Road Station. The first half of the way runs across a flat sandy tract called Mallory Heath, where the short greensward encroaches on the road, and where the eye roaming east or west or north can discern nothing except a limitless expanse of heather, broken here and there by patches of gorse and bracken, or by clumps of touselled and wind-thinned pines and Scotch firs. The tawny-coloured, sandy track is difficult to follow in the dark, and there are posts set up at intervals on the skirts of the way for travellers' guidance. These posts show out white against a starless night, and dark against the snow which sometimes covers the heath with a silvery sheet.

On a clear night the traveller can see the far-off lamps of the station at Cullerne Road a mile after he has left the old seaport town. They stand out like a thin line of light in the distant darkness, a line continuous at first, but afterwards resolvable into individual units of lamps as he walks farther along the straight road. Many a weary wayfarer has watched those lamps hang changeless in the distance, and chafed at their immobility. They seem to come no nearer to him for all the milestones, with the distance from Hyde Park Corner graven in old figures on their lichened faces, that he has passed. Only the increasing sound of the trains tells him that he is nearing his goal, and by degrees the dull rumble becomes a clanking roar as the expresses rush headlong by. On a crisp winter day they leave behind them a trail of whitest wool, and in the night-time a fiery serpent follows them when the open furnace-door flings on the cloud a splendid radiance. But in the dead heats of midsummer the sun dries up the steam, and they speed along, the more wonderful because there is no trace to tell what power it is that drives them.

Of all these things Westray saw nothing. A soft white fog had fallen upon everything. It drifted by in delicate whirling wreaths, that seemed to have an innate motion of their own where all had been still but a minute before. It covered his clothes with a film of the finest powdery moisture that ran at a touch into heavy drops; it hung in dripping dew on his moustache, and hair, and eyebrows; it blinded him, and made him catch his breath. It had come rolling in from the sea as on that night when Mr Sharnall was taken, and Westray could hear the distant groaning of fog-horns in the Channel; and looking backwards towards Cullerne, knew from a blurred glare, now green, now red, that a vessel in the offing was signalling for a coastwise pilot. He plodded steadily forward, stopping now and then when he found his feet on the grass sward to recover the road, and rejoicing when one of the white posts assured him that he was still keeping the right direction. The blinding fog isolated him in a strange manner; it cut him off from Nature, for he could see nothing of her; it cut him off from man, for he could not have seen even a legion of soldiers had they surrounded him. This removal of outside influences threw him back upon himself, and delivered him to introspection; he began for the hundredth time to weigh his position, to consider whether the momentous step that he was taking was necessary to his ease of mind, was right, was prudent.

To make a proposal of marriage is a matter that may give the strongest-minded pause, and Westray's mind was not of the strongest. He was clever, imaginative, obstinate, scrupulous to a fault; but had not that broad outlook on life which comes of experience, nor the power and resolution to readily take a decision under difficult circumstances, and to abide by it once taken. So it was that reason made a shuttlecock of his present resolve, and half a dozen times he stopped in the road meaning to abandon his purpose, and turn back to Cullerne. Yet half a dozen times he went on, though with slow feet, thinking always. Was he right in what he was doing, was he right? And the fog grew thicker; it seemed almost to be stifling him; he could not see his hand if he held it at arm's length before his face. Was he right, was there any right or any wrong, was anything real, was not everything subjective—the creation of his own brain? Did he exist, was he himself, was he in the body or out of the body? And then a wild dismay, a horror of the darkness and the fog, seized hold of him. He stretched out his arms, and groped in the mist as if he hoped to lay hold of someone, or something, to reassure him as to his own identity, and at last a mind-panic got the better of him; he turned and started back to Cullerne.

It was only for a moment, and then reason began to recover her sway; he stopped, and sat down on the heather at the side of the road, careless that every spray was wet and dripping, and collected his thoughts. His heart was beating madly as in one that wakes from a nightmare, but he was now ashamed of his weakness and of the mental *débâcle*, though there had been none to see it. What could have possessed him, what madness was this? After a few minutes he was able to turn round once more, and resumed his walk towards the railway with a firm, quick step, which should prove to his own satisfaction that he was master of himself.

For the rest of his journey he dismissed bewildering questions of right and wrong, of prudence and imprudence, laying it down as an axiom that his emprise was both right and prudent, and busied himself with the more material and homely considerations of ways and means. He amused himself in attempting to fix the sum for which it would be possible for him and Anastasia to keep house, and by mentally straining to the utmost the resources at his command managed to make them approach his estimate. Another man in similar circumstances might perhaps have given himself to reviewing the chances of success in his proposal, but Westray did not trouble himself with any doubts on this point. It was a foregone conclusion that if he once offered himself Anastasia would accept him; she could not be so oblivious to the advantages which such a marriage would offer, both in material considerations and in the connection with a superior family. He only regarded the matter from his own standpoint; once he was convinced that *he* cared enough for Anastasia to make her an offer, then he was sure that she would accept him.

It was true that he could not, on the spur of the moment, recollect many instances in which she had openly evinced a predilection for him, but he was conscious that she thought well of him, and she was no doubt too modest to make manifest feelings which she could never under ordinary circumstances hope to see returned. Yet he certainly *had* received encouragement of a quiet and unobtrusive kind, quite sufficient to warrant the most favourable conclusions. He remembered how many, many times their eyes had met when they were in one another's company; she must certainly have read the tenderness which had inspired his glances, and by answering them she had given perhaps the greatest encouragement that true modesty would permit. How delicate and infinitely gracious her acknowledgment had been, how often had she looked at him as it were furtively, and then, finding his passionate gaze upon her, had at once cast her own eyes shyly to the ground! And in his reveries he took not into reckoning, the fact that through these later weeks he had scarcely ever taken his gaze off her, so long as she was in the same room with him. It would have been strange if their eyes had not sometimes met, because she must needs now and then obey that impulse which forces us to look at those who are looking at us. Certainly, he meditated, her eyes had given him encouragement, and then she had accepted gratefully a bunch of lilies of the valley which he said lightly had been given him, but which he had really bought *ad hoc* at Carisbury. But, again, he ought perhaps to have reflected that it would have been difficult for her to refuse them. How could she have refused them? How could any girl under the circumstances do less than take with thanks a few lilies of the valley? To decline them would be affectation; by declining she might attach a false and ridiculous significance to a kindly act. Yes, she had encouraged him in the matter of the lilies, and if she had not worn some of them in her bosom, as he had hoped she might, that, no doubt, was because she feared to show her preference too markedly. He had noticed particularly the interest she had shown when a bad cold had confined him for a few days to the house, and this very evening had he not heard that she missed him when he was absent even for a night? He smiled at this thought, invisibly in the fog; and has not a man a right to some complacence, on whose presence in the house hang a fair maiden's peace and security? Miss Joliffe had said that Anastasia felt nervous whenever he, Westray, was away; it was very possible that Anastasia had given her aunt a hint that she would like him to be told this, and he smiled again in the fog; he certainly need have no fear of any rejection of his suit.

He had been so deeply immersed in these reassuring considerations that he walked steadily on unconscious of all exterior objects and conditions until he saw the misty lights of the station, and knew that his goal was reached. His misgivings and tergiversations had so much delayed him by the way, that it was past midnight, and the train was already due. There were no other travellers on the platform, or in the little waiting-room where a paraffin lamp with blackened chimney struggled feebly with the fog. It was not a cheery room, and he was glad to be called back from a contemplation of a roll of texts hanging on the wall, and a bottle of stale water on the table, to human things by the entry of a drowsy official who was discharging the duties of station-master, booking-clerk, and porter all at once.

'Are you waiting for the London train, sir?' he asked in a surprised tone, that showed that the night mail found few passengers at Cullerne Road. 'She will be in now in a few minutes; have you your ticket?'

They went together to the booking-office. The station-master handed him a third-class ticket, without even asking how he wished to travel.

'Ah, thank you,' Westray said, 'but I think I will go first class tonight. I shall be more likely to have a compartment to myself, and shall be less disturbed by people getting in and out.'

'Certainly, sir,' said the station-master, with the marked increase of respect due to a first-class passenger— 'certainly, sir; please give me back the other ticket. I shall have to write you one—we do not keep them ready; we are so very seldom asked for first class at this station.'

'No, I suppose not,' Westray said.

'Things happen funny,' the station-master remarked while he got his pen. 'I wrote one by this same train a month ago, and before that I don't think we have ever sold one since the station was opened.'

'Ah,' Westray said, paying little attention, for he was engaged in a new mental disputation as to whether he was really justified in travelling first class. He had just settled that at such a life-crisis as he had now reached, it was necessary that the body should be spared fatigue in order that the mind might be as vigorous as possible for dealing with a difficult situation, and that the extra expense was therefore justified; when the station-master went on:

'Yes, I wrote a ticket, just as I might for you, for Lord Blandamer not a month ago. Perhaps you know Lord Blandamer?' he added venturously; yet with a suggestion that even the sodality of first-class travelling was not in itself a passport to so distinguished an acquaintance. The mention of Lord Blandamer's name gave a galvanic shock to Westray's flagging attention.

'Oh yes,' he said, 'I know Lord Blandamer.'

'Do you, indeed, sir'—and respect had risen by a skip greater than any allowed in counterpoint. 'Well, I wrote a ticket for his lordship by this very train not a month ago; no, it was not a month ago, for 'twas the very night the poor organist at Cullerne was took.'

'Yes,' said the would-be indifferent Westray; 'where did Lord Blandamer come from?'

'I do not know,' the station-master replied— 'I do *not* know, sir,' he repeated, with the unnecessary emphasis common to the uneducated or unintelligent.

'Was he driving?'

'No, he walked up to this station just as you might yourself. Excuse me sir,' he broke off; 'here she comes.'

They heard the distant thunder of the approaching train, and were in time to see the gates of the level-crossing at the end of the platform swing silently open as if by ghostly hands, till their red lanterns blocked the Cullerne Road.

No one got out, and no one but Westray got in; there was some interchanging of post-office bags in the fog, and then the station-master-booking-clerk-porter waved a lamp, and the train steamed away. Westray found himself in a cavernous carriage, of which the cloth seats were cold and damp as the lining of a coffin. He turned up the collar of his coat, folded his arms in a Napoleonic attitude, and threw himself back into a corner to think. It was curious—it was very curious. He had been under the impression that Lord Blandamer had left Cullerne early on the night of poor Sharnall's accident; Lord Blandamer had told them at Bellevue Lodge that he was going away by the afternoon train when he left them. Yet here he was at Cullerne Road at midnight, and if he had not come from Cullerne, whence had he come? He could not have come from Fording, for from Fording he would certainly have taken the train at Lytchett. It was curious, and while he was so thinking he fell asleep.

Chapter 16

A day or two later Miss Joliffe said to Anastasia:

'I think you had a letter from Mr Westray this morning, my dear, had you not? Did he say anything about his return? Did he say when he was coming back?'

'No, dear aunt, he said nothing about coming back. He only wrote a few lines on a matter of business.'

'Oh, yes, just so,' Miss Joliffe said dryly, feeling a little hurt at what seemed like any lack of confidence on her niece's part.

Miss Joliffe would have said that she knew Anastasia's mind so well that no secrets were hid from her. Anastasia would have said that her aunt knew everything except a few *little* secrets, and, as a matter of fact, the one perhaps knew as much of the other is it is expedient that age should know of youth. 'The mind is its own place, and in itself can make a hell of heaven, a heaven of hell.' Of all earthly consolations this is the greatest, that the mind is its own place. The mind is an impregnable fortress which can be held against all comers, the mind is a sanctuary open day or night to the pursued, the mind is a flowery pleasance where shade refreshes even in summer droughts. To some trusted friend we try to give the clue of the labyrinth, but the ball of silk is too short to guide any but ourselves along all the way. There are sunny mountain-tops, there are innocent green arbours, or closes of too highly-perfumed flowers, or dank dungeons of despair, or guilty *mycethmi*—bellowing caves black as night, where we walk alone, whither we may lead no one with us by the hand.

Miss Euphemia Joliffe would have liked to ignore altogether the matter of Westray's letter, and to have made no further remarks thereon; but curiosity is in a woman a stronger influence than pride, and curiosity drove her to recur to the letter.

'Thank you, my dear, for explaining about it. I am sure you will tell me if there are any messages for me in it.'

'No, there was no message at all for you, I think,' said Anastasia. 'I will get it for you by-and-by, and you shall see all he says,' and with that she left the room as if to fetch the letter. It was only a subterfuge, for she felt Westray's correspondence burning a hole in her pocket all the while; but she was anxious that her aunt should not see the letter until an answer to it had been posted; and hoped that if she once escaped from the room, the matter would drop out of memory. Miss Joliffe fired a parting shot to try to bring her niece to her bearings as she was going out:

'I do not know, my dear, that I should encourage any correspondence from Mr Westray, if I were you. It would be more seemly, perhaps, that he should write to me on any little matter of business than to you.' But Anastasia feigned not to hear her, and held on her course.

She betook herself to the room that had once been Mr Sharnall's, but was now distressingly empty and forlorn, and there finding writing materials, sat down to compose an answer to Westray's letter. She knew its contents thoroughly well, she knew its expressions almost by heart, yet she spread it out on the table before her, and read and re-read it as many times as if it were the most difficult of cryptograms.

'Dearest Anastasia,' it began, and she found an outrage in the very first word, 'Dearest.' What right had he to call her 'Dearest'? She was one of those unintelligible females who do not shower superlatives on every chance acquaintance. She must, no doubt, have been callous as judged by modern standards, or at least, singularly unimaginative, for among her few correspondents she had not one whom she addressed as 'dearest.' No, not even her aunt, for at such rare times of absence from home as she had occasion to write to Miss Joliffe, 'My dear Aunt Euphemia' was the invocation.

It was curious that this same word 'Dearest' had occasioned Westray also considerable thought and dubiety. Should he call her

'Dearest Anastasia,' or 'Dear Miss Joliffe'? The first sounded too forward, the second too formal. He had discussed this and other details with his mother, and the die had at last fallen on 'Dearest.' At the worst such an address could only be criticized as proleptic, since it must be justified almost immediately by Anastasia's acceptance of his proposal.

Dearest Anastasia—for dearest you are and ever will be to me—I feel sure that your heart will go out to meet my heart in what I am saying; that you kindness will support me in the important step which has now to be taken.

Anastasia shook her head, though there was no one to see her. There was a suggestion of fate overbearing prudence in Westray's words, a suggestion that he needed sympathy in an unpleasant predicament, that jarred on her intolerably.

I have known you now a year, and know that my happiness is centred in you; you too have known me a year, and I trust that I have read aright the message that your eyes have been sending to me.

> *'For I shall happiest be to-night*
> *Or saddest in the town;*
> *Heaven send I read their message right,*
> *Those eyes of hazel brown.'*

Anastasia found space in the press of her annoyance to laugh. It was more than a smile, it was a laugh, a quiet little laugh to herself, which in a man would have been called a chuckle. Her eyes were not hazel brown, they were not brown at all; but then brown rhymed with town, and after all the verse might perhaps be a quotation, and must so be taken only to apply to the situation in general. She read the sentence again, 'I have known you now a year; you too have known me a year.' Westray had thought this poetic insistence gave a touch of romance, and balanced the sentence; but to Anastasia it seemed the reiteration of a platitude. If he had known her a year, then she had known him a year, and to a female mind the sequitur was complete.

Have I read the message right, dearest? Is your heart my own?

Message? What message did he speak of? What message did he imagine she had wished to give *him* with her eyes? He had stared at her persistently for weeks past, and if her eyes sometimes caught his,

that was only because she could not help it; except when between
whiles she glanced at him of set purpose, because it amused her to see
how silly a man in love may look.

Say that it is; tell me that your heart is my own

(and the request seemed to her too preposterous to admit even of
comment).

I watch your present, dear Anastasia, with solicitude. Sometimes I
think that you are even now exposed to dangers of whose very
existence you know nothing; and sometimes I look forward with
anxiety to the future, so undecipherable, if misfortune or death
should overtake your aunt. Let me help you to decipher this riddle.
Let me be your shield now, and your support in the days to come.
Be my wife, and give me the right to be your protector. I am
detained in London by business for some days more; but I shall
await your answer here with overwhelming eagerness, yet, may I
say it? not without hope.

Your most loving and devoted

EDWARD WESTRAY.

She folded the letter up with much deliberation, and put it back into its
envelope. If Westray had sought far and wide for means of damaging his
own cause, he could scarcely have found anything better calculated for
that purpose than these last paragraphs. They took away much of that
desire to spare, to make unpleasantness as little unpleasant as may be,
which generally accompanies a refusal. His sententiousness was
unbearable. What right had he to advise before he knew whether she
would listen to him? What were these dangers to which she was even
now exposed, and from which Mr Westray was to shield her? She asked
herself the question formally, though she knew the answer all the while.
Her own heart had told her enough of late, to remove all difficulty in
reading between Mr Westray's lines. A jealous man is, if possible, more
contemptible than a jealous woman. Man's greater strength postulates a
broader mind and wider outlook; and if he fail in these, his failure is
more conspicuous than woman's. Anastasia had traced to jealousy the
origin of Westray's enigmatic remarks; but if she was strong enough to
hold him ridiculous for his pains, she was also weak enough to take a
woman's pleasure in having excited the interest of the man she ridiculed.

She laughed again at the proposal that she should join him in
deciphering any riddles, still more such as were undecipherable; and the

air of patronage involved in his anxiety to provide for her future was the more distasteful in that she had great ideas of providing for it herself. She had told herself a hundred times that it was only affection for her aunt that kept her at home. Were 'anything to happen' to Miss Joliffe, she would at once seek her own living. She had often reckoned up the accomplishments which would aid her in such an endeavour. She had received her education—even if it were somewhat desultory and discontinuous—at good schools. She had always been a voracious reader, and possessed an extensive knowledge of English literature, particularly of the masters of fiction; she could play the piano and the violin tolerably, though Mr Sharnall would have qualified her estimate. She had an easy touch in oils and water-colour, which her father said she must have inherited (from his mother—from that Sophia Joliffe who painted the great picture of the flowers and caterpillar, and her spirited caricatures had afforded much merriment to her schoolfellows. She made her own clothes, and was sure that she had a taste in matters of dress design and manufacture that would bring her distinction if she were only given the opportunity of employing it; she believed that she had an affection for children, and a natural talent for training them, though she never saw any at Cullerne. With gifts such as these, which must be patent to others as well as herself, there would surely be no difficulty in obtaining an excellent place as governess if she should ever determine to adopt that walk of life; and she was sometimes inclined to gird at Fate, which for the present led her to deprive the world of these benefits.

In her inmost heart, however, she doubted whether she would be really justified in devoting herself to teaching; for she was conscious that she might be called to fill a higher mission, and to instruct by the pen rather than by word of mouth. As every soldier carries in his knapsack the bâton of the Field Marshal, so every girl in her teens knows that there lie hidden in the recesses of her *armoire*, the robes and coronet and full insignia of a first-rate novelist. She may not choose to take them out and air them, the crown may tarnish by disuse, the moth of indolence may corrupt, but there lies the panoply in which she may on any day appear fully dight, for the astonishment of an awakening world. Jane Austen and Maria Edgeworth are heroines, whose aureoles shine in the painted windows of such airy castles; Charlotte Brontë wrote her masterpieces in a seclusion as deep as that of Bellevue Lodge; and Anastasia Joliffe thought many a time of that day when, afar off from her watch-tower in quiet Cullerne, she would follow the triumphant progress of an epoch-making romance.

It would be published under a *nom de plume*, of course, she would not use her own name till she had felt her feet; and the choice of the pseudonym was the only definite step towards this venture that she had yet made. The period was still uncertain. Sometimes the action was to be placed in the eighteenth century, with tall silver urns and tables, and breast-waisted dresses; sometimes in the struggle of the Roses, when barons swam rivers in full armour after a bloody bout; sometimes in the Civil War, when Vandyke drew the arched eyebrow and taper hand, and when the shadow of death was over all.

It was to the Civil War that her fancy turned oftenest, and now and again, as she sat before her looking-glass, she fancied that she had a Vandyke face herself. And so it was indeed; and if the mirror was fogged and dull and outworn, and if the dress that it reflected was not of plum or amber velvet, one still might fancy that she was a loyalist daughter whose fortunes were fallen with her master's. The Limner of the King would have rejoiced to paint the sweet, young, oval face and little mouth; he would have found the space between the eyebrow and the eyelid to his liking.

If the the plot were still shadowy, her characters were always with her, in armour or sprigged prints; and, the mind being its own place, she took about a little court of her own, where dreadful tragedies were enacted, and valorous deeds done; where passionate young love suffered and wept, and where a mere girl of eighteen, by consummate resolution, daring, beauty, genius, and physical strength, always righted the situation, and brought peace at the last.

With resources such as these, the future did not present itself in dark colours to Anastasia; nor did its riddle appear to her nearly so undecipherable as Mr Westray had supposed. She would have resented, with all the confidence of inexperience, any attempt to furnish her with prospects; and she resented Westray's offer all the more vigorously because it seemed to carry with it a suggestion of her own forlorn position, to insist unduly on her own good fortune in receiving such a proposal, and on his condescension in making it.

There are women who put marriage in the forefront of life, whose thoughts revolve constantly about it as a centre, and with whom an advantageous match, or, failing that, a match of some sort, is the primary object. There are others who regard marriage as an eventuality, to be contemplated without either eagerness or avoidance, to be accepted or declined according as its circumstances may be favourable or unfavourable. Again, there are some who seem, even from youth, to resolutely eliminate wedlock from their thoughts, to permit themselves no mental discussion upon this subject. Though a man profess that he will never marry, experience has shown that his resolve is often subject to reconsideration. But with unmarrying women the case is different, and unmarried for the most part they remain, for man is often so weak-kneed a creature in matters of the heart, that he refrains from pursuing where an unsympathetic attitude discourages pursuit. It may be that some of these women, also, would wish to reconsider their verdict, but find that they have reached an age when there is no place for repentance; yet, for the most part, woman's resolve upon such matters is more stable than man's, and that because the interests at stake in marriage are for her more vital than can ever be the case with man.

It was to the class of indifferentists that Anastasia belonged; she neither sought nor shunned a change of state, but regarded marriage as an accident that, in befalling her, might substantially change the outlook. It would render a life of teaching, no doubt, impossible; domestic or maternal cares might to some extent trammel even literary activity (for, married or not married, she was determined to fulfil her mission of writing), but in no case was she inclined to regard marriage as an escape from difficulties, as the solution of so trivial a problem as that of existence.

She read Westray's letter once more from beginning to end. It was duller than ever. It reflected its writer; she had always thought him unromantic, and now he seemed to her intolerably prosaic, conceited, pettifogging, utilitarian. To be his wife! She had rather live as a nursery governess all her life! And how could she write fiction with such a one for mentor and company? He would expect her to be methodic, to see that eggs were fresh, and beds well aired. So, by thinking, she reasoned herself into such a theoretic reprobation of this attempt upon her, that his offer became a heinous crime. If she answered him shortly, brusquely, nay rudely, it would be but what he deserved for making her ridiculous to herself by so absurd a proposal, and she opened her writing-case with much firmness and resolution.

It was a little wooden case covered in imitation leather, with *Papeterie* stamped in gold upon the top. She had no exaggerated notions as to its intrinsic worth, but it was valuable in her eyes as being a present from her father. It was, in fact, the only gift he ever had bestowed upon her; but on this he had expended at least half a crown, in a fit of unusual generosity when he sent her with a great flourish of trumpets to Mrs Howard's school at Carisbury. She remembered his very words. 'Take this, child,' he said; 'you are now going to a first-class place of education, and it is right that you should have a proper equipment,' and so gave her the *papeterie*. It had to cover a multitude of deficiencies, and poor Anastasia lamented that it had not been a new hair-brush, half a dozen pocket-handkerchiefs, or even a sound pair of shoes.

Still it had stood in good stead, for with it she had written all her letters ever since, and being the only receptacle with lock and key to which she had access, she made it a little ark and coffer for certain girlish treasures. With such it was stuffed so full that they came crowding out as she opened it. There were several letters to which romance attached, relics of that delightful but far too short school-time at Carisbury; there was her programme, with rudely scribbled names of partners, for the splendid dance at the term's end, to which a selection of other girls' brothers were invited; a pressed rose given her by someone which she had worn in her bosom on that historic occasion, and many other equally priceless mementoes. Somehow these things seemed now neither so romantic nor so precious as on former occasions; she was even inclined to smile, and to make light of them, and then a little bit of paper fluttered off the table on to the floor. She stooped and picked up the flap of an envelope with the coronet and 'Fording' stamped in black upon it which she had found one day when Westray's waste-paper basket was emptied. It was a simple device enough, but it must have furnished her food for thought, for it lay under her eyes on the table for at least ten minutes before she put it carefully back into the *papeterie*, and began her letter to Westray.

She found no difficulty in answering, but the interval of reflection had soothed her irritation, and blunted her animosity. Her reply was neither brusque nor rude, it leant rather to conventionalism than to originality, and she used, after all, those phrases which have been commonplaces in such circumstances, since man first asked and woman first refused. She thanked Mr Westray for the kind interest which he had taken in her, she was deeply conscious of the consideration which he had shown her. She was grieved—sincerely grieved—to tell him that things could not be as he wished. She was so afraid that her letter would seem unkind; she did not mean it to be unkind. However difficult it was to say it now, she thought it was the truest kindness not to disguise from him that things *never* could be as he wished. She paused a little to review this last sentiment, but she allowed it to remain, for she was anxious to avoid any recrudescence of the suppliant's passion, and to show that her decision was final. She should always feel the greatest esteem for Mr Westray; she trusted that the present circumstances would not interrupt their friendship in any way. She hoped that their relations might continue as in the past, and in this hope she remained very truly his.

She gave a sigh of relief when the letter was finished, and read it through carefully, putting in commas and semicolons and colons at what she thought appropriate places. Such punctilio pleased her; it was, she considered, due from one who aspired to a literary style, and aimed at making a living by the pen. Though this was the first answer to a proposal that she had written on her own account, she was not altogether without practice in such matters, as she had composed others for her heroines who had found themselves in like position. Her manner, also, was perhaps unconsciously influenced by a perusal of *The Young Person's Compleat Correspondent, and Guide to Answers to be given in the Various Circumstances of Life*, which, in a tattered calf covering, formed an item in Miss Euphemia's library.

It was not till the missive was duly sealed up and posted that she told her aunt of what had happened. 'There is Mr Westray's letter,' she said, 'if you would care to read it,' and passed over to Miss Joliffe the piece of white paper on which a man had staked his fate.

Miss Joliffe took the letter with an attempt to assume an indifferent manner, which was unsuccessful, because an offer of marriage has about it a certain exhalation and atmosphere that betrays its importance even to the most unsuspicious. She was a slow reader, and, after wiping and adjusting her spectacles, sat down for a steady and patient consideration of the matter before her.

But the first word that she deciphered, 'Dearest', startled her composure, and she pressed on through the letter with a haste that was foreign to her disposition. Her mouth grew rounder as she read, and she sighed out 'Dear's' and 'Dear Anastasia's' and 'Dear Child's' at intervals as a relief to her feelings.

Anastasia stood by her, following the lines of writing that she knew by heart, with all the impatience of one who is reading ten times faster than another who turns the page.

Miss Joliffe's mind was filled with conflicting emotions; she was glad at the prospect of a more assured future that was opening before her niece, she was hurt at not having been taken sooner into confidence, for Anastasia must certainly have known that he was going to propose; she was chagrined at not having noticed a courtship which had been carried on under her very eyes; she was troubled at the thought that the marriage would entail the separation from one who was to her as a child.

How weary she would find it to walk alone down the long paths of old age! how hard it was to be deprived of a dear arm on whose support she had reckoned for when 'the slow dark hours begin'! But she thrust this reflection away from her as selfish, and contrition for having harboured it found expression in a hand wrinkled and roughed by hard wear, which stole into Anastasia's.

'My dear,' she said, 'I am very glad at your good fortune; this is a great thing that has befallen you.' A general content that Anastasia should have received a proposal silenced misgivings.

To the recipient, an offer of marriage, be it good, bad, or indifferent, to be accepted or to be refused, brings a certain complacent satisfaction. She may pretend to make light of it, to be displeased at it, to resent it, as did Anastasia; but in her heart of hearts there lurks the self-appreciating reflection that she has won the completest admiration of a man. If he be a man that she would not marry under any conditions, if he be a fool, or a spendthrift, or an evil-liver, he is still a man, and she has captured him. Her relations share in the same pleasurable reflections. If the offer is accepted, then a future has been provided for one whose future, maybe, was not too certain; if it is declined, then they congratulate themselves on the high morale or strong common sense of a kinswoman who refuses to be won by gold, or to link her destiny with an unsuitable partner.

'It is a great thing, my dear, that has befallen you,' Miss Joliffe repeated. 'I wish you all happiness, dear Anastasia, and may all blessings wait upon you in this engagement.'

'Aunt,' interrupted her niece, 'please don't say that. I have refused him, of *course*; how could you think that I should marry Mr Westray? I never have thought of any such thing with him. I never had the least idea of his writing like this.'

'You have refused him?' said the elder lady with a startled emphasis. Again a selfish reflection crossed her mind—they were not to be parted after all—and again she put it resolutely away. She ran over in her mind all the possible objections that could have influenced her niece in arriving at such a conclusion. Religion was the keynote of Miss Joliffe's life; to religion her thought reverted as the needle to the pole, and to it she turned for an explanation now. It must be some religious consideration that had proved an obstacle to Anastasia.

'I do not think you need find any difficulty in his having been brought up as a Wesleyan,' she said, with a profound conviction that she had put her finger on the matter, and with some consciousness of her own perspicacity. 'His father has been dead some time, and though his mother is still alive, you would not have to live with her. I do not think, dear, she would at all wish you to become a Methodist. As for our Mr Westray, your Mr Westray, I should say now,' and she assumed that expression of archness which is considered appropriate to such occasions, 'I am sure he is a sound Churchman. He goes regularly to the minster on Sundays, and I dare say, being an architect, and often in church on week-days, he has found out that the order of the Church of England is more satisfactory than that of any other sect. Though I am sure I do not wish to say one word against Wesleyans; they are no doubt true Protestants, and a bulwark against more serious errors. I rejoice that your lover's early training will have saved him from any inclination to ritualism.'

'My dear aunt,' Anastasia broke in, with a stress of earnest deprecation on the 'dear' that startled her aunt, 'please do *not* go on like that. Do not call Mr Westray my lover; I have told you that I will have nothing to do with him.'

Miss Joliffe's thoughts had moved through a wide arc. Now that this offer of marriage was about to be refused, now that this engagement was not to be, the advantages that it offered stood out in relief. It seemed too sad that the curtain should be rung down just as the action of a drama of intense interest was beginning, that the good should slip through their fingers just as they were grasping it. She gave no thought now to that fear of a lonely old age which had troubled her a few minutes before; she only saw the provision for the future which Anastasia was wilfully sacrificing. Her hand tightened automatically, and crumpled a long piece of paper that she was holding. It was only a milkman's bill, and yet it might perhaps have unconsciously given a materialistic colour to her thoughts.

'We should not reject any good thing that is put before us,' she said a little stiffly, 'without being very certain that we are right to do so. I do not know what would become of you, Anastasia, if anything were to happen to me.'

'That is exactly what he says, that is the very argument which he uses. Why should you take such a gloomy view of things? Why should something *happening* always mean something bad? Let us hope something good will happen, that someone else will make me a better offer.' She laughed, and went on reflectively: 'I wonder whether Mr Westray will come back here to lodge; I hope he won't.'

Hardly were the words out of her mouth when she was sorry for uttering them, for she saw the look of sadness which overspread Miss Joliffe's face.

'Dear aunt,' she cried, 'I am so sorry; I didn't mean to say that. I know what a difference it would make; we cannot afford to lose our last lodger. I hope he *will* come back, and I will do everything I can to make things comfortable, short of marrying him. I will earn some money myself. I will *write*.'

'How will you write? Who is there to write to?' Miss Joliffe said, and then the blank look on her face grew blanker, and she took out her handkerchief. 'There is no one to help us. Anyone who ever cared for us is dead long ago; there is no one to write to now.'

Chapter 17

Westray played the rôle of rejected lover most conscientiously; he treated the episode of his refusal on strictly conventional lines. He assured himself and his mother that the light of his life was extinguished, that he was the most unhappy of mortals. It was at this time that he wrote some verses called 'Autumn,' with a refrain of—

> *For all my hopes are cold and dead,*
> *And fallen like the fallen leaves.*

which were published in the *Clapton Methodist*, and afterwards set to music by a young lady who wished to bind up another wounded heart. He attempted to lie awake of nights with indifferent success and hinted in conversation at the depressing influence which insomnia exerts over its victims. For several meals in succession he refused to eat heartily of such dishes as he did not like, and his mother felt serious anxiety as to his general state of health. She inveighed intemperately against Anastasia for having refused her son, but then she would have inveighed still more intemperately had Anastasia accepted him. She wearied him with the portentous gloom which she affected in his presence, and quoted Lady Clara Vere de Vere's cruelty in turning honest hearts to gall, till even the rejected one was forced to smile bitterly at so inapposite a parallel.

Though Mrs Westray senior poured out the vials of her wrath on Anastasia for having refused to become Mrs Westray junior, she was at heart devoutly glad at the turn events had taken. At heart Westray could not have said whether he was glad or sorry. He told himself that he was deeply in love with Anastasia, and that this love was further ennobled by a chivalrous desire to shield her from evil; but he could not altogether forget that the unfortunate event had at least saved him from the unconventionality of marrying his landlady's niece. He told himself that his grief was sincere and profound, but it was possible that chagrin and wounded pride were after all his predominant feelings. There were other reflections which he thrust aside as indecorous at this acute stage of the tragedy, but which, nevertheless, were able to exercise a mildly consoling influence in the background. He would be spared the anxieties of early and impecunious marriage, his professional career would not be weighted by family cares, the whole world was once more open before him, and the slate clean. These were considerations which could not prudently be overlooked, though it would be unseemly to emphasize them too strongly when the poignancy of regret should dominate every other feeling.

He wrote to Sir George Farquhar, and obtained ten days' leave of absence on the score of indisposition; and he wrote to Miss Euphemia Joliffe to tell her that he intended to seek other rooms. From the first he had decided that this latter step was inevitable. He could not bear the daily renewal of regret, the daily opening of the wound that would be caused by the sight of Anastasia, or by such chance intercourse with her as further residence at Bellevue Lodge must entail. There is no need to speculate whether his decision was influenced in part by a concession to humiliated pride; men do not take pleasure in revisiting the scenes of a disastrous rout, and it must be admitted that the possibility of summoning a lost love to his presence when he rang for boiling water, had in it something of the grotesque. He had no difficulty in finding other lodgings by correspondence, and he spared himself the necessity of returning at all to his former abode by writing to ask Clerk Janaway to move his belongings.

One morning, a month later, Miss Joliffe sat in that room which had been occupied by the late Mr Sharnall. She was alone, for Anastasia had gone to the office of the *Cullerne Advertiser* with an announcement in which one A. J. intimated that she was willing to take a post as nursery-governess. It was a bright morning but cold, and Miss Joliffe drew an old white knitted shawl closer about her, for there was no fire in the grate. There was no fire because she could not afford it, yet the sun pouring in through the windows made the room warmer than the kitchen, where the embers had been allowed to die out since breakfast. She and Anastasia did without fire on these bright autumn days to save coals; they ate a cold dinner, and went early to bed for the same reason, yet the stock in the cellar grew gradually less. Miss Joliffe had examined it that very morning, and found it terribly small; nor was there any money nor any credit left with which to replenish it.

On the table before her was a pile of papers, some yellow, some pink, some white, some blue, but all neatly folded. They were folded lengthways and to the same breadth, for they were Martin Joliffe's bills, and he had been scrupulously neat and orderly in his habits. It is true that there were among them some few that she had herself contracted, but then she had always been careful to follow exactly her brother's method both of folding and also of docketing them on the exterior. Yes, no doubt she was immediately responsible for some, and she knew just which they were from the outside without any need to open them. She took up one of them: 'Rose and Storey, importers of French millinery, flowers, feathers, ribbons etc. Mantle and jacket show-rooms.' Alas, alas! how frail is human nature! Even in the midst of her misfortunes, even in the eclipse of old age, such words stirred Miss Joliffe's interest—flowers, feathers, ribbons, mantles, and jackets; she saw the delightful showroom 19, 20, 21, and 22 Market Place, Cullerne—saw it in the dignified solitude of a summer morning when a dress was to be tried on, saw it in the crush and glorious scramble of a remnant sale. 'Family and complimentary mourning, costumes, skirts, etc.; foreign and British silks guaranteed makes.' After that the written entry seemed mere bathos: 'Material and trimming one bonnet, 11s. 9d.; one hat 13s. 6d. Total, £1 5s. 3d.' It really was not worth while making a fuss about, and the bunch of cherries and bit of spangled net were well worth the 1s. 9d., that Anastasia's had cost more than hers.

Hole, pharmaceutical chemist: 'Drops, 1s. 6d.; liniment, 1s.; mixture, 1s. 9d.;' repeated many times. 'Cod liver oil, 1s. 3d., and 2s. 6d., and 1s. 3d. again. £2 13s. 2d., with 4s. 8d. interest,' for the bill was four years old. That was for Anastasia at a critical time when nothing seemed to suit her, and Dr Ennefer feared a decline; but all the medicine for poor Martin was entered in Dr Ennefer's own account.

Pilkington, the shoemaker, had his tale to tell; 'Miss Joliffe: Semi-pold. lace boots, treble soles, £1 1s. 0d. Miss A. Jol.: Semi-pold. lace boots, treble soles, £1 1s. 0d. 6 pairs of mohair laces 9d. 3 ditto, silk, 1s.' Yes, she was indeed a guilty woman. It was she that had 'run up' *these* accounts, and she grew red to think that her own hand should have helped to build so dismal a pile.

Debt, like every other habit that runs counter to the common good, brings with it its own punishment, because society protects itself by making unpleasant the ways of such as inconvenience their neighbours. It is true that some are born with a special talent and capacity for debts—they live on it, and live merrily withal, but most debtors feel the weight of their chains, and suffer greater pangs than those which they inflict on any defrauded creditor. If the mill-stone grinds slowly it grinds small, and undischarged accounts bring more pain than the goods to which they relate ever brought pleasure. Among such bitternesses surely most bitter are the bills for things of which the fruition has ceased—for worn-out finery, for withered flowers, for drunk wine. Pilkington's boots, were they never so treble soled, could not endure for ever, and Miss Joliffe's eyes followed unconsciously under the table to where a vertical fissure showed the lining white at the side of either boot. Where were new boots to come from now, whence was to come clothing to wear, and bread to eat?

Nay, more, the day of passive endurance was past; action had begun. The Cullerne Water Company threatened to cut off the water, the Cullerne Gas Company threatened to cut off the gas. Eaves, the milkman, threatened a summons unless that long, long bill of his (all built up of pitiful little pints) was paid forthwith. The Thing had come to the *Triarii*, Miss Joliffe's front was routed, the last rank was wavering. What was she to do, whither was she to turn? She must sell some of the furniture, but who would buy such old stuff? And if she sold furniture, what lodger would take half-empty rooms? She looked wildly round, she thrust her hands into the pile of papers, she turned them over with a feverish action, till she seemed to be turning hay once more as a little girl in the meadows at Wydcombe. Then she heard footsteps on the pavement outside, and thought for a moment that it was Anastasia returned before she was expected, till a heavy tread told her that a man was coming, and she saw that it was Mr Joliffe, her cousin, churchwarden and pork-butcher. His bulky and unwieldy form moved levelly past the windows; he paused and looked up at the house as it to make sure that he was not mistaken, and then he slowly mounted the semicircular flight of stone steps and rang the bell.

In person he was tall, but disproportionately stout for his height. His face was broad, and his loose double chin gave it a flabby appearance. A pallid complexion and black-grey hair brushed straightly down where he was not bald, produced an impression of sanctimoniousness which was increased by a fawning manner of speech. Mr Sharnall was used to call him a hypocrite, but the aspersion was false, as such an aspersion commonly is.

Hypocrites, in the pure and undiluted sense, rarely exist outside the pages of fiction. Except in the lower classes, where deceit thrives under the incentive of clerical patronage, men seldom assume deliberately the garb of religion to obtain temporal advantages or to further their own ends. It is probable that in nine cases out of ten, where practice does not accord sufficiently with profession to please the censorious, the discrepancy is due to inherent weakness of purpose, to the duality of our nature, and not to any conscious deception. If a man leading the lower life should find himself in religious, or high-minded, or pure society, and speak or behave as if he were religious, or high-minded, or pure, he does so in nine cases out of ten not with any definite wish to deceive, but because he is temporarily influenced by better company. For the time he believes what he says, or has persuaded himself that he believes it. If he is froward with the froward, so he is just with the just, and the more sympathetic and susceptible his nature, the more amenable is he to temporary influences. It is this chameleon adaptability that passes for hypocrisy.

Cousin Joliffe was no hypocrite, he acted up to his light; and even if the light be a badly-trimmed, greasy, evil-smelling paraffin-lamp, the man who acts up to it is only the more to be pitied. Cousin Joliffe was one of those amateur ecclesiastics whose talk is of things religious, whom Church questions interest, and who seem to have missed their vocation in not having taken Orders. If Canon Parkyn had been a High Churchman, Cousin Joliffe would have been High Church; but the Canon being Low Church, Cousin Joliffe was an earnest evangelical, as he delighted to describe himself. He was rector's churchwarden, took a leading part in prayer-meetings, with a keen interest in school-treats, ham teas, and magic lanterns, and was particularly proud of having been asked more than once to assist in the Mission Room at Carisbury, where the Vicar of Christ Church carried on revival work among the somnolent surroundings of a great cathedral. He was without any sense of humour or any refinement of feeling—self-important, full of the dignity of his office, thrifty to meanness, but he acted up to his light, and was no hypocrite.

In that petty middle class, narrow-minded and penuriously pretentious, which was the main factor of Cullerne life, he possessed considerable influence and authority. Among his immediate surroundings a word from Churchwarden Joliffe carried more weight than an outsider would have imagined, and long usage had credited him with the delicate position of *censor morum* to the community. Did the wife of a parishioner venture into such a place of temptation as the theatre at Carisbury, was she seen being sculled by young Bulteel in his new skiff of a summer evening, the churchwarden was charged to interview her husband, to point out to him privately the scandal that was being caused, and to show him how his duty lay in keeping his belongings in better order. Was a man trying to carry fire in his bosom by dalliance at the bar of the Blandamer Arms, then a hint was given to his spouse that she should use such influence as would ensure his evenings being at home. Did a young man waste the Sabbath afternoon in walking with his dog on Cullerne Flat, he would receive *The Tishbite's Warning, a Discourse showing the Necessity of a Proper Observance of the Lord's Day*. Did a pig-tailed hoyden giggle at the Grammar School boys from her pew in the minster, the impropriety was reported by the churchwarden to her mother.

On such occasions he was scrupulous in assuming a frock-coat and a silk hat. Both were well worn, and designed in the fashion of another day; but they were in his eyes insignia of office, and as he felt the tails of the coat about his knees they seemed to him as it were the skirts of Aaron's garment. Miss Joliffe was not slow to notice that he was thus equipped this morning; she knew that he had come to pay her a visit of circumstance, and swept her papers hurriedly into a drawer. She felt as if they were guilty things these bills, as if she had been engaged in a guilty action in even 'going through' them, as if she had been detected in doing that which she should not do, and guiltiest of all seemed the very hurry of concealment with which she hid such compromising papers.

She tried to perform that feat of mental gymnastics called retaining one's composure, the desperate and forced composure which the coiner assumes when opening the door to the police, the composure which a woman assumes in returning to her husband with the kisses of a lover tingling on her lips. It *is* a feat to change the current of the mind, to let the burning thought that is dearest or bitterest to us go by the board, to answer coherently to the banalities of conversation, to check the throbbing pulse. The feat was beyond Miss Joliffe's powers; she was but a poor actress, and the churchwarden saw that she was ill at ease as she opened the door.

'Good morning, cousin,' he said with one of those interrogative glances which are often more irritating and more difficult to parry than a direct question; 'you are not looking at all the thing this morning. I hope you are not feeling unwell; I hope I do not intrude.'

'Oh, *no*,' she said, making as good an attempt at continuous speech as the quick beating of her heart allowed; 'it is only that your visit is a little surprise. I am a little flurried; I am not quite so young as I was.'

'Ay,' he said, as she showed him into Mr Sharnall's room, 'we are all of us growing older; it behoves us to walk circumspectly, for we never know when we may be taken.' He looked at her so closely and compassionately that she felt very old indeed; it really seemed as if she ought to be 'taken' at once, as if she was neglecting her duty in not dying away incontinently. She drew the knitted shawl more tightly round her spare and shivering body.

'I am afraid you will find this room a little cold,' she said; 'we are having the kitchen chimney cleaned, so I was sitting here.' She gave a hurried glance at the bureau, feeling a suspicion that she might not have shut the drawer tight, or that one of the bills might have somehow got left out. No, all was safe, but her excuse had not deceived the churchwarden.

'Phemie,' he said, not unkindly, though the word brought tears to her eyes, for it was the first time that anyone had called her by the old childhood name since the night that Martin died— 'Phemie, you should not stint yourself in fires. It is a false economy; you must let me send you a coal ticket.'

'Oh, no, thank you very much; we have plenty,' she cried, speaking quickly, for she would rather have starved outright, than that it should be said a member of the Dorcas Society had taken a parish coal ticket. He urged her no more, but took the chair that she offered him, feeling a little uncomfortable withal, as a well-clothed and overfed man should, in the presence of penury. It was true he had not been to see her for some time; but, then, Bellevue Lodge was so far off, and he had been so pressed with the cares of the parish and of his business. Besides that, their walks of life were so different, and there was naturally a strong objection to any kinswoman of his keeping a lodging-house. He felt sorry now that compassion had betrayed him into calling her 'cousin' and 'Phemie'; she certainly *was* a distant kinswoman, but *not*, he repeated to himself, a cousin; he hoped she had not noticed his familiarity. He wiped his face with a pocket-handkerchief that had seen some service, and gave an introductory cough.

'There is a little matter on which I should like to have a few words with you,' he said, and Miss Joliffe's heart was in her mouth; he *had* heard, then, of these terrible debts and of the threatened summons.

'Forgive me if I go direct to business. I am a business man and a plain man, and like plain speaking.'

It is wonderful to what rude remarks, and unkind remarks and untrue remarks such words as these commonly form the prelude, and how very few of these plain speakers enjoy being plainly spoken to in turn.

'We were talking just now,' he went on, 'of the duty of walking circumspectly, but it is our duty, Miss Joliffe, to see that those over whom we are set in authority walk circumspectly as well. I mean no reproach to you, but others beside me think it would be well that you should keep closer watch over your niece. There is a nobleman of high station that visits much too often at this house. I will *not* name any names'—and this with a tone of magnanimous forbearance—'but you will guess who I mean, because the nobility is not that frequent hereabout. I am sorry to have to speak of such things which ladies generally see quick enough for themselves, but as churchwarden I can't shut my ears to what is matter of town talk; and more by token when a namesake of my own is concerned.'

The composure which Miss Joliffe had been seeking in vain, came back to her at the pork-butcher's words, partly in the relief that he had not broached the subject of debts which had been foremost in her mind, partly in the surprise and indignation occasioned by his talk of Anastasia. Her manner and very appearance changed, and none would have recognized the dispirited and broken-down old lady in the sharpness of her rejoinder.

'Mr Joliffe,' she apostrophized with tart dignity, 'you must forgive me for thinking that I know a good deal more about the nobleman in question than you do, and I can assure you *he* is a perfect gentleman. If he has visited this house, it has been to see Mr Westray about the restoration of the minster. I should have thought one that was churchwarden would have known better than to go bandying scandals about his betters; it is small encouragement for a nobleman to take an interest in the church if the churchwarden is to backbite him for it.'

She saw that her cousin was a little taken aback, and she carried the war into the enemy's country, and gave another thrust.

'Not but what Lord Blandamer has called upon me too, apart from Mr Westray. And what have you to say to *that*? If his lordship has thought fit to honour me by drinking a cup of tea under my roof, there are many in Cullerne would have been glad to get out their best china if he had only asked himself to *their* houses. And there are some might well follow his example, and show themselves a little oftener to their friends and relations.'

The churchwarden wiped his face again, and puffed a little.

'Far be it from me,' he said, dwelling on the expression with all the pleasure that a man of slight education takes in a book phrase that he has got by heart— 'far be it from me to set scandals afloat—'twas you that used the word scandal—but I have daughters of my own to consider. I have nothing to say against Anastasia, who, I believe, is a good girl enough'—and his patronizing manner grated terribly on Miss Joliffe—'though I wish I could see her take more interest in the Sunday-school, but I won't hide from you that she has a way of carrying herself and mincing her words which does *not* befit her station. It makes people take notice, and 'twould be more becoming she should drop it, seeing she will have to earn her own living in service. I don't want to say anything against Lord Blandamer either— he seems to be well-intentioned to the church—but if tales are true, the *old* lord was no better than he should be, and things have, happened before now on your side of the family, Miss Joliffe, that make connections feel uncomfortable about Anastasia. We are told that the sins of the fathers will be visited to the third and fourth generation.'

'Well,' Miss Joliffe said, and made a formidable pause on this adverb, 'if it is the manners of your side of the family to come and insult people in their own houses, I am glad I belong to the other side.'

She was alive to the profound gravity of such a sentiment, yet was prepared to take her stand upon it, and awaited another charge from the churchwarden with a dignity and confidence that would have become the Old Guard. But no fierce passage of arms followed; there was a pause, and if a dignified ending were desired the interview should here have ended. But to ordinary mortals the sound of their own voices is so musical as to deaden any sense of anticlimax; talking is continued for talking's sake, and heroics tail off into desultory conversation. Both sides were conscious that they had overstated their sentiments, and were content to leave main issues undecided.

Miss Joliffe did not take the bills out of their drawer again after the churchwarden had left her. The current of her ideas had been changed, and for the moment she had no thought for anything except the innuendoes of her visitor. She rehearsed to herself without difficulty the occasions of Lord Blandamer's visits, and although she was fully persuaded that any suspicions as to his motives were altogether without foundation, she was forced to admit that he *had* been at Bellevue Lodge more than once when she had been absent. This was no doubt a pure coincidence, but we were enjoined to be wise as serpents as well as innocent as doves, and she would take care that no further occasion was given for idle talk.

Anastasia, on her return, found her aunt unusually reserved and taciturn. Miss Joliffe had determined to behave exactly as usual to Anastasia because her niece was entirely free from fault; but she was vexed at what the churchwarden had said, and her manner was so mysterious and coldly dignified as to convince Anastasia that some cause for serious annoyance had occurred. Did Anastasia remark that it was a close morning, her aunt looked frowningly abstracted and gave no reply; did Anastasia declare that she had not been able to get any 14 knitting-needles, they were quite out of them, her aunt said 'Oh!' in a tone of rebuke and resignation which implied that there were far more serious matters in the world than knitting-needles.

This dispensation lasted a full half-hour, but beyond that the kindly old heart was quite unequal to supporting a proper hauteur. The sweet warmth of her nature thawed the chilly exterior; she was ashamed of her moodiness, and tried to 'make up' for it to Anastasia by manifestation of special affection. But she evaded her niece's attempts at probing the matter, and was resolved that the girl should know nothing of Cousin Joliffe's suggestions or even of the fact of his visit.

But if Anastasia knew nothing of these things, she was like to be singular in her ignorance. All Cullerne knew; it was in the air. The churchwarden had taken a few of the elders into his confidence, and asked their advice as to the propriety of his visit of remonstrance. The elders, male and female, heartily approved of his action, and had in their turn taken into confidence a few of their intimate and specially-to-be-trusted friends. Then ill-natured and tale-bearing Miss Sharp told lying and mischief-making Mrs Flint, and lying and mischief-making Mrs Flint talked the matter over at great length with the Rector, who loved all kinds of gossip, especially of the highly-spiced order. It was speedily matter of common knowledge that Lord Blandamer was at the Hand of God (so ridiculous of a lodging-house keeper christening a public-house Bellevue Lodge!) at *all* hours of the day *and* night, and that Miss Joliffe was content to look at the ceiling on such occasions; and worse, to go to meetings so as to leave the field undisturbed (what intolerable hypocrisy making an excuse of the Dorcas meetings!); that Lord Blandamer loaded—simply loaded— that pert and good-for-nothing girl with presents, that even the young architect was forced to change his lodgings by such disreputable goings-on. People wondered how Miss Joliffe and her niece had the effrontery to show themselves at church on Sundays; the younger creature, at least, must have *some* sense of shame left, for she never ventured to exhibit in *public* either the fine dresses or the jewellery that her lover gave her.

Such stories came to Westray's ears, and stirred in him the modicum of chivalry which leavens the lump of most men's being. He was still smarting under his repulse, but he would have felt himself disgraced if he had allowed the scandal to pass unchallenged, and he rebutted it with such ardour that people shrugged their shoulders, and hinted that there had been something between *him*, too, and Anastasia.

Clerk Janaway was inclined to take a distressingly opportunist and matter-of-fact view of the question. He neither reprobated nor defended. In his mind the Divine right of peers was firmly established. So long as they were rich and spent their money freely, we should not be too particular. They were to be judged by standards other than those of common men; for his part, he was glad they had got in place of an old curmudgeon a man who would take an interest in the Church, and spend money on the place and the people. If he took a fancy to a pretty face, where was the harm? 'Twas nothing to the likes of them, best let well alone; and then he would cut short the churchwarden's wailings and godly lamentations by 'descanting' on the glories of Fording, and the boon it was to the countryside to have the place kept up once more.

'Clerk Janaway, your sentiments do you no credit,' said the pork-butcher on one such occasion, for he was given to gossip with the sexton on terms of condescending equality. 'I have seen Fording myself, having driven there with the Carisbury Field Club, and felt sure it must be a source of temptation if not guarded against. 'That one man should live in such a house is an impiety; he is led to go about like Nebuchadnezzar, saying: "Is not this great Babylon that I have builded?"'

'*He* never builded it,' said the clerk with some inconsequence; 'twere builded centuries ago. I've heard 'tis that old no one don't know *who* builded it. Your parents was Dissenters, Mr Joliffe, and never taught you the Catechism when you was young, but as for me, I order myself to my betters as I should, so long as they orders themselves to me. 'Tain't no use to say as how we're all level; you've only got to go to Mothers' Meetings, my old missus says, to see that. 'Tis no use looking for too much, nor eating salt with red herrings.'

'Well, well,' the other deprecated, 'I'm not blaming his lordship so much as them that lead him on.'

'Don't go for to blame the girl, neither, too hardly; there's faults on both sides. His grandfather didn't always toe the line, and there were some on her side didn't set too good an example, neither. I've seen many a queer thing in my time, and have got to think blood's blood, and forerunners more to blame than children. If there's drink in fathers, there'll be drink in sons and grandsons till 'tis worked out; and if there's wild love in the mothers, daughters'll likely sell their apples too. No, no, God-a-mighty never made us equal, and don't expect us all to be churchwardens. Some on us comes of virtuous forerunners, and are born with wings at the back of our shoulders like you'—and he gave a whimsical look at his listener's heavy figure—'to lift us up to the vaulting; and some on us our fathers fits out with lead soles to the bottom of our boots to keep us on the floor.'

Saturday afternoon was Lord Blandamer's hour, and for three Saturdays running Miss Joliffe deserted the Dorcas meeting in order to keep guard at home. It rejoiced the moral hearts of ill-natured and tale-bearing Miss Sharp and of lying and mischief-making Mrs Flint that the disreputable old woman had at least the decency not to show herself among her betters, but such defection was a sore trial to Miss

Joliffe. She told herself on each occasion that she *could* not make such a sacrifice again, and yet the love of Anastasia constrained her. To her niece she offered the patent excuse of being unwell, but the girl watched her with wonder and dismay chafe feverishly through the two hours, which had been immemorially consecrated to these meetings. The recurrence of a weekly pleasure, which seems so limitless in youth and middle age, becomes less inexhaustible as life turns towards sunset. Thirty takes lightly enough the forgoing of a Saturday reunion, the uncongenial spending of a Sunday; but seventy can see the end of the series, and grudges every unit of the total that remains.

For three Saturdays Miss Joliffe watched, and for three Saturdays no suspicious visitor appeared.

'We have seen nothing of Lord Blandamer lately,' she would remark at frequent intervals with as much indifference as the subject would allow.

'There is nothing to bring him here now that Mr Westray has gone. Why should he come?'

Why, indeed, and what difference would it make to her if he never came again? These were questions that Anastasia had discussed with herself, at every hour of every day of those blank three weeks. She had ample time for such foolish discussions, for such vain imaginings, for she was left much to herself, having no mind-companions either of her own age or of any other. She was one of those unfortunate persons whose education and instincts unfit them for their position. The diversions of youth had been denied her, the pleasure of dress or company had never been within her reach. For pastime she was turned back continually to her own thoughts, and an active imagination and much desultory reading had educated her in a school of romance, which found no counterpart in the life of Cullerne. She was proud at heart (and it is curious that those are often the proudest who in their neighbours' estimation have least cause for pride), but not conceited in manner in spite of Mr Joliffe's animadversion on the mincing of her words. Yet it was not her pride that had kept her from making friends, but merely the incompatibility of mental temperament, which builds the barrier not so much between education and ignorance, as between refinement and materialism, between romance and commonplace.

That barrier is so insurmountable that any attempt upon it must end in failure that is often pathetic from its very hopelessness; even the warmth of ardent affection has never yet succeeded in evolving a mental companionship from such discordant material. By kind dispensation of nature the breadth of the gulf, indeed, is hidden from those who cannot cross it. They know it is there, they have some inkling of the difference of view, but they think that love may build a bridge across, or that in time they may find some other access to the farther side. Sometimes they fancy that they are nearer to the goal, that they walk step and step with those they love; but this, alas! is not to be, because the mental sympathy, the touch of illumination that welds minds together, is wanting.

It was so with Miss Joliffe the elder—she longed to be near her niece, and was so very far away; she thought that they went hand in hand, when all the while a different mental outlook set them poles asunder. With all her thousand good honest qualities, she was absolutely alien to the girl; and Anastasia felt as if she was living among people of another nation, among people who did not understand her language, and she took refuge in silence.

The dulness of Cullerne had grown more oppressive to her in the last year. She longed for a life something wider, she longed for sympathy. She longed for what a tall and well-favoured maiden of her years most naturally desires, however much she may be ignorant of her desire; she longed for someone to admire her and to love her; she longed for someone about whom she could weave a romance.

The junior partner in Rose and Storey perhaps discerned her need, and tried to supply it. He paid her such odious compliments on the 'hang of her things', that she would never have entered the shop again, were it not that Bellevue Lodge was bound hand and foot to Rose and Storey, for they were undertakers as well as milliners; and besides the little affair of the bonnet, the expenses of Martin's funeral were still unsatisfied. There was a young dairy farmer, with a face like a red harvest moon, who stopped at her aunt's door on his way to market. He would sell Miss Joliffe eggs and butter at wholesale prices, and grinned in a most tiresome way whenever he caught sight of Anastasia. The Rector patronized her insufferably; and though old Mr Noot was kind, he treated her like a small child, and sometimes patted her cheek, which she felt to be disconcerting at eighteen.

And then the Prince of Romance appeared in Lord Blandamer. The moment that she first saw him on the doorstep that windy autumn afternoon, when yellow leaves were flying, she recognized him for a prince. The moment that he spoke to her she knew that he recognized her for a lady, and for this she felt unspeakably glad and grateful. Since then the wonder had grown. It grew all the faster from the hero's restraint. He had seen Anastasia but little, he spoke but little to her, he never gave her even a glance of interest, still less such glances as Westray launched at her so lavishly. And yet the wonder grew. He was so different from other men she had seen, so different from all the other people she had ever met. She could not have told how she knew this, and yet she knew. It must have been an atmosphere which followed him wherever he went—that penumbra with which the gods wrap heroes—which told her he was different.

The gambits of the great game of love are strangely limited, and there is little variation in the after-play. If it were not for the personal share we take, such doings would lack interest by reason of their monotony, by their too close resemblance to the primeval type. This is why the game seems dull enough to onlookers; they shock us with the callousness with which they are apt to regard our ecstasies. This is why the straightforward game palls sometimes on the players themselves after a while; and why they are led to take refuge from dulness in solving problems, in the tangled irregularities of the knight's move.

Anastasia would have smiled if she had been told that she had fallen in love; it might have been a thin smile, pale as winter's sunshine, but she would have smiled. It was *impossible* for her to fall in love, because she knew that kings no longer marry beggar-maids, and she was far too well brought up to fall in love, except as a preliminary to marriage. No heroine of Miss Austen would permit herself even to feel attraction to a quarter from which no offer of marriage was possible; therefore Anastasia could not have fallen in love. She certainly was not in the least in love, but it was true Lord Blandamer interested her. He interested her so much, in fact, as to be in her thoughts at all hours of the day; it was strange that no matter with what things her mind was occupied, his image should continually present itself. She wondered why this was; perhaps it was his power— she thought it was the feeling of his power, a very insolence of power that dominated all these little folk, and yet was most powerful in its restraint. She liked to think of the compact, close-knit body, of the curling, crisp, iron-grey hair, of the grey eyes, and of the hard clear-cut face. Yes, she liked the face because it *was* hard, because it had a resolute look in it that said he meant to go whither he wished to go.

There was no doubt she must have taken considerable interest in him, for she found herself dreading to pronounce his name even in the most ordinary conversation, because she felt it difficult to keep her voice at the dead level of indifference. She dreaded when others spoke of him, and yet there was no other subject that occupied her so much. And sometimes when they talked of him she had a curious feeling of jealousy, a feeling that no one had a right even to talk of him except herself, and she would smile to herself with a little scornful smile, because she thought that she knew more about him, could understand him better than them all. It was fortunate, perhaps, that the arbitrament of Cullerne conversation did not rest with Anastasia or there would have been but little talking at this time; for if it seemed preposterous that others should dare to discuss Lord Blandamer, it seemed equally preposterous that they should take an interest in discussing anything else.

She certainly was *not* in love; it was only the natural interest, she told herself, that anyone anyone with education and refinement must take in a strange and powerful character. Every detail about him interested her. There was a fascination in his voice, there was a melody in his low, clear voice that charmed, and made even trifling remarks seem important. Did he but say it was a rainy afternoon, did he but ask if Mr Westray were at home, there was such mystery in his tone that no rabbinical cabalist ever read more between the lines than did Miss Anastasia Joliffe. Even in her devotions thought wandered far from the pew where she and her aunt sat in Cullerne Church; she found her eyes looking for the sea-green and silver, for the nebuly coat in Abbot Vinnicomb's window; and from the clear light yellow of the aureole round John Baptist's head, fancy called up a whirl of faded lemon-coloured acacia leaves, that were in the air that day the hero first appeared.

Yet, if heart wavered, head stood firm. He should never know her interest in him; no word, no changing colour should ever betray her; he should never guess that agitation sometimes scarcely left her breath to make so short a rejoinder as 'Goodnight'.

For three Saturdays, then, Miss Joliffe the elder sat on guard at Bellevue Lodge; for three Saturday afternoons in succession, she sat and chafed as the hours of the Dorcas meeting came and went. But nothing happened; the heavens remained in their accustomed place, the minster tower stood firm, and then she knew that the churchwarden had been duped, that her own judgment had been right, that Lord Blandamer's only motive for coming to her house had been to see Mr Westray, and that now Mr Westray was gone Lord Blandamer would come no more. The fourth Saturday arrived; Miss Joliffe was brighter than her niece had seen her for a calendar month.

'I feel a good deal better, my dear, this afternoon,' she said; 'I think I shall be able to go to the Dorcas meeting. The room gets so close that I have avoided going of late, but I think I shall not feel it too much to-day. I will just change, and put on my bonnet; you will not mind staying at home while I am away, will you?' And so she went.

Anastasia sat in the window-seat of the lower room. The sash was open, for the spring days were lengthening, and a soft, sweet air was moving about sundown. She told herself that she was making a bodice; an open work-box stood beside her, and there was spread around just such a medley of patterns, linings, scissors, cotton-reels, and buttons as is required for the proper and ceremonious carrying on of 'work'. But she was not working. The bodice itself, the very cause and spring of all these preparations, lay on her lap, and there, too, had fallen her hands. She half sat, half lay back on the window-seat, roaming in fancy far away, while she drank in the breath of the spring, and watched a little patch of transparent yellow sky between the houses grow pinker and more golden, as the sunset went on.

Then a man came down the street and mounted the steps in front of Bellevue Lodge; but she did not see him, because he was walking in from the country, and so did not pass her window. It was the door-bell that first broke her dreams. She slid down from her perch, and hastened to let aunt in, for she had no doubt that it was Miss Joliffe who had come back from the meeting. The opening of the front-door was not a thing to be hurried through, for though there was little indeed in Bellevue Lodge to attract burglars, and though if burglars came they would surely select some approach other than the main entrance, yet Miss Joliffe insisted that when she was from home the door should be secured as if to stand a siege. So Anastasia drew the top bolt, and slipped the chain, and unlocked the lock. There was a little difficulty with the bottom bolt, and she had to cry out: 'I am sorry for keeping you waiting; this fastening *will* stick.' But it gave at last; she swung the heavy door back, and found herself face to face with Lord Blandamer.

Chapter 18

They stood face to face, and looked at one another for a second. Anyone seeing those two figures silhouetted against the yellow sunset sky might have taken them for cousins, or even for brother and sister. They were both dressed in black, were both dark, and of nearly the same height, for though the man was not short, the girl was very tall.

The pause that Anastasia made was due to surprise. A little while ago it would have been a natural thing enough to open the door and find Lord Blandamer, but the month that had elapsed since last he came to Bellevue Lodge had changed the position. It seemed to her that she stood before him confessed, that he must know that all these weeks she had been thinking of him, had been wondering why he did not come, had been longing for him to come, that he must know the pleasure which filled her now because he was come back again. And if he knew all this, she, too, had learnt to know something, had learnt to know how great a portion of her thoughts he filled. This eating of the tree of knowledge had abashed her, for now her soul stood before her naked. Did it so stand naked before him too? She was shocked that she should feel this attraction where there could be no thought of marriage; she thought that she should die if he should ever guess that one so lowly had gazed upon the sun and been dazzled.

The pause that Lord Blandamer made was not due to surprise, for he knew quite well that it would be Anastasia who opened the door. It was rather that pause which a man makes who has undertaken a difficult business, and hesitates for a moment when it comes to the touch. She cast her eyes down to the ground; he looked full at her, looked at her from head to foot, and knew that his resolution was strong enough to carry to a conclusion the affair on which he had come. She spoke first.

'I am sorry my aunt is not at home,' and kept her right hand on the edge of the open door, feeling grateful for any support. As the words came out she was relieved to find that it was indeed she herself who was speaking, that it was her own voice, and that her voice sounded much as usual.

'I am sorry she is not in,' he said, and he, too, spoke after all in just those same low, clear tones to which she was accustomed—'I am sorry she is not in, but it was *you* that I came to see.'

She said nothing; her heart beat so fast that she could not have spoken even in monosyllables. She did not move, but kept her hand still on the edge of the door, feeling afraid lest she should fall if she let it go.

'I have something I should like to say to you; may I come in?'

She hesitated for a moment, as he knew that she would hesitate, and then let him in, as he knew that she would let him in. He shut the heavy front-door behind them, and there was no talk now of turning locks or shooting bolts; the house was left at the mercy of any burglars who might happen to be thereabout.

Anastasia led the way. She did not take him into Mr Sharnall's old room, partly because she had left half-finished clothes lying there, and partly from the more romantic reflection that it was in Westray's room that they had met before. They walked through the hall and up the stairs, she going first and he following, and she was glad of the temporary respite which the long flights secured her. They entered the room, and again he shut the door behind them. There was no fire, and the window was open, but she felt as if she were in a fiery furnace. He saw her distress, but made as if he saw nothing, and pitied her for the agitation which he caused. For the past six months Anastasia had concealed her feelings so very well that he had read them like a book. He had watched the development of the plot without pride, or pleasure of success, without sardonic amusement, without remorse; with some dislike for a rôle which force of circumstances imposed on him, but with an unwavering resolve to walk the way which he had set before him. He knew the exact point which the action of the play had reached, he knew that Anastasia would grant whatever he asked of her.

They were standing face to face again. To the girl it all seemed a dream; she did not know whether she was waking or sleeping; she did not know whether she was in the body or out of the body. It was all a dream, but it was a delightful dream; there was no of reflection now, no anxiety, no regard for past or future, only utter absorption in the present moment. She was with the man who had possessed her thoughts for a month past; he had come back to her. She had not to consider whether she should ever see him again; he was with her now. She had not to think whether he was there for good or evil, she had lost all volition in the will of the man who stood before her; she was the slave of his ring, rejoicing in her slavery, and ready to do his bidding as all the other slaves of that ring.

He was sorry for the feelings which he had aroused, sorry for the affection he had stirred, sorry for the very love of himself that he saw written in her face. He took her hand in his, and his touch filled her with an exquisite content; her hand lay in his neither lifelessly nor entirely passively, yet only lightly returning the light pressure of his fingers. To her the situation was the supreme moment of a life; to him it was passionless as the betrothal piece in a Flemish window.

'Anastasia,' he said, 'you guess what it is I have to tell you; you guess what it is I have to ask you.'

She heard him speaking, and his voice was as delightful music in her delightful dream; she knew that he was going to ask something of her, and she knew that she would give him anything and all that he asked.

'I know that you love me,' he went on, with an inversion of the due order of the proposition, and an assumption that would have been intolerable in anyone else, 'and you know that I love you dearly.' It was a proper compliment to her perspicuity that she should know already that he loved her, but his mind smiled as he thought how insufficient sometimes are the bases of knowledge. 'I love you dearly, and am come to ask you to be my wife.'

She heard what he said, and understood it; she had been prepared for his asking anything save this one thing that he had asked. The surprise of it overwhelmed her, the joy of it stunned her; she could neither speak nor move. He saw that she was powerless and speechless, and drew her closer to him. There was none of the impetuous eagerness of a lover in the action; he drew her gently towards him because it seemed appropriate to the occasion that he should do so. She lay for a minute in his arms, her head bent down and her face hidden, while he looked not so much at her as above her. His eyes wandered over the mass of her dark-brown wavy hair that Mrs Flint said was not wavy by nature, but crimped to make her look like a Blandamer, and so bolster up her father's nonsensical pretensions. His eyes took full account of that wave and the silken fineness of her dark-brown hair, and then looked vaguely out beyond till they fell on the great flower-picture that hung on the opposite wall.

The painting had devolved upon Westray on Mr Sharnall's death, but he had not yet removed it, and Lord Blandamer's eyes rested on it now so fixedly, that he seemed to be thinking more of the trashy flowers and of the wriggling caterpillar, than of the girl in his arms. His mind came back to the exigencies of the situation.

'Will you marry me, Anastasia—will you marry me, dear Anstice?' The home name seemed to add a touch of endearment, and he used it advisedly. 'Anstice, will you let me make you my wife?'

She said nothing, but threw her arms about his neck, and raised her face a little for the first time. It was an assent that would have contented any man, and to Lord Blandamer it came as a matter of course; he had never for a moment doubted her acceptance of his offer. If she had raised her face to be kissed, her expectation was gratified; he kissed her indeed, but only lightly on the brow, as actor may kiss actress on the stage. If anyone had been there to see, they would have known from his eyes that his thoughts were far from his body, that they were busied with somebody or something, that seemed to him of more importance than the particular action in which he was now engaged. But Anastasia saw nothing; she only knew that he had asked her to marry him, and that she was in his arms.

He waited a moment, as if wondering how long the present position would continue, and what was the next step to take; but the girl was the first to relieve the tension. The wildest intoxication of the first surprise was passing off, and with returning capacity for reflection a doubt had arisen that flung a shadow like a cloud upon her joy. She disengaged herself from his arms that strove in orthodox manner to retain her.

'Don't,' she said—'don't. We have been too rash. I know what you have asked me. I shall remember it always, and love you for it to my dying day, but it cannot be. There are things you must know before you ask me. I do not think you would ask me if you knew all.'

For the first time he seemed a little more in earnest, a little more like a man living life, a little less like a man rehearsing a part that he had got by heart. This was an unexpected piece of action, an episode that was not in his acting edition, that put him for the moment at a loss; though he knew it could not in any way affect the main issues of the play. He expostulated, he tried to take her hand again.

'Tell me what it is, child, that is troubling you,' he said; 'there can be nothing, nothing under heaven that could make me wish to unsay what I have said, nothing that could make us wish to undo what we have done. Nothing can rob me now of the knowledge that you love me. Tell me what it is.'

'I cannot tell you,' she answered him. 'It is something I cannot tell; don't ask me. I will write it. Leave me now—please leave me; no one shall know that you have been here, no one must know what passed between us.'

Miss Joliffe came back from the Dorcas meeting a little downhearted and out of humour. Things had not gone so smoothly as usual. No one had inquired after her health, though she had missed three meetings in succession; people had received her little compliments and cheery small-talk with the driest of negatives or affirmatives; she had an uncomfortable feeling that she was being cold-shouldered. That high moralist, Mrs Flint, edged her chair away from the poor lady of set purpose, and Miss Joliffe found herself at last left isolated from all, except Mrs Purlin, the builder's wife, who was far too fat and lethargic to be anything but ignorantly good-natured. Then, in a fit of pained abstraction, Miss Joliffe had made such a bad calculation as entirely to spoil a flannel petticoat with a rheumatic belt and camphor pockets, which she had looked upon as something of a *chef d'œuvre*.

But when she got back to Bellevue Lodge her vexation vanished, and was entirely absorbed in solicitude for her niece.

Anstice was unwell, Anstice was quite ill, quite flushed, and complaining of headache. If Miss Joliffe had feigned indisposition for three Saturdays as an excuse for not leaving the house, Anastasia had little need for simulation on this fourth Saturday. She was, in effect, so dazed by the event which had happened, and so preoccupied by her own thoughts, that she could scarcely return coherent replies to her aunt's questions. Miss Joliffe had rung and received no answer, had discovered that the front-door was unlocked, and had at last found Anastasia sitting forlorn in Mr Westray's room with the window open. A chill was indicated, and Miss Joliffe put her to bed at once.

Bed is a first aid that even ambulance classes have not entirely taught us to dispense with; it is, moreover, a poor man's remedy, being exceedingly cheap, if, indeed, the poor man is rich enough to have a bed at all. Had Anastasia been Miss Bulteel, or even Mrs Parkyn, or lying and mischief-making Mrs Flint, Dr Ennefer would have been summoned forthwith; but being only Anastasia, and having the vision of debt before her eyes, she prevailed on her aunt to wait to see what the night brought forth, before sending for the doctor. Meanwhile Dr Bed, infinitely cleverest and infinitely safest of physicians, was called in, and with him was associated that excellent general practitioner Dr Wait. Hot flannels, hot bottles, hot possets, and a bedroom fire were exhibited, and when at nine o'clock Miss Joliffe kissed her niece and retired for the night, she by no means despaired of the patient's speedy recovery from so sudden and unaccountable an attack.

Anastasia was alone; what a relief to be alone again, though she felt that such a thought was treasonable and unkind to the warm old heart that had just left her, to that warm old heart which yearned so deeply to her, but with which she had not shared her story! She was alone, and she lay a little while in quiet content looking at the fire through the iron bars at the foot of her bedstead. It was the first bedroom fire she had had for two years, and she enjoyed the luxury with a pleasure proportionate to its rarity. She was not sleepy, but grew gradually more composed, and was able to reflect on the letter which she had promised to write. It would be difficult, and she assured herself with much vigour that it must raise insurmountable obstacles, that they were obstacles which one in Lord Blandamer's position must admit to be quite insurmountable. Yes, in this letter she would write the colophon of so wondrous a romance, the epilogue of so amazing a tragedy. But it was her conscience that demanded the sacrifice, and she took the more pleasure in making it, because she felt at heart that the pound of flesh might never really after all be cut.

How thoroughly do we enjoy these sacrifices to conscience, these followings of honour's code severe, when we know that none will be mean enough to take us at our word! To what easilygained heights of morality does it raise us to protest that we never could accept the gift that will eventually be forced into our reluctant hands, to insist that we regard as the shortest of loans the money which we never shall be called upon to repay. It was something of the same sort with Anastasia. She told herself that by her letter she would give the death-blow to her love, and perhaps believed what she told, yet all the while kept hope hidden at the bottom of the box, even as in the most real perils of a dream we sometimes are supported by the sub-waking sense that we *are* dreaming.

A little later Anastasia was sitting before her bedroom fire writing. It has a magic of its own—the bedroom fire. Not such a one as night by night warms hothouse bedrooms of the rich, but that which burns but once or twice a year. How the coals glow between the bars, how the red light shimmers on the black-lead bricks, how the posset steams upon the hob! Milk or tea, cocoa or coffee, poor commonplace liquids, are they not transmuted in the alembic of a bedroom fire, till they become nepenthe for a heartache or a philtre for romance? Ah, the romance of it, when youth forestalls tomorrow's conquest, when middle life forgets that yesterday is past for ever, when even querulous old age thinks it may still have its 'honour and its toil'!

An old blue cloak, which served the turn of dressing-gown, had fallen apart in the exigencies of composition, and showed underlying tracts of white nightgown. Below, the fire-light fell on bare feet resting on the edge of the brass fender till the heat made her curl up her toes, and above, the fire-light contoured certain generous curves. The roundness and the bloom of maidenhood was upon her, that bloom so transient, so irreplaceable, that renders any attempt to simulate it so profoundly ludicrous. The mass of dark hair, which turned lying-and-mischief-making Mrs Flint so envious, was gathered behind with a bow of black ribbon, and hung loosely over the back of her chair. She sat there writing and rewriting, erasing, blotting, tearing up, till the night was far spent, till she feared that the modest resources of the *papeterie* would be exhausted before toil came to fruition.

It was finished at last, and if it was a little formal or high-flown, or stilted, is not a certain formality postulated on momentous occasions? Who would write that he was 'delighted' to accept a bishopric? Who would go to a levée in a straw hat?

Dear Lord Blandamer [the letter ran],

I do not know how I ought to write to you, for I have little experience of life to guide me. I thank you with all my heart for what you have told me. I am glad to think of it, and I always shall be. I believe there must be many strong reasons why you should not think of marrying me, yet if there are, you must know them far better than I, and you have disregarded them. But there is one reason that you cannot know, for it is known to very few; I hope it is known only to some of our own relations. Perhaps I ought not to write of it at all, but I have no one to advise me. I mean what is right, and if I am doing wrong you will forgive me, will you not? and burn this letter when you have read it.

I have no right to the name I am called by; my cousins in the Market Place think we should use some other, but we do not even know what our real name would be. When my grandmother married old Mr Joliffe, she had already a son two or three years old. This son was my father, and Mr Joliffe adopted him; but my grandmother had no right to any but her maiden name. We never knew what that was, though my father tried all his life to find it out, and thought he was very near finding out when he fell into his last illness. We think his head must have been affected, for he used to say strange things about his parentage. Perhaps the thought of this disgrace troubled him, as it has often troubled me, though I never thought it would trouble me so much as now.

I have not told my aunt about what you have said to me, and no one else shall ever know it, but it will be the sweetest memory to me of all my life.

Your very sincere Friend,

ANASTASIA JOLIFFE.

It was finished at last; she had slain all her hopes, she had slain her love. He would never marry her, he would never come near her again; but she had unburdened herself of her secret, and she could not have married him with that secret untold. It was three o'clock when she crept back again to bed. The fire had gone out, she was very cold, and she was glad to get back to her bed. Then Nature came to her aid and sent her kindly sleep, and if her sleep was not dreamless, she dreamt of dresses, and horses, and carriages, of men-servants, and maid-servants, of Lady Blandamer's great house of Fording, and of Lady Blandamer's husband.

Lord Blandamer also sat up very late that night. As he read before another bedroom fire he turned the pages of his book with the utmost regularity; his cigar never once went out. There was nothing to show that his thoughts wandered, nothing to show that his mind was in any way preoccupied. He was reading Eugenid's 'Aristeia' of the pagans martyred under Honorius; and weighed the pros and cons of the arguments as dispassionately as if the events of the afternoon had never taken place, as if there had been no such person as Anastasia Joliffe in the world.

Anastasia's letter reached him the next day at lunch, but he finished his meal before opening it. Yet he must have known whence it came, for there was a bold 'Bellevue Lodge' embossed in red on the flap of the envelope. Martin Joliffe had ordered stamped paper and envelopes years ago, because he said that people of whom he made genealogical inquiries paid more attention to stamped than to plain paper-it was a credential of respectability. In Cullerne this had been looked upon as a gross instance of his extravagance. Mrs Bulteel and Canon Parkyn alone could use headed paper with propriety, and even the rectory only printed, and did not emboss. Martin had exhausted his supply years ago, and never ordered a second batch, because the first was still unpaid for; but Anastasia kept by her half a dozen of these fateful envelopes. She had purloined them when she was a girl at school, and to her they were still a cherished remnant of gentility, the pallium under which so many of us would fain hide our rags. She had used one on this momentous occasion; it seemed a fitting cover for despatches to Fording, and might divert attention from the straw paper on which her letter was written.

Lord Blandamer had seen the Bellevue Lodge, had divined the genesis of the embossed inscription, had unravelled all Anastasia's thoughts in using it, yet let the letter lie till he had finished lunch. When he read it afterwards he criticized it as he might the composition of a stranger, as a document with which he had no very close concern. Yet he appreciated the effort which it must have cost the girl to write it, was touched by her words, and felt a certain grave compassion for her. But it was the strange juggle of circumstance, the Sophoclean irony of a position of which he alone held the key, that most impressed themselves upon his mood.

He ordered his horse, and took the road to Cullerne, but his agent met him before he had passed the first lodge, and asked some further instructions for the planting at the top of the park. So he turned and rode up to the great belt of beeches which was then being planted, and was so long engaged there that dusk forced him to abandon his journey to the town. He rode back to Fording at a foot-pace, choosing devious paths, and enjoying the sunset in the autumn woods. He would write to Anastasia, and put off his visit till the next day.

With him there was no such wholesale destruction of writing paper as had attended Anastasia's efforts on the previous night. One single sheet saw his letter begun and ended, a quarter of an hour sufficed for committing his sentiments very neatly to writing; he flung off his sentences '$ηδίως$,* as easily as Odysseus tossed his heavy stone beyond all the marks of the Phæacians:

My Dearest Child,

I need not speak now of the weary hours of suspense which I passed in waiting for your letter. They are over, and all is sunshine after

* gushing

the clouds. I need not tell you how my heart beat when I saw an envelope with your address, nor how eagerly my fingers tore it open, for now all is happiness. Thank you, a thousand times thank you for your letter; it is like you, all candour, all kindness, and all truth. Put aside your scruples; everything that you say is not a featherweight in the balance; do not trouble about your name in the past, for you will have a new name in the future. It is not I, but you, who overlook obstacles, for have you not overlooked all the years that lie between your age and mine? I have but a moment to scribble these lines; you must forgive their weakness, and take for said all that should be said. I shall be with you to-morrow morning, and till then am, in all love and devotion,

Yours,

BLANDAMER.

He did not even read it through before he sealed it up, for he was in a hurry to get back to Eugenid and to the 'Aristeia' of the heathens martyred under Honorius.

Two days later, Miss Joliffe put on her Sunday mantle and bonnet in the middle of the week, and went down to the Market Place to call on her cousin the pork-butcher. Her attire at once attracted attention. The only justification for such extravagance would be some parish function or festivity, and nothing of that sort could be going on without the knowledge of the churchwarden's family. Nor was it only the things which she wore, but the manner in which she wore them, that was so remarkable. As she entered the parlour at the back of the shop, where the pork-butcher's lady and daughters were sitting, they thought that they had never seen their cousin look so well dressed. She had lost the pinched, perplexed, down-trodden air which had overcast her later years; there was in her face a serenity and content which communicated itself in some mysterious way even to her apparel.

'Cousin Euphemia looks quite respectable this morning,' whispered the younger to the elder daughter; and they had to examine her closely before they convinced themselves that only a piece of mauve ribbon in her bonnet was new, and that the coat and dress were just the same as they had seen every Sunday for two years past.

With 'nods and becks and wreathed smiles' Miss Euphemia seated herself. 'I have just popped in,' she began, and the very phrase had something in it so light and flippant that her listeners started—'I have just popped in for a minute to tell you some news. You have always been particular, my dears, that no one except your branch had a right to the name of Joliffe in this town. You can't deny, Maria,' she said deprecatingly to the churchwarden's wife, 'that you have always held out that you were the real Joliffes, and been a little sore with me and Anstice for calling ourselves by what we thought we had a right to. Well, now there will be one less outside your family to use the name of Joliffe, for Anstice is going to give it up. Somebody has offered to find another name for her.'

The real Joliffes exchanged glances, and thought of the junior partner in the drapery shop, who had affirmed with an oath that Anastasia Joliffe did as much justice to his goods as any girl in Cullerne; and thought again of the young farmer who was known for certain to let Miss Euphemia have eggs at a penny cheaper than anyone else.

'Yes, Anstice is going to change her name, so that will be one grievance the less. And another thing that will make matters straighter between us, Maria. I can promise the little bit of silver shall never go out of the family. You know what I mean—the teapot and the spoons marked with "J" that you've always claimed for yours by right. I shall leave them all back to you when my time comes; Anstice will never want such odds and ends in the station to which she's called now.'

The real Joliffes looked at each other again, and thought of young Bulteel, who had helped Anastasia with the gas-standards when the minster was decorated at Christmas. Or was it possible that her affected voice and fine lady airs had after all caught Mr Westray, that rather good-looking and interesting young man, on whom both the churchwarden's daughters were not without hopes of making an impression?

Miss Joliffe enjoyed their curiosity; she was in a teasing and mischievous mood, to which she had been a stranger for thirty years.

'Yes,' she said, 'I am one that likes to own up to it when I make a mistake, and I will state I *have* made a mistake. I suppose I must take to spectacles; it seems I cannot see things that are going on under my very eyes—no, not even when they are pointed out to me. I've come round to tell you, Maria, one and all, that I was completely mistaken when I told the churchwarden that it was not on Anstice's account that Lord Blandamer had been visiting at Bellevue Lodge. It seems it was just for that he came, and the proof of it is he's going to marry her. In three weeks' time she will be Lady Blandamer, and if you want to say good-bye to her you'd better come back and have tea with me now, for she's packed her box, and is off to London to-morrow. Mrs Howard, who keeps the school in Carisbury where Anstice went in dear Martin's lifetime, will meet her and take charge of her, and get her trousseau.

Lord Blandamer has arranged it all, and he is going to marry Anstice and take her for a long tour on the Continent, and I'm sure I don't know where else.'

It was all true. Lord Blandamer made no secret of the matter, and his engagement to Anastasia, only child of the late Martin Joliffe, Esquire, of Cullerne, was duly announced in the London papers. It was natural that Westray should have known vacillation and misgivings before he made up his mind to offer marriage. It is with a man whose family or position are not strong enough to bear any extra strain, that public opinion plays so large a part in such circumstances. If he marries beneath him he falls to the wife's level, because he has no margin of resource to raise her to his own. With Lord Blandamer it was different: his reliance upon himself was so great, that he seemed to enjoy, rather than not, the flinging down of a gauntlet to the public in this marriage.

Bellevue Lodge became a centre of attraction. The ladies who had contemned a lodging-house keeper's daughter courted the betrothed of a peer. From themselves they did not disguise the motive for this change, they did not even attempt to find an excuse in public. They simply executed their *volte face* simultaneously and with most commendable regularity, and felt no more reluctance or shame in the process than a cat feels in following the man who carries its meat. If they were disappointed in not seeing Anastasia herself (for she left for London almost immediately after the engagement was made public), they were in some measure compensated by the extreme readiness of Miss Euphemia to discuss the matter in all its bearings. Each and every detail was conscientiously considered and enlarged upon, from the buttons on Lord Blandamer's boots to the engagement-ring on Anastasia's finger; and Miss Joliffe was never tired of explaining that this last had an emerald—'A very large emerald, my dear, surrounded by diamonds, green and white being the colours of his lordship's shield, what they call the nebuly coat, you know.'

A variety of wedding gifts found their way to Bellevue Lodge. 'Great events, such as marriages and deaths, certainly do call forth the sympathy of our neighbours in a wonderful way,' Miss Joliffe said, with all the seriousness of an innocent belief in the general goodness of mankind. 'Till Anstice was engaged, I never knew, I am sure, how many friends I had in Cullerne.' She showed 'the presents' to successive callers, who examined them with the more interest because they had already seen most of them in the shop-windows of Cullerne, and so were able to appreciate the exact monetary outay with which their acquaintances thought it prudent to conciliate the Fording interest.

Every form of useless ugliness was amply represented among them—vulgarity masqueraded as taste, niggardliness figured as generosity—and if Miss Joliffe was proud of them as she forwarded them from Cullerne, Anastasia was heartily ashamed of them when they reached her in London.

'We must let bygones be bygones,' said Mrs Parkyn to her husband with truly Christian forbearance, 'and if this young man's choice has not fallen exactly where we could have wished, we must remember, after all that he *is* Lord Blandamer, and make the best of the lady for his sake. We must give her a present; in your position as Rector you could not afford to be left out. Everyone, I hear, is giving something.'

'Well, don't let it be anything extravagant,' he said, laying down his paper, for his interest was aroused by any question of expense. 'A too costly gift would be quite out of place under the circumstances. It should be rather an expression of good-will to Lord Blandamer than anything of much intrinsic value.'

'Of course, of course. You may trust me not to do anything foolish. I have my eye on just the thing. There is a beautiful set of four salt-cellars with their spoons at Laverick's, in a case lined with puffed satin. They only cost thirty-three shillings, and look worth at least three pounds.'

Chapter 19

The wedding was quiet, and there being no newspapers at that time to take such matters for their province, Cullerne curiosity had to be contented with the bare announcement: 'At St. Agatha's-at-Bow, Horatio Sebastian Fynes, Lord Blandamer, to Anastasia, only child of the late Martin Joliffe, of Cullerne Wharfe.' Mrs Bulteel had been heard to say that she could not allow dear Lord Blandamer to be married without her being there. Canon Parkyn and Mrs Parkyn felt that their presence also was required *ex-officio*, and Clerk Janaway averred with some redundancies of expletive that he, too, 'must see 'em turned off.' He hadn't been to London for twenty year. If 'twere to cost a sovereign, why, 'twas a poor heart that never made merry, and he would never live to see another Lord Blandamer married. Yet none of them went, for time and place were not revealed.

But Miss Joliffe was there, and on her return to Cullerne she held several receptions at Bellevue Lodge, at which only the wedding and the events connected with it were discussed. She was vested for these functions in a new dress of coffee-coloured silk, and what with a tea-urn hissing in Mr Sharnall's room, and muffins, toast, and sweet-cakes, there were such goings-on in the house, as had not been seen since the last coach rolled away from the old Hand of God thirty years before. The company were very gracious and even affectionate, and Miss Joliffe, in the exhilaration of the occasion, forgot all those cold-shoulderings and askance looks which had grieved her at a certain Dorcas meeting only a few weeks before.

At these reunions many important particulars transpired. The wedding had been celebrated early in the morning at the special instance of the bride; only Mrs Howard and Miss Euphemia herself were present. Anstice had worn a travelling dress of dark-green cloth, so that she might go straight from the church to the station. 'And, my dears,' she said, with a glance of all-embracing benevolence, 'she looked a perfect young peeress.'

The kind and appreciative audience, who had all been expecting and hoping for the past six weeks, that some bolt might fall from the blue to rob Anastasia of her triumph, were so astonished at the wedding having finally taken place that they could not muster a sneer among them. Only lying-and-mischief-making Mrs Flint found courage for a sniff, and muttered something to her next neighbour about there being such things as mock marriages.

The honeymoon was much extended. Lord and Lady Blandamer went first to the Italian lakes, and thence, working their way home by Munich, Nuremberg, and the Rhine, travelled by such easy stages that autumn had set in when they reached Paris. There they wintered, and there in the spring was born a son and heir to all the Blandamer estates. The news caused much rejoicing in the domain; and when it was announced that the family were returning to Cullerne, it was decided to celebrate the event by ringing a peal from the tower of St Sepulchre's. The proposal originated with Canon Parkyn.

'It is a graceful compliment,' he said, 'to the nobleman to whose munificence the restoration is so largely due. We must show him how much stronger we have made our old tower, eh, Mr Westray? We must get the Carisbury ringers over to teach Cullerne people how such things should be done. Sir George will have to stand out of his fees longer than ever, if he is to wait till the tower tumbles down now. Eh, eh?'

'Ah, I do so dote on these old customs,' assented his wife. 'It is so delightful, a merry peal. I do think these good old customs should always be kept up.' It was the cheapness of the entertainment that particularly appealed to her. 'But is it necessary, my dear,' she demurred, 'to bring the ringers over from Carisbury? They are a sad drunken lot. I am sure there must be plenty of young men in Cullerne, who would delight to help ring the bells on such an occasion.'

But Westray would have none of it. It was true, he said, that the tie-rods were fixed, and the tower that much the stronger; but he could countenance no ringing till the great south-east pier had been properly under-pinned.

His remonstrances found little favour. Lord Blandamer would think it so ungracious. Lady Blandamer, to be sure, counted for very little; it was ridiculous, in fact, to think of ringing the minster bells for a landlady's niece, but Lord Blandamer would certainly be offended.

'I call that clerk of the works a vain young upstart,' Mrs Parkyn said to her husband. 'I cannot think how you keep your temper with such a popinjay. I hope you will not allow yourself to be put upon again. You are so sweet-tempered and forbearing, that *everyone* takes advantage of you.'

So she stirred him up till he assured her with considerable boldness that he was *not* a man to be dictated to; the bells *should* be rung, and he would get Sir George's views to fortify his own. Then Sir George wrote one of those cheery little notes for which he was famous, with a proper admixture of indifferent puns and a classic conceit: that when Gratitude was climbing the temple steps to lay an offering on Hymen's altar, Prudence must wait silent at the base till she came down.

Sir George should have been a doctor, his friends said; his manner was always so genial and reassuring. So having turned these happy phrases, and being overwhelmed with the grinding pressure of a great practice, he dismissed the tower of St Sepulchre from his mind, and left Rector and ringers to their own devices.

Thus on an autumn afternoon there was a sound in Cullerne that few of the inhabitants had ever heard, and the little town stopped its business to listen to the sweetest peal in all the West Country. How they swung and rung and sung together, the little bells and the great bells, from Beata Maria, the sweet silver-voiced treble, to Taylor John, the deep-voiced tenor, that the Guild of Merchant Taylors had given three hundred years ago. There was a charm in the air like the singing of innumerable birds; people flung up their windows to listen, people stood in the shop-doors to listen, and the melody went floating away over the salt-marshes, till the fishermen taking up their lobster-pots paused in sheer wonder at a music that they had never heard before.

It seemed as if the very bells were glad to break their long repose; they sang together like the morning stars, they shouted together like the sons of God for joy. They remembered the times that were gone, and how they had rung when Abbot Harpingdon was given his red hat, and rung again when Henry defended the Faith by suppressing the Abbey, and again when Mary defended the Faith by restoring the Mass, and again when Queen Bess was given a pair of embroidered gloves as she passed through the Market Place on her way to Fording. They remembered the long counterchange of life and death that had passed under the red roofs at their feet, they remembered innumerable births and marriages and funerals of old time; they sang together like the morning stars, they shouted together like the sons of God for joy, they shouted for joy.

The Carisbury ringers came over after all; and Mrs Parkyn bore their advent with less misgiving, in the hope that directly Lord Blandamer heard of the honour that was done him, he would send a handsome donation for the ringers as he had already sent to the workhouse, and the old folk, and the school-children of Cullerne. The ropes and the cage, and the pins and the wheels, had all been carefully overhauled; and when the day came, the ringers stood to their work like men, and rang a full peal of grandsire triples in two hours and fifty-nine minutes.

There was a little cask of Bulteel's brightest tenpenny that some magician's arm had conjured up through the well-hope in the belfry floor: and Clerk Janaway, for all he was teetotaler, eyed the foaming pots wistfully as he passed them round after the work was done.

'Well,' he said, 'there weren't no int'rupted peal this time, were there? These here old bells never had a finer set of ringing-men under them, and I lay you never had a finer set of bells above your heads, my lads; now did 'ee? I've heard the bells swung many a time in Carisbury tower, and heard 'em when the Queen was set upon her throne, but, lor'! they arn't so deeplike nor yet so sweet as this here old ring. Perhaps they've grow'd the sweeter for lying by a bit, like port in the cellars of the Blandamer Arms, though I've heard Dr Ennefer say some of it was turned so like sherry, that no man living couldn't tell the difference.'

Westray had bowed like a loyal subaltern to the verdict of his Chief. Sir George's decision that the bells might safely be rung lifted the responsibility from the young man's shoulders, but not the anxiety from his mind. He never left the church while the peal was ringing.

First he was in the bell-chamber steadying himself by the beams of the cage, while he marked the wide-mouthed bells now open heavenwards, now turn back with a rush into the darkness below. Then he crept deafened with the clangour down the stairs into the belfry, and sat on the sill of a window, watching the ringers rise and fall at their work. He felt the tower sway restlessly under the stress of the swinging metal, but there was nothing unusual in the motion; there was no falling of mortar, nothing to attract any special attention. Then he went down into the church, and up again into the organ-loft, whence he could see the wide bow of that late Norman arch which spanned the south transept.

Above the arch ran up into the lantern the old fissure, zigzag like a baleful lightning flash, that had given him so much anxiety. The day was overcast, and heavy masses of cloud drifting across the sky darkened the church. But where the shadows hung heaviest, under a stone gallery passage that ran round the inside of the lantern, could be traced one of those heavy tie-rods with which the tower had recently been strengthened. Westray was glad to think that the ties were there; he hoped that they might indeed support the strain which this bell-ringing was bringing on the tower; he hoped that Sir George was right, and that he, Westray, was wrong. Yet he had pasted a strip of paper across the crack, so that by tearing it might give warning if any serious movement was taking place.

As he leant over the screen of the organ-loft, he thought of that afternoon when he had first seen signs of the arch moving, of that afternoon when the organist was playing 'Sharnall in D flat'. How much had happened since then! He thought of that scene which had happened in this very loft, of Sharnall's end, of the strange accident that had terminated a sad life on that wild night. What a strange accident it was, what a strange thing that Sharnall should have been haunted by that wandering fancy of a man following him with a hammer, and then have been found in this very loft, with the desperate wound on him that the pedal-note had dealt! How much had happened—his own proposal to Anastasia, his refusal, and now that event for which the bells were ringing! How quickly the scenes changed! What a creature of an hour was he, was every man, in face of these grim walls that had stood enduring, immutable, for generation after generation, for age after age! And then he smiled as he thought that these eternal realities of stone were all created by ephemeral man; that he, ephemeral man, was even now busied with schemes for their support, with anxieties lest they should fall and grind to powder all below.

The bells sounded fainter and far off inside the church. As they reached his ears through the heavy stone roof they were more harmonious, all harshness was softened; the *sordino* of the vaulting produced the effect of a muffled peal. He could hear deep-voiced Taylor John go striding through his singing comrades in the intricacies of the Treble Bob Triples, and yet there was another voice in Westray's ears that made itself heard even above the booming of the tenor bell. It was the cry of the tower arches, the small still voice that had haunted him ever since he had been at Cullerne. 'The arch never sleeps,' they said— 'the arch never sleeps;' and again, 'They have bound on us a burden too heavy to be borne; but we are shifting it. The arch never sleeps.'

The ringers were approaching the end; they had been at their work for near three hours, the 5,040 changes were almost finished. Westray went down from the organ-loft, and as he walked through the church the very last change was rung. Before the hum and mutter had died out of the air, and while the red-faced ringers in the belfry were quaffing their tankards, the architect had made his way to the scaffolding, and stood face to face with the zigzag crack. He looked at it carefully, as a doctor might examine a wound; he thrust his hand like Thomas into the dark fissure. No, there was no change; the paper strip was unbroken, the tie-rods had done their work nobly. Sir George had been quite right after all.

And as he looked there was the very faintest noise heard—a whisper, a mutter, a noise so slight that it might have passed a hundred times unnoticed. But to the architect's ear it spoke as loudly as a thunderclap. He knew exactly what it was and whence it came; and looking at the crack, saw that the broad paper strip was torn half-way across. It was a small affair; the paper strip was not quite parted, it was only torn half-way through. Though Westray watched for an hour, no further change took place. The ringers had left the tower, the little town had resumed its business. Clerk Janaway was walking across the church, when he saw the architect leaning against a cross-pole of the scaffolding, on the platform high up under the arch of the south transept.

'I'm just a-locking up,' he called out. 'You've got your own key, sir, no doubt?'

Westray gave an almost imperceptible nod.

'Well, we haven't brought the tower down this time,' the clerk went on. But Westray made no answer; his eyes were fixed on the little half-torn strip of paper, and he had no thought for anything else. A minute later the old man stood beside him on the platform, puffing after the ladders that he had climbed. 'No int'rupted peal this time,' he said; 'we've fair beat the neb'ly coat at last. Lord Blandamer back, and an heir to keep the family going. Looks as if the neb'ly coat was losing a bit of his sting, don't it?' But Westray was moody, and said nothing. 'Why, what's the matter? You bain't took bad, be you?'

'Don't bother me now,' the architect said sharply. 'I wish to Heaven the peal *had* been interrupted. I wish your bells had never been rung. Look there'—and he pointed at the strip of paper.

The clerk went closer to the crack, and looked hard at the silent witness. 'Lor' bless you! that ain't nothing,' he said; ''tis only just the jarring of the bells done that. You don't expect a mushet of paper to stand as firm as an anvilstone, when Taylor John's a-swinging up aloft.'

'Look you,' Westray said; 'you were in church this morning. Do you remember the lesson about the prophet sending his servant up to the top of a hill, to look at the sea? The man went up ever so many times and saw nothing. Last he saw a little cloud like a man's hand rising out of the sea, and after that the heaven grew black, and the storm broke. I'm not sure that bit of torn paper isn't the man's hand for this tower.'

'Don't bother yourself,' rejoined the clerk; 'the man's hand showed the rain was a-coming, and the rain was just what they wanted. I never can make out why folks twist the Scripture round and make the man's hand into something bad. 'Twas a *good* thing, so take heart and get home to your victuals; you can't mend that bit of paper for all your staring at it.'

Westray paid no attention to his remarks, and the old man wished him good-night rather stiffly. 'Well,' he said, as he turned down the ladder, 'I'm off. I've got to be in my garden afore dark, for they're going to seal the leek leaves to-night against the leek show next week. My grandson took first prize last year, and his old grandad had to put up with eleventh; but I've got half a dozen leeks this season as'll beat any plant that's growed in Cullerne.'

By the next morning the paper strip was entirely parted. Westray wrote to Sir George, but history only repeated itself, for his Chief again made light of the matter, and gave the young man a strong hint that he was making mountains of molehills, that he was unduly nervous, that his place was to diligently carry out the instructions he had received. Another strip of paper was pasted across the crack, and remained intact. It seemed as if the tower had come to rest again, but Westray's scruples were not so easily allayed this time, and he took measures for pushing forward the underpinning of the south-east pier with all possible despatch.

Chapter 20

That inclination or predilection of Westray's for Anastasia, which he had been able to persuade himself was love, had passed away. His peace of mind was now completely restored, and he discounted the humiliation of refusal, by reflecting that the girl's affections must have been already engaged at the time of his proposal. He was ready to admit that Lord Blandamer would in any case have been a formidable competitor, but if they had started for the race at the same time he would have been quite prepared to back his own chances. Against his rival's position and wealth, might surely have been set his own youth, regularity of life, and professional skill; but it was a mere tilting against windmills to try to win a heart that was already another's. Thus disturbing influences were gradually composed, and he was able to devote an undivided attention to his professional work.

As the winter evenings set in, he found congenial occupation in an attempt to elucidate the heraldry of the great window at the end of the south transept. He made sketches of the various shields blazoned in it, and with the aid of a county history, and a manual which Dr Ennefer had lent him, succeeded in tracing most of the alliances represented by the various quarterings. These all related to marriages of the Blandamer family, for Van Linge had filled the window with glass to the order of the third Lord Blandamer, and the sea-green and silver of the nebuly coat was many times repeated, besides figuring in chief at the head of the window. In these studies Westray was glad to have Martin Joliffe's papers by him. There was in them a mass of information which bore on the subject of the architect's inquiries, for Martin had taken the published genealogy of the Blandamer family, and elaborated and corrected it by all kinds of investigation as to marriages and collaterals.

The story of Martin's delusion, the idea of the doited grey-beard whom the boys called 'Old Nebuly,' had been so firmly impressed on Westray's mind, that when he first turned over the papers he expected to find in them little more than the hallucinations of a madman. But by degrees he became aware that however disconnected many of Martin's notes might appear, they possessed a good deal of interest, and the coherence which results from a particular object being kept more or less continuously in view. Besides endless genealogies and bits of family history extracted from books, there were recorded all kinds of personal impressions and experiences, which Martin had met with in his journeyings. But in all his researches and expeditions he professed to have but one object—the discovery of his father's name; though what record he hoped to find, or where or how he hoped to find it, whether in document or register or inscription, was nowhere set out.

It was evident that the old fancy that he was the rightful owner of Fording, which had been suggested to him in his Oxford days, had taken such hold of his mind that no subsequent experience had been able to dislodge it. Of half his parentage there was no doubt. His mother was that Sophia Flannery who had married Yeoman Joliffe, had painted the famous picture of the flowers and caterpillar, and done many other things less reputable; but over his father hung a veil of obscurity which Martin had tried all his life to lift. Westray had heard those stories from Clerk Janaway a dozen times, how that when Yeoman Joliffe took Sophia to church she brought him a four-year-old son by a former marriage. By a former *marriage* Martin had always stoutly maintained, as in duty bound, for any other theory would have dishonoured himself. With his mother's honour he had little concern, for where was the use of defending the memory of a mother who had made a shipwreck of her own reputation with soldiers and horse-copers? It was this previous marriage that Martin had tried so hard to establish, tried all the harder because other folk had wagged their heads and said there was no marriage to discover, that Sophia was neither wife nor widow.

Towards the end of his notes it seemed as if he had found some clue—had found some clue, or thought that he had found it. In this game of hunt the slipper he had imagined that he was growing 'hotter' and 'hotter' till death balked him at the finish. Westray recollected Mr Sharnall saying more than once that Martin had been on the brink of solving the riddle when the end overtook him. And Sharnall, too, had he not almost grasped the Will-of-the-wisp when fate tripped *him* on that windy night? Many thoughts came to Westray's mind as he turned these papers, many memories of others who had turned them before him. He thought of clever, worthless Martin, who had wasted his days on their writing, who had neglected home and family for their sake; he thought of the old organist who had held them in his feverish hands, who had hoped by some dramatic discovery to illumine the dark setting of his own life. And as Westray read, the interest grew with him too, till it absorbed the heraldry of the Blandamer window from which the whole matter had started. He began to comprehend the vision that had possessed Martin, that had so stirred the organist's feelings; he began to think that it was reserved for himself to make the long-sought discovery, and that he had in his own hand the clue to the strangest of romances.

One evening as he sat by the fire, with a plan in his hands and a litter of Martin's papers lying on a table at his side, there was a tap at the door, and Miss Joliffe entered. They were still close friends in spite of his leaving Bellevue Lodge. However sorry she had been at the time to lose her lodger, she recognized that the course he had taken was correct, and, indeed, obligatory. She was glad that he had seen his duty in this matter; it would have been quite impossible for any man of ordinary human feelings, to continue to live on in the same house under such circumstances. To have made a bid for Anstice's hand, and to have been refused, was a blow that moved her deepest pity, and she endeavoured in many ways to show her consideration for the victim. Providence had no doubt overruled everything for the best in ordaining that Anstice should refuse Mr Westray, but Miss Joliffe had favoured his suit, and had been sorry at the time that it was not successful. So there existed between them that curious sympathy which generally exists between a rejected lover and a woman who has done her best to further his proposal. They had since met not unfrequently, and the year which had elapsed had sufficiently blunted the edge of Westray's disappointment to enable him to talk of the matter with equanimity. He took a sad pleasure in discussing with Miss Joliffe the motives which might have conduced to so inexplicable a refusal, and in considering whether his offer would have been accepted if it had been made a little sooner or in another manner. Nor was the subject in any way distasteful to her, for she felt a reflected glory in the fact of her niece having first refused a thoroughly eligible proposal, and having afterwards accepted one transcendently better.

'Forgive me, sir—forgive me, Mr Westray,' she corrected herself, remembering that their relation was no longer one of landlady and lodger. 'I am sorry to intrude on you so late, but it is difficult to find you in during the day. There is a matter that has been weighing lately on my mind. You have never taken away the picture of the flowers, which you and dear Mr Sharnall purchased of me. I have not hurried in the matter, feeling I should like to see you nicely settled in before it was moved, but now it is time all was set right, so I have brought it over to-night.'

If her dress was no longer threadbare, it was still of the neatest black, and if she had taken to wearing every day the moss-agate brooch which had formerly been reserved for Sundays, she was still the very same old sweet-tempered, spontaneous, Miss Joliffe as in time past. Westray looked at her with affection.

'Sit down,' he said, offering her a chair; 'did you say you had brought the picture with you?' and he scanned her as if he expected to see it produced from her pocket.

'Yes,' she said; 'my maid is bringing it upstairs'—and there was just a suspicion of hesitation on the word 'maid,' that showed that she was still unaccustomed to the luxury of being waited on.

It was with great difficulty that she had been persuaded to accept such an allowance at Anastasia's hands, as would enable her to live on at Bellevue Lodge and keep a single servant; and if it brought her infinite relief to find that Lord Blandamer had paid all Martin's bills within a week of his engagement, such generosity filled her at the same time with a multitude of scruples. Lord Blandamer had wished her to live with them at Fording, but he was far too considerate and appreciative of the situation to insist on this proposal when he saw that such a change would be uncongenial to her. So she remained at Cullerne, and spent her time in receiving with dignity visits from innumerable friends that she found she now possessed, and in the fullest enjoyment of church services, meetings, parish work, and other privileges.

'It is very good of you, Miss Joliffe,' Westray said; 'it is very kind of you to think of the picture. But,' he went on, with too vivid a recollection of the painting, 'I know how much you have always prized it, and I could not bear to take it away from Bellevue Lodge. You see, Mr Sharnall, who was part owner with me, is dead; I am only making you a present of half of it, so you must accept that from me as a little token of gratitude for all the kindness you have shown me. You *have* been very kind to me, you know,' he said with a sigh, which was meant to recall Miss Joliffe's friendliness, and his own grief, in the affair of the proposal.

Miss Joliffe was quick to take the cue, and her voice was full of sympathy. 'Dear Mr Westray, you know how glad I should have been if all could have happened as you wished. Yet we should try to recognize the ordering of Providence in these things, and bear sorrow with meekness. But about the picture, you must let me have my own way this once. There may come a time, and that before very long, when I shall be able to buy it back from you just as we arranged, and then I am sure you will let me have it. But for the present it must be with you, and if anything should happen to me I should wish you to keep it altogether.'

Westray had meant to insist on her retaining the picture; he would not for a second time submit to be haunted with the gaudy flowers and the green caterpillar. But while she spoke, there fell upon him one of those gusty changes of purpose to which he was peculiarly liable. There came into his mind that strange insistence with which Sharnall had begged him at all hazards to retain possession of the picture. It seemed as if there might be some mysterious influence which had brought Miss Joliffe with it just now, and that he might be playing false to his trust with Sharnall if he sent it back again. So he did not remain obdurate, but said: 'Well, if you really wish it, I will keep the picture for a time, and whenever you want it you can take it back again.' While he was speaking there was a sound of stumbling on the stairs outside, and a bang as if something heavy had been let drop.

'It is that stupid girl again,' Miss Joliffe said; 'she is always tumbling about. I am sure she has broken more china in the six months she has been with me than was broken before in six years.'

They went to the door, and as Westray opened it great red-faced and smiling Anne Janaway walked in, bearing the glorious picture of the flowers and caterpillar.

'What have you been doing now?' her mistress asked sharply.

'Very sorry, mum,' said the maid, mingling some indignation with her apology, 'this here gurt paint tripped I up. I'm sure I hope I haven't hurt un'—and she planted the picture on the floor against the table.

Miss Joliffe scanned the picture with an eye which was trained to detect the very flakiest chip on a saucer, the very faintest scratch upon a teapot.

'Dear me, dear me!' she said, 'the beautiful frame is ruined; the bottom piece is broken almost clean off.'

'Oh come,' Westray said in a pacifying tone, while he lifted the picture and laid it flat on the table, 'things are not so bad as all that.'

He saw that the piece which formed the bottom of the frame was indeed detached at both corners and ready to fall away, but he pushed it back into position with his hand till it stuck in its place, and left little damage apparent to a casual observer.

'See,' he said, 'It looks nearly right. A little glue will quite repair the mischief to-morrow. I am sure I wonder how your servant managed to get it up here at all—it is such a weight and size.'

As a matter of fact, Miss Joliffe herself had helped Anne to carry the picture as far as the Grands Mulets of the last landing. The final ascent she thought could be accomplished in safety by the girl alone, while it would have been derogatory to her new position of an independent lady to appear before Westray carrying the picture herself.

'Do not vex yourself,' Westray begged; 'look, there is a nail in the wall here under the ceiling which will do capitally for hanging it till I can find a better place; the old cord is just the right length.' He climbed on a chair and adjusted the picture, standing back as if to admire it, till Miss Joliffe's complacency was fairly restored.

Westray was busied that night long after Miss Joliffe had left him, and the hands of the loud-ticking clock on the mantelpiece showed that midnight was near before he had finished his work. Then he sat a little while before the dying fire thinking much of Mr Sharnall, whom the picture had recalled to his mind, until the blackening embers warned him that it was time to go to bed. He was rising from his chair, when he heard behind him a noise as of something falling, and looking found, saw that the bottom of the picture-frame, which he had temporarily pushed into position, had broken away again of its own weight, and was fallen on the floor. The frame was handsomely wrought with a peculiar interlacing fillet, as he had noticed many times before. It was curious that so poor a picture should have obtained a rich setting, and sometimes he thought that Sophia Flannery must have bought the frame at a sale, and had afterwards daubed the flower-piece to fill it.

The room had grown suddenly cold with the chill which dogs the heels of a dying fire on an early winter's night. An icy breath blew in under the door, and made something flutter that lay on the floor close to the broken frame. Westray stooped to pick it up, and found that he had in his hand a piece of folded paper.

He felt a curious reluctance in handling it. Those fantastic scruples to which he was so often a prey assailed him. He asked himself had he any right to examine this piece of paper? It might be a letter; he did not know whence it had come nor whose it was, and he certainly did not wish to be guilty of opening someone else's letter. He even went so far as to put it solemnly on the table, like a skipper on whose deck the phantom whale-boat of the *Flying Dutchman* has deposited a packet of mails. After a few minutes, however, he appreciated the absurdity of the situation, and with an effort unfolded the mysterious missive.

It was a long narrow piece of paper, yellowed with years, and lined with the unopened creases of a generation. It had on it both printed and written characters. He recognized it instantly for a certificate of marriage—those 'marriage lines' on which so often hang both the law and the prophets. There it was with all the little pigeon-holes duly filled in, and set forth how that on 'March 15, 1800, at the

Church of St. Medard Within, one Horatio Sebastian Fynes, bachelor, aged twenty-one, son of Horatio Sebastian Fynes, gentleman, was married to one Sophia Flannery, spinster, aged twenty-one, daughter of James Flannery, merchant,' with witnesses duly attesting. And underneath an ill-formed straggling hand had added a superscription in ink that was now brown and wasted: 'Martin born January 2, 1801, at ten minutes past twelve, night.' He laid it on the table and folded it out flat, and knew that he had under his eyes that certificate of the first marriage (of the only true marriage) of Martin's mother, which Martin had longed all his life to see, and had not seen; that patent of legitimacy which Martin thought he had within his grasp when death overtook him, that clue which Sharnall thought that he had within his grasp when death overtook him also.

On March 15, 1800, Sophia Flannery was married by special licence to Horatio Sebastian Fynes, gentleman, and on January 2, 1801, at ten minutes past twelve, night, Martin was born. Horatio Sebastian—the names were familiar enough to Westray. Who was this Horatio Sebastian Fynes, son of Horatio Sebastian Fynes, gentleman? It was only a formal question that he asked himself, for he knew the answer very well. This document that he had before him might be no legal proof, but not all the lawyers in Christendom could change his conviction, his intuition, that the 'gentleman' Sophia Flannery had married was none other than the octogenarian Lord Blandamer deceased three years ago. There was to his eyes an air of authenticity about that yellowed strip of paper that nothing could upset, and the date of Martin's birth given in the straggling hand at the bottom coincided exactly with his own information. He sat down again in the cold with his elbows on the table and his head between his hands while he took in some of the corollaries of the position. If the old Lord Blandamer had married Sophia Flannery on March 15, 1800, then his second marriage was no marriage at all, for Sophia was living long after that, and there had been no divorce. But if his second marriage was no marriage, then his son, Lord Blandamer, who was drowned in Cullerne Bay, had been illegitimate, and his grandson, Lord Blandamer, who now sat on the throne of Fording, was illegitimate too. And Martin's dream had been true. Selfish, thriftless, idle Martin, whom the boys called 'Old Nebuly', had not been mad after all, but had been Lord Blandamer.

It all hung on this strip of paper, this bolt fallen from the blue, this message that had come from no one knew where. Whence *had* it come? Could Miss Joliffe have dropped it? No, that was impossible; she would certainly have told him if she had any information of this kind, for she knew that he had been trying for months to unravel the tangle of Martin's papers. It must have been hidden behind the picture, and have fallen out when the bottom piece of the frame fell.

He went to the picture. There was the vase of flaunting, ill-drawn flowers, there was the green caterpillar wriggling on the table-top, but at the bottom was something that he had never seen before. A long narrow margin of another painting was now visible where the frame was broken away; it seemed as if the flower-piece had been painted over some other subject, as if Sophia Flannery had not even been at the pains to take the canvas out, and had only carried her daub up to the edge of the frame. There was no question that the flowers masked some better painting, some portrait, no doubt, for enough was shown at the bottom to enable him to make out a strip of a brown velvet coat, and even one mother-of-pearl button of a brown velvet waistcoat. He stared at the flowers, he held a candle close to them in the hope of being able to trace some outline, to discover something of what lay behind. But the colour had been laid on with no sparing hand, the veil was impenetrable. Even the green caterpillar seemed to mock him, for as he looked at it closely, he saw that Sophia in her wantonness had put some minute touches of colour, which gave its head two eyes and a grinning mouth.

He sat down again at the table where the certificate still lay open before him. That entry of Martin's birth must be in the handwriting of Sophia Flannery, of faithless, irresponsible Sophia Flannery, flaunting as her own flowers, mocking as the face of her own caterpillar.

There was a dead silence over all, the utter blank silence that falls upon a country town in the early morning hours. Only the loud-ticking clock on the mantelpiece kept telling of time's passage till the carillon of St Sepulchre's woke the silence with New Sabbath. It was three o'clock, and the room was deadly cold, but that chill was nothing to the chill that was rising to his own heart. He knew it all now, he said to himself—he knew the secret of Anastasia's marriage, and of Sharnall's death, and of Martin's death.

Chapter 21

The foreman of the masons at work in the under-pinning of the south-east pier came to see Westray at nine o'clock the next morning. He was anxious that the architect should go down to the church at once, for the workmen, on reaching the tower shortly after daybreak, found traces of a fresh movement which had taken place during the night. But Westray was from home, having left Cullerne for London by the first train.

About ten of the same forenoon, the architect was in the shop of a small picture-dealer in Westminster. The canvas of the flowers and caterpillar picture lay on the counter, for the man had just taken it out of the frame.

'No,' said the dealer, 'there is no paper or any kind of lining in the frame—just a simple wood backing, you see. It is unusual to back at all, but it *is* done now and again'—and he tapped the loose frame all round. 'It is an expensive frame, well made, and with good gilding. I shouldn't be surprised if the painting underneath this daub turned out to be quite respectable; they would never put a frame like this on anything that wasn't pretty good.'

'Do you think you can clean off the top part without damaging the painting underneath?'

'Oh dear, yes,' the man said; 'I've had many harder jobs. You leave it with me for a couple of days, and we'll see what we can make of it.'

'Couldn't it be done quicker than that?' Westray said. 'I'm in rather a hurry. It is difficult for me to get up to London, and I should rather like to be by, when you begin to clean it.'

'Don't make yourself anxious,' the other said; 'you can leave it in my hands with perfect confidence. We're quite used to this business.'

Westray still looked unsatisfied. The dealer gave a glance round the shop. 'Well,' he said, 'things don't seem very busy this morning; if you're in such a hurry, I don't mind just trying a little bit of it now. We'll put it on the table in the back-room. I can see if anyone comes into the shop.'

'Begin where the face ought to be,' Westray said; 'let us see whose portrait it is.'

'No, no,' said the dealer; 'we won't risk the face yet. Let us try something that doesn't matter much. We shall see how this stuff peels off, that'll give us a guide for the more important part. Here, I'll start with the table-top and caterpillar. There's something queer about that caterpillar, besides the face some joker's fitted it up with. I'm rather shy about the caterpillar. Looks to me as if it was a bit of the real picture left showing through, though I don't very well see how a caterpillar would fit in with a portrait.' The dealer passed the nail of his forefinger lightly over the surface of the picture. 'It seems as if 'twas sunk. You can feel the edges of this heavy daubing rough all round it.'

It was as he pointed out; the green caterpillar certainly appeared to form some part of the underlying picture. The man took out a bottle, and with a brush laid some solution on the painting. 'You must wait for it to dry. It will blister and frizzle up the surface, then we can rub off the top gently with a cloth, and you'll see what you will see.'

'The fellow who painted this table-top didn't spare his colours,' said the dealer half an hour later, 'and that's all the better for us. See, it comes off like a skin'—and he worked away tenderly with a soft flannel. 'Well, I'm jiggered,' he went on, 'if here isn't another caterpillar higher up! No, it ain't a caterpillar; but if it ain't a caterpillar, what is it?'

There was indeed another wavy green line, but Westray knew what it was directly he saw it. 'Be careful,' he said; 'they aren't caterpillars at all, but just part of a coat of arms—a kind of bars in an heraldic shield, you know. There will be another shorter green line lower down.'

It was as he said, and in a minute more there shone out the silver field and the three seagreen bars of the nebuly coat, and below it the motto *Aut Fynes aut finis*, just as it shone in the top light of the Blandamer window. It was the middle bar that Sophia had turned into a caterpillar, and in pure wantonness left showing through, when for her own purposes she had painted out the rest of the picture. Westray's excitement was getting the better of him—he could not keep still: he stood first on one leg and then on another, and drummed on the table with his fingers.

The dealer put his hand on the architect's arm. 'For God's sake keep quiet!' he said; 'don't excite yourself. You needn't think you have found a gold mine. It ain't a ten-thousand-guinea Vandyke. We can't see enough yet to say what it is, but I'll bet my life you never get a twenty-pound note for it.'

But for all Westray's impatience, the afternoon was well advanced before the head of the portrait was approached. There had been so few interruptions, that the dealer felt called upon to extenuate the absence of custom by explaining more than once that it was a very dull season. He was evidently interested in his task, for he worked with a will till the light began to fail. 'Never mind,' he said; 'I will get a lamp; now we have got so far we may as well go a bit further.'

It was a full-face picture, as they saw a few minutes afterwards. Westray held the lamp, and felt a strange thrill go through him, as he began to make out the youthful and unwrinkled brow. Surely he knew that high forehead—it was Anastasia's, and there was Anastasia's dark wavy hair above it. 'Why, it's a woman after all,' the dealer said. 'No, it isn't; of course, how could it be with a brown velvet coat and waistcoat? It's a young man with curly hair.'

Westray said nothing; he was too much excited, too much interested to say a word, for two eyes were peering at him through the mist. Then the mist lifted under the dealer's cloth, and the eyes gleamed with a startling brightness. They were light-grey eyes, clear and piercing, that transfixed him and read the very thoughts that he was thinking. Anastasia had vanished. It was Lord Blandamer that looked at him out of the picture.

They were Lord Blandamer's eyes, impenetrable and observant as today, but with the brightness of youth still in them; and the face, untarnished by middle age, showed that the picture had been painted some years ago. Westray put his elbows on the table and his head between his hands, while he gazed at the face which had thus come back to life. The eyes pursued him, he could not escape from them, he could scarcely spare a glance even for the nebuly coat that was blazoned in the corner. There were questions revolving in his mind for which he found as yet no answer. There was some mystery to which this portrait might be the clue. He was on the eve of some terrible explanation; he remembered all kinds of incidents that seemed connected with this picture, and yet could find no thread on which to string them. Of course, this head must have been painted when Lord Blandamer was young, but how could Sophia Flannery have ever seen it? The picture had only been the flowers and the table-top and caterpillar all through Miss Euphemia's memory, and that covered sixty years. But Lord Blandamer was not more than forty; and as Westray looked at the face he found little differences for which no change from youth to middle age could altogether account. Then he guessed that this was not the Lord Blandamer whom he knew, but an older one—that octogenarian who had died three years ago, that Horatio Sebastian Fynes, gentleman, who had married Sophia Flannery.

'It ain't a real first-rater,' the dealer said, 'but it ain't bad. I shouldn't be surprised if 'twas a Lawrence, and, anyway, it's a sight better than the flowers. Beats me to know how anyone ever came to paint such stuff as them on top of this respectable young man.'

Westray was back in Cullerne the next evening. In the press of many thoughts he had forgotten to tell his landlady that he was coming, and he stood chafing while a maid-of-all-work tried to light the recalcitrant fire. The sticks were few and damp, the newspaper below them was damp, and the damp coal weighed heavily down on top of all, till the thick yellow smoke shied at the chimney, and came curling out under the worsted fringe of the mantelpiece into the chilly room. Westray took this discomfort the more impatiently, in that it was due to his own forgetfulness in having sent no word of his return.

'Why in the world isn't the fire lit?' he said sharply. 'You must have known I couldn't sit without a fire on a cold evening like this;'

and the wind sang dismally in the joints of the windows to emphasize the dreariness of the situation.

'It ain't nothing to do with me,' answered the red-armed, coal-besmeared hoyden, looking up from her knees; 'it's the missus. "He was put out with the coal bill last time," she says, "and I ain't going to risk lighting up his fire with coal at sixpence a scuttle, and me not knowing whether he's coming back tonight."'

'Well, you might see at any rate that the fire was properly laid,' the architect said, as the lighting process gave evident indications of failing for the third time.

'I do my best,' she said in a larmoyant tone, 'but I can't do everything, what with having to cook, and clean, and run up and down stairs with notes, and answer the bell every other minute to lords.'

'Has Lord Blandamer been here?' asked Westray.

'Yes, he came yesterday and twice today to see you,' she said, 'and then he left a note. There 'tis'—and she pointed to the end of the mantelpiece.

Westray looked round, and saw an envelope edged in black. He knew the strong, bold hand of the superscription well enough, and in his present mood it sent something like a thrill of horror through him.

'You needn't wait,' he said quickly to the servant; 'it isn't your fault at all about the fire. I'm sure it's going to burn now.'

The girl rose quickly to her feet, gave an astonished glance at the grate, which was once more enveloped in impotent blackness, and left the room.

An hour later, when the light outside was failing, Westray again sat in a cold and darkening room. On the table lay open before him Lord Blandamer's letter:

Dear Mr Westray,

I called to see you yesterday, but was unfortunate in finding you absent from home, and so write these lines. There used to hang in your sitting-room at Bellevue Lodge an old picture of flowers which has some interest for my wife. Her affection for it is based on early associations, and not, of course, on any merits of the painting itself. I thought that it belonged to Miss Joliffe, but I find on inquiry from her that she sold it to you some little time ago, and that it is with you now. I do not suppose that you can attach any great value to it, and, indeed, I suspect that you bought it of Miss Joliffe as an act of charity. If this is so, I should be obliged if you would let me know if you are disposed to part with it again, as my wife would like to have it here.

I am sorry to hear of fresh movement in the tower. It would be a bitter thought to me, if the peal that welcomed us back were found to have caused damage to the structure, but I am sure you will know that no expense should be spared to make all really secure as soon as possible.

Very faithfully yours,

BLANDAMER.

Westray was eager, impressionable, still subject to all the exaltations and depressions of youth. Thoughts crowded into his mind with bewildering rapidity; they trod so close upon each other's heels that there was no time to marshal them in order; excitement had dizzied him. Was he called to be the minister of justice? Was he chosen for the Scourge of God? Was his the hand that must launch the bolt against the guilty? Discovery had come directly to him. What a piece of circumstantial evidence were these very lines that lay open on the table, dim and illegible in the darkness that filled the room! Yet clear and damning to one who had the clue.

This man that ruled at Fording was a pretender, enjoying goods that belonged to others, a shameless evil-doer, who had not stuck at marrying innocent Anastasia Joliffe, if by so stooping he might cover up the traces of his imposture. There was no Lord Blandamer, there was no title; with a breath he could sweep it all away like a house of cards. And was that all? Was there nothing else?

Night had fallen. Westray sat alone in the dark, his elbows on the table, his head still between his hands. There was no fire, there was no light, only the faint shimmer of a far-off street lamp brought a perception of the darkness. It was that pale uncertain luminosity that recalled to his mind another night, when the misty moon shone through the clerestory windows of St Sepulchre's. He seemed once more to be making his way up the ghostly nave, on past the pillars that stood like gigantic figures in white winding-sheets, on under the great tower arches. Once more he was groping in the utter darkness of the newel stair, once more he came out into the organ-loft, and saw the baleful silver and sea-green of the nebuly coat gleaming in the transept window. And in the corners of the room lurked presences of evil, and a thin pale shadow of Sharnall wrung its hands, and cried to be saved from the man with the hammer. Then the horrible suspicion that had haunted him these last days stared out of the darkness as a fact, and he sprung to his feet in a shiver of cold and lit a candle.

An hour, two hours, three hours passed before he had written an answer to the letter that lay before him, and in the interval a fresh vicissitude of mind had befallen him. He, Westray, had been singled out as the instrument of vengeance; the clue was in his hands; his was the mouth that must condemn. Yet he would do nothing underhand, he would take no man unawares; he would tell Lord Blandamer of his discovery, and give him warning before he took any further steps. So he wrote:

'My lord,' and of the many sheets that were begun and flung away before the letter was finished, two were spoiled because the familiar address 'Dear Lord Blandamer' came as it were automatically from Westray's pen. He could no longer bring himself to use those words now, even as a formality, and so he began:

My Lord,

I have just received your note about the picture bought by me of Miss Joliffe. I cannot say whether I should have been willing to part with it under ordinary circumstances. It had no apparent intrinsic value, but for me it was associated with my friend the late Mr Sharnall, organist of St Sepulchre's. We shared in its purchase, and it was only on his death that I came into sole possession of it. You will not have forgotten the strange circumstances of his end, and I have not forgotten them either. My friend Mr Sharnall was well known among his acquaintances to be much interested in this picture. He believed it to be of more importance than appeared, and he expressed himself strongly to that effect in my presence, and once also, I remember, in yours.

But for his untimely death I think he would have long ago made the discovery to which chance has now led me. The flowers prove to be a mere surface painting which concealed what is undoubtedly a portrait of the late Lord Blandamer, and at the back of the canvas were found copies of certain entries in parish registers relating to him. I most earnestly wish that I could end here by making over these things to you, but they seem to me to throw so strange a light on certain past events that I must hold myself responsible for them, and can give them up to no private person. At the same time, I do not feel justified in refusing to let you see picture and papers, if you should wish to do so, and to judge yourself of their importance. I am at the above address, and shall be ready to make an appointment at any time before Monday next, after which date I shall feel compelled to take further steps in this matter.

Westray's letter reached Lord Blandamer the next morning. It lay at the bottom of a little heap of correspondence on the breakfast table, like the last evil lot to leap out of the shaken urn, an Ephedrus, like that Adulterer who at the finish tripped the Conqueror of Troy. He read it at a glance, catching its import rather by intuition than by any slavish following of the written characters. If earth was darkness at the core, and dust and ashes all that is, there was no trace of it in his face. He talked gaily, he fulfilled the duties of a host with all his charm of manner, he sped two guests who were leaving that morning with all his usual courtesy. After that he ordered his horse, and telling Lady Blandamer that he might not be back to lunch, he set out for one of those slow solitary rides on the estate that often seemed congenial to his mood. He rode along by narrow lanes and bridle-paths, not forgetting a kindly greeting to men who touched their hats, or women who dropped a curtsey, but all the while he thought.

The letter had sent his memory back to another black day, more than twenty years before, when he had quarrelled with his grandfather. It was in his second year at Oxford, when as an undergraduate he first felt it his duty to set the whole world in order. He held strong views as to the mismanagement of the Fording estates; and as a scholar and man of the world, had thought it weakness to shirk the expression of them. The timber was being neglected, there was no thinning and no planting. The old-fashioned farmhouses were being let fall into disrepair, and then replaced by parsimonious eaveless buildings; the very grazing in the park was let, and fallow-deer and red-deer were jostled by sheep and common mongrel cows. The question of the cows had galled him till he was driven to remonstrate strongly with his grandfather. There had never been much love lost between the pair, and on this occasion the young man found the old man strangely out of sympathy with suggestions of reform.

'Thank you,' old Lord Blandamer had said; 'I have heard all you have to say. You have eased your mind, and now you can go back to Oxford in peace. I have managed Fording for forty years, and feel myself perfectly competent to manage it for forty years more. I don't quite see what concern you have in the matter. What business is it of yours?'

'You don't see what concern I have in it,' said the reformer impetuously; 'you don't know what business it is of mine? Why, damage is being done here that will take a lifetime to repair.'

A man must be on good terms with his heir not to dislike the idea of making way for him, and the old lord flew into one of those paroxysms of rage which fell upon him more frequently in his later years.

'Now, look you,' he said; 'you need not trouble yourself any more about Fording, nor think you will be so great a sufferer by my mismanagement. It is by no means certain that I shall ever burden you with the place at all.'

Then the young man was angry in his turn. 'Don't threaten me, sir,' he said sharply; 'I am not a boy any longer to be cowed by rough words, so keep your threats for others. You would disgrace the family and disgrace yourself, if you left the property away from the title.'

'Make your mind easy,' said the other; 'the property shall follow the title. Get away, and let me hear no more, or you may find both left away from you.'

The words were lightly spoken, perhaps in mere petulance at being taken to task by a boy, perhaps in the exasperating pangs of gout; but they had a bitter sound, and sank deep into the heart of youth. The threat of the other possible heirs was new, and yet was not new to him. It seemed as if he had heard something of this before, though he could not remember where; it seemed as if there had always been some ill-defined, intangible suspicion in the air of Fording to make him doubt, since he came to thinking years, whether the title ever really would be his.

Lord Blandamer remembered these things well, as he walked his horse through the beech-leaves with Westray's letter in his breast-pocket. He remembered how his grandfather's words had sent him about with a sad face, and how his grandmother had guessed the reason. He wondered how she had guessed it; but she too, perhaps, had heard these threats before, and so came at the cause more easily. Yet when she had forced his confidence she had little comfort to give.

He could see her now, a stately woman with cold blue eyes, still handsome, though she was near sixty.

'Since we are speaking of this matter,' she said with chilling composure, 'let us speak openly. I will tell you everything I know, which is nothing. Your grandfather threatened me once, many years ago, as he has threatened you now, and we have never forgotten nor forgiven.' She moved herself in her chair, and there came a little flush of red to her cheek. 'It was about the time of your father's birth; we had quarrelled before, but this was our first serious quarrel, and the last. Your father was different from me, you know, and from you; he never quarrelled, and he never knew this story. So far as I was concerned I took the responsibility of silence, and it was wisest so.' She looked sterner than ever as she went on. 'I have never heard or discovered anything more. I am not afraid of your grandfather's intentions. He has a regard for the name, and he means to leave all to you, who have every right, unless, indeed, it may be, a legal right. There is one more thing about which I was anxious long ago. You have heard about a portrait of your grandfather that was stolen from the gallery soon after your father's birth? Suspicion fell upon no one in particular. Of course, the stable door was locked after the horse was gone, and we had a night-watchman at Fording for some time; but little stir was made, and I do not believe your grandfather ever put the matter in the hands of the police. It was a spiteful trick, he said; he would not pay whoever had done it the compliment of taking any trouble to recover the portrait. The picture was of himself; he could have another painted any day.

'By whatever means that picture was removed, I have little doubt that your grandfather guessed what had become of it. Does it still exist? Was it stolen? Or did he have it taken away to prevent its being stolen? We must remember that, though we are quite in the dark about these people, there is nothing to prevent their being shown over the house like any other strangers.' Then she drew herself up, and folded her hands in her lap, and he saw the great rings flashing on her white fingers. 'That is all I know,' she finished, 'and now let us agree not to mention the subject again, unless one of us should discover anything more. The claim may have lapsed, or may have been compounded, or may never have existed; I think, anyhow, we may feel sure now that no move will be made in your grandfather's lifetime. My advice to you is not to quarrel with him; you had better spend your long vacations away from Fording, and when you leave Oxford you can travel.'

So the young man went out from Fording, for a wandering that was to prove half as long as that of Israel in the wilderness. He came home for a flying visit at wide intervals, but he kept up a steady correspondence with his grandmother as long as she lived. Only once, and that in the last letter which he ever received from her, did she allude to the old distasteful discussion. 'Up to this very day,' she wrote, 'I have found out nothing; we may still hope that there is nothing to find out.'

In all those long years he consoled himself by the thought that he was bearing expatriation for the honour of the family, that he was absenting himself so that his grandfather might find the less temptation to drag the nebuly coat in the mire. To make a fetish of family was a tradition with Blandamers, and the heir as he set out on his travels, with the romance of early youth about him, dedicated himself to the nebuly coat, with a vow to 'serve and preserve' as faithfully as ever taken by Templar.

Last of all the old lord passed away. He never carried out his threat of disinheritance, but died intestate, and thus the grandson came to his own. The new Lord Blandamer was no longer young when he returned; years of wild travel had hardened his face, and made his heart self-reliant, but he came back as romantic as he went away. For Nature, if she once endows man or woman with romance, gives them so rich a store of it as shall last them, life through, unto the end. In sickness or health, in poverty or riches, through middle age and old age, through loss of hair and loss of teeth, under wrinkled face and gouty limbs, under crow's-feet and double chins, under all the least romantic and most sordid malaisances of life, romance endures to the end. Its price is altogether above rubies; it can never be taken away from those that have it, and those that have it not, can never acquire it for money, nor by the most utter toil—no, nor ever arrive at the very faintest comprehension of it.

The new lord had come back to Fording full of splendid purpose. He was tired of wandering; he would marry; he would settle down and enjoy his own; he would seek the good of the people, and make his great estates an example among landowners. And then within three weeks he had learned that there was a pretender to the throne, that in Cullerne there was a visionary who claimed to be the very Lord Blandamer. He had had this wretched man pointed out to him once in the street—a broken-down fellow who was trailing the cognizance of all the Blandamers in the mud, till the very boys called him Old Nebuly. Was he to fight for land, and house, and title, to fight for everything, with a man like that? And yet it might come to fighting, for within a little time he knew that this was the heir who had been the intangible shadow of his grandmother's life and of his own; and that Martin might stumble any day upon the proof that was lacking. And then death set a term to Martin's hopes, and Lord Blandamer was free again.

But not for long, for in a little while he heard of an old organist who had taken up Martin's rôle—a meddlesome busybody who fished in troubled waters, for the trouble's sake. What had such a mean man as this to do with lands, and titles, and coats of arms? And yet this man was talking under his breath in Cullerne of crimes, and clues, and retribution near at hand. And then death put a term to Sharnall's talk, and Lord Blandamer was free again.

Free for a longer space, free this time finally for ever; and he married, and marriage set the seal on his security, and the heir was born, and the nebuly coat was safe. But now a new confuter had risen to balk him. Was he fighting with dragon's spawn? Were fresh enemies to spring up from the— The simile did not suit his mood, and he truncated it. Was this young architect, whose very food and wages in Cullerne were being paid for by the money that he, Lord Blandamer, saw fit to spend upon the church, indeed to be the Avenger? Was his own creature to turn and rend him? He smiled at the very irony of the thing, and then he brushed aside reflections on the past, and stifled even the beginnings of regret, if, indeed, any existed. He would look at the present, he would understand exactly how matters stood.

Lord Blandamer came back to Fording at nightfall, and spent the hour before dinner in his library. He wrote some business letters which could not be postponed, but after dinner read aloud to his wife. He had a pleasant and well-trained voice, and amused Lady Blandamer by reading from the 'lngoldsby Legends', a new series of which had recently appeared.

Whilst he read Anastasia worked at some hangings, which had been left unfinished by the last Lady Blandamer. The old lord's wife had gone out very little, but passed her time for the most part with her gardens, and with curious needlework. For years she had been copying some moth-eaten fragments of Stuart tapestry, and at her death left the work still uncompleted. The housekeeper had shown these half-finished things and explained what they were, and Anastasia had asked Lord Blandamer whether it would be agreeable to him that she should go on with them. The idea pleased him, and so she plodded away evening by evening, very carefully and slowly, thinking often of the lonely old lady whose hands had last been busied with the same task. This grandmother of her husband seemed to have been the only relation with whom he had ever been on intimate terms, and Anastasia's interest was quickened by an excellent portrait of her as a young girl by Lawrence, which hung in the long gallery. Could the old lady have revisited for once the scene of her labours, she would have had no reason to be dissatisfied with her successor. Anastasia looked distinguished enough as she sat at her work-frame, with the skeins of coloured silks in her lap and the dark-brown hair waved on her high forehead; and a dress of rich yellow velvet might have supported the illusion that a portrait of some bygone lady of the Blandamers had stepped down out of its frame.

That evening her instinct told her that something was amiss, in spite of all her husband's self-command. Something very annoying must have happened among the grooms, gardeners, gamekeepers, or other dependents; he had been riding about to set the matter straight, and it was no doubt of a nature that he did not care to mention to her.

Chapter 22

Westray passed a day of painful restlessness. He had laid his hand to a repugnant business, and the burden of it was too heavy for him to bear. He felt the same gnawing anxiety, that is experienced by one whom doctors have sentenced to a lethal operation. One man may bear himself more bravely in such circumstances than another, but by nature every man is a coward; and the knowledge that the hour is approaching, when the surgeon's knife shall introduce him to a final struggle of life and death cannot be done away. So it was with Westray; he had undertaken a task for which he was not strong enough, and only high principle, and a sense of moral responsibility, kept him from panic and flight. He went to the church in the morning, and endeavoured to concentrate attention on his work, but the consciousness of what was before him would not be thrust aside. The foreman-mason saw that his master's thoughts were wandering, and noticed the drawn expression on his face.

In the afternoon his restlessness increased, and he wandered listlessly through the streets and narrow entries of the town, till he found himself near nightfall at that place by the banks of the Cull, where the organist had halted on the last evening of his life. He stood leaning over the iron railing, and looked at the soiled river, just as Mr Sharnall had looked. There were the dark-green tresses of duckweed swaying to and fro in the shallow eddies, there was the sordid collection of broken and worthless objects that lay on the bottom, and he stared at them till the darkness covered them one by one, and only the whiteness of a broken dish still flickered under the water.

Then he crept back to his room as if he were a felon, and though he went early to bed, sleep refused to visit him till the day began to break. With daylight he fell into a troubled doze, and dreamt that he was in a witness-box before a crowded court. In the dock stood Lord Blandamer dressed in full peer's robes, and with a coronet on his head. The eyes of all were turned upon him, Westray, with fierce enmity and contempt, and it was he, Westray, that a stern-faced judge was sentencing, as a traducer and lying informer. Then the people in the galleries stamped with their feet and howled against him in their rage;

and waking with a start, he knew that it was the postman's sharp knock on the street-door, that had broken his slumber.

The letter which he dreaded lay on the table when he came down. He felt an intense reluctance in opening it. He almost wondered that the handwriting was still the same; it was as if he had expected that the characters should be tremulous, or the ink itself blood-red. Lord Blandamer acknowledged Mr Westray's letter with thanks. He should certainly like to see the picture and the family papers of which Mr Westray spoke; would Mr Westray do him the favour of bringing the picture to Fording? He apologized for putting him to so much trouble, but there was another picture in the gallery at Fording, with which it might be interesting to compare the one recently discovered. He would send a carriage to meet any train; Mr Westray would no doubt find it more convenient to spend the night at Fording.

There was no expression of surprise, curiosity, indignation, or alarm; nothing, in fact, except the utmost courtesy, a little more distant perhaps than usual, but not markedly so.

Westray had been unable to conjecture what would be the nature of Lord Blandamer's answer. He had thought of many possibilities, of the impostor's flight, of lavish offers of hush-money, of passionate appeals for mercy, of scornful and indignant denial. But in all his imaginings he had never imagined this. Ever since he had sent his own letter, he had been doubtful of its wisdom, and yet he had not been able to think of any other course that he would have preferred. He knew that the step he had taken in warning the criminal was quixotic, and yet it seemed to him that Lord Blandamer had a certain right to see his own family portrait and papers, before they were used against him. He could not feel sorry that he had given the opportunity, though he had certainly hoped that Lord Blandamer would not avail himself of it.

But go to Fording he would not. That, at any rate, no fantastic refinement of fair play could demand of him. He knew his mind at least on this point; he would answer at once, and he got out a sheet of paper for his refusal. It was easy to write the number of his house, and the street, and Cullerne, and the formal 'My lord,' which he used again for the address. But what then? What reason was he to give for his refusal? He could allege no business appointment or other serious engagement as an obstacle, for he himself had said that he was free for a week, and had offered Lord Blandamer to make an appointment on any day. He himself had offered an interview; to draw back now would be mean and paltry in the extreme. It was true that the more he thought of this meeting the more he shrank from it. But it could not be evaded now. It was, after all, only the easiest part of the task that he had set before him, only a prolusion to the tragedy that he would have to play to a finish. Lord Blandamer deserved, no doubt, all the evil that was to fall on him; but in the meanwhile he, Westray, was incapable of refusing this small favour, asked by a man who was entirely at his mercy.

Then he wrote with a shrinking heart, but with yet another fixed purpose, that he would bring the picture to Fording the next day. He preferred not to be met at the station, he would arrive some time during the afternoon, but could only stay an hour at the most, as he had business which would take him on to London the same evening.

It was a fine autumn day on the morrow, and when the morning mists had cleared away, the sun came out with surprising warmth, and dried the dew on the lawns of many-gardened Cullerne. Towards mid-day Westray set forth from his lodgings to go to the station, carrying under his arm the picture, lightly packed in lath, and having in his pocket those papers which had fallen out from the frame. He chose a route through back-streets, and walked quickly, but as he passed Quandrill's, the local maker of guns and fishing-rods, a thought struck him. He stopped and entered the shop.

'Good-morning,' he said to the gunsmith, who stood behind the counter; 'have you any pistols? I want one small enough to carry in the pocket, but yet something more powerful than a toy.'

Mr Quandrill took off his spectacles.

'Ah,' he said, tapping the counter with them meditatively. 'Let me see. Mr Westray, is it not, the architect at the minster?'

'Yes,' Westray answered. 'I require a pistol for some experiments. It should carry a fairly heavy bullet.'

'Oh, just so,' the man said, with an air of some relief, as Westray's coolness convinced him that he was not contemplating suicide. 'Just so, I see; some experiments. Well, in that case, I suppose, you would not require any special facilities for loading again quickly, otherwise I should have recommended one of these,' and he took up a weapon from the counter. 'They are new-fangled things from America, revolving pistols they call them. You can fire them four times running, you see, as quick as you like,' and he snapped the piece to show how well it worked.

Westray handled the pistol, and looked at the barrels.

'Yes,' he said, 'that will suit my purpose very well, though it is rather large to carry in the pocket.'

'Oh, you want it for the pocket,' the gunmaker said with renewed surprise in his tone.

'Yes; I told you that already. I may have to carry it about with me. Still, I think this will do. Could you kindly load it for me now?'

'You are sure it's quite safe?' said the gunmaker.

'I ought to ask *you* that,' Westray rejoined with a smile. 'Do you mean it may go off accidentally in my pocket?'

'Oh no, it's safe enough that way,' said the gunmaker. 'It won't go off unless you pull the trigger.' And he loaded the four barrels, measuring out the powder and shot carefully, and ramming in the wads. 'You'll be wanting more powder and shot than this, I suppose,' he said.

'Very likely,' rejoined the architect, 'but I can call for that later.'

He found a heavy country fly waiting for him at Lytchett, the little wayside station which was sometimes used by people going to Fording. It is a seven-mile drive from the station to the house, but he was so occupied in his own reflections, that he was conscious of nothing till the carriage pulled up at the entrance of the park. Here he stopped for a moment while the lodgekeeper was unfastening the bolt, and remembered afterwards that he had noticed the elaborate iron-work, and the nebuly coat which was set over the great gates. He was in the long avenue now, and he wished it had been longer, he wished that it might never end; and then the fly stopped again, and Lord Blandamer on horseback was speaking to him through the carriage window.

There was a second's pause, while the two men looked each other directly in the eyes, and in that look all doubt on either side was ended. Westray felt as if he had received a staggering blow as he came face to face with naked truth, and Lord Blandamer read Westray's thoughts, and knew the extent of his discovery.

Lord Blandamer was the first to speak.

'I am glad to see you again,' he said with perfect courtesy, 'and am very much obliged to you for taking this trouble in bringing the picture.' And he glanced at the crate that Westray was steadying with his hand on the opposite seat. 'I only regret that you would not let me send a carriage to Lytchett.'

'Thank you,' said the architect; 'on the present occasion I preferred to be entirely independent.' His words were cold, and were meant to be cold; and yet as he looked at the other's gentle bearing, and the grave face in which sadness was a charm, he felt constrained to abate in part the effect of his own remark, and added somewhat awkwardly: 'You see, I was uncertain about the trains.'

'I am riding back across the grass,' Lord Blandamer said, 'but shall be at the house before you'; and as he galloped off, Westray knew that he rode exceedingly well.

This meeting, he guessed, had been contrived to avoid the embarrassment of a more formal beginning. It was obvious that their terms of former friendship could no longer be maintained. Nothing would have induced him to have shaken hands, and this Lord Blandamer must have known.

As Westray stepped into the hall through Inigo Jones' Ionic portico, Lord Blandamer entered from a side-door.

'You must be cold after your long drive. Will you not take a biscuit and a glass of wine?'

Westray motioned away the refreshment which a footman offered him.

'No, thank you,' he said; 'I will not take anything.' It was impossible for him to eat or drink in this house, and yet again he softened his words by adding: 'I had something to eat on the way.'

The architect's refusal was not lost upon Lord Blandamer. He had known before he spoke that his offer would not be accepted.

'I am afraid it is useless to ask you to stop the night with us,' he said; and Westray had his rejoinder ready:

'No; I must leave Lytchett by the seven-five train. I have ordered the fly to wait.'

He had named the last train available for London, and Lord Blandamer saw that his visitor had so arranged matters, that the interview could not be prolonged for more than an hour.

'Of course, you *could* catch the night-mail at Cullerne Road,' he said. 'It is a very long drive, but I sometimes go that way to London myself.'

His words called suddenly to Westray's recollection that night walk when the station lights of Cullerne Road were seen dimly through the fog, and the station-master's story that Lord Blandamer had travelled by the mail on the night of poor Sharnall's death. He said nothing, but felt his resolution strengthened.

'The gallery will be the most convenient place, perhaps, to unpack the picture,' Lord Blandamer said; and Westray at once assented, gathering from the other's manner that this would be a spot where no interruption need be feared.

They went up some wide and shallow stairs, preceded by a footman, who carried the picture.

'You need not wait,' Lord Blandamer said to the man; 'we can unpack it ourselves.'

When the wrappings were taken off, they stood the painting on the narrow shelf formed by the top of the wainscot which lined the gallery, and from the canvas the old lord surveyed them with penetrating light grey eyes, exactly like the eyes of the grandson who stood before him.

Lord Blandamer stepped back a little, and took a long look at the face of this man, who had been the terror of his childhood, who had darkened his middle life, who seemed now to have returned from the grave to ruin him. Did he know himself to be in a desperate pass? If so it was time to make a last stand, for the issue lay between him and Westray. No one else had learned the secret. He understood and relied implicitly on Westray's fantastic sense of honour. Westray had written that he would 'take no steps' till the ensuing Monday, and Lord Blandamer was sure that no one would be told before that day, and that no one had been told yet. If Westray could be silenced, all was saved; if Westray spoke, all was lost. If it had been a question of weapons, or of bodily strength, there was no doubt which way the struggle would have ended. Westray knew this well now, and felt heartily ashamed of the pistol that was bulging the breast-pocket on the inside of his coat. If it had been a question of physical attack, he knew now that he would have never been given time, or opportunity, for making use of his weapon.

Lord Blandamer had travelled north and south, east and west; he had seen and done strange things; he had stood for his life in struggles whence only one could come out alive; but here was no question of flesh and blood—he had to face principles, those very principles on which he relied for respite; he had to face that integrity of Westray which made persuasion or bribery alike impossible. He had never seen this picture before, and he looked at it intently for some minutes; but his attention was all the while concentrated on the man who stood beside him. This was his last chance—he could afford to make no mistake; and his soul, or whatever that thing may be called which is certainly not the body, was closing with Westray's soul in a desperate struggle for mastery.

Westray was not seeing the picture for the first time, and after one glance he stood aloof. The interview was becoming even more painful than he had expected. He avoided looking Lord Blandamer in the face, yet presently, at a slight movement, turned and met his eye.

'Yes, it is my grandfather,' said the other.

There was nothing in the words, and yet it seemed to Westray as if some terrible confidence was being thrust upon him against his will; as if Lord Blandamer had abandoned any attempt to mislead, and was tacitly avowing all that might be charged against him. The architect began to feel that he was now regarded as a personal enemy, though he had never so considered himself. It was true that picture and papers had fallen into his hands, but he knew that a sense of duty was the only motive of any action that he might be taking.

'You promised, I think, to show me some papers,' Lord Blandamer said.

Most painfully Westray handed them over; his knowledge of their contents made it seem that he was offering a deliberate insult. He wished fervently that he never had made any proposal for this meeting; he ought to have given everything to the proper authorities, and have let the blow fall as it would. Such an interview could only end in bitterness; its present result was that here in Lord Blandamer's own house, he, Westray, was presenting him with proofs of his father's illegitimacy, with proofs that he had no right to this house—no, nor to anything else.

Perhaps it was a bitter moment for Lord Blandamer to find such information in the possession of a younger man; but, if there was more colour in his face than usual, his self-command stood the test, and he thrust resentment aside. There was no time to say or do useless things, there was no time for feeling; all his attention must be concentrated on the man before him. He stood still, seeming to examine the papers closely, and, as a matter of fact, he did take note of the name, the place, and the date, that so many careful searchings had failed ever to find. But all the while he was resolutely considering the next move, and giving Westray time to think and feel. When he looked up, their eyes met again, and this time it was Westray that coloured.

'I suppose you have verified these certificates?' Lord Blandamer asked very quietly.

'Yes,' Westray said, and Lord Blandamer gave them back to him without a word, and walked slowly away down the gallery.

Westray crushed the papers into his pocket where most of the room was taken up by the pistol; he was glad to get them out of his sight; he could not bear to hold them. It was as if a beaten fighter had given up his sword. With these papers Lord Blandamer seemed to resign into his adversary's hands everything of which he stood possessed, his lands, his life, the honour of his house. He made no defence, no denial, no resistance, least of all any appeal. Westray was left master of the situation, and must do whatever he though fit. This fact was clearer to him now than it had ever been before, the secret was his alone; with him rested the responsibility of making it public. He stood dumb before the picture, from which the old lord looked at him with penetrating eyes. He had nothing to say; he could not walk after Lord Blandamer; he wondered whether this was indeed to be the end of the interview, and turned sick at the thought of the next step that must be taken.

At a distance of a few yards Lord Blandamer paused, and looked round, and Westray understood that he was being invited, or commanded, to follow. They stopped opposite the portrait of a lady, but it was the frame to which Lord Blandamer called attention by laying his hand on it.

'This was my grandmother,' he said; 'they were companion pictures. They are the same size, the moulding on the frame is the same, an interlacing fillet, and the coat of arms is in the same place. You see?' he added, finding Westray still silent.

Westray was obliged to meet his look once more.

'I see,' he said, most reluctantly. He knew now, that the unusual moulding and the size of the picture that hung in Miss Joliffe's house, must have revealed its identity long ago to the man who stood before him; that during all those visits in which plans for the church had been examined and discussed, Lord Blandamer must have known what lay hid under the flowers, must have known that the green wriggling caterpillar was but a bar of the nebuly coat. Confidences were being forced upon Westray that he could not forget, and could not reveal. He longed to cry out, 'For God's sake, do not tell me these things; do not give me this evidence against yourself!'

There was another short pause, and then Lord Blandamer turned. He seemed to expect Westray to turn with him, and they walked back over the soft carpet down the gallery in a silence that might be heard. The air was thick with doom; Westray felt as if he were stifling. He had lost mental control, his thoughts were swallowed up in a terrible chaos. Only one reflection stood out, the sense of undivided responsibility. It was not as if he were adding a link, as in duty bound, to a long chain of other evidence. the whole matter was at rest; to set it in motion again would be his sole act, his act alone. There was a refrain ringing in his ears, a verse that he had heard read a few Sundays before in Cullerne Church, 'Am I God, to kill and make alive? Am I God, to kill and make alive?' Yet duty commanded him to go forward, and go forward he must, though the result was certain: he would be playing the part of executioner.

The man whose fate he must seal was keeping pace with him quietly, step by step. If he could only have a few moments to himself, he might clear his distracted thoughts. He paused before some other picture, feigning to examine it, but Lord Blandamer paused also, and looked at him. He knew Lord Blandamer's eye was upon him, though he refused to return the look. It seemed a mere act of courtesy on Lord

Blandamer's part to stop. Mr Westray might be specially interested in some of the pictures, and, if any information was required, it was the part of the host to see that it was forthcoming. Westray stopped again once or twice, but always with the same result. He did not know whether he was looking at portraits or landscapes, though he was vaguely aware that half-way down the gallery, there stood on the floor what seemed to be an unfinished picture, with its face turned to the wall.

Except when Westray stopped, Lord Blandamer looked neither to the right nor to the left, he walked with his hands folded lightly behind him, and with his eyes upon the ground, yet did not feign to have his thoughts disengaged. His companion shrank from any attempt to understand or fathom what those thoughts could be, but admired, against his will, the contained and resolute bearing. Westray felt as a child beside a giant, yet had no doubt as to his own duty, or that he was going to do it. But how hard it was! Why had he been so foolish as to meddle with the picture? Why had he read papers that did not belong to him? Why, above all, had he come down to Fording to have his suspicions confirmed? What business was it of his to ferret out these things? He felt all the unutterable aversion of an upright mind for playing the part of a detective; all the sovereign contempt even for such petty meanness as allows one person to examine the handwriting or postmark of letters addressed to another. Yet he knew this thing, and he alone; he could not do away with this horrible knowledge.

The end of the gallery was reached; they turned with one accord and paced slowly, silently back, and the time was slipping away fast. It was impossible for Westray to consider anything *now*, but he had taken his decision before he came to Fording; he must go through with it; there was no escape for *him* any more than for Lord Blandamer. He would keep his word. On Monday, the day he had mentioned, he would speak, and once begun, the matter would pass out of his hands. But how was he to tell this to the man who was walking beside him, and silently waiting for his sentence? He could not leave him in suspense; to do so would be cowardice and cruelty. He must make his intention clear, but how? in what form of words? There was no time to think; already they were repassing that canvas which stood with its face to the wall.

The suspense, the impenetrable silence, was telling upon Westray; he tried again to rearrange his thoughts, but they were centred only on Lord Blandamer. How calm he seemed, with his hands folded behind him, and never a finger twitching! What did *he* mean to do—to fly, or kill himself, or stand his ground and take his trial on a last chance? It would be a celebrated trial. Hateful and inevitable details occurred to

Westray's imagination; the crowded, curious court as he saw it in his dream, with Lord Blandamer in the dock, and this last thought sickened him. His own place would be in the witness-box. Incidents that he wished to forget would be recalled, discussed, dwelt on; he would have to search his memory for them, narrate them, swear to them. But this was not all. He would have to give an account of this very afternoon's work. It could not be hushed up. Every servant in the house would know how he had come to Fording with a picture. He heard himself cross-examined as to 'this very remarkable interview'. What account was he to give of it? What a betrayal of confidence it would be to give *any* account. Yet he must, and his evidence would be given under the eyes of Lord Blandamer in the dock. Lord Blandamer would be in the dock watching him. It was unbearable, impossible; rather than this he would fly himself, he thought he would use the pistol that bulged his pocket against his own life.

Lord Blandamer had noted Westray's nervous movements, his glances to right and left, as though seeking some way of escape; he saw the clenched hands, and the look of distress as they paced to and fro. He knew that each pause before a picture was an attempt to shake him off, but he would not be shaken off; Westray was feeling the grip, and must not have a moment's breathing space. He could tell exactly how the minutes were passing, he knew what to listen for, and could catch the distant sound of the stable clock striking the quarters. They were back at the end of the gallery. There was no time to pace it again; Westray must go now if he was to catch his train.

They stopped opposite the old lord's portrait; the silence wrapped Westray round, as the white fog had wrapped him round that night on his way to Cullerne Road. He wanted to speak, but his brain was confused, his throat was dry; he dreaded the sound of his own voice.

Lord Blandamer took out his watch.

'I have no wish to hurry you, Mr Westray,' he said, 'but your train leaves Lytchett in little over an hour. It will take you nearly that time to drive to the station. May I help you to repack this picture?'

His voice was clear, level, and courteous, as on the day when Westray had first met him at Bellevue Lodge. The silence was broken, and Westray found himself speaking quickly in answer.

'You invited me to stay here for the night. I have changed my mind, and will accept your offer, if I may.' He hesitated for a moment, and then went on. 'I shall be thankful if you will keep the picture and these documents. I see now that I have no business with them.'

He took the crumpled papers from his pocket, and held them out without looking up.

Then silence fell on them again, and Westray's heart stood still; till after a second that seemed an eternity Lord Blandamer took the papers with a short 'I thank you,' and walked a little way further, to the end of the gallery. The architect leant against the side of a window opposite which he found himself, and, looking out without seeing anything, presently heard Lord Blandamer tell a servant that Mr Westray would stop the night, and that wine was to be brought them in the gallery. In a few minutes the man came back with a decanter on a salver, and Lord Blandamer filled glasses for Westray and himself. He felt probably that both needed something of the kind, but to the other more was implied. Westray remembered that an hour ago he had refused to eat or drink under this roof. An hour ago—how his mood had changed in that short time! How he had flung duty and principle to the winds! Surely this glass of red wine was a very sacrament of the devil, which made him a partner of iniquity.

As he raised the glass to his lips a slanting sunbeam shot through the window, and made the wine glow red as blood. The drinkers paused glass in hand, and glancing up saw the red sun setting behind the trees in the park. Then the old lord's picture caught the evening light, the green bars of the nebuly coat danced before Westray's eyes, till they seemed to live, to be again three wriggling caterpillars, and the penetrating grey eyes looked out from the canvas as if they were watching the enactment of this final scene. Lord Blandamer pledged him in a bumper, and Westray answered without hesitation, for he had given his allegiance, and would have drunk poison in token that there was to be no turning back now.

An engagement kept Lady Blandamer from home that evening. Lord Blandamer had intended to accompany her, but afterwards told her that Mr Westray was coming on important business, and so she went alone. Only Lord Blandamer and Westray sat down to dinner, and some subtle change of manner made the architect conscious that for the first time since their acquaintance, his host was treating him as a real equal. Lord Blandamer maintained a flow of easy and interesting conversation, yet never approached the subject of architecture even near enough to seem to be avoiding it. After dinner he took Westray to the library, where he showed him some old books, and used all his art to entertain him and set him at his ease. Westray was soothed for a moment by the other's manner, and did his best to respond to the courtesy shown him; but everything had lost its savour, and he knew that black Care was only waiting for him to be alone, to make herself once more mistress of his being.

A wind which had risen after sunset began to blow near bedtime with unusual violence. The sudden gusts struck the library windows till they rattled again, and puffs of smoke came out from the fireplace into the room.

'I shall sit up for Lady Blandamer,' said the host, 'but I dare say you will not be sorry to turn in'; and Westray, looking at his watch, saw that it wanted but ten minutes of midnight.

In the hall, and on the staircase, as they went up, the wind blowing with cold rushes made itself felt still more strongly.

'It is a wild night,' Lord Blandamer said, as he stopped for a moment before a barometer, 'but I suspect that there is yet worse to come; the glass has fallen in an extraordinary way. I hope you have left all snug with the tower at Cullerne; this wind will not spare any weak places.'

'I don't think it should do any mischief at St Sepulchre's,' Westray answered, half unconsciously. It seemed as though he could not concentrate his thought even upon his work.

His bedroom was large, and chilly in spite of a bright fire. He locked the door, and drawing an easy-chair before the hearth, sat a long while in thought. It was the first time in his life that he had with deliberation acted against his convictions, and there followed the reaction and remorse inseparable from such conditions.

Is there any depression so deep as this? is there any night so dark as this first eclipse of the soul, this *first* conscious stilling of the instinct for right? He had conspired to obscure truth, he had made himself partaker in another man's wrongdoing, and, as the result, he had lost his moral foothold, his self-respect, his self-reliance. It was true that, even if he could, he would not have changed his decision now, yet the weight of a guilty secret, that he must keep all his life long, pressed heavily upon him. Something must be done to lighten this weight; he must take some action that would ease the galling of his thoughts. He was in that broken mood for which the Middle Ages offered the cloister as a remedy; he felt the urgent need of sacrifice and abnegation to purge him. And then he knew the sacrifice that he must make: he must give up his work at Cullerne. He was thankful to find that there was still enough of conscience left to him to tell him this. He could not any longer be occupied on work for which the money was being found by this man. He would give up his post at Cullerne, even if it meant giving up his connections with his employers, even if it meant the giving up of his livelihood. He felt as if England itself were not large enough to hold him and Lord Blandamer. He must never more see the associate of his guilt; he dreaded meeting his eyes again, lest the other's will should constrain his will to further wrong. He would write to resign his work the very next day; that would be an active sacrifice, a definite mark from which he might begin a painful retracing of the way, a turning-point from which he might hope in time to recover some measure of self-respect and peace of mind. He would resign his work at Cullerne the very next day; and then a wilder gust of wind buffeted the windows of his room, and he thought of the scaffolding on St Sepulchre's tower. What a terrible night it was! Would the thin bows of the tower arches live through such a night, with the weight of the great tower rocking over them? No, he could not resign to-morrow. It would be deserting his post. He must stand by till the tower was safe, *that* was his first duty. *After* that he would give up his post at once.

Later on he went to bed, and in those dark watches of the night, that are not kept by reason, there swept over him thoughts wilder than the wind outside. He had made himself sponsor for Lord Blandamer, he had assumed the burden of the other's crime. It was he that was branded with the mark of Cain, and he must hide it in silence from the eyes of all men. He must fly from Cullerne, and walk alone with his burden for the rest of his life, a scapegoat in the isolation of the wilderness.

In sleep the terror that walketh in darkness brooded heavily on him. He was in the church of St Sepulchre, and blood dripped on him from the organ-loft. Then as he looked up to find out whence it came he saw the four tower arches falling to grind him to powder, and leapt up in his bed, and struck a light to make sure that there were no red patches on him. With daylight he grew calmer. The wild visions vanished, but the cold facts remained: he was sunk in his own esteem, he had forced himself into an evil secret which was no concern of his, and now he must keep it for ever.

No. Had he indeed lost his self-esteem? Was there indeed so guilty a secret? Was not the whole story a phantom of his own brain?

Westray found Lady Blandamer in the breakfast-room. Lord Blandamer had met her in the hall on her return the night before, and though he was pale, she knew before he had spoken half a dozen words, that the cloud of anxiety which had hung heavily on him for the last few days was past. He told her that Mr Westray had come over on business, and, in view of the storm that was raging, had been persuaded to remain for the night. The architect had brought with him a picture which he had accidentally come across, a portrait of the old Lord Blandamer which had been missing for many years from Fording. It was very satisfactory that it had been recovered; they were under a great obligation to Mr Westray for the trouble which he had taken in the matter.

In the events of the preceding days Westray had almost forgotten Lady Blandamer's existence, and since the discovery of the picture, if her image presented itself to his mind, it had been as that of a deeply wronged and suffering woman. But this morning she appeared with a look of radiant content that amazed him, and made him shudder as he thought how near he had been only a day before to plunging her into the abyss. The more careful nurture of the year that had passed since her marriage, had added softness to her face and figure, without detracting from the refinement of expression that had always marked her. He knew that she was in her own place, and wondered now that the distinction of her manner had not led him sooner to the truth of her birth. She looked pleased to meet him, and shook hands with a frank smile that acknowledged their former relations, without any trace of embarrassment. It seemed incredible that she should ever have brought him up his meals and letters.

She made a polite reference to his having restored to them an interesting family picture, and finding him unexpectedly embarrassed, changed the subject by asking him what he thought of her own portrait.

'I think you must have seen it yesterday,' she went on, as he appeared not to understand. 'It has only just come home, and is standing on the floor in the long gallery.'

Lord Blandamer glanced at the architect, and answered for him that Mr Westray had not seen it. Then he explained with a composure that shed a calm through the room:

'It was turned to the wall. It is a pity to show it unhung, and without a frame. We must get it framed at once, and decide on a position for it. I think we shall have to shift several paintings in the gallery.'

He talked of Snyders and Wouverman, and Westray made some show of attention, but could only think of the unframed picture standing on the ground, which had helped to measure the passing of time in the terrible interview of yesterday. He guessed now that Lord Blandamer had himself turned the picture with its face to the wall, and in doing so had deliberately abandoned a weapon that might have served him well in the struggle. Lord Blandamer must have deliberately forgone the aid of recollections such as Anastasia's portrait would have called up in his antagonist's mind. *Non tali auxilio nec defensoribus istis.**

Westray's haggard air had not escaped his host's notice. The architect looked as if he had spent the night in a haunted room, and Lord Blandamer was not surprised, knowing that the other's scruples

* Neither such help nor those defences (*Aeneid*)

had died hard, and were not likely to lie quiet in their graves. He thought it better that the short time which remained before Westray's departure should be spent out of the house, and proposed a stroll in the grounds. The gardener reported, he said, that last night's gale had done considerable damage to the trees. The top of the cedar on the south lawn had been broken short off. Lady Blandamer begged that she might accompany them, and as they walked down the terrace steps into the garden a nurse brought to her the baby heir.

'The gale must have been a cyclone,' Lord Blandamer said. 'It has passed away as suddenly as it arose.'

The morning was indeed still and sunshiny, and seemed more beautiful by contrast with the turmoil of the previous night. The air was clear and cold after the rain, but paths and lawns were strewn with broken sticks and boughs, and carpeted with prematurely fallen leaves.

Lord Blandamer described the improvements that he was making or projecting, and pointed out the old fishponds which were to be restocked, and the ladies' garden arranged on an old-world plan by his grandmother, and maintained unchanged since her death. He had received an immense service from Westray, and he would not accept it ungraciously or make little of it. In taking the architect round the place, in showing this place that his ancestors had possessed for so many generations, in talking of his plans for a future that had only so recently become assured, he was in a manner conveying his thanks, and Westray knew it.

Lady Blandamer was concerned for Westray. She saw that he was downcast, and ill at ease, and in her happiness that the cloud had passed from her husband, she wanted everyone to be happy with her. So, as they were returning to the house, she began, in the kindness of her heart, to talk of Cullerne Minster. She had a great longing, she said, to see the old church again. She should so much enjoy it if Mr Westray would some day show her over it. Would he take much longer in the restorations?

They were in an alley too narrow for three to walk abreast. Lord Blandamer had fallen behind, but was within earshot.

Westray answered quickly, without knowing what he was going to say. He was not sure about the restorations—that was, they certainly were not finished; in fact, they would take some time longer, but he would not be there, he believed, to superintend them. That was to say, he was giving up his present appointment.

He broke off, and Lady Blandamer knew that she had again selected an unfortunate subject. She dropped it, and hoped he would let them know when he was next at leisure, and come for a longer visit.

'I am afraid it will not be in my power to do so,' Westray said; and then, feeling that he had given a curt and ungracious answer to a kindly-meant invitation, turned to her and explained with unmistakable sincerity that he was giving up his connection with Farquhar and Farquhar. This subject also was not to be pursued, so she only said that she was sorry, and her eyes confirmed her words.

Lord Blandamer was pained at what he had heard. He knew Farquhar and Farquhar, and knew something of Westray's position and prospects—that he had a reasonable income, and a promising future with the firm. This resolve must be quite sudden, a result of yesterday's interview. Westray was being driven out into the wilderness like a scapegoat with another man's guilt on his head. The architect was young and inexperienced. Lord Blandamer wished he could talk with him quietly. He understood that Westray might find it impossible to go on with the restoration at Cullerne, where all was being done at Lord Blandamer's expense. But why sever his connection with a leading firm? Why not plead ill-health, nervous breakdown, those doctor's orders which have opened a way of escape from impasses of the mind as well as the body? An archæologic tour in Spain, a yachting cruise in the Mediterranean, a winter in Egypt—all these things would be to Westray's taste; the blameless herb nepenthe might anywhere be found growing by the wayside. He must amuse himself, and forget. He wished he could *assure* Westray that he would forget, or grow used to remembering; that time heals wounds of conscience as surely as it heals heart-wounds and flesh-wounds; that remorse is the least permanent of sentiments. But then Westray might not yet wish to forget. He had run full counter to his principles. It might be that he was resolved to take the consequences, and wear them like a hair-shirt, as the only means of recovering his self-esteem. No; whatever penance, voluntary or involuntary, Westray might undergo, Lord Blandamer could only look on in silence. His object had been gained. If Westray felt it necessary to pay the price, he must be let pay it. Lord Blandamer could neither inquire nor remonstrate. He could offer no compensation, because no compensation would be accepted.

The little party were nearing the house when a servant met them.

'There is a man come over from Cullerne, my lord,' he said. 'He is anxious to see Mr Westray at once on important business.'

'Show him into my sitting-room, and say that Mr Westray will be with him immediately.'

Westray met Lord Blandamer in the hall a few minutes later.

'I am sorry to say there is bad news from Cullerne,' the architect said hurriedly. 'Last night's gale has strained and shaken the tower severely. A very serious movement is taking place. I must get back at once.'

'Do, by all means. A carriage is at the door. You can catch the train at Lytchett, and be in Cullerne by midday.'

The episode was a relief to Lord Blandamer. The architect's attention was evidently absorbed in the tower. It might be that he had already found the blameless herb growing by the wayside.

The nebuly coat was on the panel of the carriage-door. Lady Blandamer had noticed that her husband had been paying Westray special attention. He was invariably courteous, but he had treated this guest as he treated few others. Yet now, at the last moment, he had fallen silent; he was standing, she fancied aloof. He held his hands behind him, and the attitude seemed to her to have some significance. But on Lord Blandamer's part it was a mark of consideration. There had been no shaking of hands up to the present; he was anxious not to force Westray to take his hand by offering it before his wife and the servants.

Lady Blandamer felt that there was something going on which she did not understand, but she took leave of Westray with special kindness. She did not directly mention the picture, but said how much they were obliged to him, and glanced for confirmation at Lord Blandamer. He looked at Westray, and said with deliberation:

'I trust Mr Westray knows how fully I appreciate his generosity and courtesy.'

There was a moment's pause, and then Westray offered his hand.

Lord Blandamer shook it cordially, and their eyes met for the last time.

Chapter 23

On the afternoon of the same day Lord Blandamer was himself in Cullerne. He went to the office of Mr Martelet, solicitor by prescriptive right to the family at Fording, and spent an hour closeted with the principal.

The house which the solicitor used for offices, was a derelict residence at the bottom of the town. It still had in front of it an extinguisher for links, and a lamp-bracket over the door of wasted iron scroll-work. It was a dingy place, but Mr Martelet had a famous county connection, and rumour said that more important family business was done here even than in Carisbury itself. Lord Blandamer sat behind the dusty windows.

'I think I quite understand the nature of the codicil,' the solicitor said. 'I will have a draft forwarded to your lordship to-morrow.'

'No, no; it is short enough. Let us finish with it now,' said his client. 'There is no time like the present. It can be witnessed here. Your head clerk is discreet, is he not?'

'Mr Simpkin has been with me thirty years,' the solicitor said deprecatingly, 'and I have had no reason to doubt his discretion hitherto.'

The sun was low when Lord Blandamer left Mr Martelet's office. He walked down the winding street that led to the market-place, with his long shadow going before him on the pavement. Above the houses in the near distance stood up the great tower of St Sepulchre's, pink-red in the sunset rays. What a dying place was Cullerne! How empty were the streets! The streets were certainly strangely empty. He had never seen them so deserted. There was a silence of the grave over all. He took out his watch. The little place is gone to tea, he thought, and walked on with a light heart, and more at his ease that he had ever felt before in his life.

He came round the bend in a street, and suddenly saw a great crowd before him, between him and the market-place over which the minster church watched, and knew that something must be happening, that had drawn the people from the other parts of the town. As he came nearer it seemed as if the whole population was there collected. Conspicuous was pompous Canon Parkyn, and by him stood Mrs Parkyn, and tall and sloping-shouldered Mr Noot. The sleek dissenting minister was there, and the jovial, round-faced Catholic priest. There stood Joliffe, the pork-butcher, in shirt-sleeves and white apron in the middle of the road; and there stood Joliffe's wife and daughters, piled up on the steps of the shop, and craning their necks towards the market-place. The postmaster and his clerk and two letter-carriers had come from the post-office. All the young ladies and young gentlemen from Rose and Storey's establishment were herded in front of their great glittering shop-window, and among them shone the fair curls of Mr Storey, the junior partner, himself. A little lower down was a group of masons and men employed on the restorations, and near them Clerk Janaway leant on his stick.

Many of these Lord Blandamer knew well by sight, and there was beside a great throng of common folk, but none took any notice of him.

There was something very strange about the crowd. Everyone was looking towards the market-place, and everyone's face was upturned as if they were watching a flight of birds. The square was empty, and no one attempted to advance further into it; nay, most stood in an alert attitude, as if prepared to run the other way. Yet all remained spell-bound, looking up, with their heads turned towards the market-place, over which watched the minster church. There was no shouting, nor laughter, nor chatter; only the agitated murmur of a multitude of people speaking under their breath.

The single person that moved was a waggoner. He was trying to get his team and cart up the street, away from the market-place, but made slow progress, for the crowd was too absorbed to give him room. Lord Blandamer spoke to the man, and asked him what was happening. The waggoner stared for a moment as if dazed; then recognized his questioner, and said quickly:

'Don't go on, my lord! For God's sake, don't go on; the tower's coming down.'

Then the spell that bound all the others fell on Lord Blandamer too. His eyes were drawn by an awful attraction to the great tower that watched over the market-place. The buttresses with their broad set-offs, the double belfry windows with their pierced screens and stately Perpendicular tracery, the open battlemented parapet, and clustered groups of soaring pinnacles, shone pink and mellow in the evening sun. They were as fair and wonderful as on that day when Abbot Vinnicomb first looked upon his finished work, and praised God that it was good.

But on this still autumn evening there was something terribly amiss with the tower, in spite of all brave appearances. The jackdaws knew it, and whirled in a mad chattering cloud round their old home, with wings flashing and changing in the low sunlight. And on the west side, the side nearest the market-place, there oozed out from a hundred joints a thin white dust that fell down into the churchyard like the spray of some lofty Swiss cascade. It was the very death-sweat of a giant in his agony, the mortar that was being ground in powder from the courses of collapsing masonry. To Lord Blandamer it seemed like the sand running through an hourglass.

Then the crowd gave a groan like a single man. One of the gargoyles at the corner, under the parapet, a demon figure that had jutted grinning over the churchyard for three centuries broke loose and fell crashing on the the gravestones below. There was silence for a minute, and then the murmurings of the onlookers began again. Everyone spoke in short, breathless sentences, as though they feared the final crash might come before they could finish. Churchwarden Joliffe, with pauses of expectation, muttered about a 'judgment in our midst.' The Rector, in Joliffe's pauses, seemed trying to confute him by some reference to 'those thirteen upon whom the tower of Siloam fell and slew them.' An old charwoman whom Miss Joliffe sometimes employed wrung her hand with an 'Ah! poor dear—poor dear!' The Catholic priest was reciting something in a low tone, and crossing himself at intervals. Lord Blandamer, who stood near, caught a word of two of the commendatory prayer for the dying, the *'Proficiscere'*, and *'liliata rutilantium'*, that showed how Abbot Vinnicomb's tower lived in the hearts of those that abode under its shadow.

And all the while the white dust kept pouring out of the side of the wounded fabric; the sands of the hour-glass were running down apace.

The foreman of the masons saw Lord Blandamer, and made his way to him.

'Last night's gale did it, my lord,' he said; 'we knew 'twas touch and go when we came this morning. Mr Westray's been up the tower since mid-day to see if there was anything that could be done, but twenty minutes ago he came sharp into the belfry and called to us, "Get out of it, lads—get out quick for your lives; it's all over now." It's widening out at bottom; you can see how the base wall's moved and forced up the graves on the north side.' And he pointed to a shapeless heap of turf and gravestones and churchyard mould against the base of the tower.

'Where is Mr Westray?' Lord Blandamer said. 'Ask him to speak to me for a minute.'

He looked round about for the architect; he wondered now that he had not seen him among the crowd. The people standing near had listened to Lord Blandamer's words. They of Cullerne looked on the master of Fording as being almost omnipotent. If he could not command the tower, like Joshua's sun in Ajalon, to stand still forthwith and not fall down, yet he had no doubt some sage scheme to suggest to the architect whereby the great disaster might be averted. Where was the architect? they questioned impatiently. Why was he not at hand when Lord Blandamer wanted him? Where was he? And in a moment Westray's name was on all lips.

And just then was heard a voice from the tower, calling out through the louvres of the belfry windows, very clear and distinct for all it was so high up, and for all the chatter of the jackdaws. It was Westray's voice:

'I am shut up in the belfry,' it called; 'the door is jammed. For God's sake! someone bring a crowbar, and break in the door!'

There was despair in the words, that sent a thrill of horror through those that heard them. The crowd stared at one another. The foreman-mason wiped the sweat off his brow; he was thinking of his wife and children. Then the Catholic priest stepped out.

'I will go,' he said; 'I have no one depending on me.'

Lord Blandamer's thoughts had been elsewhere; he woke from his reverie at the priest's words.

'Nonsense!' said he; 'I am younger than you, and know the staircase. Give me a lever.'

One of the builder's men handed him a lever with a sheepish air. Lord Blandamer took it, and ran quickly towards the minster.

The foreman-mason called after him:

'There is only one door open, my lord—a little door by the organ.'

'Yes, I know the door,' Lord Blandamer shouted, as he disappeared round the church.

A few minutes later he had forced open the belfry door. He pulled it back towards him, and stood behind it on the steps higher up, leaving the staircase below clear for Westray's escape. The eyes of the two men did not meet, for Lord Blandamer was hidden by the door; but Westray was much overcome as he thanked the other for rescuing him.

'Run for your life!' was all Lord Blandamer said; 'you are not saved yet.'

The younger man dashed headlong down the steps, and then Lord Blandamer pushed the door to, and followed with as little haste or excitement as if he had been coming down from one of his many inspections of the restoration work.

As Westray ran through the great church, he had to make his way through a heap of mortar and débris that lay upon the pavement. The face of the wall over the south transept arch had come away, and in its fall had broken through the floor into the vaults below. Above his head that baleful old crack, like a black lightning flash, had widened into a cavernous fissure. The church was full of dread voices, of strange moanings and groanings, as if the spirits of all the monks departed were wailing for the destruction of Abbot Vinnicomb's tower. There was a dull rumbling of rending stone and crashing timbers, but over all the architect heard the cry of the crossing arches: 'The arch never sleeps, never sleeps. They have bound upon us a burden too heavy to be borne; we are shifting it. The arch never sleeps.'

Outside the people in the market-place held their breath, and the stream of white dust still poured out of the side of the wounded tower. It was six o'clock; the four quarters sounded, and the hour struck. Before the last stroke had died away Westray ran out across the square, but the people waited to cheer until Lord Blandamer should be safe too. The chimes began 'Bermondsey' as clearly and cheerfully as on a thousand other bright and sunny evenings.

And then the melody was broken. There was a jangle of sound, a deep groan from Taylor John, and a shrill cry from Beata Maria, a roar as of cannon, a shock as of an earthquake, and a cloud of white dust hid from the spectators the ruin of the fallen tower.

Epilogue

On the same evening Lieutenant Ennefer, RN, sailed down Channel in the corvette *Solebay*, bound for the China Station. He was engaged to the second Miss Bulteel, and turned his glass on the old town where his lady dwelt as he passed by. It was then he logged that Cullerne Tower was not to be seen, though the air was clear and the ship but six miles from shore. He rubbed his glass, and called some other officers to verify the absence of the ancient seamark, but all they could make out was a white cloud, that might be smoke or dust or mist hanging over the town. It must be mist, they said; some unusual atmospheric condition must have rendered the tower invisible.

It was not for many months afterwards that Lieutenant Ennefer heard of the catastrophe, and when he came up Channel again on his return five years later, there was the old seamark clear once more, whiter a little, but still the same old tower. It had been rebuilt at the sole charge of Lady Blandamer, and in the basement of it was a brass plate to the memory of Horatio Sebastian Fynes, Lord Blandamer, who had lost his life in that place whilst engaged in the rescue of others.

The rebuilding was entrusted to Mr Edward Westray, whom Lord Blandamer, by codicil dictated only a few hours before his death, had left co-trustee with Lady Blandamer, and guardian of the infant heir.

AT 3 O'CLOCK   New Sabbath

Bermondsey

Sheldon

Mount Ephraim